PRAISE FOR
PILGRIMAGE

"Having already reimagined the life of Geoffrey Chaucer as historical fiction in This Passing World, Michael Herzog turns his considerable talent to the Canterbury Tales, translating this cherished collection of stories into accessible modern English while also filling in the missing tales. What emerges is a splendid mix of scholarship and literary invention."
—*Jess Walter, New York Times bestselling author of*
The Cold Millions and Beautiful Ruins

After 600 years, Michael Herzog has completed the unfinished Canterbury Tales in a style entirely consistent with Chaucer's work. Surprising, entertaining, poignant, imaginative, and delightful. This translation brings a rich new coloring and texture and energy to the original and lures us into what Chaucer, better than anyone, reveals about the human psyche. Bravo!!!
—*Patrick Burke, Ph.D., Professor of Philosophy*

Herzog's expansion of Canterbury Tales is wonderfully readable. His use of contemporary language makes Chaucer accessible to new readers and non-specialists, while his deft storytelling will delight scholars of all casts. The addition of new tales and new interactions among pilgrims mirror the humor and subtlety of Chaucer's original material. Indeed, there is a seamless flow from beginning to end. The functions, titles and roles of these travelers might seem antiquated to contemporary readers, but their tales, both Herzog's and Chaucer's originals, reveal something universal about vice and virtue, about human nature and human sexuality, about the power of stories where the truth will out. Herzog has achieved his purpose in this completed Canterbury Tales: to help readers "appreciate the genius of this medieval poet."
—*Janis Haswell, PhD, Professor Emerita of English*

The idea of Pilgrimage is terrific, and it is executed with real skill. I admire the inventiveness and reach of combining the extant tales with the new ones.. Very impressive; a genuine pleasure to read.
—*Chris Anderson, PhD, Professor Emeritus of English*

Pilgrimage: The Only Complete Version of Geoffrey Chaucer's Canterbury Tales is a work of fiction. Any references to historical events, real people, or real places are used to serve this fiction. Other names, characters, places and incidents are products of the author's imagination. Any other resemblance to actual events, persons, living or dead is coincidental.

Copyright © 2022 by Michael B. Herzog. All rights reserved.

Printed in the United States of America. No part of this book may be used or reproduced in any manner without written permission except in the case of brief quotations embodied in critical articles and reviews.

For information about special discounts for bulk purchases, please contact Will Dreamly Arts Publishing:
www.WillDreamlyArts.com

FIRST Will Dreamly Arts hardcover edition

Book and jacket design by Michael B. Koep
Jacket portrait by Rajah Bose

Pilgrimage: The Only Complete Version of Geoffrey Chaucer's Canterbury Tales
is also available in eBook and ePub formats.

Library of Congress Cataloging-in-Publication Data has been applied for.

(hardcover edition)
ISBN# 978-1-734138-33-7

10 8 6 4 2 0 1 3 5 7 9

Will Dreamly Arts
PUBLISHING

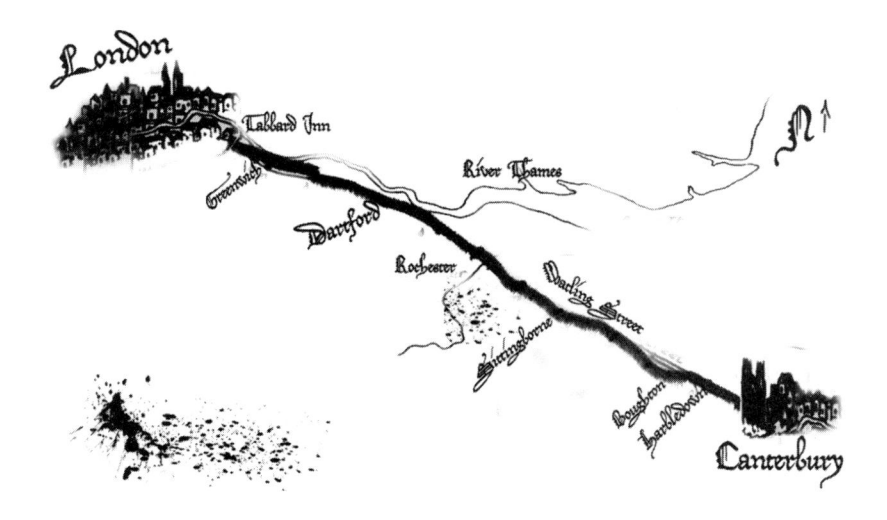

PILGRIMAGE

THE ONLY COMPLETE VERSION OF GEOFFERY CHAUCER'S
CANTERBURY TALES

Will Dreamly Arts
PUBLISHING

TABLE OF CONTENTS

Translator's Note	1
Some Cultural Idiosyncrasies of 14th Century England	7
Prologue	15
The Knight's Tale	40
The Miller's Tale	72
The Reeve's Tale	89
The Cook's Tale	100
The Man of Law's Tale	111
The Wife of Bath's Tale	134
The Friar's Tale	163
The Summoner's Tale	172
The Haberdasher's Tale	189
The Shipman' Tale	199
The Merchant's Tale	210
The Clerk's Tale	241
The Tapister's Tale	269
The Prioress's Tale	279
The Narrator's Tale of Sir Thopas	284
The Narrator's Tale of Melibee	293
The Monk's Tale	317
The Nun's Priest's Tale	329
The Carpenter's Tale	343
The Weaver's Tale	350
The Physician's Tale	359
The Pardoner's Tale	371
The Squire's Tale	383
The Franklin's Tale	398
The Dyer's Tale	421
The Second Nun's Tale	431
The Canon's Yeoman's Tale	447
The Manciple's Tale	464
The Knight's Yeoman's Tale	471

The Parson's Tale	491
Epilogue	504
Translator's Final Note	512
Acknowledgements	513
Works Consulted	515

To Jean

Translator's Note

If you are aware of the literary treasure unearthed in a London archeological dig in 2015, you know that the effort yielded two previously unknown works by the preeminent English medieval poet, Geoffrey Chaucer. One was a journal Chaucer had secretly kept and confided in for the final, tumultuous few years of his life, from May of 1398 to his death in October, 1400. That journal was translated and published in late 2019 under the title of *This Passing World*. In it Chaucer not only chronicled the remarkable events which occurred in London and England during that time but also recounted many episodes from his own personal life as courtier, ambassador, husband, father, lover and poet. In this journal he also wrote about his masterwork, The Canterbury Tales, and shared his decision, late in life, to rewrite that collection of stories, ostensibly told by a group of pilgrims on their way to the shrine of St. Thomas Becket, traveling from London to Canterbury, a journey of some 60 miles.

To the chagrin of lovers of literature and Chaucer scholars over the centuries, *The Canterbury Tales* have, previous to this, been handed down historically to audiences only in fragmentary form, much of it in verse, a few portions in prose. The *Tales* must have been very popular not only in Chaucer's lifetime but thereafter, as well, since nearly 100 hand-written fragments of various parts of the collection were produced more or less while Chaucer was still alive and shortly after his death. This is particularly impressive when one considers how expensive "books" were in the Middle Ages. Clearly Chaucer worked on *The Canterbury Tales*, his major opus, over a period of years, even decades, but sadly the world has — until now — never seen a completed version, only those aforementioned fragments and, later, once printing had been invented, various versions of those fragments organized and connected in multiple ways by various editors and scholars — that may or may not have reflected Chaucer's own intentions.

It has been accepted fact up to now that none of the several plans for the completed *Canterbury Tales* were ever carried out by Chaucer. At various spots in the extant manuscripts, the narrator of the *Tales* says that 1) each of the thirty pilgrims making up the group is going to tell a story on the way to Canterbury and one on the return trek to London, 2) that each pilgrim will tell two stories on each leg of the journey and 3) that each of them will tell one story on the way to Canterbury only. The most ambitious of these plans would have resulted in 120 (or more) stories — more because the pilgrims are joined on their path for a short time by The Canon's Yeoman, who also tells a story. Perhaps Chaucer realized over time, as did his his nearly contemporary fellow artist in Italy, Michelangelo, that the best laid pans are not always feasible. That great sculptor agreed, at one point in his life, to fashion 100 sculptures to adorn the *de Medici* tombs, but did not even come close to carrying out that effort, as the first sculpture took him — and his apprentices — four years to finish.

Whatever Chaucer's original — or final — plan was, we have historically had available to us only a *General Prologue*, in which most of the pilgrims are introduced, followed by twenty-four tales. No stories are told by the Knight's Yeoman or the Plowman, although the Nun's Priest, who is named but not described in the *Prologue*, has the opportunity to tell his tale. Also without stories are the Haberdasher, the Carpenter, the Weaver, the Dyer, the Tapister (a maker of tapestries), and the Plowman. This means that nearly a quarter of the pilgrims do not tell stories in the extant manuscripts. And, finally, even though the premise for the story-telling is that this is a contest, with the winner to be revealed after the group reaches Canterbury, we are missing any conclusion. In other words, we have had only the option to imagine the arrival of the pilgrims in Canterbury and to conjecture as to who (in the sole and incontestable judgment of Harry Bailey, the Host) won the prize.

Until now.

For, the second of the two books discovered in that 2015 archeological dig in London was this only complete version of *The Canterbury Tales*. Here, all the pilgrims are introduced and each one has the opportunity to tell a tale, and the previously missing conclusion tells us what happened once they arrived at the pilgrimage's goal. Not only that, but, as he discussed in his journal, gambling on his best guess about the future popularity of story-telling forms, Chaucer had rewritten the entire work in prose, completing it before his death in October of the year 1400.

And this is the work you have before you now — the Prologue, all of the tales, and the Epilogue — translated and retold in accessible modern English prose.

It is important to note that in translating this work, I have done only what Chaucer's narrator claims to have done: to re-tell the stories as he heard them, imperfections, warts, objectionable language and all. The modern reader may at times be surprised, if not shocked, by some of the stories and by the language used by various pilgrims, a number of whom are seemingly perpetually drunk, while others reflect the macrocosm of medieval English society, meaning that some of them are less than savory characters.

Indeed, you might well be tempted to ask precisely why certain of these characters are on pilgrimage at all?

We have to assume that then, as now, pilgrims undertake their journeys for as many reasons as there are pilgrims. Some of them certainly participate in this ostensibly faith-fueled trek for sincerely religious and pious reasons. But there are others who seem simply to enjoy the freedom of being on pilgrimage — the opportunity to be someone other than the folks at home think they know. Some are looking to have a good time. Still others may be trying to escape their dally routines or even their (real or imaginary) pursuers, or it may be as simple for them as enjoying a fresh, beautiful spring following a long, dreary winter. Whatever their reasons for going on this pilgrimage, they are depicted by Chaucer as three-dimensional humans beings who operate out of the virtues and vices that make them who they are.

Members of a modern audience must always keep in mind that Chaucer's society is pre-Puritan and pre-Victorian, and that its members have not experienced the luxury of privacy that the modern world has come to prize (pre-social media). Medieval people lived in a world without many of the assumptions and practices that make life for many of us today predictable and stable. They had to accept the formal and assumed strictures, rules, and expectations anchoring a society based on unalterable layers of social class, at the complete whim of those fortunate enough simply to be born into wealth and power. Everyone was subject to the constant, moment-to-moment possibility of a sudden end due to uncontrolled violence, accidents that maimed permanently or killed, minor illnesses — such as an infected wound or even an abscessed tooth, and major health issues — such as the plague — that no physician could deal with, even spells and curses that they believed could change everything in an instant. All activities humans might engage in — from birth to death, from lust to anger, and from sheer evil to exemplary saintliness — were carried out publicly, visible to all present.

In such a reality, one cannot stand on some of the formalities we take for granted.

Our modern taboos relating to sex, bodily activities and social/ethnic sensitivities are often not observed. Even the formal medieval taboos of abusing the name of God in cursing — paid lip service to, at best — are circumvented by some fairly obvious verbal disguises that leave no doubt about the speaker's meaning. We have to accept the fact that the Wife of Bath's diction includes four-letter words and that the Host crudely insults certain pilgrims with sexual and fecal terms. To paraphrase Chaucer's narrator: "don't blame me for reporting what actually happened and how people speak in real life. And, by the way, if you are offended by this story or that story-teller, just turn the page, and perhaps you will find something more to your liking."

So, finally, we are left with a complete — the only complete — version of a brilliant compilation of stories that explore, reflect and bring to life people and their activities in a society that precedes us by 600 years but also illumines the society we ourselves inhabit. And at last we have the tales in the order in which Chaucer placed them — long a subject of heated debate and contentious argument among academics.

Whole forests have been sacrificed to provide paper for the scholarly books that probe varied and, often, conflicting perspectives on Chaucer and his work. Most agree, however, that *The Canterbury Tales*, as they have so-far been available to us, provide various perspectives on a relatively few major themes.

Some believe that the entire collection of stories is really an exploration of and attempt to understand better the **seven deadly sins**. Others have pointed out that these stores and the interactions of the pilgrims focus on how different pilgrims think about **power**: who wields it, how it is used properly or abused, what difference is made by who has power and who is powerless, and so on. How particular pilgrims think about **relationships**, such as friendship and marriage, sexual relationships, human relationships with God — who has the power in those relationships and how and for what ends it is wielded. And what assumptions the pilgrims rely upon about **order**: whether the world is divinely controlled, or whether everything is a series of coincidental actions. Is our lived experience actually the systematic carrying out of a divine plan in accord with the natural law, under the guidance of individuals God has installed to maintain that order, or are we simply subject to a series of chaotic incidents and coincidences that are part of an unpredictable and unstable reality? And, depending on the answer to that last question, how do power and relationships reflect that order and, in turn, shape us and lives?

In this complete version of the *Tales*, Chaucer appears to have returned to another big issue that he is clearly fascinated with throughout his poetic work: **transformation** — the way in which the unavoidable fact that we live in a reality of constant change affects and shapes everything. In a number of the "new" stories here, various store-tellers explore (be that intentionally or unintentionally) how transformation plays a role in all facets of our lives, often in relation to the three other major themes the *Tales* seem interested in. This last claim about transformation, by the way, is addressed, explored and substantiated by Chaucer himself in *This Passing World*.

While Chaucer's work speaks for itself, your translator has provided the occasional footnote to explain matters that are so inherently medieval that many modern audience members are likely to be baffled or mystified by them.

And now, *Pilgrimage: The Only Complete Version of Geoffrey Chaucer's Canterbury Tales* awaits your reading pleasure.

Some Cultural Idiosyncrasies of 14th Century England

The Western Middle Ages were socially stratified and very class-conscious. Clothing (style and color), the length of an individual's hair, the kind of weapon a man (and only a man) could carry, food that could be eaten on certain days, the kind of work one could do, etc., were all regulated in various ways by law and custom.

Although Parliament is assembled at the pleasure of the king and can be manipulated significantly by the crown and the nobility, it becomes increasingly powerful during Chaucer's time. There is an extensive and complex legal system, and the English bureaucratic system is known and admired throughout Europe for its perceived efficiency.

By Chaucer's time, the spoken language (Middle English) is the Anglo-Saxon that has survived the Norman Conquest, has absorbed much French vocabulary, and undergone significant grammatical change from Old English, or Anglo-Saxon. Latin is the language of scholarship, and French is the official language of the court system (until 1362, when Chaucer is approximately twenty years old). Compared to our own times, the language is in constant flux, changing rapidly, and undergoing major alteration in grammar, vocabulary and pronunciation that make it dramatically different from the language of the author of Beowulf (400-600 years earlier) and of Shakespeare (200 years after Chaucer's death). While some of his contemporaries, like John Gower, hedged their bets and produced work in Latin, French and English (sometimes in the same book), Chaucer wrote only in English, both betting on the survival and primacy of English and helping to shape it through his writings. By writing this collection of stories almost exclusively in prose, Chaucer seems also to have anticipated and counted on a wider audience that would prefer prose to poetry.

While there was an extensive legal system, pervasive public violence made day-to-day survival uncertain. The idea that all are equal under the law was an ideal rather than reality. The rich and powerful essentially had their own police systems, paying for private protection from random violence that commoners experienced as a daily reality; on one occasion, Chaucer himself was legally charged with beating a friar; on another, he was robbed twice in one day. With the continuing disputes between the rulers of England and France over who owned large tracts of Europe, and whether Ireland, Scotland and even Wales were meant to be ruled by English monarchs, not to mention forty years of papal schism (two warring popes each claiming to be the only true spiritual head of Christianity), Chaucer's life time is filled with uncertainty and violence, public and private, personal and international.

Wealth was largely land-based, and there were enormous discrepancies between the ultra-rich and the inordinately poor. Wars are fought over land, and victory was generally measured by how many survived on each side to take control of the disputed land. An elaborate ransom system made war lucrative, in that captured combatants were ransomed by large sums of money (sometimes regulated and stipulated by law). Thus prisoners were often literally more valuable alive than dead, while royal pr noble captives were treated like cherished guests, provided with all of the luxuries they would have enjoyed at home, including the elaborate and costly ritual known as the medieval hunt.

Because water was often unsafe to drink, as streams around towns and cities tended to be toxic from human and animal waste as well as dyes used by tanners, adults and children alike imbibed considerable alcohol, including various forms of beer and wine. Diners normally used their hands to pick up food and, when eating with others, tended to share a "trencher' (large slab of bread used like a plate), wiping their mouths on their sleeves — one of the reasons that sleeves, unlike other part of clothing, were often changed out and attached to different sets of clothing (note the popular medieval song that has survived until today as *Greensleeves)*.

Privacy, as we know and value it, was rare. Most people slept in the nude in one room with the other members of the household. All human activities were practiced in such common rooms, making the sexual taboos with which we are familiar, quite impractical. Children were exposed at a very early age, to the realities of life and death, as they were sheltered from neither. Consequently, Chaucer and his contemporaries minced few words, referring to body parts and bodily functions in ways that even in our modern liberated society would be considered crude and inappropriate.

Flowers, spices, and perfumes were heavily relied on to cover the odors of a population that rarely bathed; also, spices generally both inhibited the growth of bacteria in foods and made foods more palatable.

Medical treatment was limited, and physicians were widely — and appropriately — distrusted. They tended to rely on extensive folk treatments, and astrology played a significant role in training and practice. Many people still believed in witchcraft, interpreted religious and secular signs and omens accordingly, and relied on them to explain their daily experiences as well as unusual events. Medieval physicians believed that humans were governed by four elemental body fluids, illness being both symptom and result of imbalances among these four elements. These four humors correlated to the four seasons, to the four elements that were believed to make up all of creation, to four age periods, to four basic human qualities, to four major organs and to four human temperaments.

HUMORS	SEASONS	ELEMENTS	AGES	DUALITIES	ORGANS	TEMPERAMENT
yellow bile	summer	fire	youth	warm and dry	spleen	choleric
black bile	autumn	earth	adulthood	cold and dry	gallbladder	melancholic
phlegm	winter	water	old age	cold and moist	brain & lungs	phlegmatic
blood	spring	air	infancy	warm and moist	liver	sanguine

"Bleeding," i.e., opening a vein to vent bad humors or allow an excess of particular humors to escape the body, was a common treatment for anything from fractures and stomach aches to fever and flesh wounds. Undoubtedly many patients died simply from needless blood loss. A sophisticated knowledge of natural medicines garnered from the wild, or intentionally grown, led to the development of a wide range of potions not unlike our contemporary medicinal drugs.

Time-keeping was based on the canonical hours governing the times of prayer prescribed for religious communities.

Medieval terms:	Rough modern equivalents:
lauds - or matins (at daybreak)	3 am
prime (early morning)	6 am
terce (mid-morning)	9 am
sext (midday)	noon
nones (mid-afternoon)	3 pm
vespers (dusk)	6 pm
compline (after dark)	9 pm

London could be entered only by a limited number of gates that were closed and locked at night. London Bridge provided the only permanent crossing of the Thames, but the river itself would have teemed with boat traffic of all sorts, ferrying individuals and goods across the river or up and down its length.

During daylight hours, London was extremely noisy, with the sounds of primarily horse-drawn traffic, the shouts of vendors, and the nearly constant peeling of bells from the many churches that marked intermingling parishes. City gates would be closed at sundown and curfews were enforced, no doubt to help control rampant crime.

Although London had an extensive sewer system (Chaucer was actually responsible for it for a time), chamber pots and kitchen wastes were often emptied into the street, combined with horse and other animal droppings; this made navigation through narrow and dark streets and alleys a never-ending challenge in keeping clean.

It was a time in which relatively few babies were fortunate enough to survive birth and rampant childhood diseases; infants might be eaten by a feral pig. If they reached adulthood, they could die from something as innocuous as a minor cut or as inescapable as legal execution. Everyone knew that the law was skewed to favor the rich and powerful, and even noble women were treated as chattel useful in business, politics or bettering family connections. They were generally not taken seriously and were depicted by poets and the Church either as the ideal of all beauty or the root of all evil — the madonna or the whore. The average life-span was approximately thirty-five years; the vast majority of people was illiterate; social status was forefront and rarely alterable or improvable; meanwhile, and the culture as a whole waxed and waned at the mercy of war, the weather, and pandemics. It was a difficult, complex time that, nevertheless, as such times often do, produced much great art that testified to the power and grandeur of the indomitable human spirit.

MICHAEL B. HERZOG 13

PILGRIMAGE

Prologue

~~Whan that April with his shoures soote~~
~~The droghte of March has perced to the roote,~~
~~And bathed every veyne in swich licour~~
~~Of which vertu engendered is the flour~~

~~When April and its sweet showers has pierced the drought of March to the root and has bathed the vein of every plant with such liquid that it empowers flowers to bloom~~

In sparkling Spring, when the sweet showers of April have once again prevailed over arid March, bathing each follicle of the flower in that liqueur which inspires its beauty — when Zephyrus joins in, his sweet breath awakening tender crops in every field and land, and the youthful sun has kicked its heels halfway through the season of the Ram, while small birds that sleep all night with open eyes pound out their melodies at Nature's relentless bidding — we find ourselves yearning to go on pilgrimages to well-known but far-off shrines in various lands, while seasoned pilgrims seek out new and exotic places of worship. In England, of course, they travel, near and far, from every shire, to Canterbury, eager to supplicate the holy blessed martyr who has always helped them in their ailments.

Filled with that devotion, I too decided to go on pilgrimage in that refreshing season and, one day, I found myself with twenty-nine others, randomly assembled at the Tabard Inn, in Southwerk. And, as we were all pilgrims, we agreed to ride together to Canterbury.

We had all settled in, comfortably and convivially, to the Tabard's spacious rooms and stables and, by the evening before we were to set out early the next morning, I had managed to speak briefly with each and every one of these, my new companions.

So now, while I have the time and the opportunity and before I move further into my story, let me introduce to you my fellow pilgrims — who they were, their place in the world, their appearance — at least how it all seemed to me.

I will begin with the Knight.

Our Knight was a well-respected man who, from the time he won his spurs, was known for his chivalry and integrity, his generosity, reliability and refined behavior. He had borne himself well in his various masters' conflicts, and no one had served better anywhere — in Christendom or in pagan lands. His reputation was celebrated by one and all. He had helped secure the victory at Alexandria and had often presided at the Prussian banquet of Teutonic knights; no Christian of his rank had raided Lithuania or Russia more often; he took part in the siege of Algezir in Grenada and was active in the Mediterranean Sea and in Turkey when that territory was won. Part of many noble military expeditions, he had been personally involved in fifteen deadly battles and fought for our faith in Morocco, not to mention slaying his opponents in three individual jousts. This same worthy knight had also served, at one time or another, the Lord of Balat against another pagan Turk — everywhere he went he won the highest praise for his valor and his prudence. But he carried himself as gently as any maiden and had never, in his life, been heard to say anything rude or malicious to anyone. This was a true, complete, noble knight. Although he rode a quality horse, personally he was anything but richly attired. His tunic was made of coarse cloth, and his coat of mail was stained with rust, as he had just arrived from his latest campaign and had decided to go on this pilgrimage without delay.

He was accompanied by his son, a young Squire, a lusty lover with locks as curly as if his hair had been shaped in a press. He had just turned twenty, I would guess, and was of average height, but very muscular and strikingly graceful. He had borne himself well on a cavalry expedition that took him to Flanders and northeastern France, and he was counting on that negligible record to bolster his pursuit of beautiful women. His clothing was so highly embroidered that it looked like a meadow filled with fresh flowers, white and red. He never stopped singing or playing his flute and, like the very month of May, he practically bloomed, like the very month of May. His tunic was fashionably short, and his sleeves swirled long and wide. He sat his horse handsomely and controlled it well; he could compose songs and lovely tunes, he jousted as well as he danced, and he could draw and write charmingly. He was so fixed on love that he wasted no more nights on sleep than does the ever-wakeful nightingale. The model of courtesy, he deported himself humbly, ever ready to serve and, as is only fitting, he carved his father's meat at table.

It was the knight's good fortune to be served, in addition, by a Yeoman, dressed and hooded in green, deftly carrying a sheaf of sharp, brightly-feathered arrows in his belt. His equipment was clearly well cared for: his arrows' feathers did not droop, and his mighty bow was carried firmly. His hair was closely cropped and his face tanned dark by the sun, and he knew everything there was to know about the woods and outdoors. A bright arm guard covered his arm, and on one side he wore a sword and shield, while the other sported a shining dagger, well ornamented and as sharp as a spear's point. On his chest there sparkled an image of St. Christopher, and he wore a horn on a green strap — all suggesting to me that he was a forester by training.

Among our company there was also a Nun, a prioress called Madame Eglentine, with a soft, modest smile. Her strongest oath would have been "by Saint Loy," and she intoned most fittingly — through her nose — the divine service. Her French was beautiful and elegant, according to the manner of Stratford at Bow — unfamiliar as she was with Parisian French. Her bearing at table was refined — allowing no morsels to fall from her lips, nor dipping her fingers too deeply into her sauce. She delivered safely every bit of food, not a drop spilling upon her breast, as she was devoted at all times to manifest courtly behavior. She reached for her food in a surpassing comely manner and wiped her upper lip so clean that no greasy remnants could be seen in her cup after she took a sip. Likewise, her deportment was most seemly, very pleasant and totally amiable. She took great pains to imitate the manners of the court and always to act dignified, deserving of respect. As for moral qualities, she was so filled with love and so easily stirred to pity that she would weep at the sight of a mouse in a trap, whether dead or just wounded and bleeding. She kept a brood of small dogs that she fed with roasted meat or milk and fine white bread, and she wept pitifully if one of them died or even if someone took a stick to one; she was all compassion and tenderness. Her wimple was perfectly pleated; her nose well-shaped; her eyes as clear as glass; her mouth quite elegant, with soft, red lips; her forehead, though perfectly formed, almost the span of a hand across. And I cannot say that she was undernourished. From what I could see, her cloak was very elegant and around her arm was wound a rosary, each set of ten coral beads smartly separated by a great green one, and from that holy ornamentation there dangled a shiny, golden brooch that gleamed with a large crowned A and the phrase "*Amor vincit omnia.*"[1]

Another Nun — her Chaplain –- as well as one Priest, attended her. This Nun, much older than the prioress, was wearing out the simple rosary she ran perpetually through her fingers to track the prayers ever on her lips. A woman of considerable girth, she seemed unaccustomed to riding, unsteady on her mare and frequently swatting at the hairy wart that peeked out from her coarse, simple wimple, while she puffed impatiently through her toothless mouth. Her habit was simple, and her gaze was meekly lowered, whether she was on horseback or on foot, where her strong limp did not slow her down. She was her prioress's secretary and had mentored her for a dozen years, though there was little evidence that her superior heeded her advice.

---

[1] Latin for "Love conquers all," a catch phrase associated with both Christian and courtly love.

The Nun's Priest was tall and thin, perhaps forty years of age, wearing an ill-fitting, mud-spattered, brown robe with a simple rope around his waist and an unadorned wooden cross hanging from it. Though guarded, his eyes were sharp and clearly missed nothing. He treated equally well the dogs at the Inn, the nag he rode, and everyone he met. I felt that if we had the time we might become great friends, as his serious demeanor was often broken by a quick smile. Without ever saying it directly, he allowed that there was a time when he had been a man of the world, once a soldier with John of Gaunt, in Spain. No doubt he had also been a respected voice in his diocese until his bishop exiled him to the monastery of St. Leonard to say daily Mass for the bishop's niece or, as was commonly assumed, that worthy prelate's daughter. I do not know how long he had been in service to the Prioress.

With us there was also a Monk, most strikingly handsome, his monastery's representative to the outside world — a man who loved hunting, a man's man, in due time clearly meant to be an abbot. His stable held many a fine horse, and whenever he rode out, the steed's bridle jingling in the whistling wind could be heard by all, clear and loud as the chapel bell of its master's abbey. As for the holy regulations of Saints Maurus or Benedict — well, they were old and unnecessarily strict, and this monk believed in letting go of things old to make space for the new. He obviously did not give a plucked chicken for the text that tells us that hunters cannot be holy men, or that a monk who does not observe the regulations is like a fish out of water or, as some would put it, a monk without a cloister. Such text meant less to him than an oyster, and I can't say that I disagree. Really, should he make himself crazy studying day and night, pouring over old books in a cloister? Should he devote himself to manual labor and work with his hands as St. Augustine commands? What will best serve the world? Let Augustine have all the manual labor he wants! Mounted on his steed for the hunt, our Monk was the picture of a mighty hunter before the Lord, surrounded by his greyhounds, swift as birds in flight. He desired nothing more than tracking and hunting down a hare; for that he would spare no cost. His high-stepping mount was a deep berry brown, and our Monk made no bones about preferring a nice fat swan when it came to roasted meat. I could see that his sleeves were lined with the finest fur money can buy and, to fasten his hood under his chin, he had acquired a most skillfully fashioned pin made entirely of gold and ending in an elaborate knot fashioned from that precious metal. His supple boots, his magnificent horse — this was a real prelate! His hue was not the ashen pall of a tormented spirit — no, indeed! His tonsured head gleamed like a piece of glass, and his face shimmered as if anointed with precious oils. He was the picture of a religious prince, in magnificent condition, his bulging eyes rolling in his head and quivering like a blazing forge boiling a steaming pot.

We had with us also a jovial Friar, a licensed clerical beggar who was quite full of himself and loved pleasure more than anything. I've not met a member of the four great orders of friars more sociable or better at flattery. He has personally paid for the marriage of many a young maiden,[2] and was a very pillar of his order, much beloved by and familiar with men of substance throughout the areas in his territory — as well as with the esteemed women of all the towns he claims. He proclaimed loudly that, by virtue of licensure from his order, his powers of confession were greater than those of any local curate. Known for his affable hearing of confessions and his agreeable absolutions, he gave easy penances to those who provided him with the best meal. He was not afraid to assert that a substantial gift to a poor order had the same spiritual value as a good confession; he preached that any man who donates generously is repentant. There are, he maintained, men so hard of heart they are unable to weep even though they are in great pain. In such cases, instead of crying and praying, these people should give silver to the poor friars. This Friar's hood was full of knives and decorative pins that he would give to attractive women as he addressed them

---

[2] The implication is that these are young women he has first seduced and then matched with suitable husbands.

graciously in a differential tone. He had a nice singing voice and accompanied himself most charmingly on a small harp. His neck was as white as a fleur-de-lis, and yet he was as strong as a champion wrestler. Well did he know the taverns, the inn-keepers and the barmaids of every town — much better than the lepers or the beggar women. He reasoned that it would be absolutely inappropriate for a worthy individual, as he was, to consort with such as those. It would not be respectable and, more importantly, less profitable to deal with such riff-raff, rather than with the rich and with successful merchants. And to be sure, where profits were to be made, he was the embodiment of courteous behavior and gracious humility. No one anywhere was as capable as he at his trade, and he was by far the best beggar in his convent. And he was happy to pay for the license that ensured his exclusive right to beg in a particular territory. No one performed ballads better than he did; then his eyes would twinkle in his head like the stars on a frosty night. A poor widow might not own any shoes, but his "in principio" was proclaimed so pleasantly that before he was done he had wriggled the last farthing out of her. His short cloak was made of double worsted, proof that his income far exceeded his costs. His ability to flirt could put a fawning puppy to shame, and he was famous for his ability to mediate on reconciliation days. At those times he was anything but a simple scholar, a poor cloistered man with a threadbare cape, but more like a learned master or a pope, as his carefully-chosen words emerged, perfectly formed, like a bell from the mold — a lisp added a hint of lasciviousness to sweeten the English dripping from the tongue of Hubert, this worthy begging friar.

There was with us also a Merchant with forked beard, sitting high on his horse, dressed in motley. He sported a Flemish hat of beaver, his boots had attractive elegant clasps, and his solemnly intoned remarks were limited to discussing increases in his profits. Above all else he wanted assurance that the waters between Middleburg, in Holland, and Orwell, in England, were kept safe for trade. He applied his wit and his expertise effectively to the buying and selling of currencies, and he was so careful in his various dealings and in borrowing money that no one could accuse him of being in debt. All in all, he was a worthy man, but I must admit that I did not learn his name.

We were joined by a Student from Oxford who had studied logic for many a year. His horse was as thin as a rake's handle and he himself anything but fat -- in fact, he looked hollow and was ever serious. His threadbare outer jacket showed that he had not yet managed to acquire either a religious post or a secular position. Given the choice, he would have preferred to own twenty books bound in red or black — for example, Aristotle and all his philosophy — than to have rich robes or a fiddle or a harp. Even though he had the entire wisdom of philosophy to draw on, his coffers had small gain from that. He spent any money he was able to gain from his friends on books and on learning, praying busily for the souls of those who supported him in his studies. He was focused completely on learning, saying not a single word more than necessary; and he spoke with appropriate formality and due respect, concisely but full of meaning. Every word from his lips was consistent with moral virtue, and he enjoyed nothing so much as teaching and learning.

With us was a Lawyer, a justice with the highest legal training, prudent and wise, exuding superiority; he was no stranger to the portico of St. Paul's Cathedral where plaintiffs come to seek legal counsel. He was discreet and inspired great reverence, at least he seemed to, he was so well spoken. He regularly presided over the court of assizes, both because it was in his jurisdiction and by special royal appointment. His vast expertise and excellent reputation assured him of multiple grants of annual income. There is no one who has, over time, acquired more land than he, as there is no one better at taking advantage of the unrestricted possession principle — of course his dealings were always above challenge. I have never seen a man as busy as this one and, somehow, he seemed even busier than he actually was. His library contained each and every case and judicial decision since the time of William the Conqueror. He knew well how to draft and polish legal documents, no one could find any flaws in his writing, and he knew every statute by heart. He wore a simple, multi-colored robe, though a silk belt decorated with narrow stripes encircled his waist. That's all I have to say about his dress.

His companion was a Franklin,[3] a gentleman with a beard as white as the daisy. He thoroughly enjoyed a piece of white bread soaked in wine, and his complexion was accordingly sanguine. His only goal in life was gratification, as he was ever a true son of Epicurus, who taught that pure pleasure is the only path toward real and perfect happiness. He maintained so great a household that in his part of the country he was the equivalent of St. Julian, patron saint of hospitality. The food and drink he served were uniformly of the highest quality, and no one had a wine cellar to match his. His house was never without plenty of baked meats, fowl or fish — in his home it practically snowed food and drink, and no matter what time of the year it might be, he adjusted his table's menu so that all proper seasonal delicacies were appropriately served. He kept countless fat partridges in pens, and his fishpond was well stocked with bream and pike. His dining room table was always set in the great hall,[4] covered with good cloth, utensils laid out, and the Franklin himself ready to preside as lord and governor of the meal; pity his cook if the sauce was not sufficiently spiced or piquant. He had served multiple times as knight of the shire,[5] as well as sheriff and auditor. A broad, double-edged dagger and a silken purse hung from a belt that was white as the morning's milk. Could there be a more exemplary estate holder than this?

---

[3] A "free" man, meaning that he was not indentured or financially beholden to anyone.

[4] Normally, tables for dining were set up only for meals, easily removable to make the same spaces available for other activities.

[5] The individual who represented a particular county in Parliament.

We had with us an entire group dressed in the matching livery of a dignified and respected parish guild: a carpenter, a weaver, a dyer, a tapestry maker and a seller of hats and small clothing items — a haberdasher. Their outfits were new, shiny and recently embellished; their knives were inlayed not with brass but with silver, worked neatly and precisely, as were their belts and purses. I am sure they all looked quite splendid when they were seated on the dais of their guild hall, each of them considered wise enough and possessed of sufficient property and income to serve as a suitable town official. This was surely also reflected in the behavior of their wives, not about to be belittled by anyone, expecting to be addressed as "madam," to lead the line at vigils and to preen in their rich mantles at the front of town processions.

The Carpenter appeared to be their somewhat unlikely leader, as the four others had much more in common in terms of their trades. His name was Joseph and he liked to talk about Jesus and Joseph being carpenters; his wife's name was Mary, and I fear that he believed each word he spoke to be about his own holy family. He had no sons but six daughters, and their names were inscribed on the wooden cross that hung from a gold chain around his neck. Joseph was tall and thin, and he expected his companions to treat him as he thought the biblical Joseph should have been treated. He imagined himself a carver and made good use of his sharp knife to create small cribs that held the Baby Jesus, but he expected endless thanks for each one he bestowed on some fortunate individual. His speech was drawn through his nose and he looked down that same nose at all who crossed his path.

There was a Tapister along with a Weaver of large cloth, and these two spent much of their time squabbling about their trades and which of them should be more respected for his art. The Weaver was almost as broad as one of his large rugs, while the Maker of Tapestries was as thin as one of the rods from which he hung his wares. From dawn to dusk, they were deep in their cups — one moment fighting with each other, the next, stumbling about with their arms around one another's shoulders, complaining about the cost of gold thread and the heavy taxes that would surely force them out of business. Gilbert and Ralf, as did their three companions, came from York, where they had amassed considerable wealth in the shops they inherited from their fathers. Though both of Viking stock, Ralf prided himself on that heritage, while Gilbert did not mention it. Gilbert treated everyone he met as a potential customer for his tapestries, tailor-made to fit any wall, no matter how small or large. Ralf seemed to think that his products were so wonderful that they required no such bluster, He preferred to let them speak for themselves — and his fat purse ostensibly supported this belief. These two behaved as if there was no Knight, no respected Monk, no Prioress or Man of Laws in our group, and they themselves were the acknowledged leaders of our little company. Drunk as they usually were, they were oblivious to the distain their fellow pilgrims were not loathe to display towards them, and so they made themselves the laughing stock of all but their fellow guild members.

Also of this group was a Dyer, name of Helfrich, who could not have denied his trade, had he wanted to. His hands, his neck, his face, his hair were motley, one bright color chasing another, so that he looked more like one of Gilbert's tapestries than one of God's regular children, a character who might have stepped out of a story about a far-off land where people came in bright, unexpected colors. But, on top of that, Helfrich was only too happy to proclaim and relish in his craft. He loved all things bright and spoke of colors as if they gave meaning to all parts of life. He loved to argue about the name of this or that hue, and the exact tint he assigned to someone's cape was as important to him as if it were a matter of faith, while misnaming any precise color was a great heresy worthy of death at the stake. Despite that, I found him likable and learned from him the names of colors I had never seen but could imagine on the wings of birds or sunsets glorifying our most benevolent Lady Nature.

The final one of these guildsmen was the haberdasher Garrit, a maker of hats and other small articles of clothing. He stammered when he spoke and would break into song without warning; then his sputtering would smooth out, and his voice would ring out as brightly and clearly as if it embodied Helfrich's entire palette of colors. To the chagrin of some, his songs were common and offended greatly, a thing Garrit seemed to enjoy even more than merely singing the words that created offense. Hanging from his belt there were four or five hats that he urged us, one and all, to consider purchasing, as they were the finest in the kingdom, made to keep cold heads warm and bald heads covered in the latest style. If Garrit was to be believed, his hats could cure leprosy, make invincible the weak, and lure stray women into the bed of any man who sported these creations. But his speech was always foul and full of words sure to displease anyone who valued courtesy or fair behavior.

For the occasion of this pilgrimage, these five guildsmen traveled with their own private Cook, hired to boil their chickens with marrowbones, tart spices and powdered roots. He was well acquainted with all drafts of London ale known to man and could roast and simmer and broil and fry; he could make a stew and bake a pie; and his blancmange could compete with any other. He seemed to relish Garrit's songs and urged him often to burst into unholy ditty that caused the Prioress — among others — to seek her distance from him. He had an odd habit of licking the palms of his hands, one after the other, and then wiping them on his greasy hair. While it did not seem to trouble the Guildsmen — his employers — I, for my part, I thought it a pity that his left shin was disfigured by a large oozing ulcer.

We also had with us a Sailor who could not have been more pleased by these guildsmen had they provided him with a constant stream of potent ale. He hailed from far west; for all I could tell he was from Dartmouth, and he clung to his nag as best he could in his coarse-cloth gown that fell to his knees. Under his arm I could see a dagger that was fastened to the cord that hung from his neck. I'm sure he was a good fellow, his face all browned from the hot sun. I'm also sure that he was accustomed to stealthily helping himself to many a draught of the on-board

Bordeaux wines while their merchants slept. His conscience was not troubled by details. If he had the upper hand in a fight or a brawl, he did not hesitate to return his opponents to their homes by various watery paths. But there was no one from Hull to Cartagena who matched his skill in charting tides and streams — not to mention threats to himself — or in finding harbors, predicting the positions of the moon, or practicing navigation. He was tough but cunning in judgment, and his beard had fluttered in many a tempest churning the seas and skies he knew so well — from Gotland and Cape Finister to every waterway in Britain and Spain, wherever he had sailed his ship, the Magdalen.

Another pilgrim with us there was a Physician who had no match in all the world when he spoke of medicine or surgery, as he was well versed in astrology. He knew just what astrological hours to assign two them, and he could calculate the ascendant positions of their signs and ascertain the cause of any malady. He knew where each humor was engendered and which of them were involved, be they hot, cold, moist or dry. As soon as he knew the cause or root of anyone's illness, he provided the remedy. He retained a stable of apothecaries to provide him with drugs and potions — they and he benefitted equally from their old and continuing friendships. He was thoroughly familiar with all the ancient and modern authorities: Hippocrates and Galen, Serapius, Averrose, Damascien and Constantine, as well as Bernard, John of Gaddesden and Gilbertus, though he spent little time studying the bible. He prescribed a diet of moderation that avoided excess, was full of nutrients and easy to digest. He was dressed from top to bottom in red and blue, lined with taffeta and various silks, although he was anything but a wastrel. He had saved his earnings from the plague because, as is well known, gold is good for what ails you. And he lived in accord with that old axiom, as he loved gold above all else.

There was a Woman from Bath, a goodly Wife who, unfortunately, was a bit hard of hearing. She was such a skilled cloth maker that she easily surpassed those from Ypres and Gaunt. In her entire parish no woman was allowed to precede her when it was time to take the offering to the altar, but if such an unfortunate event occurred, her anger knew no bounds. Her head coverings were so finely woven that I daresay her head was weighed down by ten pounds of a Sunday. Her tightly-laced stockings gleamed with the finest scarlet, and her shoes were made of supple leather, of course, in the latest fashion. She had a proud look on her fair, ruddy face but was somewhat gap-toothed, if I am to be honest with you. She had always been a respectable woman and — not counting other companions in her youth — she had been betrothed at church door to five husbands, but there's no reason to dwell on that now. She rode her horse comfortably and was well-versed in travel on and off the beaten path: three pilgrimages to Jerusalem, not to mention crossing many a foreign sea on her travels to Rome and Bologna, to Cologne and to the shrine of St. James of Compostella. Her large wimple was covered by an even larger hat, as broad as a buckler or a shield. She wore a rich overskirt around her wide hips and made no effort to hide the spurs on her feet. She could tell a joke and knew how to have a good time; there is no doubt but that she knew all the tricks of the trade in love, and she was well versed in remedies for love-sickness.

With us, also, was a pious Priest, a village Parson, a poor man, wealthy indeed in holy thought and sacred work. He was a learned person, educated, and completely committed to teaching Christ's gospel and devoutly serving his parishioners. He was gracious and wondrously diligent, always patient in adversity, something he proved many times over. He was loathe to excommunicate those from this flock who were too poor to pay proper tithes and would rather have given back to them the voluntary offerings at mass and those from his proper parish income. He was totally satisfied with having next to nothing. His parish was spread out with houses scattered here and there, but that did not stop him from visiting anyone who was suffering or ill, the great and small, no matter how far he had to go. On foot, a staff in his hand, he was a noble example for his sheep, tending to his flock first and teaching them later. Inspired by the words of the holy gospel, he was ever ware of this text: "if gold rusts, what chance does iron have?" For if a priest — whom we are to trust — can be corrupt, a simple man will surely corrode. And, truly, there is nothing more shameful than to have befouled shepherds leading clean sheep. It is, after all, the priest's responsibility to provide the example, through his own virtue, for all his sheep. This was not one of those parsons who leave their sheep stuck in the mud while they run off to St. Paul's, in London, seeking the highest bidder to pay for Masses for the dear departed; nor would he ever become the priest for hire of some wealthy guild. No, he remained at home and looked out for his fold, lest the wolf lead them into evil. He was a shepherd, not a mercenary. But though he was himself holy and virtuous, he did not scorn his sinful fellow humans, neither with derision nor haughty speech, as his teaching was always courteous and gentle. He saw his task as drawing people to heaven by kindness and by good example. Of course, if there was someone intractable, no matter who, great or lowly, he would rebuke such a person without hesitation. I am absolutely certain that never has there been a better priest anywhere. He did not value pomp, or ceremony, or an overly scrupulous conscience, teaching simply the story of Christ and his twelve apostles; and be lived that life by example.

This Parson was accompanied by his brother, a simple Plowman who had hauled many a cartload of dung in his life; he was a hard and true worker who lived with others in perfect peace and charity. He loved God first and foremost, with all his heart, at all times, whether life was pleasant or painful — and always he treated his neighbor as he himself wanted to be treated. Any time he was able to do so, he gladly thrashed wheat and dug ditches for anyone poor who needed help, without getting paid, all for the sake of Christ. He paid his tithes fully and fairly, both on his own labor and on what he owned. And, fittingly, he wore a laborer's tunic and rode a simple mare.

This left a Reeve, a Miller, a Summoner, a Pardoner, a Manciple and me, and that would sum up everyone.

The Miller was a stout fellow, to be sure. He was brawny in his bones and in the flesh that covered them. And he put that to good use, for wherever he came upon a wrestling match, he was sure to walk away with the prize ram. He had a thick neck, broad shoulders and great muscles; no door was safe from being lifted off its hinges or broken down if he ran his head into it. His beard was as red as is any sow or fox and as broad as a spade. On the top right of his nose he had a wart, a tuft of hair sprouting from it as rough as the bristles on a pig's ear; his enormous nostrils were black and wide, and his mouth gaped like a giant furnace. He was a buffoon who loved telling dirty stories about horrible obscenities and vicious sins. An accomplished thief of his customer's grain, he excelled at secretly triple-charging them, leaning effectively on the proverbial thumb of gold that Millers are claimed to have. He wore a sword and buckler over his white coat and blue hood, and he could blow well the bagpipe he carried, with which he played us loudly out of the town when we began our journey.

A gentle Manciple, a business manager for one of the temples dedicated to the study of law, was with us, also — this was one man whom others would do well to emulate in buying provisions wisely, whether paying in cash or buying on credit. For he was so careful to espy the moment of best opportunity that he was always ahead of everyone else, ever in the best position for the deal. I find it amazing how on God's green earth the wit of this uneducated fellow should outpace the collected wisdom of all these learned men to whom he reported: more than thirty individuals, all of them very skilled — all experts in the law. Among them there were at least a dozen respected enough to be competent stewards of the income and lands of any lord in England. Somehow our Manciple knew how to allow a noble master to live according to his full wealth, honorably and without debt (unless he were crazy!) or to live as frugally as he might choose to do; this manciple could manage an entire shire, whatever its condition, outsmarting everyone else.

The Reeve was a thin, choleric man, his beard shaved as closely as possible, his hair clipped narrowly around his ears and chopped short in front as if he were a priest. His legs were as long and lean as a staff, as if he had no calves at all. He wore a long blue surcoat, and on his hip a rusty blade. However, he rode an impressive, dappled, gray steed he called Scot. So expert was he in managing bins and grain storages that no auditor could get the better of him. And he read the weather so well that he could predict accurately what yield to expect from seed and grain. This Reeve was totally in charge of everything his lord owned: his sheep, his cattle, the dairy, the swine, all the horses, livestock and poultry. He had first contracted to manage the estate when his master was just twenty years of age, and in all that time no one had ever known the Reeve to be in arrears. There was never a bailiff, no herdsman or any servant whose tricks or ploys our Reeve was not on to, and they feared him as if he were the grim reaper himself. His handsome, well-built dwelling was situated on a heath, shadowed comfortably by great green trees. He seemed to be better at buying property than was his lord, something that had quietly made him very rich. He knew exactly how to please his lord in subtle ways; he would give and take loans on his master's goods, pocketing a tidy profit, earning the master's gratitude and a reward from him to boot. As a young man he had learned a solid craft, as he was a competent carpenter. This Reeve, who came from Norfolk, outside a town known as Baldeswell, wore his cloak tucked in all around, like friars do, and he made sure always to ride at the very rear of all our troop.

The Summoner[6] we had with us had a fire-red baby face, full of pimples and topped by swollen eyelids; his scurvy black eyebrows and scabby beard punctuated a face to scare children. Nothing could heal the pustules on his face, not quick-silver, no kinds of lead, not sulphur, nor borax or oil of tartar, no ointment of any kind that cleans or stings — nor was there remedy for his

---

[6] Someone authorized to "summon" individuals to appear before the ecclesiastical courts of the time.

swollen cheeks. On his head he wore a garland, as big as a tavern sign, and he brandished a large loaf of bread as if it were a shield. He loved his garlic, onions, and leeks and relished drinking strong wine, red as blood — then he would yell and shout as if he had gone mad. And when he was well in his cups he spoke only Latin, that is, the two or three phrases he took from some decree that he had heard — God knows he heard them all day long, and we all know that a magpie can pronounce "Walter" as well as can the pope. But if this Summoner were to be examined about anything else, the limits of his knowledge were clear, as all he knew was to repeat: "Questio quid iuris."[7] Granted, he was as lecherous and randy as a sparrow, but all in all, he was a harmless buffoon, kind in his own way; you couldn't ask for a better buddy. For a quart of wine he would allow one of his friends to spend a whole year with his own whore and hold no grudge. He was expert at swindling someone without ever being found out, and if he came across a likely apprentice, he would teach him his nefarious tricks despite the archdeacon's threat of excommunication. This Summoner had great sway with many of the young people of the diocese because he knew their secrets and served all of them with his counsel. He would tell them that "The purse is the archdeacon's hell." Now I know full well that this lie would not help them if they got in trouble, for the guilty have good reason to fear the archdeacon's power to excommunicate, for his curse means death, while absolution gives life. I say: let a guilty man fear the *Significat*.[8]

A gentle Pardoner,[9] from Rouncivalle, the Charing Cross hospital, rode with this Summoner, as they were companions and

---

[7] Latin for "What point of the law is applicable?"

[8] A term that was used when someone was remanded to prison.

[9] An individual licensed (within a certain jurisdiction) to sell pardons for sins. In return for paying certain sums of money, individuals received documents attesting that they were absolved of specific days they would have to spend in purgatory.

friends. This Pardoner, newly come from the papal court, was wont to break into loud song: "Come hither, my love, to me," and the Summoner provided a solid harmony, louder than any trumpet you could imagine. The Pardoner's hair was as yellow as wax, hanging straight like a hank of flax, in thin strands that spread all over his shoulders, one by one, and his eyes stared with the frozen glare of a hare. His voice was as high as a goat's, and he had no beard — nor would he ever have one — his face as smooth as if he had just been shaven. I suspect he was a gelding or a mare. To play up what he thought was his attractive appearance he refused to wear a hood, leaving it packed away in his knapsack. He believed to be demonstrating the latest fashion as he rode along, all loose and open, except for his cape. Into his cape was sown a small reproduction of St. Veronica's cloth, with the image of Jesus's thorn-crowned head. The knapsack in his lap was brimful of pardons so recently hot from Rome that they were still steaming. But to speak of his craft, there was no Pardoner his match between Berwick and Ware, for in his pouch he had a pillowcase that he claimed was the veil of Our Lady, the Virgin Mary. He also said that he had a piece of St. Peter's sail from the time he was a fisherman and Christ called him to follow Him. He had a cross made of alloy decorated with stones and a glass full of pig's bones. And he used these relics whenever he came across poor people in the countryside to get from them more money in a single day than they earned in two months. This is how, with false flattery and various kinds of trickery, he turned such unsuspecting folks into apes. And yet, in the end, he was considered a noble ornament to adorn any parish church, as he could read a verse or a lesson most dramatically and demonstrate his greatest skill in the manner in which he sang the offertory. He sang merrily and loudly, following it up at once with powerful preaching in his refined tongue, reaping without delay the silver he so dearly sought.

    So now I have briefly told you as much as I can about the members of our group, their social status and their appearance, as well as the reason we were gathered in Southwerk at this pleasant lodging called the Tabard, right by the Bell. I have described what we did that night we were all gathered there, and after this I will tell of our journey and the details of our pilgrimage. But first I must beseech you that in your kindness you do not attribute my plain speech in this effort to my lack of sophistication, as I intend simply to present my companions' words and behavior just as I observed and heard them. For I am sure that you know as well as do I that anyone who tries to tell another person's story must repeat each word as accurately as he possibly can — that is his responsibility — no matter how crudely or rashly that person spoke. Anything else would mean that the tale would be false, or invented, or relying on invention — a storyteller must be true to this, though he were speaking for his brother, and even if one word was as good as another. Christ himself spoke very plainly in the scriptures, and we all know that there is no villainy in the sacred text. Plato, too, says — for those who can read his work — that the words must be cousin to the deed. And I, too, beg you to forgive me if, here in my telling, I have failed to treat people properly according to their rank. You must understand that I have but limited wit.

But back to our Host, who treated each one of us with great warmth and soon had us seated at a supper consisting of the best provisions one could imagine. We were delighted to drink the good strong wine he served. Our Host was the kind of man who would have made an impressive master of ceremonies in any great lord's hall. He was a large, bright-eyed man — a finer businessman you would not find in Cheapside — direct in his speech, clever, and well-trained. He lacked nothing one might expect in a respectable man with a good sense of humor. And so, when the supper was over, he began to entertain us, speaking of many things and sharing good stories and jokes. Later, after we had all settled our bills, he spoke to the group: "Now then, masters, I truly hope you all feel most welcome here! I do not exaggerate to tell you that I have not seen so attractive a group as you here, in my lodging, in more than a year. I would love to do you some service, if I knew how, and as I think about it, even now something comes to mind whereby I can make it all more enjoyable, and it will cost you nothing.

You are all on your way to Canterbury — Godspeed — and may the blessed martyr hear your prayers and fulfill your needs. But I would guess that along the way you will share stories to entertain yourselves. We all know that riding along the road dumb as stones is neither interesting nor enjoyable. But this is where I can bring you some amusement, as I have said, and better your experience. And if you can be of one mind and agree to place yourselves under my rule and to act in accord with what I propose, tomorrow, as you ride along your way, by the soul of my dead father, if you are not entertained, may you take my head. Enough said. Hold up your hands if you agree!"

It did not take us long to make our decision. Nobody thought it worthwhile to complicate things so, without further words, we granted his intention and asked him to share with us his further proposition.

"Masters," he continued immediately, "please listen to my plan then, and hear it with an open mind. I will go straight to the point, short and clear, and ask that each of you, in order to shorten our journey, shall tell two tales on our journey to Canterbury. Listen carefully! On the way back here to London, each of you shall tell two more, stories that can be drawn from any of your experiences. Now, the one tale that surpasses all others — and by that I mean a story that has the most to say and brings us the most pleasure — that person shall have a supper paid for by all the rest, here in this same place, the Tabard Inn, upon our return from Canterbury. And," he shushed a murmur from the group, "and, only to increase your ease on this trek, I will gladly ride along with you myself — at my own cost, of course — and serve as your guide and judge. But," he raised his arm, finger outstretched in warning, "if any among you will challenge my judgment as to the best tale, that person will pay for everything that we have spent along our way." Silence. "So, if you all agree to everything I have said, tell me now, without hesitation, and I will prepare everything accordingly."

There seemed to be general agreement, judging by the nodding heads of many, but then Gilbert, the tapestry maker, noisily pushed his chair back, almost falling over in the process, unsteadily fighting the drunkenness that was threatening to conquer him.

"I . . . musht objet," he shouted, trying to find the Host where he stood on one side of the large chamber. Only some heard him, and they did not include the Host. But Gilbert was not to be ignored. Again he shouted: "I objet" and this time he was heard by all. The Host, now frowning, hushed the room and asked: "Do I hear you to object, sir?" He made a great point of pronouncing all the letters in the word, although the point was lost on Gilbert. "Yesh . . . shir," Gilbert slurred. "Not all, that ish, we are shomewhat . . . that wish . . . shome are not . . . I mean to shay that we are not, not all of ush, are not planning to return to London. Not!"

And now, Ralf, the weaver, drunk as Gilbert, entered the lists. Pulling himself up to stand, weaving dangerously, grasping at Gilbert's unsteady shoulder for assistance, Ralf burped heartily before he spoke. "Dashs right!" He burped again. "I alsho . . . I want to shay that we return to home. Norsh . . . norsh . . . norsh umbria! And we don't plan to come back . . . here." He plopped down on his bench, glaring glassily at the Host. Now it was Garrit's turn. "By God's blood, we don't want to come back to London, and we won't." Garrit, who obviously held his liquor much better than did his fellow guildsmen, sat down but then rose again: "Tell me why in bloody hell I should pay for someone else's bleeding supper. I'd rather they choke on their own vomit and slide down into the devil's arse and ask him for help — but not me."

Harry Bailey, our host, whom I have known for many years, was taken aback, for once, without the words that usually served him well. But Joseph the Carpenter stood now to speak. "My fellow pilgrims, please; these, my companions, do speak true. We did not plan to return here but to go straight home once we visited the martyr's shrine. I would ask that we consider another possibility. Perhaps . . ." he pondered, seemingly without ready solution, and then the Franklin rose: "Gentlemen, gentlemen, if I may, I dare say we are all friends here, with enough courtesy amongst us to solve this problem."

The room did quiet then, and this gentle man, softly stroking one side of his well-maintained beard, continued. "If, indeed, these gentlemen from . . . the north will not be returning to London, surely we can resolve this difficulty to everyone's satisfaction. May I suggest that we make plans just for the journey to the shrine and let everyone return as he please?"

Before this could be taken up, the Man of Laws elegantly rose to his feet and solemnly proclaimed: "I thank you, and I am certain that I speak for all, in thanking you for your suggestion, Sir, but this solves only half the problem. As someone who must judge guilt and innocence each day, I put it to you all that our lord and judge, our innkeeper and host, would be hard put to judge among so many tales. What if our Clerk tells two memorable stories and our Lady Prioress offers us two equally wondrous?"

The good Woman from Bath laughed heartily and loudly stated: "I've been accused often enough of talking too much, but four tales seems like too much even for me!"

The Man of Laws continued as if she had not opened her mouth at all. "Or if the Squire and my lord Monk and our friend Joseph here all tell memorable tales not ever to be forgotten, what then? How then is our poor Sir Host to decide among them?" He paused and I could see that all, at least those sober, in the room considered this difficulty. "I proffer that there be fewer tales all around and that the matter be more simple." He paused, turned rather elaborately toward the knight, and addressed him. "Sir Knight, I have not the pleasure of knowing your name, but I can tell that you are a man of wide experience and great wisdom. What say you, Sir, about our problem here?"

The Knight furrowed his brow and looked down, then up, meeting his questioner's intent gaze. The Lawyer sat as the Knight rose slowly to his feet. "You honor me, Sir, and I hope to satisfy your question."

"You can satisfy the blood of the sacred goat" Garrit muttered loudly enough for all to hear.

The Knight ignored it and was about to speak, but our Host had finally found his voice again. "I must protest, gentlemen. If I have overstepped my bounds I do plead guilty, as I wished only to increase your pleasure on this holy journey."

The silence that followed made it clear to him that the pilgrims sought to hear from the Knight, who responded: "It seems to me that the solution is as simple as can be. We do all travel in unison to the holy shrine, so let us agree for just that portion of our journey. The fact is that one tale told by each us will fill the time to Canterbury, and a common meal by all to celebrate that journey seems just. So, let us ask our worthy Host to make his judgment then, before we all disperse, based on a single tale from each. The martyr will bless our efforts — as he will the Host's judgment — and we will all go hence in friendship and in joyful fellowship. I am certain that our Host will judge fairly and well." He sat down and there were nods and then murmuring and then shouts of agreement and applause.

This seemed to be a solution somewhat to the Host's displeasure — perhaps because he was losing the opportunity to host a dinner in his own establishment when all returned. But it was clear that the Knight's solution was acceptable to the group, and we swore our oaths happily and assented for Harry to do as was now established — we would be governed by him, he would judge our tales and be our record keeper, determine the price of the supper and other costs, and none would challenge his decisions in any of these matters. And thus, by common assent, we reached accord and then more wine was shared before we all retired for the night. Although some lasted longer than others, quite a few began snoring long before they were jolted upright and encouraged to move to their chambers.

The next morning, with the first light, our Host arose and served as rooster for us all. Once he had gathered us into a flock, we rode two miles at a pace just faster than a walk and reached a stream called the Watering of St. Thomas. There he pulled up and said: "If you please, my lords, let me call to mind our agreement made last night. If what we said at evensong still agrees with your minds now, in the light of this glorious day, let us now determine who will begin with our first tale. As ever I drink wine or ale, whoever here refuses to abide by my decision shall pay for all of our expenses on our journey. So, before we go any further, we will draw straws, and whoever has the short straw will begin. Sir Knight," he continued, "my master and my lord, please draw now, in keeping with my decision. Come, my lady Prioress, and you Sir Clerk — let's not be shy and waste time thinking about it; come, everyone, take your turn."

And so, in time, each of us had drawn a straw and, to tell you without further delay, whether it was by chance, luck or fate, the fact is that the short straw went to the Knight. All seemed quite pleased by this, and now, just as you have already heard, in keeping with the agreement made beforehand, without further ado, it was up to the Knight to tell his tale. And, realizing that it was his task to be the first to honor our agreement, this wise and congenial gentleman said: "What? I welcome the lot I have drawn. In God's name, I shall begin the game. So, let us ride and listen to my story." And with that we set out again on our journey, and the Knight began, quite pleasantly, to tell his tale — as you will hear.

The Knight's Tale

"We hear in old stories that there once lived a Duke named Theseus, the lord and governor of Athens. In his time no greater conqueror was known to all the world, and through his wisdom and chivalry he subjugated many wealthy lands. This included the country of the Amazons, ruled by Queen Hypolita, whom Theseus married and was now, gloriously and with much splendor, bringing home with him — along with her young sister, the fair Emily.

Now, if it were not that it would take too long, I would tell you all about how Theseus managed to vanquish this land of women, about the unmatched wedding celebration, and even about the storm that threatened the voyage back to Athens, but I have a large field to plow — and, I will admit — my oxen are weak — and I certainly don't wish to hinder other pilgrims from telling their stories. After all, I want everyone to have a fair chance to win the supper by telling the best story.

So I will go on.

When Duke Theseus, prosperous and proud, had nearly reached Athens, he noticed a company of women at the side of the road, kneeling in two rows, all solemnly dressed in black. They were wailing and keening more loudly and pitifully than had ever been heard before in all the world, and they ceased only when they had managed to seize the bridle of the Duke's steed.

The Duke accosted them: 'Who do you people think you are to disturb my homecoming with such lamentation? Is this howling your way of showing how much you envy my honor? Or has someone else injured or offended you? Tell me why you are all dressed in black and what can be done to make amends?'

The oldest woman among them swooned, but then she spoke: 'My Lord, Fortune has blessed you with victory, and heaven knows we do not begrudge your glory; rather we seek your mercy and your help. Have pity on us in our distress. Please let some drop of grace fall upon us wretched women. In our lives we have all been duchesses — even queens — but, thanks to Fortune and her treacherous wheel, we have become the miserable wretches you see before you. Here, by the temple of the Goddess Clemence, we have been awaiting your arrival for this last fortnight. You have it in your power, Lord, to help us!'

She continued: 'I, wretched I, reduced to weeping and wailing, was once the wife of King Canapeus who died at Thebes — I curse the day — and all these women whom you see before you, they all lost their husbands in the siege of that town. And now that old fool Creon, Lord of Thebes, filled with wrath and wickedness, in brutal spitefulness, so as to shame and dishonor our slain lords, has — by his sole authority — ordered all their bodies to be cast onto a sweltering heap, refusing to let them be buried or burned, letting dogs devour them instead.'

Now all the women fell down and cried, most pitifully: 'Show some mercy on us wretched women and allow our sorrow to sink into your heart!'

The gentle Duke thought his heart would break at the sight of these poor women, brought from great estate to such misery and despair. His heart filled with pity, he leaped from his charger and embraced them, comforting them as best he could. He swore an oath right then and there that he would, as he was a true knight, use all his might to wreak such vengeance on Creon that the people of Greece would never forget that tyrant's well-deserved death. Right then and there Theseus unfurled his war banner and, with all his men, set out toward Thebes. He commanded Hypolita and her beautiful young sister to wait for him in Athens, but he himself did not spare even a moment to rest before he rode forth. That is all there is to say about that.

His massive white banner, fluttering with the red statue of Mars, and his pennant, embossed with the minotaur he had slain in Crete, led this conqueror's host, the flower of chivalry, directly to the fields surrounding Thebes. The outcome was that Theseus fought and slew Creon in open battle, routed the enemy, besieged the city, razed it and restored to the grieving widows the bones of their beloved men, so that proper rites could be observed. Of course it would take too long to do justice to the lamentations that accompanied the cremation of the bodies or to the generous honors Theseus bestowed upon the grieving women — and I mean to be concise.

In the aftermath of the battle, the scavengers thoroughly ransacked the corpses left on the field, stripping them of armor and clothing. And it so happened that in those piles of bodies they found, bleeding from many a wound, two young knights in matching armor, neither quite dead nor fully alive. By their heraldic devices they were soon identified as Arcite and Palamon, sons of sisters of the royal line of Thebes. The two young men were extricated from the gory piles of corpses and carefully carried to the tent of Theseus, who immediately ordered them to be taken to Athens to be imprisoned for the rest of their lives — with no possibility of ransom. And soon thereafter this worthy Duke and all his men returned home in conquering glory, where he lived out his life beloved and honored. What else is there to say?

Meanwhile, Palamon and his companion Arcite languished woefully and without hope in their tower, knowing that no amount of gold could ransom them.

And so, one day turned into another, and years passed, until one May morning, the beautiful Emily rose before dawn, as she always did, more fair than any pure white lily on its stalk of green, and fresher than a dewy field bedecked with flowers. I cannot say which was more beautiful, her complexion or the hue of a rose.

Now we all know that the month of May does not tolerate sluggards, as it pierces every gentle heart and wakens it from slumber: 'Arise and pay respect, as is proper.' Emily was happy to take part in this tradition, and so she rose, freshly attired, her golden hair in a braid down her back, a yard in length. And she walked back and forth in the garden, saluting the rising sun, gathering red and white flowers for an intricate wreath, all the while singing a tune as only an angel could.

The castle's great tower, thick and strong, was joined unto the garden in which Emily found her delight; this tower served as the castle's main dungeon, and there dwelled the two knights of whom I have told you before and will now tell you more.

On that bright May morning, this woeful prisoner Palamon had risen and was roving about in a chamber high up in the tower, from which he could see the entire city, as well as that luxurious green garden which Emily herself was enjoying. Palamon, sad Palamon, pacing back and forth, lamenting and cursing the day that he was born, happened, by chance or as fate would have it, to look out through a small square window firmly barred with iron, and there he saw Emily. Turning pale, all he could say was: 'Ah!' as if stung deep in the heart.

Arcite, hearing this moan, leaped from his bed and inquired: 'Dear cousin, what is wrong. You are deathly pale. And you cried out as if someone has done you grievous harm. For the love of God, I beg you to suffer our imprisonment with patience, for we can never escape. Fortune, perhaps Saturn — displeased with us — or some other constellation has dealt us this adversity, despite our best efforts. It was written in the stars the day we were born, and we have no choice but to endure it. That's all there is to it.'

But Palamon disagreed: 'Oh, cousin, truly, your opinion in this case is based on your faulty imagination. It was not our imprisonment that caused me to cry out, although I was wounded just now through my eye and deep in my heart by something deadly. It is the beauty of the lady I see roaming to and fro in yonder garden that is the cause of my anguish and my tears. I do not know whether she be woman or goddess, unless she be Venus herself.' And, with that, he fell to his knees and continued: 'Venus, if it is your will to appear thus in this garden before sorrowful, wretched me, I implore you to help us escape this prison. But if it is my eternally determined destiny to die in prison, have some compassion on our noble heritage, brought so low by heartless tyranny.'

But then Arcite also caught sight of Emily exploring the garden and was immediately wounded by her beauty to such a degree that if Palamon was deeply harmed Arcite was hurt as much or more, able only to mutter pitifully: 'I am slain by the peerless beauty of her who wanders here; unless I have her mercy and her grace and may at least look upon her, I may as well be dead; there is nothing left to say.'

Hearing this, Palamon responded angrily: 'Are you joking? You can't be serious!'

'By everything I believe, I am dead serious! God help me if I am joking!' That was all Arcite could say.

Palamon's brows tightened: 'It would be no great honor for you to be a false traitor to me, your cousin and your brother. Have we not sworn that nothing, never, for pain or terror, till death part us, would ever divide us? That neither one of us would ever hinder the other in love? That you would truly support me always, as I would you? This was your oath and mine, as well. You cannot disavow it! And as I have put my faith in you, you must agree. But now, suddenly, you are about to love falsely my lady, whom I love and serve and will always until death stills my heart. No, no, treacherous Arcite, you shall not! I loved her first and shared my woe with you, my sworn brother pledged to help me. And, as a knight, you are bound to aid me if it is in your power, or else, I must call you a false villain.'

Arcite responded proudly: 'It is you who is false – not I! Let me tell you why: I loved her first – as a man. You are still not certain whether she is woman or goddess. That means that yours is the affection for something divine and mine is love for a fellow human. And that is the reason I told you — as my cousin and my sworn brother — about my feelings. Let's suppose that you loved first; don't you know the old legal adage: "who would try to impose any law unto a lover?" By everything of value in my head, love is a more powerful law than may be imposed on any man. And that is why man-made laws are broken every day in the name of love. A man must love, no matter what; he cannot avoid it unless he be dead — whether it be a girl, a widow or even another man's wife; the same is true for me.

But surely you haven't forgotten that you and I are damned to prison — forever! No ransom can save us. You and I are acting like two dogs fighting over a bone the whole day, and then along comes a kite that makes off with the bone while they are growling at each other. At the royal court, my dear brother, it's every man for himself.

Go ahead, love all you want, and so shall I, and surely that will be the end of it while we live out our lives in this prison. So let each of us bear it as best he can.'

The antagonism between these two was great and did not abate — but I have no time to dwell on that. To the point. It so happened one day — I will tell it as quickly as I can — the worthy Duke Perotheus, good friend to Theseus since they were boys, came to visit his dear friend. Old books tell us that their friendship was so great that after one of them died, his friend — and this is true — went after him and sought him down in hell — but that is not the story I am telling here.

Duke Perotheus, who had come to know Arcite prior to this in Thebes and liked him well, through multiple requests and pleas persuaded Theseus to release Arcite without ransom, to go freely wherever he wished, but under the condition I will now detail for you.

This, plain and simple, was the agreement: if Arcite were ever in his life, by day or night, to be discovered for even one hour in any domain belonging to Theseus — this they all agreed to — he would be decapitated at once. There would be no other option.

So Arcite took his leave and made his way toward home. Let him be careful — his neck is his pledge.

But just consider his suffering now! He might as well be dead. He wept, he wailed, he cried pitifully; he considered how he might end it all. 'Alas the day that I was born! My prison is worse than before, for now I am condemned for all eternity not to purgatory, but to hell. How I wish I had never known Perotheus, because then I would have stayed with Theseus, chained forever in his prison. But that would have been bliss, not woe. The mere sight of her whom I serve, though I might never earn her grace, would have been enough.

Oh, my dear cousin Palamon, you have indeed won the victory here, for you remain blissfully in prison. In prison? Surely you are in paradise rather than prison! Fortune supported your throw of the dice and allows you to have sight of her, while I have none. Since you are near her and are a worthy and able knight, it is possible that, by chance, since Fortune changes constantly, you may one day attain your desire. But I, exiled and stripped of all grace, am in such despair that neither earth, water, fire nor air, nor any creature consisting of these, can help or comfort me. I would be better off dead than suffering this despair and distress. Farewell my life, my heart's desire, my happiness!

Alas, you fools, who complain about divine providence or Fortune when, in fact, you receive much more than you could ever imagine, but obscurely. We cannot anticipate how the thing we are praying for will affect us; our search for happiness too often just leads us astray. Look at me: I was so sure that if only I could escape my prison I would be bathed in joy and well-being. Instead, I find myself banished from all prosperity, since I cannot see you, my Emily. I am dead — there is no remedy.'

Meanwhile, when Palamon realized that Arcite was gone, his wailing could be heard well beyond his tower, and his shiny shackles around his ankles were bathed in his salty tears. 'Oh, Arcite, dear cousin, God knows, after all our fighting, you have walked away with the prize. As you walk freely around Thebes, I'm sure my sorrow does not weigh on you. There's nothing to prevent you from using your wit and your courage to call on our common kindred and descend on this city with such force that you will shortly gain your lady and have her as your wife — while I perish. As you are a free lord and warrior, the advantage is all yours, and all I can do is to die in this cage. I am left to weeping and wailing for as long as I live, my pain doubled by the unrequited love I will feel always.'

And the fire of jealousy so burned his heart that his outward hue was indistinguishable from the pallor of cold ashes. But he continued: 'O cruel Goddess who governs our world with your eternal and immutable decrees, your decisions chiseled into the hardest stone, why are we more obliged to obey you than are the sheep in the fields? We die like other beasts, we are captured like other animals, we suffer sickness and adversity – and all too often innocently. What good is your knowledge of what is to come when it just leads to the punishment of the innocent? Why can other animals do whatever they want, but we must curtail our desires? At least, when beasts die, their pain is at an end, but we continue to suffer after we die, no matter how horrible our lives! Only theologians can answer that question. All I can see is villains free to do their mischief and to harm good people, while I languish in prison because Saturn and Juno, long jealous of and ever angry with our beloved Thebes, have turned its vast walls to rubble — and now Venus torments me as well, with my jealousy and my fear of what Arcite will do.'

But let me leave Palamon for a time to stew in his prison while I return to Arcite.

Through the long summer, the slow nights serve merely to increase the love pangs of both the lover and the prisoner, and I am hard put to judge who suffers more. As I have told you, Palamon, as good as dead in his chains and fetters, is damned to life-long imprisonment, and Arcite is exiled forevermore under penalty of death, never to see his beloved lady again.

So I now ask you lovers this question: Who is worse off, Arcite or Palamon? One can see his lady every day but must stay forever in prison; the other is free to go where he wishes but without seeing his lady ever again. So, decide, those of you who can, while I continue the story I have begun.[10]

Returning to Thebes, Arcite spent his days swooning often and generally in such grief that no creature before or after him has ever suffered so. Without sleep or food or drink, he became

---

[10] The *demand d'amour*, a traditional element in romances, where the story-teller asks the audience to decide which of two rivals is most deserving to win fair lady's hand.

as thin and dry as a stick; his eyes were hollow — grisly to behold — his skin was yellow, and his face as pale as ash, and he was always alone, spending his nights wailing and moaning. Even music — when he was able to notice it — merely made him weep more hopelessly. So low were his spirits and so much was he changed that no one could even recognize his voice. He acted like everyone else who has ever been love-sick, isolated in his chamber, in the depths of melancholy. And before long there was nothing about this woeful lover Arcite that had not become the opposite of the person he once was.

I could spend all day on his suffering, but to what avail?

When he had endured this cruel torment, this pain and suffering, for a year or two, one night, as he slept in his bed, there appeared to him the winged god Mercury, encouraging him to be merry. Mercury was arrayed just as when he had appeared to Argus in his sleep: his sleep-inducing staff in his hand and a hat covering his bright hair. He said to Arcite: 'Go at once to Athens, for there your sadness is destined to end.' Awakened by these words, Arcite said: 'In faith, no matter how painful it may be, I will set out for Athens immediately. Fear of death will not keep me from seeing my lady, whom I love and serve, for I am not afraid to die if only I can be in her presence.' Then he caught a glimpse of himself in a large mirror and realized that his complexion and his entire appearance had changed so much that he looked nothing like his former self. The torments he had suffered had so disfigured his face that if he did not draw attention to himself, no one in Athens would know who he was — but he would have the joy of looking upon his lady every day.

And so he changed into the clothes of a poor laborer and, accompanied only by a faithful squire also disguised as a poor man, he sought out the nearest road to Athens. Once there, he went to the palace and offered his services to draw water and do any low work needed and soon found steady work with a court attendant who was in Emily's retinue, a man in a position to determine which servants were capable and worthy of advancement and which were not.

Now Arcite, young and strong, could hew wood and carry water with the best of them, capable of carrying out any chore asked of him. He called himself Philostrate and served like this in the household of the beauteous Emily for a year or two. In truth, there was no one at the court in his position who was half so well-beloved as was this Philostrate; so gentle was his behavior that his renown spread throughout the court, and many said that it was only right that Theseus should advance him and find more noble use for him, employment that would allow him to exercise his full abilities. The fame of his actions and of his eloquence continued to grow and, before long, Theseus took an interest in him and made him a squire of his chamber with earnings enough to look and dress the part. Of course Arcite was also secretly receiving an annual income from Thebes, but he spent his money wisely and carefully, raising no suspicions. He lived like this for three years, through peace and war, and by then no man was more dear to Theseus. So, let me now leave Arcite in this current good fortune and speak a bit of Palamon.

For seven long years Palamon has languished, distressed and sad, in his dark, horrible, impenetrable prison. Can you imagine the dual sorrow and depression he has experienced, so enchained by love that he is nearly mad? Not to mention that his captivity will last forever — forever! Who could do justice to his martyrdom in English? Clearly, not I. So I will just let it be.

It so happened, then, in May of the seventh year, on the third night (this is what it says in old books that tell this story in greater detail), perhaps it was chance, perhaps fate — since, as we all know, when something is destined, it must happen — some time after midnight, with the help of a friend, Palamon escaped and fled the city. He had drugged his jailor with the best Theban narcotics available, so that the man could not have been awakened no matter how hard anyone might shake him. The night was short, and Palamon realized that he had to hide; so, filled with dread, he slipped into a grove by the wayside, thinking that he would seek shelter there during the day and then continue on to Thebes under cover of night. There he would gather his friends to help him make war on Theseus, so that he would soon either lose his life or gain Emily as his wife. This was, in short, his plan.

Now I turn back to Arcite, who could not have anticipated how Fortune's snare was about to increase his suffering.

Joyfully, the lark announced the dawn and fiery Phoebus once more lit up the shining day, drying the dew drops on the leaves; Arcite, now the main squire of Theseus, rose and spurred his majestic steed into the fresh countryside to pay his respects to this lovely season. After a mile or two, he found himself — entirely by chance — by that same grove I mentioned earlier. Here he dismounted and began to make a garland out of honeysuckle and hawthorn branches and leaves, heartily singing a song inspired by the warm sun: 'Welcome fair, fresh May, bedecked with beauteous flowers; help me to find and enjoy the green outdoors.' All this time he was on the path right next to where Palamon was hiding, filled with dread that he might be seen and would have to forfeit his life. He had no idea that this singer he heard might be Palamon; God knows he could not have imagined it.

Here, my friends, is why we should always act as if the fields have eyes and the woods ears, for we can never know whom we will meet unexpectedly. Certainly, Arcite had no idea how near was his comrade, cowering silently in the bushes, close enough to touch.

Having finished his song, Arcite suddenly sank into despondency, as lovers, in their curious way, do. For they dart up and then dash down more than a well-used bucket in a well. And so, Arcite sat down heavily and sighed: 'Alas that I was ever born. How long, Juno, will you continue to assault fair Thebes so cruelly? You have brought to ruin the royal blood of Amphion and of Cadmus, the first to build that great city and its first ruler. And I, his direct descendant, that same royal blood coursing through my veins, am now enslaved, a wretched captive to my mortal enemy, serving him as a poor squire.

But Juno simply piles shame upon shame for me, as I dare not even acknowledge my own name. Once I was known as Arcite; now I am the useless Philostrate. Oh, fierce Mars and Juno — how you have destroyed our royal lineage, leaving only me and wretched Palamon, now a martyr in Theseus's prison. And to top it all, love has so cruelly struck his fiery dart through my faithful, sorrowful heart, that my death was destined even before I was born. Oh, Emily, you slay me with your eyes. You are the cause of my death! None of my other cares are equal to a fraction of that sorrow. I would give anything only I could please you.' And with that he fell into a silent trance, as if he were dead.

Palamon felt as if a cold sword had suddenly sliced into his heart. Shaking with anger he could not be silent and, with ashen face, he leaped out of the woods as if demented, shouting: 'You foul, wicked traitor, Arcite — now you are caught, you, so insistent in loving my lady for whom I suffer all this pain and woe! You, my blood and my sworn comrade, have you now changed your name and thus falsely tricked Duke Theseus? Either I or you must die here, on this spot! You shall not love my lady Emily, for she is mine and mine alone, for I am Palamon, your deadly enemy. I have no weapon now, having just now escaped my prison, yet I doubt not that you shall die unless you spurn the love of Emily forever. Make your choice, for you cannot escape!'

As soon as Arcite heard his words and recognized Palamon, scornful and fierce as a lion, he drew his sword, replying: 'By the eternal God who reigns above, were it not that you are sick and mad with love and have no weapon, you should never leave this grove alive but die at my own hand. I renounce the oath of brotherhood you claim that I have sworn! What? You fool! Do you not know that love is not restrained by oaths? Or do you think that all of your force will keep me from loving?

But as you are yet a worthy knight, willing to let battle decide, hear now my promise: I swear that I shall return here tomorrow, without the knowledge of any others, as a faithful knight, with armor for both of us; and you can choose the best of that armor and leave the worst for me. And, before that, this night I will bring you food and drink and accouterment for your rest. And if you win my lady by killing me here in these woods, she shall be yours.'

Palamon answered: 'I agree to all of that.' And thus they parted until the next day, when they had pledged their word to meet.

Oh Cupid, who disdains all claims of equality by other gods! Here Arcite and Palamon have discovered that love will have no equal but will reign supreme.

Arcite rode back at once to Athens where, by the next morning, he had quietly gathered armor for the two of them to decide this battle in the field and brought it to the grove, just as he and Palamon had agreed to do. Grimly, they prepared for this fight that would lead to the death of one or both. No good wishes, no greetings, no words of any kind were exchanged as each helped arm the other, as brothers or friends would do, and then, at once, they began to thrust at one another with their sharp spears. Palamon might as well have been a mad lion as he fought, and Arcite a cruel tiger; like wild boars they came together, frothing at the mouth with pure anger, in blood up to their ankles.

So let them fight while I tell you of Theseus.

So strong is Destiny, that divine purveyor of God's providence everywhere, that even if all the world had sworn the opposite, what is ordained will nevertheless happen at just the intended moment, as it was meant to be. Whether it be war or peace or hate or love — all is governed by foresight from above.

Now this is what I must say about mighty Theseus: so eager — particularly in May — is he to hunt the great hart, that there dawns not a single day on which he does not dress for the hunt, with hunters, hounds and horns at his side. Such delight has he in hunting that his joy and desire are completely set on killing the hart for, second only to Mars, Theseus now serves Diana.

As I said earlier, the day was clear, and Theseus rode out joyfully, with his fair queen Hypolita and with Emily, all in royal hunting green, straight to a nearby grove where his men told him there was a hart. Anticipating a course or two for himself and his hounds, Theseus crossed a brook and rode straight to the clearing where the hart was heading. But when he came to the clearing and shaded his eyes from the sun, he saw Palamon and Arcite, fighting like two fierce boars. Their gleaming swords cut back and forth so violently it seemed that they were chopping down mighty oaks. Theseus, with no idea as to who they might be, drew his own sword and rode straight between the two fighters: 'Hold! Cease upon penalty of losing your head! By mighty Mars, whichever of you strikes another blow shall die. Now, tell me at once what sort of men you are, so bold to fight here in this manner, without judge or other officer, as if you were engaged in sanctioned combat.'

Palamon was quick to answer: 'Without wasting words, Sir, we both deserve to die, for we are but two woeful wretches, two prisoners who find our very lives burdensome. And, as you are a just lord, grant us neither mercy nor refuge — but, for the love of God, kill me first, and then my compatriot. Or start with him because, although you do not know it, that is your mortal foe, Arcite, banished from your lands upon penalty of death, and thus deserving of execution. He has mocked you for many a year by coming into your retinue under the name of Philostrate, and you made him your chief squire, while he had returned there only because he loves Emily. And since my death is imminent, I will tell you plainly that I am Palamon, who discourteously escaped from your prison. I am your mortal enemy, but I love the fair Emily so passionately that I willingly die here in her sight. I accept your justice and my death, as long as you also slay my comrade here, as we both deserve to die.'

Theseus answered without hesitation: 'You have handed down a concise judgment. You are damned by your own words, your own confession, and I herewith announce your sentence; there is no need to torture you into further admissions. By bloody Mars, you shall die!'

But now the queen, a wonderful woman, as well as Emily, began to weep openly, as did all the other women there. They thought it a pity that immediate death should be the fate of these two gentlemen of great estate, and all because of love — for that was the heart of this issue. Seeing the wide wounds of the two knights gushing blood, they cried out in unison: 'Oh noble Lord, have mercy upon all of us here.' They fell onto their knees and tried to kiss his feet and, as pity runs deep in noble hearts, Theseus soon calmed down. And though he had been so angry that he was shaking and trembling, he reconsidered both the crime and its cause. And, in the end, even though his just wrath arose from their guilt, his reason excused them both. He realized that any man in love would, if he could, escape from prison, and he felt compassion for the weeping women; so, in his gentle heart he reconsidered: 'Cursed be a lord without mercy, who, like an unchangeable lion, responds the same to a fearful man repenting and to a proud, spiteful man who cannot change. A just lord cannot weigh pride and humility as equal, with no distinction and exhibiting no discretion.'

Now no longer angry, he smiled gently and said to those assembled there: 'Blessed be the god of love. How mighty and great a lord he is! He should indeed be called divine for working such miracles, as he is capable of shaping any heart into the service of love. Behold here Arcite and Palamon, each successfully escaped from my prison, free to live like kings in Thebes. Knowing that I am their mortal enemy and that their lives rest in my hands, nevertheless they were led by love to this place where they would surely die. Is this is not the height of folly? Is there a greater fool than a man in love? For God's sake, look at them. See how they bleed! Are they not well adorned? This is how the god of love has paid their wages for serving him! And yet lovers believe that they are wise, no matter what they suffer.

But the irony is that the woman for whom they undergo such delights has no more reason to thank them for their efforts than she does me. For she is as unaware of their hot passion for her as is a cuckoo in a tree or a hare in the fields. Of course, I understand it all too well myself, for I have been a lover in my time. As one who was myself too often trapped in love's snares, I have felt love's pain and know what it can make a man do.' He turned to the two knights. 'So now, at the request of my queen, kneeling here, and of Emily, my dear sister, I forgive the two of you. But you must swear to me here and now that nevermore will you threaten my country nor make war upon me, by day or night, but be my friends forever in everything you do. And, with that, I hereby pardon you of all misdeeds.'

Of course these two knights swore agreement to his request, were grateful for his mercy and asked to serve his lordship, all of which he granted and said: 'Speaking of royal lineage and affluence, even though she is a queen and a princess, each of you would clearly be worthy to marry my sister Emily — when the time comes. As for her, for whose sake you suffer all this strife and jealousy, I need not tell you that she cannot marry two men, no matter how long you fight over her or how jealous or angry you may be. Thus, I now place this decree upon you in order to make sure each of you achieves his destiny. So, hear now what will happen.

This is my decision, my final word — and I will hear no objection, as I hope you see the good in it: each of you shall go from here to wherever you like, freely, without ransom or resistance, to return fifty weeks from this day — no more, no less — along with 100 knights, armored and prepared to decide here the right by combat. And, on my word as a true knight, I promise you that whichever one of you wins the victory, that is either, with his 100 men, slays his opponent or drives him from the lists, to him, so graced by Fortune, I will give Emily to be his wife. Here, in this very place, I shall have the lists constructed and, as God is my witness, I shall be an even-handed and fair judge. One of you must accept the inevitable end: you will be either dead or captive. And if you agree to this, say so now and profess yourselves satisfied. This is how we will end and conclude this.'

Who is smiling now, if not Palamon? Who is jumping for joy, if not Arcite? Who could possibly do justice to the delight that fills everyone there after Theseus has acted so graciously? All present fell to their knees and thanked him with all their might and, in good spirits and full of hope, Palamon and Arcite turned their horses homeward, toward the wide walls of Thebes."

Here the Squire graciously handed his father a draft of wine, and the Knight gratefully took it before he nodded to his son and continued his story, the outcome of which all of us were eager to hear.

"I fear I will be accused of negligence if I fail to acknowledge the vast expenditures Theseus committed to constructing an arena so noble that the world has never seen the like. Round, like a compass, a mile around, the walls of stone were surrounded by a ditch and filled with rows of seats sixty feet high, so cunningly that no one's view was blocked. Nowhere in the world was there an artisan skilled in geometry or arithmetic, a sculptor or painter, who was not sought out and paid well to design and create this theater. And, in praise of Venus, Goddess of Love, Theseus had built at the eastern gate an altar and a chapel and, at the western gate, likewise, one in praise of Mars — each of them costing a cartload of gold. And on the north, in a wall turret, he ordered a richly adorned chapel of white alabaster and red coral to be built, dedicated to the chaste goddess Diane.

But I have yet to describe all the wondrous carvings and portraits that filled these three places of worship.

First, the walls in the temple of Venus were covered with depictions of the suffering that love's servants endure: the interrupted sleep, the sighing and the tears, the lamentations, the fires of desire and all the other annoyances of love. There was Narcissus, Solomon in all his folly, Medea and Circes with their magic, all showing that nothing compares to the power of love. There were many others caught in love's snare, and I could mention a thousand more, but these will have to do. The statue of Venus was naked, floating in the sea, a zither in her hand and a garland of roses in her hair, and beside her was her blind son, Cupid, clutching his shining bow and sharp arrows.

Let me not slight the decorations of the temple of Mars, beginning with an enormous forest covering the wall, devoid of man or beast, rumbling with a mighty wind, a storm threatening to break every branch. On a hill stood the temple of mighty Mars, in burnished steel, the door of impenetrable adamant, each pillar a ton of bright, shiny iron. There was Wickedness, cruel Anger, pale Dread, treasonous murder in bed, open warfare, Strife with bloody knife, suicides, clammy death, Madness laughing with rage, armed Discontent, Unrest and Violence; there were tyrants, ravaged villages, the sow chewing up the baby in its cradle, the carter run over by his cart. And above them all, mighty Conquest, enthroned in honor, his sharp sword hanging high by a thread. There you could see the slaughter of Julius, Nero and Antonius, though yet unborn — as who shall be slain is written in the stars; these few examples will have to do. The statue of Mars was riding a chariot, armed, grim as madness, a red-eyed wolf before his feet, gnawing at a human body — the story of Mars in all his glory.

Now let me hasten to the temple of chaste Diana, decorated with scenes of hunting and modest chastity — here the sorrowful Calisto, turned from a woman into a bear by the angry Diana; there, Daphne, turned into a tree; then, Atalanta turned into a deer as punishment for seeing the naked Diana. And depicted there were many other wonderful stories which I will not now rehearse. Diana herself was shown sitting on a mighty hart, small dogs all about her feet that rested on the moon; she was dressed all in green, a bow in her hand and arrows in her quiver.

When Theseus saw that the lists were completed — at his own great cost — he was well pleased by the temples and the entire arena. But let me leave him for a while and return to Palamon and Arcite.

The assigned day for their return came, and each had kept his covenant and assembled 100 well-armed knights. If we are to speak of knighthood and prowess, never had such a noble group been assembled; every man who loved chivalry clamored to be part of this contest, just as, if there were such an opportunity tomorrow, you know that every young knight who loves passionately — be he in England or elsewhere — would be grateful to fight for such a lady. Oh, it was a wondrous sight to see!

To name but one warrior on each side, there, with Palamon, was Lygurcus himself, the king of Thrace, with black beard and manly visage, looking about like a griffin. He had the skin of a bear, long hair that streamed down his back, and a large, gem-studded golden wreath on his head. Twenty or more white muzzled wolfhounds milled about his chariot and more than 100 mighty warriors surrounded him, armed to the teeth and grim at heart. On the other side, Arcite had with him the great Emetreus, king of India, riding — like Mars himself — a steel-armored warhorse, covered in gold cloth. His golden curls glittered like the sun, his lips were full, his aspect ruddy, and he cast his eyes around him like a lion. Proudly he led his entourage of 100 duke's, earls, and kings, ever with a snow-white eagle on his arm and a swirl of tame leopards and lions weaving all around him.

Now Theseus made certain to house and feed them well, each according to his status; no one could have wished for more. I will not describe the minstrels, the feasts, the gifts for each and everyone, the adornments of the palace, nor who sat first or last on the dais, which ladies were the best at dancing or singing, who spoke most feelingly of love, nor the hawks perched on arms or the hounds on the floor. Instead, I will come straight to the point, so listen carefully.

On Sunday night, before dawn, hearing the first lark, Palamon rose to make his pilgrimage to the altar of Venus, goddess of love, and there he knelt to pray: 'Oh, fairest of the fair, my Lady Venus, daughter of Jupiter and Vulcan's spouse, have pity on my bitter tears and take to heart my humble prayer. My heart cannot reveal the depth of my suffering; I am so confused I don't know what I am saying. Have mercy on my misery, as I will forevermore be your faithful servant, ever at war with chastity!

I do not boast of warfare; nor do I ask for victory tomorrow; neither fame nor glory matter to me. I will gladly die in your service if I but possess fully my Emily. You decide how I can embrace my lady as my own, and I will forever sacrifice at your altar. But if this be not your will, sweet lady, than I pray that tomorrow Arcite's spear pierces me through the heart. Thus I beseech you to reward me by giving my beloved to, oh, blissful dear lady.'

Somberly he made his sacrifice with all appropriate observances, although I will not detail that. But then the statue of Venus shook and made a sign, which he took as acceptance of his prayer. Although there had been a small delay before the response, he was certain that his plea was answered and, with a joyous heart, he made his way home.

The sun rose and, with it, Emily, on her way to the temple of Diana, accompanied by her maidens with fire and incense, the robes and all else necessary for their sacrifice. This gentle Emily washed at a sacred well, her bright hair unbound, well combed, and covered with a green oak circle. She kindled two fires on the great altar and spoke, most piteously, to Diana: 'Oh, chaste goddess of virgins and the green woods, queen of Pluto's empire, goddess of chaste maidens, you have known my heart for many years and you know that I desire nothing but to remain a virgin all my life. Ever of your company, I want to be no man's love or wife, as I desire only to hunt freely in your woods — I want never to be a wife or bear a child.

I seek no man, despite the love that Palamon and Arcite may feel for me. I beg you to shower them with love and peace so that they may turn away from me, their devotion and fiery love extinguished or directed elsewhere.

But if you are unable to grant me this grace and one of them is indeed my destiny, please send me him who loves me most. As you are virgin and guardian of us all, preserve my virginity and let me serve you always in perfect chastity.' Immediately one of the two fires went out and then relit, followed by the extinguishing of the other fire; there was a whistling sound and then drops of blood escaped from the burning brands. Not knowing what this might portend, the terrified Emily, nearly mad and weeping, then saw Diana, bow in hand, dressed for the hunt. She spoke: 'Dear daughter, cease your weeping. You shall be married to the one who loves you most but, for now, you cannot know which one it is.' Then she was gone, leaving the astonished Emily to pray: 'I know not what this means, but I place myself under your protection and your disposition.' And so she, too, returned home.

An hour later, Arcite made his way to the temple of Mars, god of war, to carry out his sacrifice and to say, with sorrowful heart and high devotion: 'O mighty god, who holds the bridle of war in every land and empire, accept my pitiful sacrifice and have mercy on my pain for the sake of the fiery desire with which you burned for the beauty of the fair, young, fresh Venus when Vulcan discovered you lying in her bed; have mercy upon my suffering, as I am young and ignorant, and she who makes me endure all this woe cares not whether I sink or swim.

Well do I know that I must win her in combat and that without your help or grace my strength alone cannot prevail. So help me, lord, in tomorrow's battle and grant me victory. In return I will honor your sovereign temple above all and devote my labor to your craft and cause. I will sacrifice to you my beard and my hair, untouched till now by razor or by scissors and will ever be your faithful servant. Oh lord, have mercy on me now and grant me victory — I ask for nothing more.' When the rings on the temple doors and the doors themselves began to shake, Arctic was quite terrified. The fires burned brightly on the altar and lit the entire temple, and a sweet smell rose from the ground. The very armor on the statue of Mars began to ring, and when Arcite heard a murmured: 'Victory,' he leapt to his feet and returned home filled with joy and hope.

But now the prayers of these three humans initiated such strife in the heavens above between Venus, goddess of love, and Mars, stern god of war, that Jupiter was forced to intervene and pale, cold Saturn had to reach deep into his trove of experience that contained solutions for any and all problems. We all know that age always has the advantage, both in wisdom and in experience: we can outrun our elders but not outwit them. So

Saturn, although it is anything but normal for him, set out to provide a solution that would end the fighting.

'Dearest daughter Venus,' Saturn said, 'my vast orbit contains more power than anyone can possibly comprehend. In the house of Leo I govern the setting of the sun, the dark cells of prisons, the churls' rebellion, secret poisoning, all vengeance and all punishment. Mine is the ruin of great halls, the destruction of towers and walls; I slew Sampson shaking the pillar, and I control malicious treason and heinous plots; my very aspect causes plague. So, stop your weeping, I shall ensure that Palamon, your knight, shall have his lady as you have promised. Of course Mars will help his knight; yet, there shall be peace between you two. I am your grandfather, ever ready to help. Weep no more; I will fulfill your wish.'

But now I must leave Mars and Venus and their heavenly strife and return to my original story.

There was great celebration in Athens that day, and the merry season of May put everyone in such a mood that from, sunrise to sunset they competed at games, danced, and served the commands of Venus. That morning the people awoke to the clatter of horses being harnessed and armor strapped on throughout the hostelries, with groups of mounted men making their way by many roads to the palace, which was filled with conversations, here three, there ten, discussing their expectations for these two Theban knights, some saying this and others saying that; some betting on him with the black beard, some on the bald, others on the hairy one; this one noted for his groomed looks; that one said to wield a battle-ax of twenty pounds. The hall rang with multiple predictions all day long.

Although the great Theseus was awakened by the noise and the sounds of minstrels, he remained in his chambers until the Theban warriors had been honorably led to the palace. Sitting at a window, a god enthroned, he was the subject of great interest by the people, all pressing in to see and honor him, as well as to hear what he had to say. A herald on a scaffold blew his trumpet to still the noise, and when all were shushed, he shared the mighty duke's will: 'Our gracious lord has, in his discretion, decided that battle to the death in this contest would lead to the spilling of much gentle blood. Therefore, to ensure that all shall live, he has altered his original plan: upon pain of death, may no man bring into the lists any kind of arrow, battle ax, or short knife; nor may any man use a short sword or ride a single course at an opponent with a sharply ground spear; only defensive thrusts will be allowed. Whoever fails to obey these rules will not be killed but will be captured and chained to a stake on either side for the rest of the battle. And if the leader of either side go down, be captured or slain, the tournament shall end at once. God speed; go forth to fight your fill with mace[11] and long sword. This is the will of our lord.'

The people responded so enthusiastically that their roars could be heard in the heavens: 'God save such a lord, so concerned for his people that none of their blood be shed!' The trumpets blew and the companies formally processed to the lists through the city decorated with gold cloth.

In lordly manner the great duke now rode forth, the two Thebans at his side, followed by Emily and the queen, and then the various members of the two combatant companies, one warrior after the other, according to rank. They passed through the city and, before mid-morning, Theseus, Hypolita and Emily, as well as other ladies of high degree had reached their seats in the awesome ring constructed for this tournament, and the common people had taken their places, as well.

Through the western gate, beneath the temple of Mars, entered Arcite, red banners waving over his hundred men; at the same moment, through the eastern gate, came Palamon and his hundred, passing under the statue of Venus, white banners snapping in the breeze. In all the world were there never two companies so evenly matched; no matter how observant, no one could have seen on either side an advantage in nobility, rank or

---

[11] A kind of club with a blunt — but sometimes spiked — end that could smash but not cut an opponent as do swords or spears.

age, as they arranged their ranks for the fight. The gates were shut, the combatants all acclaimed by name, and shouts rang out: 'Now do your duty, proud young knights.' The heralds ceased riding up and down, and now the lances are firmly in place, spurs pierce horses' flanks, and all can see who rides well and who can joust.

Lances twenty feet and longer rise in the air but then shiver and break on thick shields; heavy blows land on chests; brilliant swords are torn from their sheaths; helmets are cut and shredded; streams of blood explode everywhere; mighty maces burst bones; one thrusts himself through the thickest throng of the enemy; strong steeds stumble and fall; yet another rolls under foot like a ball; this one, unhorsed, stabs with his spear and brings down a rider, horse and all; that one, despite all his efforts, is heartily wounded and taken to the stake, where he must abide, as was agreed. At the appropriate time Theseus decrees a time to rest, to refresh and have a drink, if they so wish.

Multiple times during the course of that day did the two Thebans meet and bring each other woe; twice they unseated one another from their steeds. There is no tiger in the valley of Gargaphia, whose whelp has been taken, that is more intense in the hunt than is Arcite. Nor is there an angrier lion in Morocco, hunted and mad for hunger, who so seeks the blood of his prey more than does Palamon in his attempts to slay his foe Arcite. Their vicious strokes bite into each others' helmets and each one's armor is discolored by his own blood and by the blood of his adversary.

But all things must end and, before sunset, the mighty king Emetreus has captured Palamon as he is fighting Arcite, a sharp sword biting deep into Palamon's flesh; now twenty more surround him, unyielding to the end, and tie him to the stake. In trying to rescue Palamon, mighty king Lygurcus falls and king Emetrius, for all his strength, is knocked from his saddle, so hard is he hit by Palamon before he is overcome. But all is for naught. Despite his fearless heart, Palamon is captured and brought to the stake, and there he must abide by force and by prior agreement.

Who weeps now but this woeful Palamon, unable to continue the fight. But as soon as Theseus noted this, he shouted to the fighters: 'Halt! No more! It is over. I will be a faithful judge, without bias. Arcite of Thebes shall have Emily, for it is his fortune to have won her fairly.' And such a joyful noise arose among the people that it seemed the lists would collapse.

What recourse does fair Venus up above now have? What can she say? What can the queen of love, her will frustrated, do but weep until her tears might overflow those very lists below. She said: 'I am filled with shame; of that I am certain.' But Saturn replied: 'Daughter, keep your peace. Mars has had his will: his knight has gained all he asked but, by my head, you shall be soothed soon enough.'

The loud music of the trumpeters, the shouting and yelling of the heralds — they feel no pain in their joy at Arcite's victory.

But stop your noise for a moment and listen, to hear what miracle occurred.

Fierce Arcite has taken off his helmet to show his face to all as he charges his courser from one end of the arena to the other, looking up at fair Emily, who returns his look with friendly eye (for women generally do follow the favor of Fortune) and filling his heart with pleasure.

But now, suddenly, an infernal fury, sent by Pluto at Saturn's behest, starts up out of the ground, frightening Arcite's horse and causing it to turn and stumble as he leaps to avoid it. And before Arcite can react, he is thrown down on his head to crumble there as good as dead, his chest smashed by his saddle pommel. He lies as black as coal or any crow, so covered is he now with his own blood. Quickly he is carried to the palace of Theseus, where they cut him out of his armor and place him gently in a bed, yet alive, his wits still about him, asking for his Emily.

The Duke and his retinue returned to his palace with great solemnity and Theseus made certain that all the combatants were cared for and ministered to. No one had died in the lists and some even now predicted that Arcite would not succumb to his grievous wound. Though many were badly hurt, one with a great wound in his chest, and some with broken arms, they were helped with salves, charms with sage, and other herbs. Their noble host made comfortable and honored every man and entertained and fed everyone the whole night through. He considered no one dishonored there, as being captured and tied to the stake by twenty men without yielding is to be expected in such adventure. And the duke ordered all rancor and envy to cease and all to treat their erstwhile opponents as brothers. He showered gifts on them and feasted everyone for three days before fittingly escorting each king on his homeward journey. And all went on their way as was proper, with no words other than: 'Fare thee well and good day!'

But let us turn again to Palamon and Arcite.

Arcite's chest swelled with great pressure on his heart; no matter what the physicians tried, his clotted blood decayed and remained in his body. Nether blood-letting nor cupping nor herbal drinks brought relief. His lungs were filled and every muscle in his chest was destroyed by the poisoned fluids. Nature failed and, where nature fails, medicine cannot avail.

You may as well carry him to church now!

Feeling his life ebb away, Arcite called for Emily and his dear cousin Palamon, and said: 'As I am dying there is but one thing I would say to you, dearest lady of mine, whom I love above all and to whom I bequeath the service of my spirit. Alas, the pain that I have suffered for you so long; alas, death; alas, my Emily; alas, my leaving you; alas, queen of my heart; alas, my wife, lady of my heart, ender of my life. What is this world? What do men seek in it? One moment I am with my love, the next in my cold grave, alone, without anyone else. Farewell, my beloved enemy, my Emily; take me gently in your arms, for the love of God, and do what I ask. I have had here with my cousin Palamon many a day of strife and rancor for the sake of your love, caused by my own jealousy. Now, as I am his true servant — who has pursued truth, honor, knighthood, wisdom, humility, and noble kinship — with my welfare in mind, Jupiter has guided me to see that in all the world there is none so worthy to be loved as Palamon, who has served you and wants to serve you all his life. Thus, if you ever shall be a wife, do not forget Palamon, this gentle man.'

And, with that, his speech began to fail, as death crept from his feet to his chest; his arms lost strength and, as his heart was overcome, so did his intellect cease to function. His eyes were overshadowed and his breath failed as he cast his last look at his lady and uttered his final words: 'Have mercy on me, my Emily.' His spirit left his body to go where I have never been and cannot describe. I am no theologian; I cannot depict what those who have gone there have not themselves told us about. Arcite is cold; his soul is in the care of Mars.

So I will speak of Emily.

This lady shrieked and Palamon howled; Theseus took his swooning sister away from the corpse. I could easily spend a day to tell about how Emily wept both morning and night; in cases like this, women feel such sorrow that it can end only in death

Boundless were the sorrow and the tears for the death of this Theban throughout the town, for young and old, child and man alike. Surely there was no greater weeping when Hector was brought, freshly slain, back to Troy. Alas, the sadness that was there — the clawing at faces, the tearing out of hair. Women cried: 'Why would you die when you had all the wealth in the world and Emily, as well?' Theseus himself could not be soothed except by his father, Egeus, who knew well how the ways of the world change, going up and down, bringing joy after sadness, and sorrow after happiness. He shared with Theseus many examples: 'No man has ever died who did not live; nor has anyone who lived not died. This world is but a stop on our journey, and we are pilgrims passing through. Death cures all worldly pain.' And he said many more things like this as, in his wisdom, he exhorted the people to console themselves.

Duke Theseus thought long and carefully about the location and the details for Arcite's tomb. Finally he decided on that the lush, green grove, where Arcite and Palamon had first begun the battle for Emily's love — site of amorous desires and of laments, where the coals of red-hot passion would fuel the fire of funereal rites. So he commanded to have the old oaks cut down and stacked in rows for the fire, and he himself ordered a bier to be provided, covered with cloth of gold, as was Arcite. On his head the corpse wore a crown of laurel and in his white-gloved hands they placed a sword as, weeping heartily, Theseus accompanied the bier into the great hall before departing for the grove.

And here came the woeful Theban Palamon, with unkempt beard and rough, ashy hair, all in black, bespattered with tears; and there Emily, surpassing all others in weeping, the most pitiful person there. In order to make this the noblest of funerals, Theseus brought forth three brightly armored steeds with riders carrying, respectively, Arcite's shield, his spear and his Turkish bow (the case and the trappings were all of refined gold), and forth the company rode with sad faces. The noblest of the Greeks carried the bier on their shoulders, slow paced, eyes red and wet, down the main street that was all draped in black. On the right side was old Egeus; on the left, Theseus; along with golden vessels filled with honey, milk, blood and wine. They were followed by Palamon and his retinue, and then Emily, bearing the fire for the proper burial rituals.

The fire, built with great skill and careful preparation, twenty fathoms abroad at the base, reached the very heavens. I won't name the trees — the oak, birch, aspen, alder, poplar, elm, plane, ash, laurel, maple, beech, hazel, yew — nor how they were layered, nor how the forest gods — the nymphs and fawns — uprooted by his funeral, ran about, nor the flight of the birds from those woods, nor the shock of the bright sun where once was all darkness, nor how there was a layer of straw and then one of dry sticks and then green wood and gold cloth and garlands and spices, nor Arcite's rich array, nor how Emily lit the fire, nor how she swooned, nor what she said, nor what valuables people threw into the fire — some their shields and some their spears — nor how the cups of blood and wine and milk were tossed into the madly burning fire, nor how the Greeks rode around the fire three times in one direction and then in the other, nor how the ladies wept, nor how Emily was led home, nor how Arcite was burned to cold ashes, nor how the wakes lasted the entire night, nor who won the wrestling matches, nor how everyone finally returned to Athens when it was all over. Rather I will come immediately to the point and end my lengthy story.

As all things must, after some years, the grieving of the Greeks came to an end. And at a certain parliament there was discussion of alliances, particularly, with Thebes. It was then that the noble Theseus sent for gentle Palamon, who arrived all dressed in black, ignorant of the reason for Theseus's command to appear. That great Duke sent also for Emily and, when they were all there, Theseus paced back and forth a bit and then spoke: 'When the First Mover of all things initially created the great chain of love, he bound together fire, air, water and earth in a lasting accord. He also granted to everything living a certain number of days that cannot be exceeded, though they may be reduced. By all this we can see that the Mover is eternal and consistent. Only a fool would not recognize that all parts derive from this whole. Nature emerges from perfection before devolving into something corruptible. And wisely, Divine Providence has so well shaped creation that rather than being eternal, species and natural processes succeed one another. All this is clearly seen by everyone. Behold the oak that takes so long to grow, lives for a long time but, in the end, dies. Consider the stones that are worn by our feet, broad rivers that dry up and mighty cities that come and go — all proving that everything ends. The same is true of us: young or old. king or page, all shall die. Everything is governed by Jupiter, the King, ruler and cause of all things, overseeing everything according to his will, against which no creature may prevail.

Thus, wisdom calls us to make virtue of necessity and embrace what we cannot change rather than choose the contrary, which is to complain, to be sad for that good man Arcite, the flower of chivalry who left before us the foul prison of his life with all proper honor. But why should his cousin and his wife, who loved him so deeply, lament? Can he show them his gratitude? By God, he cannot. And so I conclude my lengthy argument with this: after we have grieved, Jupiter wants us to feel joy and so, before we leave this place today, I suggest that we turn two woes into one perfect joy, changing the deepest sorrow into the greatest happiness.

My dear sister, Emily, this is my opinion, reached with the advice of parliament: that gentle Palamon, your own knight, who serves you with all his will, heart and might, and has done so ever since you first knew him, shall have mercy bestowed on him as you take him for your husband and lord. Give me your hand, for this is our judgment. Show us now your womanly grace. He is a king's brother's son, but even were he simply a poor young knight, as he has served you so many years and has suffered so much on your behalf, this must be honored. Noble mercy ought to rule justice.'

And then he spoke to Palamon: 'I trust you need no persuasion to agree to this. Approach and take your lady's hand.'

At once they reached agreement on that bond we call matrimony or marriage, in accord with the counsel of the nobles. And so, in all bliss and harmony, Palamon wed Emily, and God, Who has made all this world, bestowed on him His love, so dearly earned, for now is Palamon completely happy, living in bliss, in wealth and in health. Throughout their lives, Emily loved him so tenderly and he served her so gently that there was never a word of jealousy or strife between them.

This then is the story of Palamon and Emily; may God save all of you in our fair assembly. Amen."

When the knight had told this story, there was no one, neither young nor old, who disagreed that it was a noble story and worthy of being remembered, especially by the gentle folk, each and every one of them.

Our Host laughed and swore: "As God is my witness, this is going alright; well-loosened is our bag of tales. So, let's see who will tell us another story. Damn me if the game has not begun well. Now, Sir Monk, tell us, if you can, a tale to respond to the Knight's."

But the Miller, so drunk as to be pale, scarcely able to maintain his saddle, ever impolite, too proud to doff his hat or hood for any man, now bellowed like Pilate in the mysteries,[12] and swore: "By God's arms, and by his blood and bones, I know a noble tale for right now, with which I will respond quite well to the Knight's tale. And . . . it will be a damn sight shorter than his."

Our Host, seeing clearly that the Miller was drunk, tried to intervene: "Wait a moment, Alan, my dear brother; let some better man first tell us another; wait for now, and let's do this the right way."

"By God's soul," the Miller swore, "not a chance. Either I speak or I go on my way."

Our Host answered: "Well then, what the hell! Tell your damn story. You are a fool and not in control of your wits."

"Now listen!" continued the Miller, "one and all! First" — he belched heartily — "let me proclaim that I am stinking drunk; I can tell by how I sound." He snorted like a great sow, and then laughed long and hard at his own gaff. "So, if I misspeak or say something wrong, I pray that you blame it on the Southwerk ale, for I mean to tell you a tale about the life of a carpenter and his wife and . . . how a clerk made a fool of that carpenter."

The Reeve, a carpenter by trade, interrupted from way back among all the other mounted pilgrims to shout: "Why don't you shut your trap and stop with your lewd smut. Enough of your drunken bawdiness. It is a sin, not to mention, utter stupidity, to injure any other or to slander him, or to bring wives into ill repute. There are plenty of other things to tell stories about."

The drunk Miller responded at once: "Dear brother Oswald; the man who has no wife is not a cuckold. But God forbid that you think I am calling you one — or that this story is about you."

He paused, as if trying to remember something he had forgotten.

---

[12] The Mystery Plays about biblical events, performed for holidays by members of the community or actors.

"The world is full of good wives; I daresay there are a thousand good for every one who is bad — and well you know that yourself, when you are in your right mind."

The Reeve had forced his way froward through the troop by now, and the Miller actually reached out for the Reeve's sleeve but missed it, nearly falling off his horse in the attempt before he continued.

"But . . . for the life of me, I can't tell why you are angry with my story already? I have a wife, God knows, as do you. And yet, by the oxen that pull my plow, I would not assume any more than I need to, nor would I think that I myself would be a cuckold; I trust that I am not."

He snorted again.

"A husband would do well not to dig too deep into God's or his wife's secrets, lest he discover God's plenty there . . . for then . . . he will need nothing more."

All I can tell you is that this Miller would hold his tongue for no man and was intent on telling his churlish story in his way.

And so, I have no choice but to retell it here as told.

Consequently, I beg every gentleman and lady, for the love of God, to believe that I have the best of intentions, as I must re-narrate all their tales, be they better or worse, lest I be false to my material.

Thus, if you do not choose to hear this tale, turn the page and choose another; you will find any number of true stories here that support noble behavior, true morality and real holiness.

I beg you not to blame me if you do not choose wisely.

The Miller is an oaf — so much is clear — and so was the Reeve and others. As you will see, and both of these churls ended up telling vulgar stories on our pilgrimage.

So, be forewarned; don't hold me accountable, and let no one take seriously a silly joke.

The Miller's Tale

"Once upon a time — or so I am told — there was a rich old churl who lived in Oxford. He was a carpenter by trade, but he also rented out rooms."

"May you and your old churl be damned to hell," the Reeve interrupted angrily. I dare say he would have tried to pull the Miller from his horse, but he was too far removed from him to do so. But the Miller was not perturbed. He laughed heartily and shrugged off his rival: "Come, come, Oswald. Not every story of an old carpenter who is about to be cuckolded is about you." The Reeve muttered something unintelligible and the Miller continued: "Maybe this one, but —" he laughed again and, ignoring the sputtering Reeve, went on with his tale.

"As I was saying — this old carpenter rented out rooms, and one of his boarders was a poor student who had studied the usual arts but whose real interest was astrology. He had mastered some axioms and some basic procedures from this science so that he could provide plausible answers to people's questions about when they might expect droughts or showers or when other things might happen in the future — I don't know what else.

This student. called 'clever Nicolas' by some, from personal experience knew all about secret affairs and passion and satisfaction. But he was so sly and discreet that he had people fooled into thinking that he was as timid as a girl. He had a room by himself that was always filled with the odor of sweet herbs, and he himself smelled as sweet as a licorice root or ginger. On the shelves by his bed he kept Ptolemy's treatise on astrology and other books, his astrolabe — essential for his study of the stars — and the counters for his abacus. His cupboard was covered with a rough red cloth, and there he kept his lute, which rang out with the mellow music he coaxed from it in the evenings. With his pleasant voice he would sing the 'Angelus of Mary' or the

'King's Tune.' And this is how this charming clerk spent his time, living off his meager income and the generosity of his friends.

Now the carpenter, his host, was newly married to a wife he loved more than his own life. She was just eighteen, and he was insanely jealous and would — if he could -- have kept her in a cage, because she was young and sexy, and he was along in years and rightly worried about being a cuckold. The fact was that he was not that smart and paid no heed to Cato's advice that a man should only marry his counterpart, someone in the same stage of life as himself, because young and old are often not a good match. But, since he was already ensnared in that trap, he simply had to live with it, as have many others.

The carpenter . . . did I mention that he was old? And did I say that his young wife was beautiful, her body as slender and delicate as a weasel's? And did I tell you that she knew how to dress herself to perfection? Oh, yes! Her belt was striped with silk, and her hips flashed a ruffled apron as white as the fresh morning milk. Her dazzling alabaster smock was embroidered all around the collar with coal-black silk, inside and out; the ribbons on her dazzling white cap matched the blush of her complexion, and on her belt there hung a leather purse covered with tassels and adorned with brass. Her silken headband sat high on her head, and her eyebrows -- dark as any blackthorn — were plucked and curved just so. Her neck boasted a broach as broad as the buckle on a shield, and her shoes were laced high up her legs. She was more luscious than a ripe pear, softer than newly-cut lamb's wool and, truth be told, she was quite a flirtatious little thing. I dare say that you could look around as long as you like anywhere in the world and, no matter how smart you might be, you could not find another such spicy little doll . . . or living, breathing wench. Her face shone more brightly than the new gold coins minted in the Tower of London, and she could sing as beautifully and as brightly as any swallow perched on a barn. On top of that she was very playful, skipping as lustily as any newborn calf or colt following its mother. Her breath was as sweet as mead, as fragrant as newly-picked apples on a bed of hay or a freshly-mown meadow. As skittish as a spirited foal and as straight and upright as a mast or arrow, she was a regular primrose, a prickly thistle for any lord to bed, or for any man to wed.

So, on a day not that different from others, this courteous Nicolas fell into teasing and flirting with this young wife while her husband happened to be away at Osney and, as these crafty and clever young students do, slyly he managed to grab her pussy, saying: 'As God is my witness, I am so at the mercy of my secret love for you that I will overflow and die right here and now if I don't have my way with you.' Boldly he embraced her thighs and continued: 'My darling, love me now or I am a dead man, God save my soul.' But she bolted like a colt in harness and turned her head away, saying: 'I will not kiss you, by my faith! Why, stop! Leave me alone! Let me be, Nicolas, or I will have to shout "help . . . rape," or even "oh, dear"! Take your hands from me and behave yourself!'

Of course, Nicolas begged her to forgive him but spoke to her so charmingly and pressed his suit so effectively that, before long, she granted him her love and swore by St. Thomas of Kent that she would be at his command as soon as the opportunity presented itself. 'My husband is so jealous that if we don't find the right time and place, I will be as good as dead,' she said. 'This can happen only if we manage it in absolute secrecy.'

'Don't you lose any sleep over that,' Nicolas winked. 'A student who can't fool a simple carpenter has definitely wasted his education.' And so they agreed and swore to wait for the right moment, just as I have told you.

When Nicolas had done with her everything he had a desire to and patted her private parts enough, he kissed her tenderly and went off with his lute to sing sad songs.

Soon, on some holy day or another, this good wife went to the parish church to worship the miracles of Christ. Her forehead was brighter than the sun, so hard had she washed it after she had finished her work. Now at the church there was a parish cleric named Absolon, his curled red hair shiny as gold, spreading out from his head like a fan, with a perfect, straight part dividing it evenly. His complexion was ruddy and his eyes as grey as those of a goose; his legs were tightly encased in elegant red hose and shoes that had St. Paul's window carved into them. His clothes were a good fit, in high fashion, topped with a light blue tunic that was richly adorned with lace. On top of that he wore a beautiful surplice as white as the fresh bud on a twig. Goddamn me, if he wasn't a merry lad. He was known for cutting hair perfectly and shaving and letting blood expertly, as well as for writing incontestable deeds and property releases. He knew the twenty latest dances, traipsing around in the Oxford manner, his legs going this way and that, all the while playing songs on a small fiddle, accompanying himself in a loud high treble, or quite charmingly playing his lute. Every tavern or ale house in that town blessed with a merry bar maid was favored with his entertainment. But . . . and you'll have to take it on my word . . . for now . . . he was fussy in his speech and just a bit squeamish about farts.

So this Absolon, lusty and joyful, on one particular holy day boldly swung his censer at the wives of the parish, looking at them most lecherously, especially at this carpenter's wife. She was so proper and sweet and sensuous that he found looking at her most delightful. If you ask me, had he been a cat and she a mouse, he would have snatched her up right then and there. This parish cleric, this jolly Absolon, was so devoted to love that he accepted no offerings from any wife there — for the love of God, he explained.

That night the moon shone brightly, as Absolon, with his guitar, decided to devote his entire night to the service of love. So he went out, chipper and horny, and found himself at the carpenter's house just after the first cock crow. He positioned himself under a hinged window on the carpenter's house wall and began to sing softly and gently: 'Now, dear lady, if it be your will, I pray for your mercy on me,' accompanying himself beguilingly on his guitar. The carpenter woke up, heard him singing and said to his wife: 'Hey, Alison, don't you hear

Absolon singing under our alcove?' But all she said was: 'Yes, John, God knows I hear him all too well.'

And that is how things were — what else is there to say?

This foolish, jovial Absolon woos Alison until he is frustration itself. He cannot sleep, whether it be day or night; he combs his hair out and puts on a happy face; he harasses her through go-betweens and middle-people; he swears that he will be her secret servant; he sings to her like a trilling nightingale; he sends her spiced wine, mead, ale, and cakes piping hot from the fire; and, because he thinks she is a worldly girl, he even offers to pay her — you know how some folks can be won over by riches, some by force, and some by gentleness? To show off his agility and his skills, he takes on the role of foolish Herod in the mysteries, but nothing can help him in his suit. She is so in love with Nicolas that Absolon might as well try to push water uphill with a rake; all his work has earned him nothing but scorn.

Alison made a monkey of poor Absolon, treating all of his serious efforts as jokes. The proverb speaks truth — it is no lie — people say so correctly: 'The sly one nearby makes the distant one less attractive.' No matter how angry or mad Absolon was, because he was farther away, the ever-present Nicolas blocked him from her sight.

Now do your best, handy Nicolas, while Absolon wallows and fusses and moans: 'alas'!

And so it happened that on a Saturday the carpenter had to go to Osney, letting handy Nicolas and Alison hatch a plan that would allow Nicolas to deceive this stupid, jealous old husband; and if it worked accordingly, she should sleep all night in his arms; and this was his desire as well as hers. And so, without delay, Nicolas slyly carried food and drink for a day or two to his room and told Alison that if her husband asked for him she should say that she did not know his whereabouts; that she had not seen him all day but that she thought he might be sick because. no matter what the servants did . . . no matter how loudly they called his name . . . there was no answer.

The whole of Saturday passed like this, with Nicolas lying silently in his room, eating, sleeping, doing whatever he wanted, until Sunday night, when the sun set. Our simple carpenter was very concerned about what might be ailing poor Nicolas, saying: 'by St. Thomas, I am afraid that there is something terribly wrong with Nicolas. God forbid that he might suddenly die. The world is an unpredictable place, after all. Just today I saw them carry a body to church that I last saw working on Monday. Go on up,' he ordered his man, 'pound on his door — no, use a stone to knock on it– see how he is doing and tell me at once.'

Boldly this servant climbs up to the room and knocks loudly and shouts as if he were mad: 'Hey! What? Nicolas? What are you doing, Master? How can you sleep for an entire day?'

All for naught — no sound, nor response.

But then the servant found a hole in a board low on the wall, a hole the cat used to creep in and out, and he looked carefully through that hole until he could see Nicolas himself. And there he was, sitting upright, staring straight up to the ceiling as if he were considering the new moon. So the man went back down and told his master in what condition hd found Nicolas.

The carpenter blessed himself many times over and said: "Help us now, most holy St. Frideswide! This shows how little we know about what will happen to us next. Surely this man has fallen into some sort of madness, what with his astronomy and all, or maybe some fit. I'm not at all surprised. There are things that God does not want us to know. Yay, blessed be the ignorant that believe only what they know!

I have heard of another student who had the same thing happen to him because of his astronomy. He went out in the country to gaze at the stars and see the future, and he fell into a clay pit that he could not see. And yet, by St. Thomas, I feel really bad for handy Nicolas. I will have to scold him for his studying, by Jesus, heavenly king. Give me a staff so I can pry from below while you, Robin, heave off the door. I have no doubt but that we must save him from all this studying.'

And with that he approached the chamber door. This servant was a strong fellow to have around and he immediately ripped the door off by its hinges, where it fell to the floor. But Nicolas sat as still as a stone and kept staring up into the air. The carpenter, sure that he was in a deep depression, shook him hard by his shoulders and cried out loudly: 'What! Nicolas! What! How! What! Look down! Awake and remember the passion of Christ. Be gone, all you demons and evil spirits!' And then he pronounced the night spell in the four quarters of the room and on the threshold where the door had been: 'Jesus Christ and Saint Benedict, bless and keep this house from all evil spirits, especially those who walk by night. And so I proclaim this white pater-noster — where have you gone, St. Peter's sister?'[13]

At this, finally, handy Nicolas began to sigh deeply: 'Alas, shall nothing then keep the world from perishing so soon?'

The carpenter asked him: 'What? What are you saying? Remember your creator, as do all working men.'

Nicolas now responded to the carpenter: 'Bring me something to drink. And then I have to speak privately with you about things of utmost importance to us both. But — and may I perish — I will not tell this to any other man but you.'

The carpenter went back down and returned with a mighty jug of ale. And, after each of them had had several generous swigs, Nicolas shut the door tightly and sat the carpenter down by his side.

He said: 'John, my dear friend and esteemed host, you must swear by all you value, here and now, that you will share with no man living what I tell you now. For I am going to reveal to you Christ's own instructions. But if you tell anyone, you are lost. This is the punishment you shall suffer if ever you whisper a word of it: you shall go mad.'

'No, Christ forbid, by his holy blood,' sputtered this pitiful man. 'I'm no blabbermouth. Nay, nay, you can believe me, I am

---

[13] "Sister" would have rhymed with "noster" in this portion of a magic charm or spell.

not one to yap. Tell me anything; I will never repeat it to child or wife, by Him who shattered hell."

'Now, John" Nicolas continued, I cannot lie; God's truth, I have discovered through my astrology, as I have studied the bright moon, that Monday next, when the moon is quarter full, we shall have a mighty rain — one so powerful and dreadful that Noah's flood was never half so bad. The entire world will drown in less than an hour, so fearful will be this rain; it will drown all mankind — all will lose their lives.'

The carpenter answered: 'Alas, my precious wife! Will she drown, too? Alas, my Alison!' This made him so sad he nearly swooned. But finally he asked: 'Is there nothing to be done?'

'Why, yes, there is,' said handy Nicolas. 'If you are willing to act in agreement with learning and good advice rather than following your own ideas. Solomon, who never spoke a falsehood, told us: 'Always act in accord with good counsel and you will never regret it.' And if you are willing to follow good advice I promise that, even without mast or sail, I will save her and you and me. Don't you remember how Noah was saved when our Lord warned him that all the world would be lost to the flood?'

'Oh, yes,' said this carpenter, 'many years ago.'

'And have you not also heard,' continued Nicolas, 'how much trouble Noah had convincing his wife to get on the boat? Given the choice, he would have traded all of his black sheep for her to have had a boat to herself, alone. And so, you know what will be best? The situation demands haste, and when something demands haste, there is no time to preach or to sit around. So, as fast as you can, procure large kneading troughs for us, or, if not that, big beer brewing tubs — that is, one for each of us three. But make sure they are large enough for us to be afloat as if we were on barges. Make sure each of them has enough food for a day — we won't need more. The water will drop and dry up by mid-morning of the next day. But neither Robin your servant nor Jill your maid can get wind of this — I cannot save them. Don't ask me why; no matter how often you ask me, I can share no more of

God's secret plan. Be satisfied with this: if you don't go crazy on me now, you shall be as showered with grace as was Noah. And have no doubt — I will, of course, save your wife.

Now on your way and get busy. And when you have gotten these three tubs, for her and you and me, hang them high in the roof of your house but without letting anyone see your preparations. And after you have done as I told you and have filled them each with good food, along with an ax to cut the rope when the water comes, so that we can make a hole way up high in the gable, on the garden side, and freely float away on our way over the stable. So then, after the great rain has passed we shall all swim away just like the white duck behind the swan. Then I will shout: "Well, Alison? Well, John? Rejoice because this flood will soon be gone." And you will answer: "Hail Master Nicolas! I see you well on this brand new day." And then we shall be the lords of all for our entire lives, just like Noah and his wife.'

But I must warn you of one final thing. Be sure, on that night when we have boarded our separate boats, that we do not speak to one another — no crying out, no shouting, just quiet prayer; that is God's specific decree. You and your wife must hang far apart so that there can be no sin between you, no more in looking than in deed. That is God's law.

Go now and godspeed. Tomorrow when everyone is asleep we will crawl into our kneading tubs and sit there, waiting for the grace of God. Now go; I don't have the time to preach about this any longer. As people say: "a word to the wise is sufficient." And you are so wise that you require no more teaching. Go, save our lives, I beg of you.'

This simple carpenter went on his way, stopping occasionally to mutter an, 'alas,' or 'woe is me.' He told his wife this great secret — of course, she was well aware and knew all about these curious events much better than he did. Nevertheless, she acted as if she was terrified that she would die, and complained: 'Alas! Go on your way then at once and help us to escape or we are all dead. I am your faithful wedded wife — go, dearest spouse, and do what you can to save our lives.'

Behold the power of emotions! People can die simply because of what they imagine; so deeply can simple impressions be felt.

This ignorant carpenter literally trembled with fear as he imagined Noah's flood come surging like the sea, drowning Alison, his sweet honey. He wept, he wailed, he was wretched; he sighed many a deep and sorrowful sigh; and he went to procure a kneading trough as well as a tub and a beer-brewing vat and had them sent secretly to his house. There, all by himself, he hung them near the roof and then made, with his own hands, three ladders by which they could climb step by step up into the rafters where the tubs were hanging. Then he filled the tubs and the trough with bread and cheese and good ale in jugs — enough of each for a day. But before he did all that he sent his servant and his maid away to London on business, and on Monday, as night drew near, he shut his door but lit no candles, making sure everything was as it should be. And then the three of them climbed up into their ships and sat quietly for a time.

'Say an "Our Father" and then shush,' Nicolas finally commanded, and 'shush' answered John, and 'shush' echoed Alison. The carpenter said his evening prayers and sat still as a mouse, praying, waiting, listening for the rain.

Tired as he was, the carpenter soon fell into a dead sleep, more or less around curfew time, I would say. The suffering of his spirit caused him to groan loudly, and the awkward position of his head made him snore loudly. Hearing that, Nicolas and Alison quickly snuck down the ladders and, without another word, went to bed. There, where the carpenter would lie, they reveled in harmonious unity. So Nicolas and Alison spent the night together, hard at work in their joy and pleasure, until the bells began to ring well before sunrise and the friars could be heard singing in their chapels.

That parish cleric, the amorous Absolon, who was so hopelessly in love, had gone with some friends to Osney that Monday to entertain and distract himself, and there he took the opportunity to ask a monk — privately, of course — about John the carpenter, and this monk asked him to follow him outside of the church, where he admitted: 'I don't know; I have not seen him here for work since Saturday. I suspect he is out looking for timber, sent by our abbot. It is usual for him to go looking for timber and to stay on some farm there for a day or two. Or else he is probably at home. I can't really say where he might be.'

This made Absolon feel better, as he thought: 'This is the time then not to waste the night on sleep; I haven't seen John anywhere around his place all day. As I thrive, when the cock crows, I will softly knock on the window that is low in the wall of his bower. There I will tell Alison all about my love and my desire for her and I will be sure at least to earn a kiss. Certainly I will receive some comfort. All day my mouth has been itchy — a sure sign that there's a kiss in my future. On top of that I dreamed the whole night through that I was at a banquet. So, I will get a couple of hours of sleep and then be awake all night, ready to play.'

So, at the first crow of the cock, this cheery lover Absolon jumped out of bed and dressed in his finest, paying attention to every detail. Even before he had combed his hair, he chewed cardamom and licorice to sweeten his breath. Certain that this would make him irresistable, he even placed a sprig of paris[14] under his tongue.

Thus he arrived at the carpenter's house and stood quietly under the closed window — it was low, about chest-height for him — and softly, gently cooed: 'What are you doing this night, my honey comb, my sweet Alison, my beautiful bird, my sweet cinnamon? Awake, dearly beloved of mine, and speak to me! I know you do not think of my suffering, though for your love I sweat wherever I am — no wonder that I grow faint and perspire for such love. I moan like the lamb for the mother's teat. Yes. My beloved, I am so filled with desire that I can eat no more than does a young girl, and I yearn for you like the eternally faithful turtledove.'

---

[14] An herb thought to guarantee true love.

'Get you gone, you jackass — get away from my window — begone,' Alison answered. 'God knows you you won't be hearing me ask you for a kiss. I love another — not that it's your business — much more than you, Absolon, so help me Jesus! Get on your way before I throw something at you. Let me go back to sleep — the devil himself take you!'

'Alas,' moaned Absolon, 'woe is me. Was true love ever rewarded with such nastiness? At least then give me a kiss, since I can hope for no better, for the love of Jesus and for my sake.'

'Will you go away then?' she asked.

'Yes, truly I will, my eternally beloved,' he answered.

'Then get ready, because I'll be right there,' she said. And to Nicolas, she said: 'Watch this. You'll die laughing.'

Meanwhile, Absolon knelt and said: 'I feel like a king right now; and I'm sure this is only the beginning. Oh, my beloved, grant me your mercy; sweet bird, give me your grace.'

Alison quickly opened the window. 'Alright already,' she said. 'Hurry up and be quick about it before the neighbors see you.'

Absolon wiped his lips in preparation as, there, in the night, dark as pitch or maybe as coal, Alison pushed her ass out the window and Absolon, who couldn't tell the difference, kissed it full on with his mouth, with great relish, not knowing what he was kissing. But then he jumped back — something was amiss — because whatever he had kissed was rough and hairy, and he knew full well that a woman has no beard. He could only ask himself: 'Whoa! Hell and damnation! What have I done?'

'Teehee,' Allison laughed and slammed the window shut, leaving Absolon to wallow in sadness.

'A beard! A trick,' shouted handy Nicolas. 'By God's body, you've outdone yourself with this prank!'

Absolon could hear this clearly and, now furious, began to bite his lip, muttering revenge to himself: 'I'll get you for this!'

Poor Absolon — how he rubs and scrubs his lips with dirt, with sand, with straw, with cloth, with wood chips, all the while bemoaning what has happened to him, cursing and swearing:

"Goddamn! I would rather bequeath my soul to Satan for eternity than to call this whole dirty town my own, if only I could be avenged for this insult! Damn, why didn't I turn away when I could?' His fiery, hot love had now completely cooled and its fire was quenched; from the moment he had kissed her ass all his interest in love had disappeared. Healed of his malady, he now ranted at and insulted the very idea of romance, at times weeping like a beaten child.

But then he gathered himself and crossed the street to the smithy of a man called Gervaise, known for making harnesses, sharpening shears and repairing plow shares. Absolon pounded on his door, demanding: 'Open up, Gervaise; I need you right now.'

'What's that? Who is it? What do you want?'

'It is I, Absolon,'

"What? Who? Absolon? For Christ's sweet cross, why are you up so early. God be with you, but what's wrong with you? God knows you look as if some sweet young thing has caused you a bit of a problem? By St Neot, it's obvious you know what I'm talking about, right?'

Absolon was not amused, and he had no interest just then in banter. There was more flax on his distaff than Gervais could possibly know. He said: 'Listen, my friend. I need you to loan me that hot poker fired up in your chimney. I need it now, right away, but I'll bring it back shortly.'

Gervais answered: 'Sure thing. Take it — I would lend it to you even if it were made of gold or were worth as much as a whole bag full of gold coins. As I am a true smith, you shall have it if you want it. But, by Christ's foe, what are you planning to do with it?'

'Don't you worry about that,' answered Absolon. 'I'll tell you all about it in good time.'

With no further delay, he grabbed the glowing poker by its cool handle and quietly slipped into the night — back to the carpenter's house. Again he coughed quietly and then knocked at the window, just as before.

Alison answered the knock : 'Who is it now? What? Who's knocking? Nicolas, listen — I think there might be a thief at the window.'

'No, no — God forbid,' Absolon answered. 'God knows, my sweet beloved, it is I, your Absolon, my darling. And I have brought you a ring made of gold. As God be my witness, my mother gave it to me. It is a thing of beauty, with a lovely inscription, and I want you to have it. All I ask in return is that you give me a kiss.'

Now Nicolas was up to take a piss and thought he could improve on Alison's joke, meaning that Absolon should kiss his ass, as well, before the day could dawn. So he quickly opened the window and stuck his ass out there, the whole buttock, all the way to his thigh. Then Absolon, our good cleric, said: 'Speak to me, sweet bird, so that I may know exactly where you are.'

At that, Nicolas let fly a fart like a thunderclap — completely blinding poor Absolon — who held ready his hot poker and now struck Nicolas smack on the ass with it. That poker burned his skin a hand's breadth all the way around his rump, and it hurt so much that he thought he was going to die. He started to shout as if he had gone mad: "Help! Water! Water! Help, for God's sake! Water! Water!"

That woke up the carpenter, who heard someone in great distress yelling 'water,' and he thought: 'Dear God! It's time! Here comes Noah's flood!' And without another word, he sat up in his tub and cut the rope that held it up, and down he went. There was no time to sell ale or brew beer before he smashed into the ground — and there he lay, knocked out.

By now Nicolas and Alison had run into the street, shouting 'Wake up' and 'Come out.' Their neighbors, young and old, came running to stare at this man in his tub, still unconscious, pale and wan, now with a broken arm, and without anyone but himself to account for it all. When he finally tried to speak, he was drowned out by Nicolas and Alison who told everyone that he had gone mad — that he was so afraid of Noah's flood that, in his fantasy and foolishness he had bought three great kneading tubs to hang high from the roof and had begged them, for the love of God, to join him there, to keep him company.

Of course the townspeople laughed at him and mocked him then; they looked at the roof and gaped at what the carpenter had done, turning everything that had happened to him into a joke. No matter what he said, they ignored it; no one was interested in his side of the story. Overcome by all their oaths, he was considered to be mad by everyone from then on, and all the students would point him out and agree: "That man is crazy, my brothers!" And that is how John became the butt of every joke.

So, the carpenter's wife was screwed, despite all his jealousy and his efforts to guard her, and Absolon kissed her lower eye, and Nicolas is branded on the rump.

My tale is done; may God save us all who travel together."

After most of the pilgrims had stopped laughing at this outrageous tale of Absolon and handy Nicolas, various pilgrims had diverse responses to it but, for the most part, they laughed and took it as good sport. I didn't see anyone upset except Oswald, the Reeve; I assume because he was older than the Miller and was, by trade, a carpenter, he might have found the tale about a foolish old carpenter a bit too much. At any rate, he now began to complain and criticize.

"I swear," he said, "if all I wanted to do was to be crude, I could tell you a story about completely tricking a Miller, but I'm old and have no interest in getting even like that. I won't play that silly game. The grass has been harvested and is now forage for the stable; my white top makes my age clear, and my heart and my hair are both stale. I am something like the open-ass pear, a fruit that gets worse the older it is, until it rots in the rubbish or the straw; I fear that is how it goes with us old men, too.

We are not ripe until we are rotten; we skip to the world's tune as long as we can. Our desire always has a snag, because we have a white head but a green tail. But, make no mistake. We are like the leek: our ability might be gone but our will still seeks folly, and will not be stopped. But since we are too old to act, we just talk; yet our old ashes still cover glowing embers.

We old men possess four coals, and I will tell you about them. They are boasting, lying, anger and avarice — these four embers glow long, well into old age. Our aching limbs may well be feeble, but our desire never ceases, and that's the truth. I still have a colt's tooth, no matter how many years it's been since the stream of my life first began its flow. I mean to say that from the moment I was born, death immediately tapped the keg of my life and let it start to run out and, ever since, that tap has been opened, and now the keg is nearly emptied. My stream of life sinks below the rim. Foolish tongues may well ring and chime about all the horrible things that happened long ago; all we old people have is our dotage."

When our Host had heard enough of this sermon he simply began to talk over it: "What, may I ask, is the point of all this ancient wisdom? Why are we wasting time speaking of scriptures. It's the devil who sends a Reeve to preach or turns a cobbler into a sailor or a physician. Quit wasting our time, and tell us your story. Look, we are nearly at Deptford and its half way mid-morning. Down the road is Greenwich, a town known to be full of shrews. It's past time for you to start your tale."

Oswald, the Reeve, answered: "Very well, then, sirs; I ask only that you take no offense when I answer now and, to some extent, make a fool of this drunk Miller, because I think we can all agree that it is right to meet force with force. He has told us how a Carpenter was tricked and made a fool of, no doubt to get at me, a carpenter by training. And, with your permission, I shall pay him back. I will tell a story using the same churlish language as he did, and I pray to God that, in the meantime, He break this fellow's neck. This one," he pointed at the Miller, "can easily see the straw in my eye but not the beam in his own."

"Ha!" snorted the Miller, "let him try. Let him tell a story that will show his own foolishness as an old man who can do no better than bemoan the fire that has gone out and tell stories about a great past that never was. At least my story told the truth. What red-blooded young man would reign in his willing steed so long and wait till he was old to bed his willing lover, like that Palamal or even his friend Arctate, or whatever their names were. I ask you all: do you know anyone who would?"

At this the Host again stepped in and said: "Enough of this; be glad that you have told your bawdy tale and have insulted our noble Knight. And you, Sir Reeve, speaking out of turn as much as did the Miller — nevertheless, go on with it now and start your tale, seemly or not."

And so the Reeve began his story.

The Reeve's Tale

"In Trumpington, not far from Cambridge, there runs a bubbling brook, and over that brook stands a bridge with a mill.

Now listen up, as every word of what I am about to tell you is true.

For many years the mill was run by a churl known as proud Symkin. He was as cocky and showy as a peacock; he could play the bagpipes, was good at fishing and mending nets, and he usually won drinking games, wrestling matches and bow and arrow contests. At his belt he always had a long blade as sharp as any sword might be, and everybody was scared of him and would not dare lay a hand on him, fearing that Sheffield knife. His face was round, he had a pug nose, and his skull was as bald as an ape's. He was a total bully, and no one dared challenge him for he was known to carry out his revenge on all who might try. Of course he was a thief of grain and ground meal, always stealing from his customers.

Since his wife's father was the village priest, she was considered to be of "noble" stock. Her dowry had included many a brass pan, enough to persuade Symkin to ally with her family. She had been raised in a nunnery, and Symkin had always said that he would take no wife who was not well-educated and a virgin, so that his status as a free man would never be in question. And she was as proud and arrogant as a magpie. The two of them made quite a picture; on holy days he would walk a few steps in front of her, the tip of his hood wound tight around his head, and she would follow in her red mantle, matching Symkin's hose. No one dared address her with anything but "lady," and none along the way were foolish enough to tease or flirt with her — unless they wanted to be the victim of Symkin's sword or dagger. Jealous men are always dangerous — at least they want their wives to believe as much. Of course, because her parentage was somewhat questionable, the Miller's wife was as proud as ditchwater, filled with disdain and scorn for everyone else. She believed that a lady should be aloof, what with her lineage and the education she had attained in the nunnery.

Between them they had a daughter, twenty years old, and no other children except a sweet little boy of half a year that lay in a cradle. The girl was well developed and a bit chunky, with a pug nose and eyes grey as glass, broad buttocks and high, full breasts. And, I will not lie, her hair was quite fair.

But Symkin made marriage for her difficult, as he intended to bestow her nobly into some house with respectable ancestry. After all, the property of Holy Mother Church may not be wasted or split but must be bestowed only on someone of proper lineage, descended also from Holy Church's blood. And that was the Miller's intent, on the sacred honor of this blood, even if it meant eating up Holy Church in the bargain.[15]

This Miller had a very profitable monopoly, grinding all the grain in the entire region, including the wheat and malt belonging to a great college nearby, known as King's Hall at Cambridge. And it so happened that this college's manciple was taken so ill, over time, that everyone thought he would die. Of course, that encouraged the Miller to steal a hundred times as much grain and ground meal as he usually did because, up till then, he had just stolen diplomatically, but now his thievery became excessive and undeniable. The master of the college raged and fussed, but the

---

[15] One of the main forces for insisting on celibacy for priests was the Church's need to control its property. As long as priests had no legitimate children, the many-faceted valuable properties belonging to the Church could not be inherited and dissipated among such offspring. In Chaucer's time it was common, especially in rural villages, for priests to have women "housekeepers," and there were few local secrets about the identity of clergy bastards. In this one short passage, the Reeve mocks both his tale's greedy Miller's questionable snobbery and his supposed interest in protecting Church property, as the Miller's wife is the daughter of the local priest, making the Miller's daughter the priest's granddaughter.

Miller did not give a tinker's dam. He blustered fiercely and swore loudly that no one could prove him to have done wrong.

Now, at the college there were two young students, headstrong and eager for adventure; so, merely for their own entertainment and pleasure they cajoled their master into allowing them a little time off to go to that mill and to watch their grain being ground — so sure of themselves that they wagered their necks that the Miller would be unable to steal even half a peck of their corn by stealth, nor rob them by force. The master finally gave in and let them go.

One of these students was John and the other Allen — both came from a town known as Strother, far in the North — I'm not sure where exactly.

So, like knights setting out to slay a marauding dragon, they prepared their gear and put it on a horse, along with an empty sack; then the two young paladins went forth, sword and buckler at their sides.

John knew the way — he needed no guide — and, arriving at the mill, he laid down his sack.

Allen spoke first: 'A grand day to you, Simon![16] How are your fair daughter and wife?'

'By God, you are welcome, Allen,' answered Symkin. 'And John, too! But what brings you here?'

'Simon,' said John, 'in God's name, necessity is not conquered by rules. The man without a servant must take care of himself, or else, as the learned tell us, he is a fool. Our manciple's teeth hurt so much in his head that I expect he will soon be dead. Thus, Allen and I have come in his stead with our grain to be ground, so we can take it back to the college. I pray you do it speedily, so that we may be on our way.'

'So shall I do then,' said Symkin, 'by my faith. And what will you do you while you wait?'

---

[16] Symkin is a nickname for Simon.

'By God, I will stand right by the hopper,' declared John, 'and watch the corn as it goes in. I swear by my father that I have never had the chance to see a hopper going back and forth.'

Allen added: 'Is that what you will do, John? In that case I will go underneath, by my crown, and watch the meal fall through into the trough — that shall be my entertainment. For John, just like you, I have been no more a miller till now than have you.'

The Miller smiled at their foolishness and thought: 'I'm onto their sly little tricks. They are cocksure that no one will deceive them but, by God, before this day is out I will blind them, no matter how much philosophy they bring to this effort. The more clever tricks they think up, the more I will steal; instead of flour, I will leave them with bran. Their cleverness does not worry me in the least. As the wolf said to the mare: "The great scholars know little enough of the world."

Quietly he stole out the door, and looked around until he found the clerks' horse, hobbled, behind the mill, under an arbor. He approached it gently and quickly stripped off the bridle, and the horse, as soon as it was free, loped toward the bog where wild mares run about, neighing along the way with gusto, charging through thick and thin.

Returning just as quietly as he had left, the Miller went about his business, now and then chatting with the clerks until the corn was well ground and, when the meal was sacked and bound, John went out, only to see that the horse was gone. He began to shout: 'Oh hell' and 'Woe is me. Our horse is lost, alas, for God's bones, get on your feet and hurry up right now! Alas, our warden's palfrey has been lost.' And Allen forgot all about the corn and the meal — he lost track of everything. 'What? Where has he gone?' he shouted helplessly.

The Miller's wife came running out of the house and told them: 'I'm sorry, boys, but your horse ran off toward the bog as fast as he could run to join the wild mares — I'd blame whoever hobbled the horse too loosely or did not tighten the reins better.'

'Damn me,' said John. 'Allen, for pain of Christ, let's take off our swords and go after the nag. I know she is fast, as she is a roe, but God knows I'm as swift as a deer — by God's heart, he cannot get away from both of us. Why didn't you tie him up in the barn? Bad luck to both of us! By God, Allen, you are such a fool.' And, with that, these foolish clerks, Allen and John, were off toward the bog. And when the Miller was sure they had gone, he took half a bushel of their flour and gave it to his wife to bake a loaf of bread, saying: 'I know they thought they were clever as the devil himself, but a miller can still tweak a clerk's beard, for all his smarts — let them go after their horse. Look at them run! Sure and let the children play all they want — they won't capture their horse that easily, by my head.'

The foolish clerks, in the meantime, ran hither and yon, shouting after their horse: 'Stop! Stop! Stand still! Stop! Down here! Watch out! Whistle for him and I'll try to grab him.' But for a long time, till it got dark, they could not catch their horse, though they tried with all their might — he was so much faster than they were — until finally they caught up with him in a ditch.

Weary and wet, like animals in the rain, these two foolish clerks began their return to the mill. 'Damn us both to hell,' said John, 'I rue the day I was born. So now we are the objects of contempt and scorn for the Miller — and when this gets out, for everyone in the countryside. Our corn is stolen and the world will call us fools, the warden as well as our fellow students — and so will the Miller, damn him, too!'

John complained all the way back to the mill, all the while leading Bayard by a rope. And at the mill there was the Miller sitting by his fire, for now it was dark and they had no shelter for the night. For the love of God they begged him for food and a place to stay, of course at their cost. The Miller said: 'You shall have what we can spare. My house is small but, no doubt, with your learning I'm sure you can stretch into a mile a place that's only twenty feet wide. We'll see whether you find enough room in our house or whether you will, by logic and argument, make it huge with your wise words.'

'Now, Simon,' said John, 'by St. Cuthbert, you're always ready with a joke — my compliments. And it is certainly true that: "A man has to make do with what he finds or make sure he brings what he needs with him." So, I beg you, dear host, for some food and drink and good company, and we will pay well for everything. We know that an empty hand never lures a hawk; look, here's our money — we are ready to spend it as needed.'

The Miller sent his daughter into the village for ale and a roasted goose, while the two students tied up their horse in the barn so firmly that it would never get loose, and their host made them a bed, covered with sheets and warm blankets, no more than ten or twelve feet from his own. Not far from there, in that same chamber, the daughter had her own bed, all to herself. This was as good as it could get, and do you know why? There was no other chamber in that place. So they ate and entertained themselves by chatting comfortably, and they drank good strong ale and finally went to bed around midnight.

The Miller had imbibed so much that his bald head was shiny with sweat — so drunk was he that his usual ruddy complexion was pale as ashes. He belched and spoke through his nose as if he were hoarse or had a cold. So off he went to bed, along with his wife — a woman as light and as lusty as a jay — her whistle was wet, too, but she nevertheless made sure the cradle with her baby boy was placed at the foot of her bed. There she could rock it and nurse him, if need be. And when the crock of ale was finally completely empty, the daughter also went to bed, as did Allen and John. No one there needed a sleeping potion that night. The Miller had drunk so much that in his sleep he farted like a horse; he cared little as to what his arse was doing. His wife accompanied him with a bold bass; you could have heard her snoring two furlongs away; and the daughter lovingly joined in to create a memorable three-part harmony.

Hearing this melody, Allen, our student, poked his friend John in the ribs and asked: 'Hey! Are you asleep? Have you ever heard such music in your life? Listen to this evensong. May all three of them be devoured by a ferocious skin rash. Who in the world has ever been forced attended such a concert? But listen, I intend to make the best of this mess. I don't plan to waste a moment of this night on sleep. Even now I foresee a better ending.

But, John,' he said, 'God bless me if don't figure out a way to screw that wench tonight; legally, I think I am entitled to some compensation. As you know, John, the law stipulates that if a man be aggrieved in one way, he may be assuaged in another way. There is no doubt but that our grain has been stolen and we have been injured in more ways than one today. Since my losses cannot be made up in any direct way I can see, I will make sure that I get even in another way, so help me God!

John answered: 'Allen, don't be rash! This fellow is a dangerous man, and if he happens to wake up, we will both be the worse for it.'

Allen responded: 'He's no more dangerous than a fly.' He rose from the bed and crept over to where the wench was sleeping, flat on her back, snoring the night away. Before she could possibly have noticed, he managed to get close enough to where it would have been too late for her to cry out. And, not to put too fine a point on it, they were soon one.

So, play, Allen — play to your heart's content, while I relate what John did.

John lay still for a short time, feeling sorry for himself: 'Damn me,' he thought, 'if I'm not the butt of this joke. It's clear now that I'm the fool here. At least my buddy is getting something in return for his loss; he's got the Miller's daughter in his arms. He took a risk and got his needs met and I'm lying here in my bed like a helpless bag of crap. And when they tell this story, and you know they will, I'll be the idiot, the sad sack weakling. By Jesus, I'll get up and I'll take a risk myself. It's like they say: "he who is timid wins nothing."'

So he too arose and quietly crept to where the cradle stood, picked it up and noiselessly moved it to the foot of his own bed.

Not long after, the wife's snoring stopped abruptly, as she woke up and went out to piss; when she came back she noticed that the cradle was gone and that wherever she groped in the dark, she couldn't find it. 'Hells bells,' she thought to herself, 'I almost made a big mistake and climbed into that student's bed. Bless me, that would have been a fine pickle!' And so she groped around some more in the dark, feeling for the cradle until she found the bed she thought she was looking for, because the cradle was sitting at its end. In the dark, she didn't know exactly where she was, and so, of course, she crept into bed next to the student. And there she lay quietly, waiting to fall asleep again, but now John leaped up and went to work on this good wife with such a vengeance that, truly, she had not been served so well in a long while. He thrust as hard and deep as if he'd gone mad, and so both students made the most of their time that night until the third cock's crow.

Allen had grown weary by then, having screwed the night away, so he said: 'Farewell Mallene, sweet wench. The dawn is here and I cannot abide; but no matter where I go or ride, I am yours. I am your faithful student, on my very soul.'

And like any beloved lady in every sweet romance, she answered: 'My dearest love, fare thee well. But before you leave me there is one thing I must tell you. As you ride homeward past the mill, look behind the door as you pass, and you will find there a half bushel cake made with your very own grain that I helped my father steal from you. So, my sweet love, God save and keep you.' And with that she nearly began to cry.

Now Allen sat up and thought: 'Before the first light, I'd better go back to sleep next to my buddy.' Searching around, he soon found the cradle and realized: 'Good God, I am totally turned around. I must still be dizzy from all the drinking — I nearly went to the wrong bed. The cradle clearly shows where I've gone wrong; I just about lay down with the Miller and his wife.' So he crawled on, twenty feet or so until he got to the bed where the Miller was sleeping.

Thinking that he had found his friend, John, Allen quickly crawled in next to him, grabbed his neck and whispered in his ear: 'Hey, John, you pig's head, wake up, for Christ's sake and listen to this; by Saint James, three times have I screwed the Miller's daughter straight up during the night, while you were cowering here, all afraid.'

The Miller shouted back: 'Have you so, you false son of a whore? You deceptive asshole! You evil student! For this you will die, so help me God! No one dare besmirch my daughter, born of such noble stock.' And with that he grabbed Allen by the throat and struck him over and over, his fist landing on Allen's nose and making a broad stream of blood run down his chest.

And there they wallowed on the floor, like two pigs in a poke, one falling over the other and then back, until the Miller stumbled over a stray stone and fell down backward on top of his wife, who was unaware of this wild fight, as she had just fallen into a deep sleep after all her hard work with John during the night.

And being awakened so suddenly from her sleep, she brayed: 'Help me, by the holy cross of Bromeholm: Into your hands, O Lord, I commend my spirit. Jesus, Lord, help me. Wake up, Simon, the devil has fallen on top of me and has broken my heart. I am dying here! Someone is lying on my stomach and someone on my head. Help me, Symkin, these treacherous students are having a fight.'

Now John, too, jumped up as fast as he could and pawed about the wall for a staff of some kind while the wife, who knew the place much better than John, of course, did the same and soon found one. When she saw a little shimmering of light from the moon finding its way through a crack in the wall, she was able to see both of the men fighting, but she did not know who was who, seeing only a flash of white. But she thought she remembered that one of the students had worn a white night cap, so she crawled closer and closer to it with her staff and, thinking it was Allen, she hit the Miller hard on his bald shiny head, and he went down, yelling: 'Jesus, bless me. I've been killed.'

The clerks finished the job of beating him, hastily dressed, took their horse, grabbed their flour and were on their way, not forgetting their bushel and half of a cake behind the door.

So, the proud Miller was well rewarded, losing the ground corn and more than paying for the supper of John and Allen, who beat him soundly. His wife got screwed, as did his daughter — enough said!

Behold, this is what happens when a Miller is a false scoundrel. And that is why the proverb is completely true, that 'those who do wrong will find themselves in jail.' Now may God, sitting high in all majesty, save all in this company, except for this churlish Miller that rides ahead of me!

And this is how my story answers his."

The London Cook was so delighted by this tale that he thought his soul's deepest itch had been scratched. He laughed again and again: "By the passion of Jesus, this Miller got the right payment for his generous hospitality. No wonder that wise King Solomon advised us well not to bring just any stranger into our house. A good night's hospitality can be a dangerous thing, and a man might well think again about whom he has brought into his home.

As I am known as Roger of Ware, I pray that God punish me with sorrow and care if ever I have heard a Miller get what's coming to him any more justly. His joke was repaid well enough in the dark of night. But God forbid that this is where we stop — so, if you will allow me and listen to my story, as well, though I be but a poor man, I will tell you a tale, as best I can, about something that happened in our very own town."

Our Host sighed and answered: "Fine, go ahead and tell your story but, Roger, make sure it's a good story, because I can tell that many a meat pie had given its life blood for you, and you have no doubt sold many other pies of your own, twice heated and twice cooled before they sold. I know you've earned the curse of quite a few unsuspecting pilgrims who have fared the worse for the parsley they consumed along with the stubble-fed goose they bought in your fly-infested shop. So go ahead, then, my friend Roger, as you are called, and all I ask is that you do not let anger affect our game, as jokes and teasing can also tell the truth."

"Agreed," said Roger, "you are dead right in what you say. But, as the Flemish say: a true joke is a bad joke and, therefore, Harry Bailey, I hope you won't be angry with me before we're all done if I tell a story about an innkeeper. But I won't do that for now – not in this story — I just hope you won't be be mad at me if I get even with you before we have finished our journey together." He was quite happy with himself and laughed as he began this story, which you will now hear.

The Cook's Tale

"I once knew a baker's apprentice in our city, a fellow as happy as a goldfinch singing in the woods. Brown as a berry and topped with black curls always combed out just so, he was a drinking buddy who had no equal, and he was known for his dancing — in fact, he was known as Perkin Partyboy. He was horny and as full of passion as a hive is with sweet honey. Any wench he hooked up with could count herself lucky, and no wedding could be called successful without his singing and dancing.

Of course he enjoyed the tavern much more than the shop. If there was a procession or any other kind of to-do in Cheapside, he was out the door and wouldn't be back until he had seen all there was to see and danced as if it were his very last time. Along the way he would collect folks like himself to dance and weave and move and enjoy; and then they would make plans to meet again, to play at dice in some street, for truly there was no apprentice in the whole town who could throw dice like Perkin.

Now when his master was not looking, Perkin was generous to a fault with everything that had its home on his master's cupboards. Of course, we all know that an apprentice reveler who spends his time gambling, partying and chasing women is making his master pay, even though the master does not enjoy the revelry himself, because using up other peoples' things is just another way of stealing. Whether you accompany them by guitar or fiddle, revelry and truth are always at each other's throats in anyone of low morals. We can all attest to that.

So, even though he was constantly being rebuked by his master and even once or twice led off to debtors' prison at Newgate, this jolly apprentice persisted to the end of his apprenticeship, and the day finally came for his master to give him his official release, no doubt thinking of the proverb: 'Better to throw out the rotten apple than to let it ruin the whole barrel.' This is how it is with a dissolute servant: better to let him go than to let him ruin all the other servants. So his master let him go, along with deeply-felt wishes of bad luck.

And so our jolly apprentice was free to go, free to party all the night but, as we all know, there is no thief without an accomplice who helps him to spend and waste everything he can beg, borrow or steal. So, the first thing Perkin did was to have his bed and all his things sent to the house of a companion who was just like him, who also loved gambling, partying and idleness. This fellow had a wife who, for appearance sake, kept a bakery shop but, in fact, screwed for a living, with her husband as her pimp.

Now Mack and Zona had married for no other reason than that it allowed them to live comfortably off Zona's screwing. It was Mack's job to find customers for Zona, and they had developed a thriving business; in fact, they lived in a large house with two separate bedrooms above their struggling bakery — all inherited from Zona's mother, also a whore. And they were so discreet that they were able to keep their neighbors from guessing what they were really doing. In fact, they had told no one, including Perkin, about their real business.

'Well met, my friend Perkin,' Mack greeted his drinking buddy. 'There is always room under our roof for one more jolly fellow. You are welcome to stay with us as long as you need. And now that you are no longer an apprentice, your help with the bakery will be most timely.'

Now Zona was even more sensuous and attractive than was the young wife in my friend's, the Miller's, story. But on top of that she also knew all the tricks of her trade, including the appearance of innocence. This was in no small part what allowed Mack and Zona to keep up their pretense of being respectable shopkeepers. And with Perkin added to their household, they could now rely on him to produce much of the baked goods they had — up to now — been selling only after secretly buying them from another baker who lived far from their house.

Since she was usually working when Mack and Perkins and their friends were out at night, making the streets of the town unsafe for normal folks, Perkin had never met Zona. So, when he first laid eyes on her, he was thunderstruck. He was sure that he had never seen any woman this beautiful. But he also knew that she was his friend's wife — his friend who was taking him in, giving him a roof over his head and a place to keep his bed. For someone who was never at a loss for something seductive to say to a woman, Perkin was dumbstruck. He could only stammer something that might have been a greeting. Mack and Zona exchanged a quick smile, for they had both noted all they needed to see. As soon as Mack had shown him where to put his bed, Perkin went there and struggled through a long quiet session of sadness and self-pity, for he knew he could not betray his friend — yet he was desperately stricken and knew that he had no choice but to pursue this beautiful creature until she was his.

After a time, Mack came to him and sat on the side of his bed, asking: 'Buddy, what's wrong. You're sad and upset. How can I help you?'

Perkin only shook his head and sighed: 'My friend, it's hopeless. I can't talk about it.'

'Oh come, Buddy. Since when do we have secrets between us? Don't we share everything?'

'Some things cannot be shared.'

No matter how much Mack tried to persuade his friend, Perkin was mum. Finally, Mack said that he had business to take care of and went his way, while Perkin continued to mope and moan ever more loudly. Zona could not help but hear him, so she crept quietly into his room and asked him gently what was the matter. Perkin was not shy with her: 'Oh, my dearest Zona, you cannot know how deeply I suffer with love for you, and how hopeless I feel to be in love with the wife of my good friend. But unless you appease my passion, I will surely die.'

'Oh, my dear Perkin,' she answered, without hesitation, 'I blush to hear this. I am taken aback and quite astonished,' she said, as she gracefully moved to sit on the side of his bed, were she gently took his hand in hers and smiled a sweet innocent smile at him. 'What in the world shall we do about it,' she asked him.

"What can we do about it?" he asked plaintively.

"My dear, simple Perkin,' she answered, gently placing his hand on her ample bosom above her boldly beating heart, 'have you not thought that I might feel the same way about you?'

'Dare I hope? Is it possible?'

'Who can explain the ways of love?' she asked, blushing as if this were a new feeling for her. 'I love my husband and am ever faithful to him, but I love you more, even though I have just met you. From the moment I saw you, I was smitten. Dear Perkin, do with me what you will.'

With such an invitation, Perkin did not hesitate. The two of them explored each other's bodies thoroughly that afternoon, and it was only after several hours that Zona finally said, 'we must stop now, lest Mack get home and find us like this.' They swore undying love and affection for one another and parted, agreeing, of course, to meet again the next time Mack left the house on business.

For some time things went along like this. Perkin baked and sold their goods, while Zona whored and Mack pimped — and all thrived, especially Perkin, who thought he had everything he wanted. There were times when Perkin found himself thinking that his hosts did not produce much in the way of baked goods, but he was happy to do his part, especially since he and Zona had reached such a mutually rewarding agreement. He also noted that Mack and Zona spent much time in their room, where he could hear the sounds of people making love at all hours of the day and night. But since he and Zona managed to find time to be together readily, he happily went along with this arrangement that allowed him to be with the woman he loved, even if she happened to be married to his best friend.

But then, one afternoon, Perkin saw a stranger leave Mack and Zona's room. It was a young man he had never seen before, and it roused Perkin's suspicions. He watched the strange man leave and then went to the door and knocked. Zona brightly announced: 'Come in.' When he did, there was Zona, quite naked, sitting up in the bed, with a welcoming smile on her beautiful face. Seeing Perkin, her smile faded a bit, but not completely. Perkin was shocked, but Zona simply said: 'Oh, dear! Ah well, it was only a matter of time. Dear Perkin, I think it's time you and I had a talk.'

'A talk?' he blustered. 'A talk? We're going to have a talk about you and this stranger?' He did not know what to do, but he finally sat down on the side of the bed, flustered by his nude lover and totally confused.

'Oh come, Perkin. Surely you have noticed how little baking Mack and I do and how often we are not in the shop? Did you not have suspicions?'

'Suspicions? About your baking? About what? This? This? This — what is this?' He looked away from her. 'Please put on some clothes. I can't talk to you like this.'

'Why not?' she asked sweetly, as she threw on a shift. 'You usually don't have any trouble talking to me like this.'

Perkin just shook his head and began to sob; Zona moved to him and embraced him, slowly pulling him down until his head was in her lap.

'But I thought you loved me,' Perkin gasped out between sobs.

'I do love you. Of course I love you. But love does not buy bread, or wine, or cheese, or this house. And surely you don't think that the bakery brings in enough money to pay for how we live.'

And now Mack also entered the room; to Perkin's surprise, Mack was no more shocked by what he saw than Zona had been to be discovered. He simply pulled over a stool to sit, nodding, and said: 'Aha, I see our little secret has been discovered.' He smiled at the couple on the bed, while Perkin was even more confused than before.

'Hello, dearest,' Zona greeted her husband. 'You come in good time. Please help me explain a few things to our friend Perkin.'

Perkin looked at Mack and then at Zona and then back at Mack, who finally said: 'I'm sorry — we're sorry — but we could say that it's really your fault.'

'My fault?' Perkin asked, feeling some anger.

'Well, yes,' answered Mack. 'You had to fall in love with Zona, and that's why we couldn't tell you. If you had just moved in and baked, as we agreed—'

'I did not choose to fall in love with her. It was love. It was — just look at her!'

'Yes,' Mack agreed. 'I know. I know. She is a very Venus.' He paused. 'It's why all this has worked so well.' Zona chuckled. 'It has indeed worked well,' she observed.

Perkin was still angry. 'So this is what you have been doing all the time — even before I moved in?'

'Why, yes,' answered Mack. 'How were we to know that you would fall in love with Zona?'

'I wish to God I had not!'

'Well,' Zona said cheerfully, 'we need to get on with it. Here we are, and it's water under the bridge, and I have work to do.' She winked at. Mack and Mack laughed.

You can imagine that it took poor Perkin some time to come to grips with all of this. While he could not understand much of what he had to accept, he did know that he was as much in love with Zona as ever. And once he realized this, he came to another decision, which he burned to share with her as soon as possible. So, a few days later, when Mack was out of the house and Mona was alone, he went to talk to her.

'Please listen to me carefully,' he begged her. 'I know that you do not want to live like this.' Zona merely smiled. 'And I know that I still love you. And I believe that you love me, too. So I have come to the conclusion that you and I must find a way out.'

'A way out?' Zona asked innocently.

'Yes, a way out of this life for you and me — so we can live happily together forever. Oh, I know Mack will be hurt, but he does not truly love you as I do, and so I'm sure he will find someone else to pimp for, and you and I will be fine.'

Zona smiled at him cheerfully.

'Well, what do you say?' he asked.

She continued to smile and then spoke. 'Here's what I say. I can tell that you truly love me, and I do love you, also. And there is a way, but it won't be easy.'

'If you know of a way, just tell me and I'll do it — anything to make this happen.'

'Alright. Now it's your turn to listen carefully to me! I inherited this house from my mother, but Mack has always wanted to own his own brothel and would be happy to let me go if he could do that. But such a thing is possible only with a lot of money. Now, Mack is very greedy and can be talked into anything that looks like he will get lots of money out of it. So, here's the plan. One of my customers is a money lender who will do anything I ask of him. If I send you to him, he will happily loan you the 500 Marks it will take to make Mack happy. Once we have the money and give it to Mack, he will give it to me for the house, we will give it back to the money lender, and you and I will simply disappear in some other city — maybe we'll go to Paris. And then we will live happily ever after.'

Perkin assured her that he would do anything for her, and Zona promptly arranged for him to meet her friend the moneylender; there, Perkin quickly agreed to the terms for the short-term loan, which the money lender said he would do without charging interest. And soon thereafter, Zona, Mack and Perkin met again in that same bedroom in which Perkin had first learned of their real work.

Zona led it off. 'My dear Mack and my dearest Perkin, since last we met Perkin has managed to acquire a great deal of money which, dear husband, he will give to you so that you can acquire your own brothel.'

Mack was delighted. "Dear friend," he said, "why do you do this generous thing for me?"

Zona answered for Perkin. "Of course, he does ask for something in return."

"Anything," said Mack, "anything he wants." He turned to Perkin. "Well, friend, what is it? What can I do for you?"

"I feel strange asking this, but Zona assures me that you will find it acceptable. I ask that you let Zona and me leave your life, never to see you again, and that you allow us to go away together.'

Without hesitation, Mack said: "Done and done. Zona will be difficult to replace but I am getting here just exactly what I want, so it is only fair that you and she get what you want. We have an agreement.'

And right there, on the spot, Perkin gave Mack 500 Marks.

I won't describe how happy the three all seemed to be, since they were all getting what they wanted but, suffice to say, they emptied several bottles of joy before they agreed that the next morning Zona and Perkin would meet at prime and then depart together, leaving Mack the house.

The next morning, before prime, Mack and Zona were having breakfast, discussing how Perkin would react when they broke the news to him that Zona had no intention of going away with him, and that he had been duped into taking up a large loan that he would be paying off for the rest of his life. But Perkin did not join them at prime or for some time after. Finally, they went to his room, only to discover that it was empty of Perkin and all his belongings. As puzzled as they were by this, they were even more surprised when the moneylender appeared and presented them with the note — payable by Mack — for a loan of 1,000 Marks, that had already accrued interest at 10 Marks and contained a clause that prohibited the loan from being rescinded or paid off before it was due.

So, Mack and Zona, who screwed and pimped for a living, were screwed by Perkin, who loved but who was not blinded enough by love to be fooled. I am told that Perkin joined a monastery around York and became a beloved confessor for young married women — and that he was well-known for baked goods that looked like purses full of money."

The Cook finished his story, and the Host opined at once: "Well, Roger, that was told much better than I had feared, considering how drunk you are already. And it was a tale well-fit to respond to the Miller and the Reeve."

"I must respectfully disagree," the Man of Laws intoned, as if he were summing up an argument before a group of jurors. "We heard a beautiful story about undying love from our esteemed Knight, followed by a disgusting tale of lust that the Miller shared at the expense of the Reeve, who could think of nothing better than a story about using sex to get even with a Miller — and now this tale in praise of whoring and pimping but without a moral point to makes us all better, and I, for one, am tired of it."

Several of the pilgrims joined to agree with the Lawyer, who felt the wind behind his sails and continued: "Therefore, I propose that we hear a moral tale from someone like the Parson or the Monk, rather than continue down this road toward more vile behavior and the worst of human activity."

At this the Franklin pushed his horse forward into the very path of the Host, to say: "Our noble Man of Laws is right. Let us hear some upstanding story from a pillar of our society rather than," he inhaled as if he had smelled something awful, "the dregs of our communities." He paused for a moment: "Perhaps the Squire would entertain us with something uplifting, a noble tale of gentle men and women and fashion at the court." But the Squire was busy whispering something into the ear of the Prioress, who blushed — at least that part of her face that could be seen — and smiled coquettishly until the frown from the Second Nun caused her to frown, as well.

Our Host could see that the bright sun had run a quarter of its path across the sky and maybe another half hour or more and, though he had not learned about astrology formally, he was aware that it was the eighteenth day of April, the month that precedes

May. He also noted that the shadows of all the trees were exactly as long as were the trunks that threw these shadows, and so, from these shadows he took it that Phoebus, shining brightly in the sun on this clear day, had climbed forty-five degrees and that for this day, at our latitude, it was 10 o'clock, or so he concluded.

He now abruptly pulled his horse about to say: "Gentles, I must call to your attention that the fourth part of this day has passed and therefore I urge us all to waste no further time, as best we can. My dear companions, time wastes day and night, and already we are robbed of the time we sleep, not to mention what we lose with our own negligence during the day of this stream that runs from the mountains unto the plains and is never returned to us again. No wonder Seneca and many other philosophers speak of time as more valuable than coffers of gold or, as he put it: 'You can always make up for lost cattle, but loss of time is unrecoverable ruin.' Never fear, it will not come again once it has passed, no more than does Malkin's virginity after, in her wantonness, she has lost it. Therefore, let us not wallow in idleness. Sir Man of Law, God bless you, tell us, without further delay, a tale to advance our case. You have been called, although by your own free assent, to take the stand in this case under my judgment; now is the time to acquit yourself of your obligation and, at the very least, to do your duty."

"My dear Host," the Lawyer answered, "in God's name, I agree; it is not my intent to get ahead of ourselves. A promise is a promise, and I will keep the entirety of my word; I can offer nothing more than that. For whatever law a man prescribes for another, it is only right that he should, at the very least, keep it himself. So we are told by many texts. Nevertheless, the sad fact is that I cannot think of a single suitable tale that that fellow Chaucer, though he knows precious little about meter or skillful rhyme, has not already told a long time ago in such English as he is capable of — this is commonly known —and, fellow travelers, if he has not told the story in one book than he's done it in some other; he has told more stories of lovers, here and there, than even

Ovid mentioned in his ancient epistles. Why should I tell again what has already been told?

In his early days this Chaucer began with Ceys and Alcione and followed that with the stories of all the other noble women and their lovers. If anyone takes the time to examine his giant tome that he calls the Legends of Saint Cupid, there he will witness the wide bleeding wound of Lucretia and of Babylonean Thisbe; the sword Dido intended to use on her unfaithful Aeneas; the tree of Phyllis and her Demophon; the complaint of Dianira and of Hermione, of Adrian and Hypsipyle — on that barren island, jutting from the sea — Lisander who drowned for Hero; the tears of Helen and the sorrow of Briseyd, and you, Ladomya; your cruelty, Queen Medea, that let you hang by the throat your own little children to punish Jason for his betrayal of your love. O Hypermnestra, Penelope, Alcestis — he praises you as wives above the best.

And yet he has not written a single word about the wicked example that was Canace, who loved her own brother sinfully — fie on such cursed stories, I say — or else of Apollonius of Tyre, or how the cruel king Antiochus took his own daughter's maidenhead — so horrible a tale to read — before he crushed her on the unforgiving pavement. Of such things, no doubt after careful consideration, he would never write in any of his sermons, not of such unnatural abominations, nor will I, given the choice, retell any such stories.

But what shall I choose for a tale here today? I would rather not be likened to the muses people call Pierides — just check the Metamorphosis to know what I mean. And don't think for a minute that I would give a rat's ass even if I were to follow him with a poor dish of baked hawthorn berries — I leave the rhymes to Chaucer and speak in prose." And hard upon that rather puzzling conclusion, he began the tale you are about to hear.

The Man of Law's Tale

"I have no choice but to begin with a denunciation of the lowest and most deplorable of human estates: poverty — that plight so unconditionally full of harm! You, those who are mired in poverty — you are distressed, thirsty, cold, hungry! Too deeply ashamed are you to ask for help. Yet, if you do not ask, you will be even more needy, and your very destitution only exposes your secret wounds. Despite your best intentions, your indigence forces you to steal, to beg, or to borrow to survive. So you blame Christ and denounce Him bitterly for so wrongly apportioning temporal wealth; you maliciously charge your neighbor with having too much while you have too little. 'As God is my witness,' you say, 'the day of reckoning will come for you who refused to help those in need when you could have — your very tail will burn in the coals of the fire then.'"

"What ails the man," loudly interrupted the Wife of Bath this litany about poverty, "what is wrong with him to assail so heinously those among us who have the misfortune of suffering from poverty?"

The Man of Laws merely frowned, while the Wife continued: "Did not our gracious Lord Himself, Jesus, source of all kindness and virtue, did He not Himself call for the poor to come unto Him like the little children?"

At this compression of biblical texts, the Man of Laws made no effort to hide the smirk that crossed his face, but still, he said nothing.

But the Wife was not finished.

"Surely the learned clerics and religious companions on this pilgrimage will know that this attack is wrong and should not continue."

An awkward silence greeted her words. And after a few moments of this, the Man of Laws simply went on, as if the Wife had never spoken at all.

"Just listen to what wise men teach us: 'Even death is better than indigence; your very neighbors despise you when you are poor,' and 'the poor will always be wicked.' Say goodbye to respect if you are poor. My advice then is to be careful and never to get to that point. If you are poor, your brother will hate you and all your friends will flee from you."

Having reviled the poor — apparently to his satisfaction, he now turned his attention to the wealthy.

"Oh, you rich merchants, you are good, as you are all noble, prudent folks. Your bags are not full of riches because you threw snake eyes but because of the fives and sixes that created your run of good luck. Well may you dance at Christmas celebrations. You gain lands and seas with your winnings and you know your value, as all wise people do. You are the makers of news and stories about peace as well as conflict."

The Wife's muttering had done little to block the path the Man of Law's had clearly claimed as his own. But he seemed, at last, to have reached the beginning of his tale.

"And so it was that I first heard this story from a successful merchant, now gone many years. Without him, I would have no tale to share with you.

Once upon a time, in Syria, there lived a group of wealthy merchants, wise and trustworthy men, who traded their goods everywhere, far and wide: gold cloth, richly colored satins, merchandise so valuable and fresh that the whole world was eager to do business with them, trading and selling their wares.

One day the leaders of those merchants arranged a trip to Rome; it may have been for business or perhaps for their amusement; the fact is that they just wanted to go to Rome. And when they arrived, they took their lodging in a place that they thought suited for their plans. And there they stayed as long as it pleased them to do so. At that time the superb reputation of the Emperor's daughter, Lady Constance, was the talk of the town, and it was reported to these Syrian businessmen in great detail, day after day, just as I shall now describe it all for you.

The general judgment of all was this: 'Our Emperor of Rome, may God protect him, has a daughter who, in all the history of the world, has never had an equal in goodness or in beauty. We pray that God sustain her honor always; more so, we wish she were the queen of all Europe. She is amazingly beautiful but without pride; she is young but neither immature nor foolish. In everything she does, she is guided by virtue, and her humility makes it impossible for her to be cruel. She is the very mirror of courtesy and her heart is the home of holiness, her hand the very agent of generosity in giving alms.'

And all these things the people said about her were absolutely true, as true as God Himself.

But to the point: when these businessmen had loaded their ships with much attractive merchandise, and after they had seen this blessed young woman for themselves, they sailed back to Syria and went about their business as they had done for years before, living well; I have nothing to add about that..

Now it so happened that these merchants enjoyed the good will of the Sultan of Syria, and whenever they returned from a foreign place he would, of his own high graciousness, entertain them and eagerly hear their tales of various kingdoms, wanting to learn all about the unusual things the merchants had heard or seen. Among other things, then, the merchants told him about the Lady Constance, omitting no details of her wonderful nobility. In response, the Sultan became so intent on his perceived image of her that all of his passion and his entire concern were turned to loving this woman for the rest of his life.

Sad to say, it was no doubt already written when he was born — in that immense book people call the stars — that he would die for love; for certain, God knows, embedded in the stars is the death of every man, plainly anticipated and recorded, clearer than glass, for those who know how to read it. Many a winter before they were born, the deaths of Hector, Achilles, Pompei, Julius were all recorded already. The Theban wars, the death of Hercules, Samson, Turnus and Socrates; sadly, human wits are so dull that no one understands all this fully.

The Sultan sent for his privy council and, without delay, declared to them that unless he could earn the grace of Constance's hand as soon as possible he was as good as dead; and he charged them formally to find some remedy for his problem. Of course various counsellors argued at length and considered alternatives, putting forth many a subtle argument. They even spoke of magic and deception, but finally, they all reached one conclusion: there was no way to satisfy the Sultan's desires other than marriage. But immediately there too they could see no way to avoid great difficulties because of the differences in beliefs, knowing that 'no Christian prince would ever agree to have his child marry under the laws of our sweet religion, as taught to us by Mohamed, our Prophet.' But the Sultan responded: 'Rather than losing Constance, I will be happy to convert. I must be hers; I cannot choose another. I pray you keep your arguments to yourselves; save my life and do not, in your negligence, keep me from winning this woman who holds my life in her hand, for I cannot long endure like this.'

Why waste any more words? With the help of ambassadors, by agreeing on certain treaties and accepting the pope's mediation, the entire church, and all of chivalry, agreed that for the sake of destroying Islam and increasing the sway of Christ's dear law — as you shall hear — the Sultan and all of his noble followers should be baptized; in return he should have Constance in marriage and a certain amount of gold — I don't know exactly how much — and all of this was sworn to by both sides and supported with appropriate collateral.

Now, Constance, may God guide you!

I suppose some of you expect that I will now tell you all about the preparations that the Emperor, in his great nobility, has made for his noble daughter, the noble lady Constance. But we all know that such great efforts may not be described appropriately in a few words, so, all I will say is that numerous bishops were charged to accompany Constance, along with lords, ladies, renowned knights and plenty of other attendants. And official exhortations were proclaimed throughout Rome that everyone should pray for Christ to accept this marriage, look upon it favorably, and bless the entire undertaking.

The day for their departure has come; I call it a sad, fatal day. Without further delay, her ladies prepare Constance who, overcome with sorrow, has risen and dressed for the trip, as she can well see that she has no other option. Who can blame her for weeping at the prospect of being sent to an alien land, far from the friends who have always kept her so tenderly, to be subject to a man about whom she knows nothing. Of course wives can attest to the fact that all husbands are good, and thus it has always been. Far be it from me to say anything more than that.

'Father,' Constance demurely approached the Emperor, 'I am your wretched child Constance, your own young daughter raised nobly by you and my mother, the two people who are my greatest delight, save for Christ himself. Hear me, your child, as I commend myself repeatedly to your grace, for I must be off to Syria, and I shall never again see either of you. Sadly I must depart for the pagan world in accordance with your will; I pray to Christ, who died for our salvation, that He may give me the grace to carry this out. Poor wretched woman that I am, my life will be no loss, of course, for women are born into servitude and penance, and to be under the governance of men.'

I am certain that at Troy, when Pyrrhus destroyed the wall, or when that city or the city of Thebes burned, or even when Rome was vanquished for the third time by Hannibal, that there was no weeping as tender as could be heard in that chamber as Constance prepared to depart. But leave she must, weeping or singing with joy.

Oh, Prime Mover! Oh, cruel firmament! Your daily motion pushes and propels everything from east to west, no matter what direction it might choose on its own. Your power sets the heavens on such a path that even at the very start of this cruel voyage, Mars has already mercilessly doomed this marriage. Oh, inauspicious, oblique, ascending sign, beyond any other power, alas, you fall out of your angle into the astronomical house below. Alas that Mars must be the dominant now! Oh, feeble moon, unfortunate is your path, as you move into a conjunction where you are less than welcome. Banished are you from a path that might have resulted in some good. And you, imprudent Emperor of Rome, woe upon woe! Were there no philosophers in your city to advise you? Might there not have been a better time for such a journey? Is not the high nobility blessed with the power to make decisions about such travel? Did no one know the relevant date of birth for Constance? Alas, humanity! We are either too stupid or too slow in wits!

Thus is this beautiful cursed maid brought to ship, solemnly, with all due pomp. Her last words to those she left behind were: 'Now may the Lord Jesus be with you all!' And all they could respond with was 'Farewell, fair Constance!' I leave her for now, as she sets sail, struggling to keep her composure, and I turn to other aspects of my story.

The Sultan's mother was the very wellspring of evil, and she was filled with wrath at her son's intention to betray the established manner of religious sacrifice in that land. She sent for her council and said what I tell you here. 'Lords,' she said, 'all of you know that my son is about to turn his back on the holy laws of our Koran, given to us by God's messenger, Mohammed. But I say to you that I would rather my life left my body here and now than have Mohammed's law leave my heart. What could possibly happen for us under this new law except enslavement of our bodies, suffering and, after that, eternal damnation to hell because we will have renounced our faith in Mohammed? But, my Lords, if you hear me out and swear your agreement to my plan, I shall save us all.'

Each and every man there swore to abide by her words unto death, to stand with her to the best of their ability and to support her decisions. And so she took charge, continuing: 'We will initially pretend to become Christians — a little cold water won't hurt us — and I will host a feast sure to please the Sultan. But in the end, however white his wife's dress may be, she will have much red to wash out, even if she brings with her a whole font full of water.'

Oh, Sultaness, you root of iniquity! Virago! You are a snake masquerading as a woman. You are in league with that serpent that resides deep in hell. Oh, deceptive woman, everything that destroys virtue and innocence is bred in you by your malice; you are the nest of every vice. Oh, Satan, envious since the day you were chased from our heritage; how well you know the way to a woman's heart. You made Eve bring us into bondage and now you want to prevent this Christian marriage! You do indeed — more's the pity — make woman your instrument when you practice your deception.

Why delay any further in telling you what this Sultaness, whom I blame and curse forever, now does? She quietly disbands her council, and tells her son that she too wants to renounce her faith and receive Christendom at a priest's hand, repenting only the fact that she has taken so long to do this. She beseeches her son to honor her by letting her host all the Christians when they arrive, promising that 'I will do everything I can to please them.' The Sultan responds joyfully: 'Let us do exactly as you request' and, on his knees, he thanks her, so happy that he is speechless; she, in turn, kisses her son and returns home to her preparations.

The day came that these Christian folks landed in Syria with great ceremony, and the Sultan swiftly sent his messenger to his mother and all of his nobles to request that they ride out to meet his queen and bolster his honor appropriately. When the Romans and Syrians met, it was a great crowd, richly appareled, and the Sultan's mother, sumptuously dressed, received Constance with the kind of welcome any mother might express to a dear daughter. Then, with much fanfare, they rode together to the nearest city. I dare say that the triumphant entrance of Julius Caesar that Lucan describes so ostentatiously was no more regal or wondrous than was the assembly of this joyful host. But through it all, this scorpion, this wicked demon, this Sultaness, for all her flattery, was simply planning to place her deadly sting.

The Sultan himself arrived in such resplendence that it is hard to do it justice, and he welcomed Constance with every joy and jubilation. And thus, in celebration and elation I will let them be, as I attend to the gist of my story. Finally came the time this old Sultaness had designated for the feast that I told you about and so, the Christian folk, young and old, all turned their attention to it. Here there was feasting, royalty to admire and more delicacies to taste than I can describe, but they paid all too dearly for it.

Oh, sudden tragedy, always sure to follow earthly bliss, sprinkled with bitterness, the inevitable end of all the joy that comes from our worldly efforts! Sorrow is always the end of our delight. Listen to my advice if you want to be safe: on any day you experience happiness never lose sight of the woe and the harm that accompany it.

But quickly now, without further ado, I must tell you that the Sultan and every one of the Christians, with the sole exception of the Lady Constance, were stabbed and cut to pieces even as they sat at their dinner. The Sultan's old mother, cursed krone — along with her friends — carried out this evil act because she wanted to be the country's only ruler. Every single Syrian who had converted or had agreed to the Sultan's plan was ripped to shreds that day before he could escape and, as God is my witness, Constance herself was abruptly thrown into a rudderless boat, humiliated and mockingly told that she better learn how to sail if she wished to return home again to Italy.

To be fair, before pushing it out to sea, they supplied the boat with certain valuables that she had brought with her, plenty of food and even her own clothes. Oh, dear Constance, so full of goodness; oh, innocent daughter of the emperor, may the Lord of Fortune Himself be your rudder.

Constance blessed herself and, with a most tremulous voice, prayed to the cross of Jesus: 'Oh, beautiful blessed altar, holy cross, so pitifully red with the blood of the lamb that cleanses the world of ancient iniquities, keep me from the fiend and from his claws on the day I succumb to the ocean deep. Victorious tree, protector of all that is true, only tree worthy of bearing the King of Heaven with His fresh wounds, white lamb, wounded with a spear, banisher of demons from men and women over whom you extend your holy shadow, keep me and help me to amend my life.'

For days, months and years this poor creature drifted across the eastern Mediterranean and finally, as fate would have it, through the Straight of Gibraltar. She had consumed many a sorrowful meal and often thought her death was near before the wild waves bore her to this destiny. You might well ask why she was not also slain at the feast? Who it was that saved her? And I answer that question with another: 'Who saved Daniel in that terrible cave where everyone else, master or slave, had served merely to appease the lion's hunger?' No other but God himself, whom he carried in his heart. And so it pleased God to show his wondrous miracle in Constance, so that we should see his mighty works.

As learned men know, Christ, who is balm for every wound, often does things for certain ends that are totally beyond human understanding, beyond the comprehension of creatures like us who, in our ignorance, cannot comprehend God's divine providence. So, since she was not murdered at the feast, who then kept her from drowning in the wide ocean? Who kept Jonah in the mouth of the fish till he was spewed up at Nineveh? We all know that it was no other than He who kept the Hebrew people from drowning, their feet dry throughout their passage through the sea. Where might this woman find food and drink to last for years and more? How can she possibly not run out? Who fed the Egyptian Mary in the cave? Or in the desert? No one but Christ, without a doubt — in one great miracle He fed five thousand with only five loaves and two fish; God sent His plenty to meet the people's need that day.

And so she drove forth into our ocean, through wild seas until the waves atlas deposits her near a castle on the shore of Northumberland, where the boat stuck so fast in the sand that the tide could not lift it; it was Christ's will that she should stay there. The castle's warden went down to see this wreck, and in the boat he discovered this weary, care-worn woman as well as the valuables she had with her. In her own language she begged him to be merciful and to end her life — to deliver her from her suffering.

Even though she spoke a kind of corrupt Latin, she was nevertheless understood by this warden. Finally on land, she knelt and thanked God for everything, but who or what she was she intended to tell no one, for better or worse, even if that meant her death. What she said instead was that, as God was her witness, she was so bewildered by the sea that she lost her memory. The warden felt great pity for her, as did his wife, and they wept at the mere thought of Constance's troubles. The wife was very diligent, and to see her was to love her; moreover, she was intent on serving and pleasing everyone around her.

This Hermingold and her husband, the warden, were, as were all the people in that country, pagans. But she cared for and loved Constance, as did Constance her and, in due time, as the result of prayer and many tears, Constance converted the Lady Hermingold to believe in Jesus. Now this was a land in which Christians were loathe to assemble, as they had all fled to Wales, to escape the pagans who had conquered their homeland. And yet, no matter how many had been exiled, there were some that deceived their heathen neighbors and secretly worshipped Christ. In fact, there were three such who lived near that castle. One of them, who was blind, could see well with the eyes of the mind that blind folks learn to use.

One summer's day, to enjoy the brightly shining sun, the warden and his wife and Constance went to the beach in order to entertain themselves and, on their journey they happened to meet the blind man, old and bent over, his eyes fast shut. But this blind Breton cried out: 'Lady Hermingold, in the name of Christ, give me back my sight!' Hearing this, the lady was deeply afraid that her husband would kill her for her love of Christ, but Constance emboldened her and encouraged her, as daughter of the Church, to carry out Christ's will. The warden was taken aback by all this and could only wonder at what was happening there. But Constance answered him: 'Sir, through the power of Christ people can escape the snares of the devil.' And so persuasively did she explain our teachings that before that day ended she had converted the warden to the gospel of Jesus.

Now this warden was not the lord and master of that place where he had found Constance but kept it well for many a year for Alla, the king of all Northumberland, most wise and renowned for his battles against the Scots. But let me return to my story.

Satan, ever lying in wait to deceive us, saw the perfection that was Constance, and thought long and hard about how he might harm her. So, he made a young knight in the town fall so passionately in lust with that young lady that he was sure that he would perish if he did not have his way with her. He wooed her fruitlessly, but there was no way she would enter into sin. And in his anger and resentment he decided to make her die a most shameful death, and so he waited for the warden to be away and stealthily crept into Constance's chamber where she slept. She, along with Hermingold, wearied from constantly praying, were asleep there. Then this knight, prodded by Satan's temptation, found the bed and stealthily slit the throat of the Lady Hermingold, leaving the bloody knife next to Constance before disappearing into the night — may God punish him with eternal suffering!

When the warden returned home and discovered his wife, slain so ruthlessly, he was beside himself with grief, wringing his hands and weeping. But then he saw the bloody knife in the bed next to Lady Constance. Dear God, what could she say in her defense, so filled with sorrow that she could barely think?

The whole sad story was soon told to King Alla, including how Constance had been found on her ship, just as I have told you already. The king's very heart shook with pity at the sight of this gracious creature so smitten by distress and adversity. For there she stood before him, like the lamb being led to its slaughter. And the treacherous knight who carried out this betrayal was the very man who accused her of the deed.

Of course there was great sadness among the people who all said that Constance could not be guilty of such great wickedness.

All they had ever seen was her great virtue and that she loved Hermingold more than her own life. Everyone in the castle bore witness to this, except the one who had actually slain Hermingold. King Alla was so moved by all these witnesses that he was certain he needed to delve more deeply into the case if he was to discover the truth.

Oh, dear God! Poor Constance, you have no champion to fight for you; more's the pity! May He who died for our salvation and shackled Satan — who still writhes there where he was vanquished — be your very own champion this day! For unless Christ works a clear miracle, you shall surely be executed today, innocent though you are!

Constance fell to her knees and prayed: 'Immortal God, you who saved Suzanna from her false accusers, and you, merciful virgin, Mary, daughter of St. Ann, before whose child the angels sing hosanna — as I am innocent of this foul crime, come to my aid, lest I perish.'

Surely each of you has seen a pale face in the midst of a crowd, the face of someone being led to his death, hopeless, of such a hue that everyone could see that face stand out among all the others there. This was Constance as she looked around her.

Oh, all you queens, living in prosperity, all you duchesses and ladies, have pity on her calamity. Here stands an emperor's daughter, alone, in great peril, with no one to call on, though she be of royal blood, far from friends in this hour of her need.

King Alla was filled with such great compassion, his gentle heart overflowing with pity, that tears welled in his eyes and ran down his cheeks like water. 'Now quickly fetch a book,' he commanded, 'and if this knight will swear that she has slain this woman, we must then think carefully about how to achieve justice here.' A sacred Breton book was brought forth and, no sooner had the knight sworn on it that she was guilty, at once a mighty hand smote him so hard on the neck that he fell down and was unconscious, with both of his eyes bursting from his face in full sight of everyone. And a mighty voice was heard by all: 'You have slandered the innocent daughter of our holy Church in the presence of the Almighty; this you have done, and this is my judgment.' Of course all present were greatly astonished by this miracle, fearful of God's vengeance, save Constance herself.

Among those who had been erroneously suspicious of this blessed innocent, Constance, there was great fear and repentance but, to sum up, through this miracle and by Constance's mediation, the king, and many others there, were converted, thanks to God's grace. Despite the great pity Constance felt for him, the false knight was quickly executed by order of King Alla. Soon after this, Jesus, in his mercy, had Alla marry — in great solemnity — this holy virgin Constance, shining in all her beauty. And thus has Christ made Constance a queen.

But I must tell the whole story — who alone was filled with sorrow at this wedding if not Donegild, the king's mother, a woman of tyranny? She thought her wicked heart would burst, for she did not want her son to do this; she thought it an outrage that he should take so foreign a creature to be his mate.

Now I will not create a long tale from the chaff, nor the straw, but draw only on the grain. I will not list all the royalty present at the wedding, or which course precedes another, or who blew a trumpet or a horn. The fruit of my tale is simply this: they ate, they drank, they danced, they sang, they played. Then, as was right and proper, they went to bed. And, though wives may be holy vessels, they must endure at night such necessary things as may please those who have wed them with rings, laying aside for a while their holiness — this is as it must be.

Shortly the king impregnated his wife with a boy child and, when he had gone to Scotland to engage his enemy, he entrusted the care of his wife to a bishop and to his warden. Now, fair Constance, so humble and meek, was far enough along in her pregnancy to keep to her chambers, in accordance with Christ's will. And when the time came, she had a boy, who was to be baptized Mauricius.

The warden sent a messenger to King Alla about this blissful event but, seeking personal gain, this messenger rode first to the castle of the king's mother, greeting her graciously in their native language: 'Madame, you have reason to be happy and joyful and thank God a hundred times or more. My Lady the Queen, to the great rejoicing of the land, has delivered a baby boy. Behold here the sealed letters that I am charged to deliver to the king with all haste. If there is anything you wish to send to your son, I am your servant, both day and night.' Donegild said: 'No, nothing right now. But please rest here for the night and I will give you my messages tomorrow.'

The messenger devoted himself to steady drinking and, while he slept like a pig, his letters were secretly taken from his bag and stealthily replaced with counterfeit ones— constructed most sinfully — supposedly from the warden to the king. And they said that the queen had been delivered of so horrible and fiendish a creature that no one in the castle dared to stay there while it was present. This birth clearly demonstrated that foul magic or the fiend himself had turned the mother into an abhorrent evil spirit.

Sorrowful indeed was the king when he had read these lies, but he said nothing to anyone else about it and sent back a response in his own hand: 'Having heard this news, I welcome now and forever whatever Christ sends my way! Lord, your will and pleasure are most welcome; my own desires will be controlled by your will. Keep and care for this child, be it foul or fair, as well as my wife, until I return again. When it pleases Him, Christ may yet send me an heir more to my liking.' Privately weeping, he seals this letter to be taken to the messenger, who rode forth at once — that is done.

Oh, messenger, compatriot of drunkenness, your breath is as strong as your limbs are weak, and you betray all confidentiality. You have lost your mind, you jangle like a jaybird, and your face turns with the wind. There, where drunkenness governs the group, no counsel can be kept, that is certain.

Oh, Donegild, I wish I had the words to do justice to your malice and your cruelty! All I can do is to consign you to the devil: let him write of your treachery. Curses on your unwomanly spirit, Curses! No, no, by Christ — on your fiendish spirit, because I can testify to the fact that though you may walk among us your spirit dwells in hell.

This disgraceful messenger left the king's court but once again stopped to see the king's mother on his way. And she, very pleased with him, provided him with everything he could want. He drank and filled his belly; he slept, snoring the whole night, until the sun arose. Again his letters were stolen and counterfeited ones substituted, that said: 'The king commands his warden, upon pain of hanging and the threat of terrible justice, that he shall not allow Constance to remain in his realm for more than three days and the length of a tide. He shall place her in the same ship as she was found, she, her offspring, and all her belongings and push her out into the sea and command her never to return.'

Oh, my dear Constance, well may thy spirit feel unrest, sleeping, while Donegild shapes such an edit.

The messenger went on his way to the castle and took the letter to the warden who, when he saw what this tragic letter contained, many times uttered: 'Alas and woe is me,' asking: 'Lord, Christ, how may this world endure when so much of it is filled with sin? Oh, mighty God, if it be your will, since you are our rightful judge, how is it that you will allow innocent blood to be spilled and wicked people to rule in prosperity? Oh, good Constance, woe is me, alas that I must be your tormentor or die a shameful death; there are no other options.'

Young and old alike in that place wept bitterly as the commands in this cursed letter were carried out. With a deadly, pale countenance, Constance was led to her ship on the fourth day, ever and always certain that Christ's will is for the best. Kneeling on the beach, she said: 'Lord, ever welcome be Your will. He who kept me from being falsely convicted when I was in this land can surely keep me from harm and shame on the salty sea — though I know not how. As powerful as ever, so is He now, and I trust in him and in His sweet mother who is ever my rudder and my sail.' Her babe lay weeping in her arms, as she knelt and pathetically assured him: 'Peace, my lovely baby boy, I will not harm you.' She took the kerchief from her head and laid it over his little eyes and lulled the baby fast asleep in her arms while she looked up to heaven: 'Mother and bright virgin, Mary, it cannot be denied that it was through the instigation of woman that mankind was lost and condemned to a life that ends in death — the reason your child was stretched on the cross — your blessed eyes witnessing all of His torment. Thus, there can be no comparison between your suffering and what any one of us may sustain. You saw your child killed before your eyes, but my little child yet lives, by my faith.

Now, shining lady, to whom all those filled with woe lift up their cries, You glory of womankind, oh, lovely virgin, haven of refuge, bright day star, have pity on my child as you pity all who need it. Oh, my child, alas, what can you possibly be guilty of since, God knows, you are still innocent? Why does your cruel father want to have you killed? Oh, mercy, dear warden, if you cannot let my child live here with you, and if you are not able to save him without paying a terrible price, at least kiss him once in his father's name.' And then she cast one final glance at the land: 'Farewell, cruel husband,' and arose to walk toward the ship, followed by all the people, shushing her baby as she went. She took her leave, blessed herself with all good intentions and entered that well-supplied ship — praise be to God. May He favor her now with good weather and wind to bring her home. This is all I can say as she embarks upon the wide ocean.

Soon after this, King Alla returned home to his castle to ask after his wife and child. The constable's heart felt a chill as he told him plainly everything as you have already heard — I cannot tell it better — showing the king his letter with his own seal, saying: 'Lord, as you commanded me upon pain of death, so have I done.' Of course they tortured the messenger until he revealed where he had spent his nights and thus soon determined the source of all this evil. They identified the handwriting of the forgery and all the venom of this cursed deed, how exactly, I am not sure, but the final outcome was this: without mercy, Alla executed his mother for betraying him as she did — you can read about that for yourselves in history books. Thus ends old Donegild; may she be ever cursed!

But no tongue can do justice to the sorrow that Alla suffers night and day for his wife and child.

Now let me return to Constance, floating miserably and painfully in the great sea for five years and more — all in accord with Christ's will — before she neared land. Finally the sea cast up Constance and her child beneath a heathen castle whose name I cannot find in my source. Our Almighty God, who saved all of us, has Constance and her child ever in His care, though she has fallen often into heathen hands and has come near to death. Soon, people came down from the castle to inspect the ship and Constance but shortly thereafter, at night, the local lord's steward — may God curse him to hell — a practiced thief who had renounced our Christian belief, came to the ship alone and commanded her to be his lover, whether she agreed or not.

More woe has now begun for this wretched woman. Her child wailed and Constance wept pitifully, but the Blessed Virgin helped her in her need for, struggling mightily with her, the thief fell overboard and drowned in the sea; and that is how Christ kept Constance undefiled.

Oh, foul lecherous lust, behold, this is your end! Not only do you weaken men's minds but truly you want to destroy their bodies; the outcome of your effort is simply lamentation. How many men have there been over time who have been slain or destroyed either for the intent to commit this sin and for carrying it out?

Of course you may ask how this weak woman found the strength to defend herself against this villain? Oh, Goliath, gigantic in stature, how did David manage to defeat you, when he was so young, without armor or arms? How did he dare look upon your dreadful face? Well can we see here that it was nothing but the grace of God. Who gave Judith the courage or hardiness to slay Holofernes in his tent and to deliver the people of God from their wretchedness? I tell you that just as God sent the power of His spirit to save them from evil, so did he send His power and spirit to Constance.

Meanwhile, her ship continued through the narrows between Gibraltar and Morocco, heading sometimes west, sometimes north, sometimes south, and sometimes east for many weary days, until Christ's mother — may she be blessed always — decided, in her eternal goodness, to bring all this distress to an end.

But let us leave Constance for now and turn to her father, the Roman emperor, who, through various emissaries, has learned about the slaughter of all the Christians in Syria and the dishonor done to his daughter by a false traitor, by which I mean the cursed, wicked Sultaness who slew more or less everyone at that feast. In response, the emperor sent his Senator, along with a royal army and all the necessary support — God knows, many soldiers — to take high revenge on the Syrians, and they burned and slew them and brought their foes to a sad end.

They were making their way back home when, so the story tells us, they came across the boat in which Constance sat, not knowing where she was or why, or what her situation might be, unable to describe her status even if threatened with death. The Senator brought her back to Rome and put her and her son in the care of his wife. Behold how Our Lady is able to deliver Constance and many others out of woe. So Constance lived with the Senator's family for some time, doing charitable work, as was her way. The Senator's wife was actually her aunt, but she did not recognize Constance any more.

Let me not tarry here any longer but return to King Alla, whom I have spoken of before, who continues to weep and mourn for his wife, while I leave Constance in the care of her aunt's household.

This King Alla, who had slain his own mother, came to feel such remorse for all that had happened that, to sum it up in a nutshell, he went to Rome to do penance, putting himself under the governance of the pope in all matters and seeking forgiveness from Christ for all the wickedness that had been done. The story of King Alla's pilgrimage was soon told throughout Rome by the servants who traveled ahead to prepare his way, and so the Senator and many others, as was customary, rode out to meet Alla, both to demonstrate their own noble state and to honor this arriving king. The Senator and Alla properly greeted each other and treated each other most honorably, so much so that within a day or two the senator was asked to a banquet with Alla and, if I am to be true to my narrative, I must tell you that Constance's son accompanied him there.

Some say that it was at the request of Constance that the Senator took her son to the feast. Obviously, I cannot be responsible for every detail — however it happened, there he was at the banquet — there he was, in the same room with Alla, who was struck by his appearance and inquired of the senator: 'Who is that beautiful child over there?' 'I cannot say for certain,' the Senator answered, 'as God and St. John are my witnesses. He has a mother but no father that I know of.' And then he briefly summed up for Alla how the child had been found. 'But God knows,' the senator continued, 'so virtuous a person as his mother I have never seen or even heard of in all my life. I swear on my life that she would rather have a knife plunged in her breast than do anything wicked. No one in the world could bring her to do anything evil.'

Now the child looked as much like Constance as could be and, of course, Alla well remembered the face of his lady Constance. So, at once, he began to wonder whether the child's mother could possibly be his wife. He sighed, privately, and left the banquet table. 'By God,' he thought, 'is this some sort of fantasy? I should not doubt, if I am reasonable, that my wife is dead in the salty sea.' And then he considered another possibility: 'What if Christ has sent my wife here by sea, just as He sent her to my country from wherever she came from then?'

At the end of the feast, Alla accompanied the Senator to his home to see whether this miracle had indeed occurred. The Senator treated Alla with great honors and sent for Constance, but you should know that this request hardly made her feel like dancing, since she did not know why she was summoned and, so, she was scarcely able to stand there without swooning.

When Alla beheld his wife, he greeted her warmly, weeping so hard that it was a pity to watch. He knew, at the first look, that truly it was she, while she, in sadness, stood silent as a tree, so wounded was her heart as she remembered his unkindness to her. Twice she swooned in front of him, but he wept and excused himself most pitifully: 'May God and all his saints have mercy on my soul if I am not as innocent of any harm done to you as is Mauricius, my son, who looks just like you. Else may the devil himself take me now!' After much sobbing and overcoming of bitter pain, Constance's woeful heart finally eased. It was most pitiful to hear her husband's pain as it only increased her own. Even I am not certain I can continue with this effort; I may not be able to do justice to their suffering until tomorrow, so difficult is it to speak of such sorrow.

But finally, when it was clear that Alla was guiltless, they must have kissed a hundred times. And then there was such bliss between the two of them that, with the exception of eternal joy, no creature has seen or ever will see its like, while the world lasts.

Now Constance asked her husband most meekly, in order to relieve her long-held pain, that he would invite her father to deign to dine with them on a given day, but she insisted that he should say nothing about her to her father. Some people say that Mauricius delivered the invitation to the emperor, but my guess is that Alla was not so foolish as to send a child to invite him who is the flower of all Christians; it makes more sense that he himself would have made the invitation in person.

Of course the emperor most graciously agreed to attend a dinner, and Alla made all the arrangements, as appropriate, to have a fitting feast. The day came and Alla and his wife dressed to meet the emperor; they rode forth in all joy and happiness and when she saw her father on the road, Constance slipped down from her horse and knelt at his feet: 'Father,' she said, 'I'm sure you have forgotten completely your young child Constance, but I am that self-same dear daughter that you once sent to far off Syria. I am she who was set out alone in the salt sea, condemned to die. So now, good father, grant me mercy and never again send me away again to a heathen but rather be grateful with me to my lord here for all his kindnesses.'

Who can possibly do justice to the joy the three of them now feel, now that they are rejoined?

But let me make an end of my tale without further delay.

The day passed quickly, and they all sat down to dinner. I will let them enjoy the bliss they feel — a thousand times more than I can suitably describe.

Since that time this child Mauricius was made emperor by the pope, and he lived a true Christian life, doing great honor to Christ's church. But my tale is of Constance, and not of him. If you want to know more of Mauricius's life, you can find it in the old Roman chronicles — I have not committed it to memory.

When Alla saw that it was the right time, he and Constance, his holy wife so sweet, made their way back to England. They lived there, joyfully and peacefully but only for a time, I must tell you, as time will not wait for joy to last, as days and nights change with the tide. Who among us has lived a single day without being troubled by conscience or anger or desire or some relative's disturbance, envy or pride or passion or offense?

I say all this simply to make my point: that the joy and bliss of Alla and Constance lasted but a short while, for Death, who collects what is owed to him by high and low alike, after a single year took Alla out of this world, leaving Constance heavy with sorrow. And so she returned to Rome, where she found her friends hale and hearty. When she met her father again, she fell on her knees before him, weeping joyfully to see him again. And for this she praised God a thousand times over. And so they all lived virtuously, with generosity to the poor, and they never again parted; they lived like that until death took them.

So now, may you all fare well; my tale is at an end. May Jesus Christ, who has the power to send joy after sorrow, govern us in his grace and keep all of us who are in this place. Amen."

And now our Host stood up in his stirrups and proclaimed: "I hope, good people that you all listened carefully. This was the right tale at the right time!"

"Right time, my ass," the Shipman interrupted him. "If I have to listen to one goddamn word more about how God protected this poor woman who spent her life on the ocean, attacked again and again by villains, pursued by evil women and terrible men and God knows what else, I'll be damned if I'm not willing to pay for everyone's dinner now."

The Wife could not hide a broad smile at this, the Prioress crossed herself a few times, and the Host, turning quite red and clearly upset, responded to the Shipman: "By God's bones—" but then he stopped and turned, instead, to the Parson, who rode near to him: "Sir Parish Priest," he intoned, "tell us a tale, by God's bones, as you agreed to do. I know that learned men such as you have much to teach us, for the grace of God."

But the Parson objected: "May God bless us, sir, but what is wrong with you that you should swear so sinfully?"

Rankled by this, the Host responded: "Oh, little Johnny, is it you? I smell a Lollard[17] in the wind." And then, with raised voice, so all could hear, he addressed our whole troop: "Now then, good people, listen to me. By the sacred passion of Christ, I think that we are about to enjoy a sermon from this Lollard, who apparently wants to enlighten us."

But the Shipman was not done: "That he shall not, by my father's soul. There will be no more preaching here. He shall neither gloss the gospel nor teach us anything else he believes. We all here believe in God, but this priest intends to sprinkle weeds among our pure grain, and rather than that, oh, Host, I give fair warning: I myself will tell you a tale that shall sound to you like a merry bell and wake up everyone here. It shall have

---

[17] Followers of John Wycliffe, who translated the Bible into English and espoused radical religious views, some of which became the theological base of the Reformation. In Chaucer's England, Lollards were not infrequently executed for heresy.

nothing to do with philosophy, nor with ornate terms of law or old law cases. There is little enough Latin in my craw."

But this was too much for the good Wife of Bath, whose smile had now turned into peals of laughter. "Not so fast, young man," she commanded with enough authority to make any shipman take note. "I think it's time for a woman's voice to be heard."

The shipman scoffed: "And I supposed you're the woman."

"Indeed I am," she continued, "unless you think you are man enough to stop me?"

She paused only for a moment, but there was no need.

"Just as I thought. So, having cleared that up, let me proceed to tell you all a thing or two about something our learned Man of Laws, who speaks with the authority of great power, seems not to understand about the ways of the world, much less about the life of a simpering refined young lady like Constance — or any woman, for that matter. In the world I have inhabited for lo these many years — no reason to count," she stared at the Host. "In my world and the world I know, I suppose there are marriages like the one you have heard about, but I am not a woman who has ever followed a man around by the apron strings or would let herself be auctioned off to some king in a pagan land, no matter how rich he might be."

The Host, who had not been willing to argue with the drunken Shipman, was even less inclined to stop this Wife; he looked hopelessly toward heaven, frowned, shrugged his shoulders and allowed her to proceed. And proceed she did.

The Wife of Bath's Tale

Making a great show of adjusting her broad skirts so that she was more comfortable in the saddle, she began.

"God knows I need no Father of the Church to teach me about the woes of marriage; my experience is more than enough for me.

By your leave, ladies and gentlemen, since I was legally able to wed when I was twelve years of age, thanks be to the eternal God above, I have taken five husbands at church door — if it is possible to marry five times — all, in their own ways, worthy men. But I was told, not too long ago, that since Christ attended only the wedding in Cana, by this example He meant to teach me that I should be wed only once — and I have not forgotten the sharp words Jesus, God and man, had for the Samaritan woman at the well: 'Woman, you have had five husbands, and the man that has you now is not your husband.'

I'm not about to argue that He did not say these words to her.

But what He meant by them is another matter. I can only ask why that fifth man was not the Samaritan woman's husband? How many, exactly, could she marry? In all my life I have never heard anyone specify this number. Men can argue and gloss up and down, but I know full well, clearly, without a lie, that God commanded us to increase and multiply. That gentle text I understand completely, just as I know Jesus said my husband should leave his father and his mother and cleave unto me. But he never mentioned a number that might add up to bigamy or octogamy! So why do men speak such evil about it?

Remember the wise King Solomon who, I know for sure, had more than one wife. I wish to God it were legal for me to be refreshed half as often as he was! What a divine gift he must have given to each of his wives! Surely there is no man alive today who could match it. God knows that this noble king, as I see it, had many a merry romp with each of them on their first night, seeing how much he enjoyed life.

I thank God for my five marriages. I always chose the best, based on the size of their monetary treasure chest and the size of their lower physical treasure." Here she broke into a large grin and winked broadly at those of us whose eye she could catch. "Diverse learning makes for perfect students, and diverse practice in various skills surely makes for a perfect worker. I have the benefit of being schooled by five husbands; the sixth is welcome, whenever he may appear.

Believe me when I say that I have little use for chastity. As soon as my husband leaves this world, another Christian man shall soon wed me. For then, the Apostle tells me, I am free to marry, by God, whomever I choose. He says that to be married is no sin: better to marry than to burn! What do I care whether people speak ill of the biblical bigamist Lamech? I am sure that Abraham was a holy man and Jacob, too, as far as I know; and each of them had more wives than two — as did many other holy men.

I pray you, name a time when the High Lord God expressly forbade marriage? Please show me exactly where he required virginity? I know as well as anyone that the Apostle, when he speaks of maidenhead, was speaking — and this I know for certain — of something he himself did not have. Men may advise women to be virgins, but advice is not law. God left it for us to decide, for had He commanded virginity He would have damned marriage with the same breath. And, please, if no seed is sown from what exactly shall virginity grow? Surely, Paul could not command something that his master did not command.

First prize may well be reserved for virginity — more power to whoever enters this race. Consider me on pins and needles to see who's the fastest runner.

Of course Paul's words are not meant for everyone, may it please the Almighty. I can well believe that the Apostle was a virgin; nevertheless, even if he wrote and taught that he wanted everyone to follow his example, it was no more than his advice to consider virginity. He certainly gave me leave and permission to marry; so there is no shame in marrying again and no worry about bigamy if my mate dies. Though he said that it was good not to touch a woman, he was no doubt speaking of doing that in a bed or on a couch, because it is dangerous to put fire and flax in proximity."

She winked again. "You know what I'm talking about.

Here's the bottom line: he held virginity in greater esteem than marriage because of human weakness. Call it weakness. Fine. But if a man and woman want to live in chastity, I say let them. I do not envy them, even if virginity is more highly prized than bigamy. They choose purity of body and spirit.

By the same token, I don't take undue pride in my own status; as you well know, no lord has in his household only golden dishes; some are made of wood and serve their master just fine. God calls people to Him in various ways and from Him each of us receives a special gift — some give Him one thing, some another — just as it pleases God.

Virginity may well be the perfect way to live, as is commitment to continence, but Christ, the source of all perfection, did not ask everyone to go sell everything he has and give it to the poor, and thus to follow in His footsteps. He said that to those who wanted to live perfectly.

Trust me — I am not one of them. I intend to relish all the acts and fruits of marriage in every stage of my life.

Enlighten me: tell me for what purpose our procreative parts were made by our perfectly wise creator? I am quite sure that they were not made for nothing. You can interpret as much as you want to and keep saying that they were made merely for discharging urine and that our two small things were made merely to tell apart male and female and for no other purpose — do you really believe that?

Our experience makes it clear that it's just not true!

But lest the learned scholars be angry with me, I say this: they were made for both purposes, that is, for bodily function and for pleasure in procreation.

Unless you think you know better than the Creator!

Why else do learned writers tell us in their books that a man shall pay his wife her debt? Just what exactly shall he make his payment with if not his blessed instrument? You can't argue with what's obvious: these parts were given to us both for purging urine and for procreation.

Of course I am not saying that every man who has the equipment is obligated, as I have told you, to make use of it in procreation. That would mean that chastity has no value. Christ, shaped like a man, was a virgin, just like many saints the world has seen since it began — they lived their lives in perfect chastity.

I am not envious of virgins — let them be white bread made of pure wheat and let us married women be known as barley bread. Of course, I remember Mark telling us that Jesus satisfied 5,000 with barley bread.

I'm not fussy. I am happy to live the life God has called me to. As a wife I will use my instrument as freely as my creator has given it to me. May God punish me, if I am stingy with it! My husband shall have it both morning and night — whenever he wants to come forth and pay his debt. I intend to have a husband — and I will be satisfied with nothing less — who shall be both my debtor and my servant, and while I am his wife, his flesh shall fully bear the burden. I — not he — shall rule his entire body for my whole life. This is what the Apostle told me when he bade our husbands to love us well — now that's a teaching I can get my head around."

At this the Pardoner roused himself and said: "Now, now Madam, by God and by Saint John, you are indeed a noble preacher on these matters! I have considered getting married, but I never will now, if I must pay for it so dearly with my flesh. I think I had rather not wed a wife any time soon."

"Just wait," she answered, "I'm only just getting started. Before I'm done here today, you'll be drinking from a keg you didn't see coming, one that will likely taste a whole lot worse than ale. And by the time I have finished my story of the trials and tribulations of marriage, something my age makes me an expert in — and I freely admit that I myself have often enough been the whip — then you can decide whether you want to knock back a drink from the keg that I will open here. Be careful, before you take me on, as I have more than ten examples: 'Let him who will not learn from the example of others be himself the example from which others learn.' Thus wrote Ptolemy, as you can read for yourself in his Almagest."

"Please, Madam, I beg you, if it be your pleasure," the Pardoner responded, with a mocking low bow, "carry on as you have begun and tell your story; spare no one and teach us young people your practices."

"I will do so gladly," she said, "and then we'll see how you like it."

She looked around at the other pilgrims.

"Of course, I ask everyone here not to take affront at anything I say, as I intend to speak as the spirit moves me — after all, I'm just here to have a good time.

But let me get on to my story, as I must; whether I drink wine or ale, I shall speak truly.

Of the husbands I have had, three were good and two were bad. The three good ones were rich and old — they were barely able to carry out the conjugal duty they were sworn to do.

I'm sure you all know what I mean — am I right?" This time she was rewarded with a round of titters, guffaws and snorts before she continued.

"So help me God, I can't help but laugh when I think back on how hard I made them work at night. And, have no doubt, I was not easily impressed. They had given me their land and their money; I didn't have to spend time or effort winning their love or treating them well. By God above, they loved me well enough, to where I didn't have to worry about it. If she's smart, a woman who is not loved will do whatever it takes to gain love. But since I had their bodies in firm control and they had given me all their land, why in the world should I make any effort to please them, unless it were for my own profit or pleasure? I put them through their paces, in faith, and many a night could they be heard moaning: 'Oh, dear God!' Rest assured that they did not enjoy the bacon that the men of Essex at Dunmow can earn.[18] But I ruled them so well, true to my own expectations, that they were each one happy and eager to bring me beautiful things from the fairs. God knows, I scolded them so mercilessly that they were blissful anytime I spoke nicely to them.

Now, listen up, you women who want to know what's what, so you understand how to do the right thing, as I have always done. This is how you do it: accuse your man for no good reason — there's not a man alive who can match a woman in swearing and lying. This is not about those times when we wives act prudently, but the moments when we find ourselves in the wrong. That's when a smart wife, if she's clever, will lie about being found out and force her own maid to swear in support of that lie.

This is the sort of thing I would say to my husband: 'Why, you old dotard, is this how it's going to be? Why is my neighbor's wife always so happy? Wherever she goes, she is honored, while I sit at home. I don't have a thing to wear! What are you doing at the neighbor's? Is she beautiful? Are you so horny? What do you have to whisper about with our maid? God bless me! You old lecher, you, stop your fooling around! Why, if I innocently go to see a close friend, you scold me like the devil himself, just because I have gone to her house to entertain myself. You come home drunk as a mouse, and then, worse luck to you, you preach at me from your high horse. You're always telling me how terribly expensive it is to marry a poor woman; but if a woman be rich and from a respectable home, then you proclaim what torture it is to suffer her pride and her moods. If she's beautiful, you rotten knave, you say that every lecher wants to have her — there's not a chance, you say, that she might be faithful — this is how you attack us, no matter what.

---

[18] A village known for its tradition of awarding a flitch (side) of bacon to married couples who went for a year and a day without quarreling. The winners "took home the bacon."

You proclaim that some men want women for their wealth, some for their bodies, some for their beauty, some because they can sing or dance, some for their status or social skills, and some for their slender arms and hands. But according to you, we are all going to the devil; you tell everyone that any castle wall that is attacked long enough will finally collapse. And if a woman is ugly, you accuse her of lusting after every man she sees, panting to jump on him like a dog in heat, until she finds one willing to take her up. You tell us that even the oldest goose in the pond will finally find a mate. Even as you're falling asleep, you lout, you proclaim that no man with a brain has any use for marriage, certainly none who value salvation. May thunder and lightning break your scrawny neck! You like to tell us that there are three things that make men desert their own homes: leaky roofs, smoke, and nagging wives. God help you, how do old men become such yammerers?

You claim that we wives hide our faults until we are securely married and show them only then — only a villain would say such a thing! You remind us that before we purchase an ox or an ass or a horse or a hound we check them out, more than once; basins and bowl, stools and kitchen tools, pots and pans, clothing and dress — all are examined carefully before we buy them — but women have to pass no such test until after they are married. Only then you say — you haggard old hypocrite – only then do they show their vices.

And on top of that, you silly old bastard, you tell the world that I will be out of sorts unless you constantly praise my beauty and gaze lovingly at me and call me 'my fairest lady' in public; or arrange for a big to-do on my birthday and entertain me and make me smile, and pay respect to my old nurse and my maid and my father's family and their friends — that's what you claim, you hollow old barrel of lies!

And, although you are wrong, of course you suspect that I am interested in our apprentice, Jankin, because he has curly hair that shines like fine-spun gold, and he attends me here and there and all around. If you were dead tomorrow, I would not want him!

But tell me this: why — and mat you be damned for it — do you keep the keys to my own chest where I can't find them? It contains what belongs to me as well as to you, by heaven! What? Do you think you can make a fool of the lady of the house? By St. James of Compostela, you will not — though it drive you mad — be lord of both my body and of my possessions. One of those you will forego, God curse your eyes! Good luck with trying to keep track of me or spying on me! Maybe you'd like to lock me up in my own house?

If you had any brains, here's what you would say: "Wife of mine, go wherever you like. Enjoy yourself. I will ignore gossip about you because I know you to be a true and faithful spouse, Lady Alice." Women will not love men who keep track of what we do or where we go; we want to be in charge of ourselves.

Surely, the brilliant astrologer, Lord Ptolomy, must be praised above all other men, for giving us this proverb in his Almagest: "He is wisest who does not concern himself with who controls the world." This proverb teaches us that if we have all we want we should not be troubled by the happiness of others. So, rest assured, you old bag of wind, you need not worry whether you will have enough pussy in the evening. A man who refuses to let another light a candle from his lantern is a true miser, for God knows he will not have less light by doing so. You have what you need; you need not complain about the things enjoyed by others.

I've also heard you say that if we get dolled up and wear our finest clothing we are asking to be seduced. Unfortunately — you poor slob — you can't help yourself but echo the Apostle, who said: "You women shall dress in clothing chaste and modest; never in coiffed hair and rich array with pearls or shiny precious stones made of gold." I, for one, will pay as much attention to your text and your teaching as does a housefly.

Once you compared me to a cat, telling me that if you singe a cat's skin, she'll never run away, but if her skin is sleek and shiny, she won't stay with you for half a day — before dawn she will run out to show off her fur and go caterwauling. In other words, Sir Scoundrel, if I look good, I will immediately show off my burlap dress to the world.

Sir Ancient Fool, what do you gain by spying on me? Even if you prayed to Argus with his hundred eyes to be my bodyguard, as best he could, there is no way he could control me, unless I let him. I could beard him anytime I wanted to, God help me.

And then you babble on about three terrible things that trouble everyone, and a fourth that no one could possibly bear. O dear Sir Villain, may Jesus end your life now! You just keep preaching that a hateful wife must surely be one of these things. Is there nothing else you can come up with to fill up your parables but a foolish wife?

You compare a woman's love to hell, to a desert without water, even to Greek fire: the more it burns, the more it wants to burn up everything in sight, you claim, like worms destroying a tree — that's how wives destroy husbands. Everyone who has been married knows this, you claim.'

So, Gentlemen, this is how I would convince my elderly husbands that these were the things they said to me when they were drunk and, to pull it off, I made Jankin and my niece be my witnesses. Oh Lord, the suffering and pain I made them go through while, if I am honest, they had done nothing. Though I was in the wrong, I could bite and whinny like a horse in my accusations — otherwise I would have been ruined more than once. 'First to the mill is first to grind her corn.' I attacked; so I won the war. I would charge them with whoring when they were too sick to get out of bed, and they would then gladly apologize for things they had never done.

And still I knew how to tickle their itch because I made them believe that I was deeply fond of them. I would swear that the only reason I went out at night was to find the wenches they were screwing. I had lots of fun with that; after all, we women are born knowing such tricks. As I live and breathe, deceit, weeping and spinning are God's gracious gifts to women. By trickery, force or never-ending grumbling and complaining, I always came out on top — I claim that proudly.

They paid a price, particularly in bed. There I would scold and deny them all pleasure. If I felt an arm coming over my side, I would get out of bed and stay there until my man had rewarded me appropriately. Then, and only then, would I fulfill his desire. And this is my lesson to every man: profit who may, because everything is for sale. No one lures a hawk with an empty hand. For my own benefit I was willing to endure their lust; I even pretended to enjoy it, even though I have never been a fan of old, cured meat.

I became a constant nag — if the pope had sat beside us at the table, I would not have spared my old man; no lie, I always gave him as good as I got. So help me almighty God, if I had to make my deathbed confession right now, I could swear that I repaid him word for word. By my own wit I managed to get from my husbands everything they had; otherwise they would never enjoy a moment's peace. My husbands might roar like crazed lions but, in the end, they would lose.

When it was useful, of course, I could also purr: 'Sweetheart, listen to me. Oh, my sweet Willie, my little sheep, how meek you look now! Come here, my dear, and let me kiss your cheek. You must be patient and sweet, with your scrupulous conscience, since you preach so much about Job's patience. You, too, must suffer constantly, as you preach so well, and if you don't, I will gladly teach you that it is good to have a satisfied wife. Clearly, one of us must give in and, since a man is so much more reasonable than a woman, you must also be more able to bear suffering. What is wrong with you, that you grumble and groan like this? Is it that you desire to have my pussy all to yourself? Why then, take all of it! Whatever! Have every bit of it. By Saint Peter, damn you, if you don't! If I wanted to sell my beautiful thing, I could be the belle of the ball; but I will keep it for your pleasure alone. But only you will be to blame, by God, I am telling you no lie!'

This is how we would carry on. But let's move on to my fourth husband.

He liked his fun — and that included having a lover — and I was young and lecherous, stubborn and bent on enjoying myself. You should have seen me, after a draft of sweet wine, dancing to the small harp and singing, by God, like any nightingale. That swine Metellius, foul villain, clubbed his wife to death just because she had some wine. If I had been his wife, he would not have frightened me away from drinking.

And once I had wine, of course, my thoughts moved to Venus — as we all know, just as a cold spell leads to hail, so does a lusty mouth require a lecherous tail. Experience teaches all lechers that a drunk woman is defenseless.

Ah, but, Lord Christ, when I let myself think back on my youth, it tickles me to the depth of my being. To this day it warms my heart that I lived life fully when I could. Alas, age, that poisons everything, has stolen my beauty and my vigor. Ah well, let it go. Farewell. Go to the devil! The flower has bloomed. There is no more to say. As best I can, I must now sell the bran. But I can yet find joy in my life. So let me tell you about my fourth husband.

I told you that I was often wracked with fear that he might find delight with another. But I managed to get even, by God and Saint Judocus. I turned that same wood into his cross. Not by debauching my own body — never — but I managed to pay enough attention to others to fry my husband in the grease of his own anger and jealousy.

God knows I was his purgatory here on earth, for which I hope his soul has found heavenly glory by now. As God is my witness, he used to sit and sing in full voice when I know his shoe was pinching him pretty painfully. No one, other than he and God, will ever know just how deeply I tortured him. He died when I returned from my pilgrimage to Jerusalem and now lies buried under the rood beam in the church, although his tomb is not nearly so elaborate as that of Darius, wrought so cleverly by the Jewish architect Appelles. It would just have been wasteful to bury him expensively. I wish him farewell; God rest his soul. He lies in his grave, nailed forever in his coffin.

But I must tell you about my fifth husband — may the Good Lord always keep his soul from hell. Still, he was the most shrewish to me. My ribs, each one, still remember, and they will to my dying day. But in our bed, when he wanted my lovely thing, he was exciting and rambunctious, and he knew just how to flatter me. Even if he had beaten every bone in my body, he was always able to win my love again in no time.

I think that I loved him best because he played hard to get. We women, if I'm going to be honest, have a curious disposition toward that. Whatever we cannot easily have is the thing we will cry after and crave all the time. Whatever is forbidden, that is what we desire. Beg us and we will surely flee, but standoffishness makes us bring out all of our merchandise. Great demand at market drives prices up, and too good a bargain undercuts value. All women learn that from experience.

I chose my fifth husband, God bless him, for love rather than wealth. He had been a student at Oxford but left his studies and took room and board with one of my good friends in our town. God rest her, she was named Allison, and she knew my heart and soul and all my secrets, better than our parish priest, if I'm going to be honest. I shared my deepest thoughts with her. I would have told her and one other good woman and my beloved niece my husband's every secret, whether he did something silly, like pissing on someone's wall, or something perilous, for which he might lose his life. And in fact I did so all the time, God knows, even though his face turned red and hot for shame and he regretted having ever told me any of his deep secrets.

And so, there was that one Lent, when I was constantly gossiping with my friends and loved being out and about, going from house to house in those springtime months of March, April and May, sharing all the stories we heard — it was Jankin, the student, and my best friend Allison and I who went together into the fields. Because my husband had gone to London for all of Lent, I was free to enjoy myself — to see, and be seen by, young lovely folks. How was I to know how or where my fate was being shaped? I attended vigils and processions, sermons and local pilgrimages, miracle plays and weddings — always sporting my bright scarlet dresses. No worms or moths or mites ever bothered my outfits in Spring — you know why? — because they were in constant use.

Now let me tell you what happened. As I said, we were walking in the fields and we started to flirt so much, this student and I, that I began to tell him about my situation and even said that, if I were widowed again, he should marry me. Of course, and I'm not bragging, I was always thinking about my future, marriage and all else. I don't think much of a mouse that has only one hole to go to — she's done, if that one fails her.

I accused him of casting a spell on me — a little something I learned from my mother — and I also told him that I had dreamed of him during the night, that he had tried to kill me and my bed was full of blood, and yet, I said, 'I believe that you would be good to me, because blood promises gold, or so I was told.' And that was all lies; I had no such dream but was simply following my mother's advice, in this as in many other things.

But, let me see, where was I? What was I saying? Oh yes, thank you, Jesus, I have the thread again.

When my fourth husband was laid out, of course I wept and showed great sadness, as wives are supposed to — it's expected, after all — and I covered my face with my kerchief, but I didn't weep all that much since, as I said, my next marriage had been arranged already.

So, in the morning my husband was carried to the church by our grieving neighbors, with Jankin, our student, among them. God help me, when I saw him walking behind the bier, I was so struck by his beautiful legs and his feet so clean and fair, that I gave him my heart right then and there. I suppose he was about twenty, and I — to be truthful — was forty.

But I've always liked young men. My teeth are set wide apart, one of my good features, and from birth, I was marked by Saint Venus. By God, I was a lusty wench. And good looking and rich and young and in fortunate circumstances and, I won't lie, as all my husbands told me, I had the best sweet thing they could imagine. Clearly I am all Venus in my feelings, even if my heart is Mars: Venus gave me my lust, my randiness; Mars my strength and boldness. I had Taurus in the ascendant and Mars in his house.

Alas! What a pity that love was ever thought to be a sin. I've always followed my stars . . . as set in place by my horoscope. I was made never to withhold my chamber of Venus from a good man. And yet I have the mark of Mars on my face and in another . . . private . . . place. As God save me, I was never able to love prudently but have always given in to my appetite. Whether a man was short or tall, black or white, poor or of whatever rank, I have never paid attention, so long as he fancied me.

What can I say? Within a month this lusty, clever student, Jankin, married me with a great celebration, and I gave him all my land and the wealth I had accumulated by then.

And that I came to regret bitterly.

As it turned out, he didn't give a rotten fig for what I wanted. I swear to God, just because I tore a page out of his book, he gave me such a thwack on the ear that I am now deaf on that side. Of course I was as stubborn as a lioness and the greatest chatterbox you've ever heard. I wanted to go about as I always had, gossiping from one house to the next, even though he commanded me not to. He had books that were the source of his constant preaching to me about stories of the ancient Romans — how Simplicius Gallus left his wife for good, only because she had looked out her door one day without her head covered. Another Roman, whose name he told me but I don't remember, also left his wife because she had gone to midsummer revels without his knowledge. And then he would look through his bible for Ecclesiastes where it explicitly declares that a husband shall forbid his wife from roaming about wherever she wants. And then he would tell me in no uncertain words: 'A man who builds his house out of willows, and spurs his blind horse over the fields, and allows his wife to go on pilgrimage, should be hanged on the gallows!'

What a waste of time all that was! I couldn't have cared less about his proverbs and his old saws; I wasn't about to be corrected by him! I can't stand people who point out my flaws and, God knows, I'm not the only one in that. I was not about to put up with all his nonsense, and he finally boiled over!

So, by St. Thomas, let me tell you the reason I tore out that page from his book and he dealt me a blow that made me deaf.

He had one favorite book — he called it Valerius and Theofrastus — that he loved to read, day and night, purely for his entertainment, constantly reviewing it. The book also had the writing of a Roman cleric by the name of St. Jerome, a cardinal, who wrote a book against Jovinian, and there was stuff by Tertullian, Crissipus, Trotula, and Heloise — the abbess not far from Paris – also parables by Solomon and Ovid's 'Ars,' and more, all bound together in one volume. And it was my husband's custom, any day or night when he had time and was not busy with other worldly pursuits, to read about wicked wives in this book. He knew far more stories about bad wives than you can find stories about good ones in the Bible because, trust me, it is impossible for a cleric to say anything good about women, unless the women are already saints — but surely never of any other women.

You tell me whether the painting of a man killing a lion was painted by the lion!

As God is my witness, if the stories put out by clerics in their chapels had been written by women, there would be more stories about the wickedness of men than all of Adam's heirs could atone for. Scholars, who are the children of Mercury, and lovers, who are the children of Venus, always oppose one another. Mercury loves wisdom and science, while Venus loves debauchery and extravagance and, because of their varying astrological placement, each overlaps the other's sign. So, Mercury is powerless in Pisces, where Venus rules, and Venus falls where Mercury rises. And that is why no woman is ever praised by a cleric. When they are old — these clerics — and no more able to carry out the works of Venus than is an old shoe, then they sit down in their dotage and write that women cannot keep their marriage vows.

But back to my story — why, as I told you, I was beaten over a book, God keep me. One night, Jankin, the master of our house, sitting by the fire, was again reading to me from that book, starting with Eve, whose wickedness brought about all of our wretchedness on this earth, for which Jesus Christ Himself was crucified so that He could redeem us with His own blood. Oh yes, here you can find clearly stated that woman was the cause of mankind's destruction.

Then he read to me how Samson, fast asleep, lost his hair when his lover cut it off with her shears — which betrayal also led to the loss of both of his eyes. He also read to me, and I am telling you nothing but the truth, the story of Hercules and his Dianira, who managed to set him on fire. Of course Jankin did not omit the care and woe that Socrates suffered with his two wives: how Xantippe poured piss over his head and that good man sat as still as though he were dead; he wiped his head and dared to say nothing more than: 'Before the sound of thunder rolls to an end, there will be rain.'

Jankin called the evil story of Pasiphae, queen of Crete, sweet — bah, I will not recount it, that grisly tale of her perverse lust. But he read, in great detail, how Clytemnestra, lecherous as she was, killed her husband. And he reveled in the tale of Amphiorax of Thebes losing his life because — so the story goes — his wife, Eriphyle, for an ounce of gold, told the Greeks where her husband was hiding — and that certainly did not end well for him. And, of course, the tale of Livia and Lucia, who killed their respective husbands, one for love and one for hate. Livia hated her husband and one evening gave him poison; lusty Lucia, on the other hand, loved her husband so much that she wanted him never to forget her, so she gave him a love-potion that made sure he never saw the sunrise.

In Jankin's book, husbands always got the worst of it.

After that he told me of Latumyus bemoaning to his friend Arrius that his garden contained a tree on which his three wives had all hanged themselves in misery. 'Oh, my brother,' answered Arrius, 'please give me a seed of this blessed tree so that I may plant it in my own garden.' He also claimed that in more recent rimes he had heard of wives murdering their husbands in their bed and having their way with their lovers all night, while the husbands' corpses bled out on the floor; some killed their sleeping husbands with nails driven through their brains, while others put poison in their husbands' drink.

He described more evil than anyone can imagine and, on top of that, knew more relevant proverbs than there are blades of grass in the world. 'It's better,' he would say, 'to live with a lion or a beastly dragon than with a nagging woman.' 'Better,' he'd continue, 'to live alone high up in an attic than in the house with an angry wife; they are so wicked and contrary that they hate anything their husbands love.' He'd say: 'Women drop their shame the moment they drop their dresses,' and then 'A beautiful woman who is not chaste is like a ring in a sow's nose.'

No one can know, or even imagine, the sadness and pain that I had to live with!

So, when I realized that he was likely to read to me every night — forever — from this cursed book, I suddenly — without warning — ripped out three pages, even as he was reading, and hit him so hard on his cheek that he fell backward into the fire. And he jumped up as angry as a crazed lion, and he punched me in the face with his fist, so that I lay there on the floor, as if dead. But when he saw how still I was, he became frightened and wanted to flee until, finally, I came to and said: 'Oh, you wicked man, have you killed me now? Have you finally murdered me for my land? Yet, before I die, I want to kiss you.'

Then he came close to me and kneeled down gently and said: 'Dear Sister Allison, so help me God, I will never strike you again. You are to blame for what I have done. But I seek your forgiveness; please grant it to me.' But first I slapped his cheek and said: 'Villain, with this I am avenged. Now I will die; I can say no more.'

But in the end, after much care and woe, we reached agreement, the two of us, because he let me have the bridle in my hand, and so I had control over my house and land, as well as over his tongue and hand. Of course I made him burn that book at once. And when I had so skillfully claimed all mastery over him, he said: 'Mine own true wife, do as you wish for the rest of your life. May you maintain your honor and my reputation.' After that day we never had another disagreement. God knows I was as kind to him from then on as is any wife between Denmark and India — as well as faithful, as he was to me. I pray to God in all His majesty that He always keep Jankin's soul in His mercy.

So now I will tell you my tale, if you want to hear it."

The Friar laughed out loud and said: "As God is my witness, dear lady, this has been is a long preamble for a story."

But the Summoner, on hearing the Friar, proclaimed: "Behold, by God's two arms! A Friar will always interfere wherever he goes. Listen, good people, flies and Friars will always fall into every dish and every issue. What do you know about preambles? What? Amble or trot; piss or sit down! You're just getting in the way of our good fun now."

"Oh, is that how it's going to be, Sir Summoner?" asked the Friar. "No, by my faith, before I am done I will tell such a tale — or maybe two — about a Summoner that will make everyone here die laughing."

"If that be so," answered the Summoner, "I curse in your face, and I will curse myself if I don't tell two or three stories about friars before we reach Sittingborn – enough to cause you real heartburn. I can see that even now you are losing self-control."

At this our Host cried out: "Alright now! Peace! And I mean right now! Let the woman tell her story. You two, quit acting like common drunks. Please, Madam, tell us your tale; that would be best."

"I am fully ready, Sir," she said, "Just as you wish. With the permission of this worthy Friar!"

"Yes, Madam," he said, "just go on. I promise to listen."

"I hope so," she said, and then she began her tale.

"In olden days, during the time of King Arthur, whom all of Britain holds in great esteem, this land was filled with fairies. With her joyful court, the Elf-Queen often held dances in green meadows. At least this is what people say, and I am talking about a time hundreds of years ago. Now, of course, you can't see elves anymore, because of the activities and prayers of begging friars who are found on every piece of land and near every stream — they're as thick as motes in a sunbeam, blessing halls and chambers and kitchens and houses and cities and fortifications and castles and great towers and villages and barns and stables and dairies — all of which means that there are no more fairies. Where once walked a fairy there now walks a begging friar, from early morning till late, saying his prayers and his holy sayings as he covers his territory. Nowadays women need not be afraid of who may be hiding in a bush or behind a tree because there the only evil spirit would be a friar — and we know that we have nothing to fear from their like!"

The good Wife smirked at the Friar but continued before he could interrupt her.

"So, in King Arthur's court there was a fine young knight who happened to be riding along the river and saw before him a young woman walking along all alone, and so he stopped and despite her unwillingness, he took, by force, her maidenhead. The news of this wrong was greeted with such an uproar and so many claims for justice before the king that Arthur, as was the law, condemned the young knight to death, and he would have lost his head — it seems such was the custom then — but the queen and many other ladies entreated the king so persistently that he granted the knight's life to the queen, leaving the young man's fate entirely in her hands.

The queen thanked the king sincerely and then, after she had made her decision, said to the knight in open court: 'As of this moment, you remain subject to execution. But I will grant you life, if you can tell me one thing: what is it that women most want? Be careful now and answer this question correctly, if you want to keep your neck from the executioner's axe. And, as I do not expect you to know what to say right now, I will give you a year, that is, twelve months and a day, to seek out and discover the right response to this question. So, before I release you, I must have your pledge that you will return to yield your body at this place a year from now.'

The knight was filled with sorrow and heaved a great sigh. But what was he to do? He had no choice, and so he agreed to go and to return at year's end with whatever answer God deigned to let him discover. Ay once, he took his leave and went on his way.

He sought out every house and every place where there was a possibility of learning the answer to this question. But no matter where he went to find his answer he never found even two people who agreed. Some told him that women loved wealth above all, some said honor, some said fun; some claimed it was beautiful dresses, some said great lust in bed, or to be married and widowed multiple times.

Some told him that our hearts are most at ease when we are flattered and pampered. This, I will admit, came close to the truth, because certainly flattery will win our hearts, and attention and care will trap us, some more, some less.

Some said that we want above all to be free and do whatever we want, with no man chiding us for our flaws, but always complimenting us and never holding us to be foolish. For truly there is not one of us who will not react if you aggravate our sore spot — if you doubt me, try it and you will see it borne out. For however vicious we may be inside, we want to be thought of as wise and unblemished.

Yet other said that we want to be considered constant and discreet, able to stay on track and not betray what men tell us secretly. But that opinion is not worth a rake handle. God knows we women can't keep a secret to save our souls. Remember Midas? Let me tell you that story.

Along with lots of other stories, Ovid tells us that Midas had, under his long hair, two ass's ears growing out of his head, something he cleverly managed to keep from everyone around, except his wife, who knew about it. Now he loved her more than anyone and trusted her with his secret. Of course he begged her not to tell anyone of his disfigurement, and she took an oath: 'Never,' even if she were offered the whole world, would she be so evil as to risk her husband's dishonor and shame — as well as her own. But then she got to a point where she thought she would die if she could not tell someone. So she ran down to a marsh, her heart beating out of her chest and, like a marsh bird, she placed her mouth right next to the water and whispered: 'Do not betray me, water, with your sound, as I tell this to you and no one else: my husband has two long ass's ears. Now my heart has calmed down, now that it is out; I could not hold it in longer, without a doubt.' Here you can see that though we can do it for a time, it must come out — we simply cannot keep a secret.

But if you want to know how this story ends, you will have to read Ovid.

The knight whom my story is primarily about, though, when he saw that he was coming no closer to achieving his goal — that is to know what women want most — his breast was filled with sadness. He turned his steed toward home; he dared not linger as he had only a few days left to get home. And it so happened, as he rode sorrowfully by a forest, he came across four and twenty — maybe more — ladies joined in dance, and he drew near them, hoping to learn something useful there. But as he came closer, they vanished without a trace — there was suddenly no sign of them.

Now he could see no one, except for one old woman sitting there on the green — a woman so foul that words cannot do justice to her appearance — and she rose as he approached and said to him: 'Sir Knight, here you will find no path to further your journey. By your faith, though, tell me what you seek and maybe I can help — old folks like me know many things.'

'My dear ancient mother,' he replied, 'I am dead, for certain, unless I can learn what it is that women most want. If you can tell me that, I will reward you most handsomely.'

'Give me your word here in my hand' she answered, 'that you shall do whatever I ask of you, if it lie in your ability and, before nightfall, I shall tell you the very thing you seek.'

'Here is my word,' said the knight, 'I so consent.'

'In that case,' she said, 'I assure you that your life is safe, and I will stand by that. Upon my soul, the queen will say the same thing that I will tell you. I don't care if she is the proudest of women, whether she wears a kerchief or a crown on her head, she will not gainsay what I shall teach you. Let us go together back to the court without further ado.' She then whispered something in his ear and bade him be glad and of good cheer.

When they got to the court, it soon became known that he had kept his word and had returned as promised. Many a noble woman and many a maid and many a widow, who had seen it all, assembled there, with the queen herself sitting in judgment — all had come to hear his answer. And when, in due time, the knight himself appeared, all were asked to be silent so that he could tell the assembled audience what it was that women want. The knight wasted no time standing stand dumb as a beast before this crowd but answered the question shortly in a manly voice, so all the court could hear.

'My liege lady' he announced, 'generally women want to have a husband who loves them and they want sovereignty over him and to be his master. This you desire most, whether or not you decide to kill me. Do with me as you wish; I am here at your demand.'

In all the court there was neither wife nor maid nor widow who contradicted him, but all said that he had saved his life with what he said. And then the old woman, whom the knight had first met on the elfin green, rose.

"Mercy,' said she, 'my sovereign lady, the Queen. Ere you disperse this court, do right by me. I taught this knight his answer, for which he gave his word that he would do the first thing I asked, if it lay in his power. And in front of this court, I pray thee, Sir Knight,' she turned to him, 'that you take me as your wife, for you know well that I have kept you alive. Tell us, by your faith, if what I say is true.'

The knight answered, 'Alas and woe is me. I know well enough to what I agreed. For the love of God, choose something else — take all of my possessions but not my body.'

'Never,' said she. 'I am horrible to look at and old and poor on top of it, but I would not give up being your wife and your love for all the precious metal or the golden ore that can be dug up or found on earth.'

'My love?' he asked. 'No, rather my damnation! Alas that any member of my family be degraded by a union with such as you.'

But it did him no good, for in the end he had no choice: he had to wed the old hag, take her as his wife and go to bed with her.

Now some among you may complain that I neglect to spend time on the festivities and the celebration that were to take up the entire day, but to them I've got to say that there was no joy and no celebration; there was just sadness and sorrow, for he wed her privately the next day and hid away like an owl after that, so hard it was for him that his wife was hideous.

You can imagine the despair with which the knight brought his bride to his bed that night; he writhed and turned to and fro — all the while his old wife lay there smiling. Finally she said: 'Bless you, dearest husband! Is this what all knights do on their wedding night? Is this the custom at King Arthur's court? Are all his knights so standoffish? I am your own love and your lawful wife; not to forget, I am the one who saved your life. What did I ever do wrong to you that you treat me like this on our first night together? You act like a man who has lost his wits. Of what am I guilty? For the love of God, just say it, and all shall be well.'

'Well? How can all be well?' asked the knight. 'Alas. Never. Never! Things will never be well again! You are so ugly, and so old and, on top of that, you come from such a low level of society — it is little wonder that I toss and turn and twist about in this bed. I wish to God that my heart would simply burst!'

She asked: 'Is that what's troubling you?'

He answered: 'Yes! You're surprised at this?'

'Now, Sir," she said, 'if I wanted to, I could make all this well in less than three days, if you treat me as I deserve to be treated. You blather on about nobility that comes from a heritage of old wealth and that makes you noble, and I have to tell you that your arrogance doesn't have the value of an old hen. Instead you ought to pay attention to who is most virtuous, who does the right thing whether anyone is watching or not, and who strives to do all the noble acts possible — that is the noblest person of all. Christ wants us to claim our nobility from him, not from our ancestors and from their wealth. Though our ancestors give us all the riches that allow us to claim noble descent, they cannot give us — no matter how hard they may try — the virtuous acts that earned them their nobility and that serve us as a model to follow.

Dante, that wise Florentine poet, said it very well in his teaching, telling all of us: "The small branches of human accomplishment seldom grow, for God, in His goodness, wants us to claim our nobility from Him, because we can claim from our ancestors only temporal things that may maim and hurt us." You know, as well as I, that if nobility were inherited naturally, the descendants of a noble line would never cease to act nobly and to do the right thing. They would never do anything wrong or evil — and our experience shows the contradiction in that.

Take some fire and carry it to the darkest house between here and the mountains of the Caucusus, while you shut the door and leave the remaining fire behind — it will burn as brightly as if twenty thousand people were looking at it; it will do its duty and burn, so help me God, until it dies out.

In this example you can see how nobility has nothing to do with wealth, since people — unlike my fire — are not always constant and true to their traditions. For, as God is my witness, people often see the son of a noble man act shamefully, like a villain. He who claims nobility only because he was born in a noble household and had virtuous ancestors who acted nobly, while he himself does not act like a gentleman nor follow in his dead ancestors' noble steps, he is no noble — I don't care if he is a duke or an earl, for his villainous, evil deeds make him a churl. For then your nobility is nothing more than the reputation of your ancestors, and it is alien to your nature. True nobility is a gift of grace from God alone; it is not automatically given to us with our station on earth.

And there is no villainy in being poor. Just think how noble that Tillius Hostillius was who, as Valerius tells us, rose from poverty to the highest status possible. Read Seneca and Boethius, and there you shall see, without a doubt, that doing noble deeds is what makes one noble.

And so, in conclusion, dear husband, perhaps I come from simple ancestors, but the high God may, and so I hope, will grant me the grace to live virtuously. Then, when I begin to live nobly and to abandon sin, then I am noble. And when you reprove me of my poverty, remember that the high God, whom I believe in, chose to live in poverty and, surely everyone, whether man or maiden or wife, full well knows that Jesus, the King of Heaven, would not voluntarily choose to live an evil life. Truly happy poverty is an honest thing — this is what Seneca and other scholars tell us. Whoever is content in his poverty, I count wealthy, even if he does not have a shirt to his name.

On the other hand, anyone who is covetous is the one who is truly poor, for he wants that which is not his, the opposite of anyone who has nothing and is not covetous — he is the one who is truly wealthy, though you may think he is no more than a knave. Juvenal tells us that true poverty sings a happy song: "The poor man merrily goes on his way, singing and playing in the very face of thieves." Poverty is a hateful good, it seems, and a great remover of cares, as well as a great shaper of wisdom for anyone who faces it with patience.

Although it seems miserable, poverty is, in truth, the possession that no one claims. Often, when a man is down, poverty is what makes him know himself and his God better. Poverty, it seems to me, is a pair of spectacles by means of which someone may know his true friends. And, therefore, sir, since I do not cause you grief, I hope that you will no longer reprimand me because I am poor.

But now, good sir, you also hold it against me that I am old. And truly, even if no authorities ever said so in any book — although I'm certain I could find such a book — you honorable nobles tell us that an old man should be honored and should be called father because of his nobility. Now when you accuse me of being ugly and old, just remember that you need have no fear of being cuckolded.

For ugliness and old age, so bless me God, are great guardians of chastity.

Nevertheless, since I know what you desire, I will fulfill your worldly appetite. Choose now,' she said, 'one of these two options: you can have me be ugly and old until the day I die and thereby be to you a true and humble wife, never displeasing you my entire life, or else you can have me be young and beautiful and take your chances with all those who come to our house or any other place because of me. But you must choose, right now, one of the two, whichever you desire.'

The knight heaved a great sigh and pondered his choice carefully. Finally he spoke: 'My Lady and my Love — my dearest wife — I place myself under your wisdom and governance. You yourself choose which you will find most pleasant and which will honor both you and me more. I don't care which of the two you choose, because I will be happy with whatever makes you happy.'

She responded: 'Then I have mastery over you, since I may choose and govern myself as I like?'

'Yes, indeed, my wife; I think that would be best.'

'Kiss me, then,' she said, 'and let us be angry with each other no more for, by my word, I will be both to you, that is to say, both beautiful and true. I swear to God before you, that may I die in complete madness, unless I be to you as good and true as ever wife was to husband, since the world was first created. And if I am not as beautiful as ever was any lady, empress or queen, that lived between east and west, you can do with my life and my death as you wish. Draw up the curtain and behold what you see.'

And when the knight saw that she was now beautiful and young, he took her in his arms, filled with joy, his heart floating in a veritable bath of bliss. A thousand times over and over he kissed her, and she did everything that might do him pleasure or be to his liking.

And they lived in this perfect joy and harmony for the rest of their lives.

And so, my fellow pilgrims, may Jesus Christ send us husbands who are gentle and young and fresh in bed and the grace to outlive those we marry. But I also pray that Jesus shorten the lives of men who chose not to be governed by their wives — these old, angry misers who spend nothing — may God send them the plague itself!"

As soon as the Wife had ended her tale, the Clerk spoke up: "Worthy Madam, if I may, are you not troubled by some of the things that happen in your story?"

"What do you mean? Do you disagree with what this story tells us about what women want? May the Lord above save me from yet another man who tells me what I mean to say."

"Not at all — my experience hardly allows me to judge the validity of your argument. Nor do I mean to tell you what your story tells us. That is not it. What I am wondering about is whether you are not troubled by telling a story in which a rapist is ultimately rewarded with wedded bliss?"

"What? Oh, I suppose that is true, but that was not the point of my story."

"Nevertheless, that is what the story says."

"I suppose so, if you want to be picky about it."

"But if that was not the point of your story, what was?"

"Clearly, that if men allow women to be in charge, all will enjoy a happy life."

"Yes, I suppose that is what you were trying to say, but the story ends happily only because of magic — have you ever known a marriage in which the woman is in charge while she continues to be ever beautiful and always faithful?"

Before the Wife could answer, the Clerk continued.

"Your own life story suggests that while you may finally have been in charge in your marriages, ever-lasting beauty and constant faithfulness were not part of the bargain. Indeed, with all due deference to yourself, at least one of those qualities is not under human control."

The Wife frowned, seemingly trying to understand what the Clerk was saying, but before she could answer, she was pre-empted.

Much of the time that the Wife of Bath had been telling us her tale, our worthy begging Friar had been scowling at the Summoner but, perhaps, for the sake of propriety he had said nothing villainous to his adversary lest he interrupt the Wife. But now he did, ignoring the questions the Clerk had raised, as this Friar had other things on his mind: "Madam, may God give you a long and good life. You have touched here, as God is my witness, on matters that scholars find to be most perplexing. I dare say that you have said some things very well, but if I may, Madam, as we ride along here we should just speak of entertaining things only and, in God's name, leave such weighty matters to the preachers and to the learned scholars. But," he continued hastily, lest he be interrupted, as well, "if it please this company, I will tell you a little something about a Summoner. Now you know, I would hope, that by his very name there is no good that can be told of a Summoner, and I pray that no one here is offended by what I say. A Summoner is nothing more than a fellow who runs here and there with letters of fornication, someone beaten at the entrance and the exit of every town."

Our Host then spoke up: "Oh, dear Sir, I was hoping for more gentility and appropriate speech from you, befitting a man of your estate. Sir, I must insist that we have no hostility among the members of our company. Just tell your story and let the Summoner be."

"Nay, nay," chimed in the Summoner, "let him say to me whatever he wants to; when it comes to be my turn, by God, I will give as good as I get. I will tell you all what a great honor it is to be a flattering begging Friar, and of many other crimes I will not mention for now. And I will tell you exactly how he carries out his duties, I swear."

Our host retorted, "Peace. No more of this!"

And then he turned to the Friar: "So, dear Master, go ahead and tell your tale.

The Friar's Tale

"Once upon a time, in the part of the country I call home, there lived an Archdeacon,[19] a man of great nobility, who boldly carried out the laws that punished fornication, witchcraft and pandering, slander, adultery, church robbery, usury and simony, as well as those which governed wills, contracts and failure to observe the sacraments. But surely he was the greatest scourge of lechers — if caught, they would definitely sing their song — and those who cheated on their tithes; if anyone turned them in they were in for severe punishment. He never failed to collect a fine, however small. Anyone who made any insufficient tithe or offering could be heard complaining pitifully — even before the Bishop caught them with his hook,[20] they were already in the archdeacon's book. His jurisdiction gave him the power to punish them as he saw fit. And, at his command he had a Summoner who had no match in slyness anywhere in England. This Summoner governed a secret network of spies that kept him well informed of all that went on, and he was happy to spare a particular lecher or two because they led him to twenty-four others. Though this Summoner was mad as a country hare, I will not go easy on him. I will lay bare all of his wickedness, because we are out of his jurisdiction and he has no power over us here or ever shall."

"Holy St. Peter," interrupted the Summoner, "so are the women of the Bishop's brothels not under our jurisdiction!"

"Peace," jumped in our Host, "bad luck to you! Let him tell his story. Now tell on. Ignore this Summoner's complaining. Spare no details, my own sweet Master!"

---

[19] Primary assistant to and representative of the bishop; in Chaucer's time, the chief judge of the ecclesiastical court.

[20] A bishop's staff, or crook, ends at the top in a kind of hook, a reminder that bishops are shepherds of Christ's sheep.

Unperturbed, the Friar continued: "This false thief, this Summoner, could reel in his spies, the same way hawks are always lured back to their master's hand. They told him everything they knew, as their acquaintance with him was well-established. They were his secret agents, part of very profitable business, of which the Summoner's master knew little enough. This lewd man could, without formal orders, but on pain of excommunication, summon folks who were happy to fill his purse and to treat him to great feasts at alehouses all about. He was as big a crook as was Judas, thief of what little money the apostles had — his master never saw more than half of what he was due.

He was, if I am to give him his due, a thief as well as a summoner, and a pimp. He had any number of wenches in his crew who whispered in his ear whenever Sir Robert or Sir Hugh, or Jack or Ralph — or whoever it might be — had lain with them. They were in on it with him, and he would get a forged summons and make them both appear at the Archdeacon's court, where he would let the wench go and swindle the man. He would say: 'Friend, for your sake I will strike her name out of the book, and you need not worry yourself about this matter more. Think of me as your friend, only here to help you.' It's a sure bet that he was involved in more briberies than I could tell you about even if I had two whole years to do so. For in this world there is not a hunting dog who can tell a wounded deer from a whole one better than this Summoner could sniff out from a mile away a sly lecher or a panderer or a lover. And since that was the source of all his income, he was ever intent on it.

And so it happened one day that this Summoner, always looking for prey, rode out to summon an old widow on a false charge, just because he was looking for a little extra money. And as it happened, near a forest, he came across a jolly Yeoman, with bow and arrows bright and shiny, wearing a green jacket and a hat with a black fringe.

'Sir,' said the Summoner, 'hail and well met.'

'Welcome,' said the other, 'as are all good fellows! What brings you to this green wood?'

He continued: 'Are you going far today?'

The Yeoman answered: 'Not too far. I am close to where I was going, here nearby; I was riding out to collect a fee that is owed my lord.'

'So you are a Bailiff, then?'

'Indeed,' he answered, ashamed that he was a Summoner and not daring to admit such a disgusting thing.

'By God, then, dear brother,' said the Yeoman, 'you are a Bailiff and so am I. But unfamiliar with this country as I am, I am pleased to make your acquaintance and to be of your brotherhood, if you will allow it. In my belongings here I have lots of gold and silver; if ever you come to my part of the country, I am happy to share it with you, as much as you like.'

'Mercy,' answered the Summoner, 'by my faith, indeed!'

And so they swore eternal brotherhood and kinship to one another and rode along together in good company and friendship.

But our Summoner, as full of gossip as are these butcher-birds full of venom, was always eager to know every little thing.

"Brother,' he asked, 'what do you call home — if I should ever come to look for you at some other time?'

This Yeoman answered him kindly, 'Brother, I dwell far off in the north country where I also hope to see you some time. Before we say our goodbyes today you shall be so clear about my home that you will have no trouble finding me.'

'Now, brother,' said the Summoner, 'I pray you, teach me some clever thing, while we are riding along, since you are a Bailiff, as am I. Tell me, in good faith, how I may gain the most, and do not spare to tell me for fear of my sensitive conscience or for committing some sin, but, as a brother, tell me how you do what you do.'

'Now, to tell the truth, dear brother,' answered the Yeoman, 'I'll tell you no lies: my wages are limited and small, my master is hard on me and demanding, and my work is very hard. So I live by extortion, in truth, and take anything that people give me.

I take things any way I can, by deception or by force, and from year to year I earn my living. In faith, that's all I can tell you.'

'I'll be damned,' said the Summoner, 'that's the same with me. I'll take anything that's not nailed down or too hot to handle, God knows. Anything useful I learn in confidence, I go after — my conscience is not bothered by it. Were it not for extortion, I couldn't make a living — and I have no concern about being forgiven for such acts. I have neither compassion nor a conscience, and I say let these father confessors go to hell. Well met are we, indeed, by God and St. James! But, dear brother, won't you tell me your name,' the Summoner ended, while the yeoman smiled a little smile.

"Do you want me to tell you then, brother,' he asked? 'I am a devil, and I make my home in hell. I am riding about here looking for ways to gain profit, to take whatever it is that people will give me. What I gain in this way is my total income. You are doing the same thing I am: riding about to find something profitable, without a care as to how you do it — just so am I. I would ride to the end of the world looking for a likely mark.'

"Bless me,' said the Summoner, "I don't believe it! I truly thought you were just a Yeoman, and here you are shaped like any other man, just like me. Tell me, do you look like this then in hell, when you are in your own home?'

'Not at all,' he answered, 'there we don't have a shape at all. But when we want to, we can slip into one or make you think that we have one. Sometimes I appear as a man, or as an ape; I can even look like an angel. It's not a big deal for us to do that. Every lousy conjurer can deceive you and, I hope to God, I am far more clever than a simple conjurer!'

'So,' the Summoner pressed on, 'as you ride about you take up any shape you like, rather than the same one all the time?'

'Sure,' he said, 'we take up whatever shape our prey finds most acceptable.'

'Why do you go to all this trouble?'

'For many reasons, my dear Summoner,' said this fiend, 'but all in good time. The day is short, it is past prime, and I have not yet gained a single thing. If you will allow me, I will turn my attention to gaining something rather than to telling you all about us. For, dear brother, the truth is that even if I told you, you are not smart enough to really understand it.

But since you asked why we go to all this trouble — sometimes we are the instruments of God and the means by which His plan is carried out in the way He wants it to affect his creatures, in different ways and different manners. Without Him we are powerless, for sure, if He chooses to stand in the way.

And sometimes we get permission to attack only the body and not trouble the soul — I'm thinking of Job, whom we made quite miserable — and sometimes we are given power to attack both, the body and the soul, I mean. And other times we are allowed to trouble a man's soul, and not his body — and that's about as good as it gets.   When a man resists our temptation, it leads to his salvation, even though that was not our intention. He is saved, even though we tried to destroy him. And still other times we are sent to serve humans, like the Archbishop Dunstan. Once I was even assigned to serve the apostles!'

'But you have to tell me,' said the Summoner, 'in truth, do you always make your new bodies of the elements?'

The devil answered: 'Nah! Sometimes we go in disguise and sometimes we bring dead bodies back to life, in various ways, and then we speak as readily and as well as Samuel did to Phitonissa. (I know that some men say it was not really he, but I pay no attention to your theology!) But I promise you one thing, and this is no joke: you will know soon enough exactly how we are shaped. My dear Brother, you will shortly come where you will not need me to teach you, for you shall know through your own experience, and you will hold the professorial chair that teaches all this better than did Virgil while he was alive or even Dante. So let's be lively and ride on, for I would enjoy our company until you give up on me.'

'Nay," answered the Summoner, "that will never happen. Everybody around here knows that I am a Yeoman, and I will keep my oath to you though you were Satan himself. I will keep my word to my brother just as I have sworn — a pledge we have made, one to the other — always to be your true brother in this matter, as we both go about our business. You take your part of all that people give you, and I'll take mine —thus, we will both make our living. And if either have more of it than the other, then he will be true and share it with his brother.'

"By my faith,' swore the Devil, 'I agree!'

And having reaffirmed their pledge to each other, they rode on to the entrance of the town to which the Summoner was riding, where they saw a hay cart which the cart-driver was taking on its way. And the cart was stuck deep in the mud, while the driver whipped the horse and yelled at it as if he had gone crazy: 'Giddy up, Brook! Giddy up, Scot! Did you think you would just stop pulling! May the devil take you, body and bones, as sure as you were born. Look at all the suffering you bring me! May the devil take all of you: horse, cart and hay!'

The Summoner said: "Now, here's some fun!' And he drew near the Devil and whispered in his ear, as if he were sharing a private joke: 'Listen, my brother, listen, by your faith! Don't you hear what the cart-driver is saying? Take it, since he has given you all three: cart, horse and hay!'

'No,' said the Devil, 'God knows, it's not so! Trust me, he didn't mean it. Ask him yourself, if you don't believe me. Or else just wait a minute and you'll see.'

Then the cart-driver patted the horse on its behind and soon enough it began to heave and to pull. 'Giddy up, now may Jesus Christ bless you,' he said then, 'and all He has made, all of it! That was well-pulled, mine own dappled boy. I pray God and Sr. Loy save you! Now is my cart out of the mud again, by God!'

'You see, brother,' asked the Devil, 'what did I tell you? Here you can see, my own dear brother, that the churl said one thing but he meant something else. So let's be on our way. By law, I have nothing to gain here.'

After they had ridden some ways beyond the town, the Summoner stealthily told the Devil: 'Brother, near here lives an old widow that would rather lose her neck than to give away any of her goods. I know that she'll go crazy but am going to demand twelve pence from her, lest I summon her to our hearings. I don't know a thing she has done wrong, if the truth be told, but you will have me as an example, even if you can't earn enough here to cover your expenses. '

With that, the Summoner knocked on the widow's gate. 'Come out,' he called, 'you old hag! I'll bet you have some friar or priest in there with you!'

"Who's that?' the woman said, 'God bless me! God save you, Sir, what is it you want with me?'

'I have here,' the Summoner said, 'a bill of summons. On pain of excommunication you are ordered to appear before the Archdeacon's court to answer certain charges.'

'Oh, Lord,' she answered, 'Christ Jesus, King of Kings, help me, as I am helpless here. I have been sick for many a day now, and my side hurts so much that I cannot go very far or ride without risking death. May I see the written indictment, Sir Summoner, and have my representative answer that which I am accused of?'

'Of course,' said the Summoner, 'but if you pay me, right now, let's see, twelve pence, I can acquit you. I will have little enough profit by doing so; my master, rather than I, has the profit. Hurry up, and I will leave you alone. Give me the twelve pence, so I can be on my way.'

'Twelve pence,' she cried out, 'now, Blessed Lady, St. Mary, in your wisdom help me from this care and from all sin; even if I were to win the whole wide world, I would never have twelve pence in my possession. I beg that you show mercy on me, poor wretch that I am.'

'In that case,' the Summoner said, 'the foul devil himself take me if I excuse you, though you die in the process!'

"Oh Lord,' she said, 'God knows, I am guilty of nothing.'

'Pay me,' he persisted, 'or by sweet Saint Anne herself, I will take your new pan in return for the debt you owe me from long ago. When you cuckolded your husband I personally paid your fine.'

'You lie,' she said, 'by my salvation, for never before today was I, widow or wife, summoned before your court. Nor was I ever in my life unfaithful! May the devil, black and foul in looks, take you and my new pan both!'

And when the Devil heard her curse the Summoner like that on her very knees, he asked: 'Now Mabel, dear old mother, is this, what you say, exactly what you want?'

'Unless he repent here and now,' she repeated, 'may the devil take him and my new pan.'

'Never, you old cow,' spoke the Summoner, 'I have no intention of repenting for anything I am taking from you. I wish I had your smock and every piece of cloth you own, too!'

'Nay, brother," said the Devil, 'don't be upset. Your body and this pan are mine by right, and this very night you shall go with me to hell, where you will know all of our secrets, far better than any master of divinity does!'

And with that the foul fiend grabbed him and he went, body and soul, with the Devil to he very pace where Summoners come from to begin with. And may God, who made us in His own image, save and guide us, all mankind, and may He perform a wondrous miracle and change these Summoners into good people."

"Gentlemen," this Friar turned to all of us, "if had I the time, I could have told you such things about this Summoner — all consistent with the texts of Christ, Paul and John, and many of our good Doctors of the Church — as would make your hearts ache, though no tongue could do justice in the course of a thousand winters to the pains of this cursed house of hell. But to keep us from that evil place, wake and watch with our Lord Jesus so that His grace keep you from that tempter, Satan.

Listen closely! Be careful, as I tell you: 'The lion is always lying in ambush to slay the innocent, if he can.' Dispose your hearts to withstand the fiend that wants to enthrall and keep you in bondage. Remember that he cannot tempt you more than you are able to withstand because Christ will be your champion and your knight, and pray with me that these Summoners repent for their misdeeds before the Devil can take them!"

Now the Summoner stood up straight in his stirrups; he was so angry with the Friar that, in his rage, he was shaking like an aspen leaf.

"Gentlemen," he said, "the only thing I ask is that, as you have heard this false Friar lie, by your leave, I be allowed to tell my story, as well. This Friar boasts that he knows hell and, small wonder, by God, that he knows it so well. There is very little difference between Friars and Devils, for all you know the story of how a Friar was taken to hell once in a vision and, as an angel was showing him around, displaying all the ways of suffering available there, he didn't see a Friar anywhere, even though he saw plenty of other people there.

And the Friar finally asked: 'Now, Sir, are Friars so filled with grace that never a one has come to this place?'

'Oh, yes,' answered the angel, 'there are many millions here.' And he led him down to Satan himself. 'As you can see,' he said, 'Satan has a tail that is broader than is the sail of a large sailing ship. Lift up your tail,' he asked Satan, 'show us your ass and let this Friar see the nest of Friars lodging there in that place.' And for minutes there streamed, like bees from a hive, out of the devil's ass more than twenty-thousand friars all together, and they swarmed about hell and returned again as fast as they had left and crept back again into Satan's ass. He clapped down his tail again and just lay there. This Friar, when he had looked all about and had seen all the torments of that horrible place, had his spirit restored to his body again by God and he awoke, still shaking with fear. He could not keep the Devil's ass out of his mind, the very abode of his own kind. God save you all, except for this accursed Friar; this is how I will end my prologue and begin my tale." And so he, too, told his story.

The Summoner's Tale

"Gentlemen, I am told that in Yorkshire there is a marshy stretch of land that goes by the name of Holderness. Once there was a begging Friar who was known to go all around that area to preach and, no doubt, to beg. And so, it happened that one day this Friar had preached at one of the churches, encouraging the faithful, above all, to sponsor trentals at his monastery[21] and to make donations in the name of God, that would fund more holy houses where divine services would be honored, not places where all is wasted and devoured — no, no need to give to those clergy living on endowments, thanks to be to God, so that they can live in wealth and abundance. 'Trentals,' he would preach, 'deliver friends' souls from penance, be they young or old, yes, even though they be hastily sung — they don't keep a priest, who only says one mass each day, young and in hay. Deliver the souls right now, with no delay! It is most painful to be clawed with flesh hooks and awls or to burn and bake in fire. Now, in Christ's name, do it without delay!' And after this Friar said his piece he left immediately, leaving behind only his *qui cum patre*.[22]

When the people in the church had given him what he wanted, as I said, he would be on his way without delay. With his satchel and his iron-tipped staff, and his skirts tucked up, he would go from house to house, peeping, prying and begging for flour and cheese or maybe corn. His assistant, with his horn-tipped staff, had a pair of ivory writing tablets and a sharp stylus, that he used to write down the names, as he stood watching, of all the folks that gave anything to the Friar, as if he intended to pray for them. 'Give us but a bushel of wheat or malt or rye, an alms cake or any kind of cheese, or anything else you can spare — we

---

[21] Thirty Masses, said on each day for thirty days, for the repose of a departed soul.

[22] "Who with the Father," the opening words of a formal Latin blessing.

are not picky — an alms halfpenny or a mass penny, or else give us your bran, if you have any, a piece of your unfinished blanket, dear Lady, our dear sister — behold, here I write down your name — bacon or beef, or anything you can find around the house.' A brawny servant — the local innkeeper's man — followed behind him and bore away everything he could fit into the sack he carried on his back. And as soon as the Friar was out the door, he erased all the names that had just been written in his tablets, and thus he served the people with foolish falsehoods."

"Such a thing never happened, by God," interrupted the Friar, "you are a foul liar, you Summoner, you!"

"Peace," cried out the Host, "for the sake of Christ's dear mother! Just tell us your story and don't spare anything."

"As I live and breathe," said the Summoner, "that I shall!

So this Friar went from house to house, until he came to one where he was accustomed to being received more warmly than he was in most other places. The good man to whom that place belonged lay sick, bedridden on a low couch.

'*Deus hic*,'[23] this false Friar intoned when he entered, 'dear Thomas, my friend, good day to you.' And he continued in a courteous and soft manner: 'Thomas,' he purred, 'God bless you! Many a time have I fared well upon your bench, and here have I enjoyed many a merry meal.' And with that he drove the cat away off the bench, put down his walking stick and his hat, as well as his texts, and sat down. His companion, along with his servant, had walked into the town to the inn where he intended to spend the night.

"Oh my dear Master,' groaned the sick man, 'how have you been since March began? I haven't seen you this fortnight . . . or more?'

'God knows, I have been working hard, and especially for your salvation have I been saying many a special prayer — and for our other friends, God bless them! This very day I said Mass

---

[23] A medieval greeting, like *Adios*; "Deus hic est," Latin for "God is here."

and preached a sermon — as well as my wit allows — at your church. Not just the words of the holy scriptures — hard enough for your simple wit —but don't worry — I will teach you the proper interpretation. Interpretation is a wonderful thing, for, as we clerics say, the letter of the law kills. So I teach my people to be charitable and to spend their goods where it is for their own good — and there I saw your Lady – ah, where is she?'

'Outside,' the man said, 'in the yard, I think. She will come in shortly.'

'Aye, Master, welcome by St. John,' said the wife when she entered, 'how are you these days, truly?

The Friar rose courteously, embraced her in his spindly arms and kissed her sweetly, chirping like a sparrow all the time: 'My Lady,' he says, 'very well, indeed, your servant in every way. Thanks be to God who gave you soul and life! I have never seen so fair a woman today in the entire church, so God save me.'

"Indeed, may God amend my faults. You are always welcome, by my faith.'

"May God grant me mercy, Lady, this I have always found to be true here. But, by your leave, of your great goodness I would beg to have a moment alone with Thomas here so that I can speak privately with him. These parish priests are notoriously negligent and slow to explore tenderly a conscience in the confessional; but my very expertise is in preaching, especially the words of Peter and Paul. I go everywhere to fish for men's souls, giving Jesus Christ His proper due, spreading His word, as is always my intention.'

'Oh, by all means, dear Sir! Chide my husband hard, in the name of the Trinity! He is as angry as an ant, even though he has all he can desire. I cover him well at night, keep him warm, and lay my leg or my arm over him; yet, he groans like the pig that roots in our sty. I have no delight of him in any other way; nothing I do pleases him.'

'O Thomas, *je vous dy*,[24] Thomas, Thomas! This is the devil's doing and it must be amended. Anger is something the most High God forbids, and I have a word or two to say to you about it.'

'Now, dear Master,' said the wife, 'will you have a bite to eat before you go? What is your pleasure? I will make whatever you want.'

'O, dear Lady,' he answered, 'now *jai vous dy sans doute* — "something simple. I would have just the pâté of a turkey, and of your soft white bread maybe a sliver, and then a roasted pig's head — of course I would hate to see any beast slaughtered on my account. I would be pleased to have this simple sustenance with you, as I am a man of few needs; my spirit is fed by the holy writ. The body is always so weak and capable of suffering, however, that my stomach is a wreck. I pray you, dear lady, don't be annoyed that I share with you so readily my own private musings; God knows, I would do so with very few others.'

'Now reverend Sir, one more thing before I leave you with my husband to prepare the food you requested. My child died less than two weeks ago, shortly after you visited us last.'

"Rest assured that I saw his death in a vision, in the dormitory at our abbey. Trust me when I say that less than half an hour after his death I saw him carried into heavenly bliss, as God is my witness. So did our Sacristan, as did the Friar in charge of the infirmary, both of them true Friars for these fifty years. They are about — thanks be to God's grace — to celebrate their jubilees together. And I rose from my bed, as did our entire convent, with tears rolling down my cheeks, but without a sound or the clinging of bells, we sang *Te Deum*[25] and no other song, along with my prayer to Christ thanking Him for this vision.

---

[24] French for "I tell you." A few lines later, the Friar says *Je vous dy sans doute*: "I tell you without a doubt." Both carry the sense of "Trust me!"

[25] A traditional Latin hymn of thanksgiving or rejoicing: *Te Deum laudamus*, meaning, "God, we praise You."

My Lord and Lady, trust me, our prayers are more powerful and we know more of Christ's secrets than other folk, even were they kings. We live in poverty and abstinence while others revel in riches, surrounded by food and drink in their foul delight. We despise the desires of the world. Lazarus and Dives lived very different lives, with different rewards that came of those lives. Whoever prays must fast and be clean of sin, fattening his soul while making his body lean. We live as the apostle told us to: so long as we have clothing and food, even if they are not very good, our lack of sin and the fasting make Christ more receptive to our prayers.

You know that Moses fasted for forty days and forty nights before the High Almighty God spoke to him on Mount Sinai. On an empty stomach, after fasting for all those days, he received the law that was written with the finger of God. Also, Elijah, who is our lives' healer, before he ever spoke to Almighty God, fasted long and contemplated much.

Aaron, in charge of the temple and of all the other priests, would not allow the other priests to enter the temple when they were to pray for the people, nor would he let them taste any drink that others might make for them, unless they had been awake and prayed in abstinence, lest they perish. Listen to what I say! Unless they be sober when they pray for the people, be aware that — I will say no more, for what I have said suffices.

Our Lord Jesus, as the holy scriptures tell us, Himself gave us the example of prayer and fasting, and that is why we mendicants,[26] we blessed Friars. take vows of poverty and continence, in charity, humility, and abstinence, persecution for righteousness, weeping mercy and cleanness. This makes it easy to see that our prayers, ours as Friars, as mendicants, are more acceptable to God Almighty than are yours, what with your daily feasts. It was for the sin of gluttony, and here I do not lie, that man was first chased out of paradise, and in paradise humans

---

[26] Religious orders of Friars who took vows of poverty and supported themselves by begging.

were chaste, so help me God. I thank God every day for my life of abstinence and avoidance of fine and abundant delicacies.

But now listen to what I say to you, Thomas. I suppose I don't have a specific text for it, but I can surely find it in some interpretation that our sweet Lord Jesus Christ was referring specifically to Friars when He said: "Blessed be the poor in spirit," etc., as the gospel tells us— most like our profession, not those drowning in possessions. Fie on their pomp and their gluttony! Cursed be their ignorance.

To me they are like Jovinianus, fat as a whale and waddling like a swan, reeking of wine like the bottle in the pantry. Their prayers are full of great reverence when they say the psalm of David for the departed; when they say, '*cor meum eructavit*'[27] it comes out with a belch.

Who else follows Christ's gospel and his path, but those of us who are humble, chaste, and poor?

We who are active servants of God, rather than mere listeners?

Therefore, just as a hawk springs into the air, just so our prayers produced by chaste, hard-working Friars, spring to the ears of God.

Thomas, Thomas! By St. Yvo, whether I walk or ride, unless you commit to being our true brother, you shall not thrive. Day and night we pray to Christ in our chapter that He send you healing and the power to mend your body with all due speed.'

"By God's bones,' Thomas said, 'Christ knows I haven't felt any benefit from that, though I have for many a year spent many a pound on many a Friar. And yet I feel no improvement. In truth, I have nearly wasted all of my goods on this — farewell, my gold, because it is all gone!'

'Oh, Thomas!' the friar answered, 'what are you saying? Why do you seek out other Friars? What need has he who has a perfect healer, to seek out other healers in town? Your lack of faith will be your ruin! Do you really think that my prayers, along with

---

[27] Latin for "my heart has uttered" (Psalm 44).

those of my convent, are not enough for you? Thomas, such a joke is not worth a Flemish farthing!

Your problem is that we have not been given enough! Hah, you give that convent half a quarter oats! Hah, give that other convent twenty four groats! Hah, you give that Friar a penny and send him on his way! Nay! Nay! Thomas! You cannot go about it this way!

I charge you to tell me what a farthing is worth after you have divided it into twelve parts?

Behold! Anything that is united in itself is stronger than when it is divided up.

I'm not going to flatter you, Thomas! It seems that you want to have all our labor for free, but God Almighty Himself, who has created this entire world, tells us that the worker is worth his hire. Thomas, I want nothing of your treasure for myself but only for our convent, who are ever so faithfully praying for you and, of course, to build up Christ's own Church.

Thomas, if you want to learn about doing good works to support our Church you will find all about it in the life of St. Thomas of India. You lie here, angry and spiteful — no doubt this is the work of the devil — and you scold the blessed innocents, like your wife, so virtuous and patient. But trust me, Thomas — and you must — fighting with your wife is no good; rather, remember what wise men tell us: "Act not the lion in your own home; do not oppress those who are subject to you and do not force those you know to flee."

And, Thomas, I charge you rid yourself of the anger that resides in your heart, because it is like a serpent that creeps slyly through the grass and stings ever so subtly. Beware, my son, and listen carefully to the stories of twenty thousand men who lost their lives in strife with their sweethearts and wives. What cause have you, Thomas, to strive with a wife as holy as yours? There is no serpent as cruel when you step on its tail, half so mean, as an angry wife; then all they desire is vengeance.

Anger is a sin, one of the deadly seven, an abomination in the eyes of God above and destruction itself. Any ignorant vicar or layperson can see that anger leads to homicide and is indeed, the executor of pride.

I have so much to say about anger, I could talk about it until tomorrow, and so I pray both day and night that God send an angry man no power. It can cause great harm and great sorrow to empower an angry man with a high degree.

It is Seneca who tells of an angry judge, during whose rule two knights rode out one day and, as Fortune decided it, only one came home that night. He was immediately brought before this impassioned judge, who declared: 'You have killed your companion and for that I sentence you to die,' and he commanded another knight to lead that knight out to his death. And it so happened as they went on their way the knight that people thought had died came riding back. So they thought it made most sense to take both the knights back to the judge. They said: 'Behold, the knight did not slay his fellow, for he is alive and well." But the judge answered: 'He shall be dead, so may I thrive! By that I mean the first, the second, and the third.' He said to the first knight: 'I condemned you; therefore, you must die.' To the second: 'You, too, must die, for you caused your companion's death.' And to the third knight he said: 'You did not do as you were commanded to do.' And then he executed all three of them.

Angry Cambises was given to drunkenness and took great delight in being a scoundrel. It so happened that a lord of his household who loved virtuous morality, one day said privately to Cambises: 'My Lord, I am compelled to say to you that a vicious Lord is a lost Lord; and drunkenness is also a terrible reputation for any man to have, particularly a Lord. Many eyes and many ears are trained on a Lord, and he may not even know it. So, for the love of God, Cambises, drink more moderately. Wine causes men to lose control of their minds and of every one of their limbs!"

But Cambises answered: 'You are dead wrong and shall, without delay, witness the opposite. And you shall prove by your own experience that wine does not do what you say it does. No amount of wine has ever made me lose power of my hands or feet, nor of my eye sight.' And to spite this Lord, Cambises drank a whole lot more, a hundred times more than he had before and then this angry, cursed wretch had the son of this Lord brought before him. And, without warning, he took his bow in hand, pulled the string to his ear, and let fly an arrow that killed the son right then and there. 'Now tell me,' he asked, 'whether I had a sure hand or not? Are all my might and my mind gone? Have I lost control of my own eyes?'

What matters now the answer of the other Lord? His son was dead; there is nothing else to say. Beware therefore how you play with Lords; sing *Placebo*[28] and "I shall, if I can." A poor man can point out another poor man's vices, truly, but never to a Lord, though he should go to hell because of it.

Behold angry Cyrus, that Persian, how he destroyed the river Gyndes because one of his horses drowned in it when he was conquering Babylon. In his anger he made sure that all that was left of the river was so insignificant that women could wade through it.

Nay, what did Solomon tell us, he who can teach so well? 'Don't befriend anyone who is angry, nor walk with a man who is mad, lest you pay for the privilege.'

But I have said all I will say on the matter.

Now Thomas, dear brother, let go of your anger and you shall find me as true as a carpenter's square. Do not hold the devil's knife to your own heart; your anger is all too painful to yourself — but rather share with me all your sins in a good confession.'

'No, indeed, by Saint Symon,' disagreed the ailing man, 'I already went to confession today to my own parish priest. I told him everything I have to say about my life and I need no more to speak of it unless, in humility, I wish to do so.'

'In that case, why not give me some more of your gold to finish our cloister,' continued the Friar, 'for while other men are living well at their leisure, we must make do with a few mussels and oysters, and that is what we have been eating while we build

---

[28] Latin for "I shall please."

our cloister. And yet, God knows, scarcely have we been able to lay the foundation, and we have not yet been able to lay a single tile of the floor on which we will live. By God, we owe forty pounds for the very stones we have laid up to now.

So help us, Thomas, for the sake of Him who harrowed hell! Else we will have to sell all our books, and if you must go without our preaching the world will go to hell. For those who want to take us away from the world, so God save me, Thomas, by your leave, they want to take away the sun from the world, for who else can teach and work as we can?

And that has been true for a very long time,' he continued; 'ever since Elijah there have been friars — that is a matter of record — in charity, thanks be to God. Now, Thomas, help us, for the sake of Saint Charity.' And with that he sank down to his knees.

This sick man was nearly mad with anger; he silently wished that this Friar had been on fire with all of his lies and deception. 'Whatever I have to give,' Thomas said, 'why that is all I can give, and nothing else. You have told me yourself that you are my brother.'

'But certainly,' said the Friar, 'you can trust that completely; I myself have taken your petitions, sealed in a letter, to Our Lady.'

"Well, then,' he said, 'while I still live, I have something to give to your holy convent, and you shall have it in your very hand, on one condition. You must share it, my dear brother, so that every Friar shall partake of it equally, one as much as the others. This you must swear to me on your profession, without fraud or quibbling.'

"I swear to that,' said the Friar, 'by my faith!' And with that he placed his hand in Thomas's: 'Behold, I give you my word; you can count on me!'

'In that case, put your hand down my back and grope around beneath my buttock until you find something I have been holding privately just for you.'

'Aha,' thought this Friar, 'this is going well!' And he launched his hand down to the man's cleft in the hope of finding the gift.

And when the sick man felt this friar groping about his hole, here and there, into his hand he let go such a great fart that no horse, drawing a cart, could have equaled that sound.

The Friar was livid and jumped up like a crazed lion: 'Oh, you lying scoundrel,' he yelled, by the crushed bones of Christ! You have done this only to spite me, but you shall pay for this fart if I have anything to say about it!'

Thomas's man, who had heard the fray, came running in to chase out the Friar, who left, his heart filled with anger. He looked like a wild boar; he was so furious that he was grinding his teeth as he made his way down to the court, where a man of great honor lived for whom he served as the regular confessor. This worthy man was the Lord of that village, and when the enraged Friar came to him he was at table, eating. The Friar was hardly able to speak, but he finally squeezed out a 'God bless you!'

The Lord took one look at him and said: 'Great God Almighty, what in the world is wrong with you, Friar John? I can see that you are upset about something, for you look as if the wood were full of thieves. Sit right down here and tell me all about it, and it shall be amended, if possible.'

'I have,' he sputtered finally, 'this day had such an insult down in your village that the poorest page in the entire world has not had to suffer such a humiliation as I received in your town. And yet, what I am most upset about is that this old churl, with hoary hair, has blasphemed against our holy convent!'

'Now, now, Master, I beseech you—'

'No master, sir, but servant only, though I have earned that honor in my studies, but God does not want us to be called teacher, neither in the market place nor in the great hall.'

'I understand, but tell me what troubles you.'

'Sir,' said this friar, 'a horrible crime has been committed this day against mine order and me, and therefore, *per consequens*,[29]

---

[29] Latin for "as a consequence," used in an effort to justify the Friar's need for revenge.

in the same degree against Holy Mother Church — may God amend it soon!'

"Sir,' answered the Lord, 'you know what must be done. Don't be angry; you're my confessor; you are the salt and the flavor of the earth; for the love of God, settle yourself and tell me all your grief.'

And the Friar quickly blurted out as you have heard it before — I need not repeat it here.

The lady of the house was silent as she listened to the Friar, but then she responded: 'Ay, by the Mother of God, that blissful virgin! Is there anything else you want to tell us.'

"Madam, is this not enough? What do you think of all this?'

'What do I think?' she said, 'as God's infinite love speed me, I say that a churl has acted like a churl. What should I say? May God never let him prosper! His sick head is filled with vanities. I think of him as being somewhat crazed.'

'Madam,' he continued, 'by God, I shall not lie about this! I know I cannot be otherwise avenged, but I plan to defame him everywhere I go, to everyone I meet, with malice — this false blasphemer who charged me to divide what cannot be divided.'

Meanwhile the Lord sat quietly, musing and mulling over everything in his heart: 'How did this churl have the imagination to pose such a problem to the Friar? Never before have I heard anything like this. I have to believe that the Devil put it in his mind. Up to now, no one has ever heard of such a question in assmetric. Who can possibly show how every man can have his equal share of the sound and smell of a fart? Damn such a silly proud churl! Bad luck to him! Who ever heard of such a thing before this? To each man his equal share? Tell me how. This is impossible; no, it cannot be.

Ay, foolish churl, may God let you never prosper. The rumbling of a fart and any sound is but reverberation of the air, and it wastes away little by little. No one can, by my faith, judge whether it was shared equally. But behold this churl, look how shrewdly he spoke this day to my confessor? He was no doubt possessed by a demon!

Now enjoy some of the delicacies we have here for your dinner, my dear Friar — the churl be damned. Let him hang himself in the name of the Devil, for all I care.'

All this time the Lord's Squire was standing quietly next to the table, carving his meat but taking in every word the Lord, his wife and the Friar had uttered. 'My Lord,' he finally said, 'I hope it does not displease you, but if I were to be rewarded with the cloth necessary for a new gown, I could tell you and the noble Friar — if you be not angry with me — how this fart may be divided evenly among the twelve members of the convent, if it please you.'

'Do that,' said the Lord, 'and you shall indeed have a new gown cloth at once, by God and by St. John!'

'My Lord,' he explained, 'when the weather is right, without a breeze or any other disturbance of the air, let a cartwheel be brought into this hall. But make sure that it has all its spokes, all twelve of them — as cartwheels do commonly have twelve spokes. Then bring out twelve Friars.

Let me explain why.

If I am told rightly, a convent has thirteen members,[30] and your confessor here, because of his extraordinary worthiness, shall round out the numbers of his convent. On command, they shall all kneel down with their noses each at the end of one of the spokes and your noble confessor — God save him — shall hold his nose right under the center of the wheel. And then let the churl, his belly stiff and full like a drum, be brought out and have him placed over the center of the wheel and make him let a fart.

I bet my life that you shall see, and it shall be proven completely, that the sound of the fart as well as the smell shall pass equally unto the ends of the cartwheel — only this worthy man, your confessor, because he is a man of great honor, shall have the first fruit of it, as is only right.

---

[30] To honor the twelve Apostles, convents were usually composed of twelve Friars and a superior (Abbot).

The worthy friars have a rule that the worthiest of them shall be served first, and certainly he has deserved this. Earlier today he taught us much that is useful through his preaching as he stood in the pulpit of our church, and I can vouch for it and can say honestly that he was the first to smell three farts there, too.

Now, if this is done as I suggest, he and all the members of his convent shall share this gift equally, appropriate to his good and holy manner.'

The Lord, the Lady, and everyone there, except the Friar, agreed that the Squire had spoken as wisely as ever did Euclid or Ptolomy. They also concluded that Thomas, the churl, had spoken very well and it was his high wit rather than any demon that made him speak as he did.

No fool he.

On top of that, Jankin, the Squire, won himself a new gown.

This is the end of my tale and, behold, we have nearly reached another town."

"Well-told, my friend," the Host responded to the Summoner's Tale, "every profession has a rotten apple, I must admit, and even holy Friars are not always holy. But you have more than requited our Friar, as good and holy a man as he appears to be."

Before either the Friar or the Summoner could respond to this comment, one of our guildsmen, the Haberdasher, jumped into the conversation, and it was clear that he would not be gainsaid.

"Wh-wh-why, d-d-d-amn my bl-bl-beedin b-b-ullocks if I don't kn-kn-kn-kn-ow many a F-f-friar no better than this. And m-many a one of them are m-m-much better ac-cu-cu-quainted with the D-d-d-devil than with the s-saints. I c-c-could tell you a t-t-ale of the Devil that would m-m-make your bl-bl-bleedin hair stand on end. I d-d-don't sup-pp-ppose you all have heard the s-s-ong about the F-f-friar?"

And without waiting for an answer, he continued in a kind of chant, during which he did not stutter at all.

"There once was a Friar named John
As a beggar he wanted to con

All that he met, if only they'd let
Friar John pull his con on their john."

"Oh, for the love of Sweet Jesus," the Host interjected, "there's no need for this ribaldry and this kind of talk on a pilgrimage such as ours."

"And w-w-what k-k-k-kind of t-t-t-talk w-w-would that be th-th-that's not alright f-f-for everywo-wo-wone here?" the Haberdasher answered, only to be interrupted by his friend, the Carpenter, "Oh, come now, my dear Ralf, behave yourself. You're not at the York Fair now, and it behooves you to act accordingly."

"C-c-ordingly, that reminds m-m-me of another li-li-ttle d-d-ditty that r-r-rings my *c-c-cor*d ingly, and th-th-that m-m-mightily.

There's a curious thing that hangs,
Dangles, one might say, by a friar's hairy thigh,
covered by his robe, with an eye on its head;
stiff and hard, but born firmly, it brings reward,
when the friar pulls up his robes and
pokes the head of that hanging thing into the old,
well-known hole it fits perfectly,
just like it has so often in the past.
What is it?"

Now, the Wife of Bath was laughing so hard, I thought at first that she was choking, but she was guffawing instead of producing words, while the Second Nun also nearly choked, but on her mumbled prayers.

Here, Joseph, the Carpenter, quickly put an end to the disapproval — as well as the guesses — arising from many a one of our companions, loudly and peremptorily announcing: "Of course, it is a key, naught else. Simply a key."

The Cook snorted in joy, clapping the Haberdasher on his back: "Well-said, my brother Ralf, well-said. I surely thought it was something else!" And produced his version of a broad wink.

At this the Knight intervened with a loud harrumph and asked the assembled group to settle down and let the story-telling continue. And the Haberdasher, to the chagrin of the Host, took him up on it.

"I will m-most g-g-g-gladly t-t-ell you a st . . . st . . . st . . . st-st-ory of the D-d-d-devil that will m-m-make you s-s-soon forget our bl-bl-blessed F-f-friar's tale of his D-d-devil and some p-p-ooor sh-sh-shlop of a ch-ch-cheating s-s-summoner, and I c-c-can do it w-w-without offending anyone here. I w-w-will be c-careful with my t-t-tongue and use it only for st-st-story-t-t-telling." And, unabashed, ignoring the objections of many of our companions to this, his latest vulgarism, like it or not, he continued.

"A-a-as you all n-n-n-know, I am a w-w-w-eaver and, I m-might add, a l-l-l-lover of sm-sm-small r-r-ugs" — at this the Carpenter gave him a mighty shove, nearly knocking him from his horse — "f-f-fine, I will behave m-yself, and, as I was s-s-saying, a m-m-maker of hats s-s-so f-f-fine they will grow h-h-hair on the h-h-head of b-b-ald men l-l-ucky enough to w-w-wear them and c-c-cure w-w-warts for any man unf-f-f-ortunate enough to have g-g-got them from — all r-r-right, I n-n-know; I will k-k-keep a c-c-civil t-t-tongue.

Our w-w-worthy F-f-friar t-t-old you his t-t-tale about the S-s-ummoner who wanted to c-c-consort with the D-devil, but now you w-w-will hear about how one pu-pu-uts the devil back into h-h-hell, something neither our F-f-friar nor our S-s-ummoner seemed able to t-t-tell us, m-m-uch less could actually d-d-do.

But since I am interested in l-l-love in all of its m-m-any f-f-forms and m-manifest-t-tations, I w-want to make it c-c-clear that this is also a l-l-love s-s-story, for it is a s-s-story about l-love and the D-d-devil, two parts of human l-life that are never too far s-s-eparated."

"That may be true in your world," interrupted the blessed Wife of Bath, "but it is not so where I come from. In my world, love has little to do with the Devil and much more to do with pleasure."

"I th-th-thank you for th-th-that, f-f-fair l-l-lady, b-b-but hear m-m-me out and you w-w-will l-learn s-s-omething, alth-th-th-

though we know where I hail from th-that th-th-things are never as s-s-simple as they ap-p-ppear."

"Come now, Madam," the Host joined in, addressing the Wife, "you told us a story in your own time, and some — not I — found it to be quite long. Please let this maker of hats do the same — although," he looked around rather helplessly, "I suspect we're in for a lengthy tale."

"Th-th-thank you, S-s-sir Host; I do ap-p-ppreciate y-y-your w-words, and I w-will c-c-continue. Y-y-you n-need have n-n-no f-fear," and here he pointed at his own back-side," ab-b-bout m-m-y t-t-tale's l-l-length."

He managed to avoid the swat directed at him by Joseph and then began a kind of chant which, while monotonous, did end his stuttering at once.

The Haberdasher's Tale

"Those of us who are experienced in the arts of love know full well that the Lord of Love, although he favors the rich palaces and the luxurious mansions of those with leisure and easy money to the hovels of the poor — nevertheless, he loves to exert his power also in the middle of overgrown forests, peaks that thrust up into the sky" — here the Haberdasher received another forceful elbow in the side from his fellow, the Carpenter, but he simply continued, hardly chastened by this physical interjection — "yes, alright, well, as I was saying, and in the private desert cavities—"

At this the Carpenter threw his arms into the air: "I give up. There is no controlling this man, and he will speak as he does. I apologize in advance for his crudeness and his language, ladies and blessed clerics here with us, but I have done all I could. From here on, you must take him as he comes. "

"Th-th-th-thank you for th-t-hat, my b-b-brother Jo-jo-joseph. I th-th-ank you for your w-w-words but I will c-con-continue as I m-must, or as you p-p-put it so aptly, you m-m-must t-t-take me as I c-c-ome." He laughed mightily at his own little joke, joined in by a few others but not most, before he continued in his chant.

"The point I was making is that love is all-powerful, not to be limited by any single vessel, and we must accept that all are subject to his power and his rule, thanks be to Venus and her blind son, Cupid.

To begin with my story, then — once there was a very rich merchant, living far from here in a land which had people of many faiths, who managed to exist with each other in harmony and, I am happy to say, coupling in harmony, as well. Now this wealthy man, by the name of Ali Beck, had many children by various of his wives — a custom I find personally reasonable and right for humans, for why should a man not sate his appetite with many wives? After all, who among us — given the choice — would choose to wear the same hat or eat the same food daily, or nightly, at the same table, for our entire lives?

Well then, Ali had many beautiful children, the most lovely among them perhaps a fair young maiden by the name of Millicent. Millicent, like her father, was not a Christian but she was curious about that faith because she heard many good things about it. So she inquired of Christians she knew who praised frequently the goodness of their God and the many benefits of following in Christ's footsteps. She asked them to tell her more, specifically how one might best serve God most directly and do what God wished us to do in this world. The answer she got from many of them was that those who followed Christ most directly were those who gave up the things of the world and left them behind in favor of a life of solitude in the nearby desert.

Now Millicent, who was a simple, earnest girl, barely of marriageable age, although well-formed, that is, with the body of a ripe woman voluptuously holding the mind of an immature girl, secretly left her luxurious home at the next dawn and, without anything but the clothes that covered her buxom body, made her way toward the desert. She reached it after a few days of wandering without food or water and soon thereafter found the hut of a man living the simple life of a hermit all alone in the wilderness. He was quite astonished to see another human being, especially one so young and voluptuous as Millicent. He was not at all surprised, however, that she was hungry and thirsty, for he knew how difficult it was to live in the desert off the meager fruits that arid land provided.

He invited her into his hut and fed her, careful that she did not eat or drink too much all at once and, when she had eaten and drunk her fill, gently inquired as to what she was doing there in the desert. Millicent enthusiastically told him that she was eager to follow in the footsteps of Christ, whom she had heard about in her home, and that she was looking for someone who would instruct her and guide her in doing that.

Now the hermit was only human, and he immediately realized that, as beautiful and innocent as Millicent was, he would quickly reach the limits of his ability to withstand the snares of the evil one and would then, no doubt, ravish his guest. Knowing that, he generously shared with her the fruits and nuts, herbs and water he had, all the while assuring her that he was not the one to meet her needs. But, he informed her, there was a holy man, far holier than he himself was, not too much farther into the desert, who was much better prepared to guide and teach Millicent in the way that she sought to learn the ways of Christ.

So he put her on the path to another hermit, who had the same response to her as had the first one, and who hastened to point her toward a third hermit, even further into the desert who, he assured her, would be able to teach her all she needed to know to achieve her goals.

Thus, Millicent went on her way from hermit to hermit, totally unaware of how close she had come to being seduced by these holy men who, in the end, and particularly with her end in sight, were only human. And soon she found her way to the domicile of a young hermit, a devout and good young man named Peter, to whom she made the same request she had made of his two compatriots.

Now Peter was a devout but lusty young man who had experienced in full the pleasures of the flesh before accepting that the only way to control his carnal desire was to live a life of solitude, far away from the temptations he had succumbed to all too easily in the time before. Hearing Millicent's story now and noting at once the bountiful charms of her supple body, Peter decided fairly quickly that perhaps it was time to put to the test his own constancy and his ability to withstand temptation in its most attractive forms. So, unlike his fellow hermits, he determined that he should try the strength of his convictions with none other than Millicent. So, he agreed to tutor her in the ways of the Lord and welcomed her by making a bed of palm leaves for her to sleep on.

It did not take long for temptation to overcome Peter's resolve to test out his powers of resistance and not much more time for the forces of temptation to put to rout his resolves to withstand once again the pleasures and wonders of the flesh. Peter quickly turned tail and gave in, giving up his devout thoughts, prayers and mortifications of the flesh in favor of planning his attack on the fortifications that protected Millicent's innocence, prudence and . . . succulent body. Soon he was thinking through his strategy for winning her, ideally without letting her realize that he was simply besotted with the flesh and totally devoted to nothing but sensual pleasure.

He began by asking her many questions about what she believed, what she knew and what she had experienced in life. It did not take long before he realized he had before him an innocent virgin who knew nothing about the pleasures women can have with men, and so he began to lay the snares that would make her his —- under the pretense of bringing her closer to God — when all he really sought was to bring her body closer to his. His opening gambit was to talk at length about the enmity between the devil and God, stressing the fact that the greatest service any human could carry out for God was to put the devil back into hell, where he had originally been condemned to spend eternity, even before Adam's unfortunate fall in the Garden of Eden.

When Millicent's asked how this was to be done, Peter explained: 'If you but do as I do, we shall soon succeed in this endeavor.' He proceeded to take off the few clothes he was wearing and stood before her naked as he was born. Innocent as she was, Millicent followed his example, and soon they were facing each other just as Adam and Eve had encountered one another in Paradise. Then Peter fell on his knees, inviting Millicent to do the same, so that they might pray the devil back into hell in unison, leaning their naked bodies together for the glory of God.

When Peter saw the beautiful Millicent like this, his desire overcame any resolve he might have still felt, and he demonstrated a visible rising of his flesh, something which surprised his innocent companion, and she asked him: 'Peter, what is happening? You have something that protrudes in a startling manner, and try though I might, I cannot imitate you because I have not such a part.'

'Oh, my dear daughter in Christ," Peter answered her, "you remember my warnings about the devil? Now you see the Prince of Darkness in all his glory. He is tormenting me most painfully and I am scarcely able to stand it.'

'Praise the Lord,' she said, 'I can see now that I am much better off than you, for I have no such devil torturing me.

'You speak the truth, my daughter,' Peter answered her, 'but instead you have something that I do not have.

'Oh my,' she said, 'what do I have that you do not possess?'

'You, my dear child," he readily answered, 'you possess hell itself. And I tell you now that it is my belief that God has sent you to this very place in order to save my soul. For this devil, that tortures me in this manner and continuously does so, can be defeated, if in your compassion you would only allow me to place him in your hell. Doing so would afford me immediate and lasting solace, while pleasing God enormously and serving him in the way solely you can. Of course that is the case only if you have come to this desert and to me in order to serve God.'

All in good faith, Millicent answered him, 'Since I seem to have hell as a place for your devil to be put, be it as God ordains and as you, and when you, my earthly father, will it.'

'May God and all the angels in heaven eternally bless you, my daughter in Christ,' Peter said, continuing, 'let us go together then to the bed and I will place my devil in your hell so that he will leave me in peace.'

Saying this, he then gently led Millicent to the bed and taught her exactly what position she had to assume so that he could imprison his devil in her hell, drawing out this accursed spirit and sending him back to whence he came.

Now Millicent had never before put any devil in her hell and, since this was her first time, she felt some pain when the devil entered her hell, causing her to ask Peter: 'It would seem, holy father, that you have told me the truth about this fellow, the devil, being evil as you say, and a great enemy to God, because there is indeed sorrow in hell when he is placed there, and I feel some pain then.'

'Indeed, my daughter,' he answered, 'rest assured that this will not always be the case; in time there will be no pain in your hell when my devil enters there.'

And to prove his point and to assure her of this truth, he put his devil into her hell six times before they were finished with this first lesson in how to serve God. This allowed him so thoroughly to defeat his devil that Peter was appeased for the time.

But of course the devil would reappear, and Millicent was always obedient and quite willing to assist Peter in returning his devil into her hell in order to manage the devil, and the time came when she began to find this game more than agreeable and she made a point of saying to Peter: 'Blessed father, now I see and understand that it was all true, when the holy people from my home would tell me that the service of God was truly a delight and that the more I devoted myself to God, the more wonderful I would find it. I cannot remember anything I did in the past that filled me with so much pleasure as does the solace I feel from allowing you to place your devil in my hell. And that is why I think it folly for anyone who cares to do anything but to love a life of devotion to the service of God.'

And from then on she would often come to Peter and say: 'My father, I came here to serve God rather than to while away my time in idleness; let us go then and put the devil back into hell.' And while they were doing so, she eventually observed: 'There's one thing I don't understand, Peter, and that is why the devil keeps escaping from hell; if only he were as ready to stay there as hell is ready to receive and retain him, he would never leave it.' Consequently, Millicent came to request and exhort Peter to the service of God so often that at last there came a time when Peter had so thoroughly lightened his load that he found himself shivering where others would have sweated.

And so he began to teach Millicent that the devil needed to be corrected and put back into hell only when his head was swollen with pride, and he explained that 'through God's grace and their service they had brought the Devil to reconsider his position so much that he now prayed to be left alone, in peace and quiet.' And through that teaching Peter did manage to keep Millicent quiet in her increasing need to defeat the devil. But they eventually got to a place where Peter felt little need to put the devil into hell, and Millicent finally said to him: 'Peter, your devil may be so controlled now that he is no longer troubling you, but my hell, for its part, grants me little peace. So I think it only fair that since my hell assisted you in placating your devil, in turn your devil can now do his job in appeasing the discomfort of my hell.'

Now we must remember that Peter lived primarily on roots and on water, and he did not always have the strength to fulfill Millicent's desires. So he tried to appease her by telling her that it would take many devils to ease the tortures of her hell, but that he would do what he could to help her.

In accord with that lie he tried to satisfy her needs occasionally, but it was so seldom that it was like trying to satisfy a lion's hunger by throwing a single bean into his maw. Now Millicent began to grumble about not being able to serve God as much as she wanted to.

And about this same time as Peter and Millicent had their disagreements about how often the devil needed to be placed in hell, there was a tremendous fire in Millicent's home city and it burned her father's home to the ground, killing him and all the other members of her family. This meant that Millicent alone became the heiress of the entire estate her father had amassed and governed.

Obviously, she knew nothing about this.

But a young man named Nebulon did. Now this Nebulon had spent all he possessed on satiating his hungers for the world, the flesh and the devil, but he had heard that Millicent was alive, living in the desert. So he set out in search of her, found her, and forced her to accompany him back to their home town, where he made her his wife. And because the court had not yet taken over Millicent's father's estate, Nebulon, by way of his wife, Millicent, claimed Ali Beck's considerable estate.

After Millicent had returned to the city but before Nebulon had lain with her, she came to spend time with the other women of her class, and they importuned her to tell them exactly how she had served God in the desert and she freely answered that she had been occupied with putting the devil back into hell, a service to God that Nebulon had interrupted inappropriately, indeed, clearly against God's will. At this her lady friends asked: 'How does one put the devil back into hell?' And Millicent happily explained, partly with words, partly with gestures, what she meant by that. Her friends began to laugh so hard at her explanation that they might still be laughing to this day, for all I know. They then told the confused young Millicent: 'Don't you worry, dear friend; that is done here all the time, and Nebulon will soon serve God completely and thoroughly with you in this manner.'

In due time, this story was told and retold so often in that city that it became a common saying that the most pleasing service one could carry out for God was to put the devil back in hell, and that phrase is still popular there as it has become in many other places in the world.

Now, gentle ladies," the Haberdasher turned his chant to the women on the pilgrimage, "I hope you have all learned from this not only how love can take many different forms but that you, too, can serve God by allowing men to put the devil back into hell. I, for one, am willing and ready to serve God with any of you who are filled with the desire to serve God in this manner. In the meantime, I have told you a story that certainly beats the Friar's tale of the Summoner and the Devil, and herewith my tale is done."

Well, you can imagine that such a bawdy tale had both its admirers and its detractors and, for some time, the pilgrims were in quite an uproar, with much shouting among the group members, and even some warnings as to what might happen next. I rather enjoyed watching Harry attempt to regain control, if he ever had any, as it was difficult to tell who was yelling what, although there was much noise and turmoil.

At last, things quieted down enough to where Harry could be heard, exhorting all to peace and to quiet and promising to restore order and proper decorum if only he was given the opportunity to do so. It seemed to me that once the initial hubbub was over, most could laugh at the Haberdasher and at the story he had told, and so we went on our way, reaching shortly after this the Black Bull, a large inn that accommodated us all in Dartford — the first — and shortest — day of our pilgrimage completed. By that time, it was nearly dusk, and most of our troop was interested only in something to eat and, for some of them more importantly, to drink, and a bed for the night, as we knew we would leave at dawn the next morning, to wend our way toward Rochester and finally the shrine of the blessed martyr at Canterbury.

The next morning dawned slowly. It was a gray and overcast day, or at least, it began that way. After all had broken their fast, our Host assembled us in the courtyard of the inn, which took some time, as some of us were much slower than others to be ready, but the time came for the Host to address us.

"Now Lords and Ladies," he began, a bit pompously, "if I may have a moment of your time to remind you all of the rules to which you agreed before we left London."

But before he could continue, the Man of Laws ostentatiously cleared his throat several times and then spoke most forcefully. "I believe, my dear Host, that we have heard the rules and all know them. It is not a matter of knowing the rules but following them. And so far, I believe, with the occasional member of our troop stepping in and taking his or her" —- he managed a slight bow in the direction of the Wife of Bath, who was rather loudly, and unsuccessfully, trying to control her horse while she settled her broad skirts around her again after having somewhat laboriously climbed up from a short stool to her steed — "as I was saying, taking a turn perhaps somewhat earlier than you, our Host, had planned or anticipated, but all in all I think the rules have been observed and we don't need them to be rehearsed."

The Host was visibly not pleased at this, but he accepted his better's comment and merely said: "Very well, then, let us commence and make our way forward, as agreed. I believe it would be a good time for you, Sir Monk, to share a tale with us."

But even as he was saying this, about a third of our troop had escaped the yard, following the Shipman, who, already in his cups even at such an early time, looked back for a moment to proclaim loudly, and to the obvious delight of the Cook and several of the Guildsmen: "Nay, nay, Sir Host, I believe I am ready to tell a tale that will quite match the delightful story my dear friend the Haberdasher shared with us late yesterday — and which I am still laughing about every time I think of it — putting the devil back into hell — nothing better than that — I'm damned if that was not a terrific tale. Never heard better! And, by God, I well believe that our own worthy Monk may regret this story that I will tell before this day is done."

Our Host clearly considered for a brief moment trying to regain his control over the events unfolding, once again, rather differently than he had intended but then seemed to think better of it and acquiesced: "Fine! That will do, and we will look forward to hearing your tale." He muttered something under his breath as he turned his horse to join the stream of pilgrims departing the inn but I could not hear what he said, over the chorus of "a moral tale, a moral tale," that arose among a certain portion of our troop.

But the die had been cast for this day and, as soon as we had all squeezed through the inn's gate and had more or less reformed so that we could hear the story teller, the Shipman began.

The Shipman's Tale

"There was once was a Merchant" — here, the Shipman passed for a moment, waiting until he thought he could be heard by all — "from St. Denis near Paris. Because he was rich, many thought he was also wise. He was married to a woman of exceptional beauty, a woman who was very social and a friend of good times. Now we all know that such traits only cause men to have more expenses than are worth all the good times and the attention that is paid to his wife at festivals and at dances. Such bowings and scrapings and courtesies pass as quickly as does a shadow cast on a wall, with the husband not only left holding the bag but continuing to kick in endlessly. Those foolish husbands pay and pay, clothing their wives and paying for their fine dresses, to raise their own honor accordingly. But if they don't pay, or if they are so foolish as to object to funding such expenses, thinking them wasteful and silly, why then another will pay for these wives, or loan them the money they require — and that is even more perilous.

Now, this noble Merchant of whom my story tells, maintained a generous household and, as a result of his largesse and his beautiful wife, his house had so many visitors that you would all be amazed; but hear me out. Among those guests, some great, others unimportant, there was a certain Monk, good looking and in his prime — I suppose he was about thirty years old — who was always visiting there. This young Monk, so good-looking, was as close to the good Merchant, his host, as any friend could be, and had been for a long time. The Merchant and the Monk were both from the same village, and the Monk claimed the Merchant as his kin, and *vice versa*. Neither denied this and the Merchant was as happy about it as a hen is at dawn. It was a source of great pleasure for them that they were knit together in this eternal alliance, and they assured each other that their brotherhood would last for their entire lives.

Father John was generous and known for bringing gifts to the members of the household, as he was ever set on making others happy, and for this purpose he spent much money. He never forgot even the lowliest page in the house, and he gave gifts appropriate for each person — the master and all those who toiled for him. Whenever he came, he had just the right thing for everyone. Consequently he was very popular, and they were as happy when he showed up as is a chicken at the rising of the sun. But this is enough about that; let's move on.

It so happened that this Merchant was preparing himself for a trip to Bruges for business, to buy there some of the goods that he sold; and for this reason he had a messenger sent to Paris who requested that Father John come to St. Denis to amuse himself with the Merchant and his wife for a few days before the Merchant had to leave for Bruges.

This noble Monk that I am telling you about was respected as a man of great judgment, and he had the permission of his abbot to ride about the country to inspect, as he wished, their storage barns and outlying acreage, so he came at once to St. Denis. Was anyone ever welcomed more by the Merchant than was the courteous Father John, the Merchant's dear kin? Of course he brought with him — as he always did — a large jug of malmsey and of another wine, white Italian, and game fowl, and for several days they ate and drank and amused themselves, this Merchant and his cousin.

On the third day that Father John was there, the Merchant rose early and prepared for his journey, beginning with a visit to his counting house to make sure he knew the exact status of his books — how the year had treated him, how much he had spent and whether he had prospered or not. To do so he placed all his books and his bags in front of him on his counting-board and, because he had lots of money and owned many other things, he shut and carefully bolted the door of that room, as he did not want to be disturbed by any one for as long as it took him to count all that he owned. And he was at this task until after prime.

Father John had also risen early that day and was walking about the garden reciting his morning devotions.

About this time the Merchant's wife came to walk about privately in that same garden, greeting Father John when she first saw him, as she was want to do. She was accompanied by a little girl, whom she was pleased to guide and tutor.

'Oh, my dear cousin, Father John,' the wife said, 'is anything wrong that has you up and out of bed so early in the day?'

'My dear niece,' he answered, 'five hours of sleep for one night ought to be enough for any man who is not old and feeble, as are some of these married men that lie and doze as if they were hares in the field on the watch for small and great hounds. But my dearest niece, why are you so pale? I'll bet it's because our good friend has put you to work the whole night so that you got little enough sleep.' And with that he laughed very heartily at his own words and turned a little red at the thoughts he was thinking.

But this lovely woman shook her head most sadly and sent the little girl into the house before she said, 'Indeed, by our God who knows all,' she said, 'that is hardly the way things stand with me, dear cousin. For by the God who gave me spirit and life, in all the kingdom of France there is no wife that has less pleasure than I in that sad game; I may indeed sing "alas, alas, that I was ever born," but I may do so to no man,' she said. 'I dare not say how it stands with me — it is because of that very thing that I am thinking constantly of running away or else to make an end of myself, so full am I of care and sadness.'

The Monk stared at this beautiful woman in disbelief and said: 'Alas, my niece, God forbid that you hurt yourself, no matter how sad or hurting you are. Rather tell me everything. Maybe I can be of council or help to you in your misery. Tell me everything; I shall keep your secret. On my breviary, I swear that never, so long as I live, come good or bad, shall I ever betray your trust.'

'And I say the same to you,' she said, 'I say, as God is my witness, I swear by this holy breviary that even if I were to be torn to pieces I shall never, at the peril of my soul, betray a word of anything you tell me, not for kinship nor for family allegiance, but truly in love and trust.' Thus the two were sworn to each other; they kissed and, from this moment on, each told the other everything.

'Cousin,' she began, 'if I only had the time — and clearly in this place I have none — I would tell you the story of my life and how much I have suffered since I became a wife to my husband, albeit he is your kin.'

'Nay,' said the monk, 'he is no more cousin to me than is this leaf that hangs from this tree. I call him kinsman, by St. Denis of France, simply so I have more reason to spend time with you, whom I have loved above all other women; truly, I swear this to you on my vows. Tell us all about your grief before he comes down here, and do it quickly now while we have time.'

'My dearest love,' she said, 'oh my dear John, I would much rather hide these private thoughts, but they must out; I can't take it any longer. My husband is the worst man to me there ever was since the beginning of the world. But since I am a wife, it is wrong for me to share the secrets of our private life, both as they pertain to our wedding bed or to other things. God, in his eternal grace, forbid that I should share these things. A wife should have nothing but honorable things to say about her husband, this I know; and I will tell only you that his worth in bed is not that of a common fly, so help me God.

And yet the most miserable part of my life comes from his miserliness. Now you know as well as I do that women naturally desire six things: they want their husbands to be strong, wise, rich, generous, compliant to their wives's wishes, and energetic in bed. In the name of that same Lord who bled for us, I try to look my best, to honor my husband, and because of that I owe a hundred franks that are due next Sunday, and I am at my wits end for how I will repay them. Yet I would rather never have been born than that I cause my husband a scandal or any other evil thing, and if he finds out about this I might as well give up everything as lost, and so I pray you to lend me this sum, or I will die.

Father John, please lend me the hundred franks, and by God, I will not fail to express my gratitude to you, if but you choose to do as I beg of you. For I will pay you back on a day certain, and I will do for you whatever pleases and serves you, just as you ask me to. And if I do not, may God take vengeance on me, as foul as ever did Ganelon[31] on France.'

The gentle Monk answered her like this: 'No, truly, my own dear beloved; I feel such enormous compassion for you, I swear to you, pledging my word, that as soon as your husband has gone off to Flanders, I will deliver you from all your troubles. I will bring to you the hundred franks you need.' And as he said that, he grabbed her luscious buttocks and embraced her hard and kissed her over and over. 'Now, on your way, swiftly and ever gently, and let us meet again to dine, as soon as possible, for as near as I can tell, it is hard upon prime now. Go, now, and be as true to me as I am to you.'

"May God forbid anything else,' she said and went on her way, as happy as pie, and ordered the cooks to shake a leg — get moving, for people wanted to eat. Then she went to her husband's counting room and boldly knocked on the door.

'*Quy la*?' he asked.[32]

'For the love of Saint Peter, it is your wife," she answered. 'Listen up and tell me just how long you want to wait to have breakfast? How much longer will you be counting and stacking your money and balancing your books and doing whatever you're doing? The Devil take all this balancing. God knows, you have enough of His bounty. Be done in there and let your bags stand where they are. Aren't you ashamed that you've made Father John fast this long, practically the whole morning? Come on, let's hear a Mass and then finally have something to eat.'

---

[31] As the betrayer of Charlemagne in the tales of Roland, Ganelon is the medieval Judas.

[32] Who is there?

'Wife,' he answered, 'you understand little enough of this serious business that we working stiffs have to deal with, as save me God and that blessed Lord we call St. Yvo. Scarcely two out of every twelve will thrive consistently — as things are these days. Oh, sure, we put a good face on it and act happy, and we let the world see our best side and keep mum about the real state of affairs that we endure till death takes us, or we pretend piety and go on pilgrimages, or we just go our way and do as best we can. And that is why I go to all this trouble to deal with this tricky world, because we live in constant fear of some accident or any of the terrible things that can happen in our business dealings.

At day break I am off to Flanders, but I plan to return as soon as possible. And so I must ask you, my dear wife, to be as obedient and meek as you can and to be ever on the lookout for our welfare and to govern the house well and honestly. You know well how I see to it that you have plenty of everything you could ask for to keep a goodly household; you are lacking neither in dress nor in nourishment; and you always have some silver in your purse.'

And with that he shut his counting room door and graciously joined everyone in the house without further delay. Mass was quickly said, and speedily the tables were set, and they sat down to eat, with this Merchant lavishly feeding this Monk.

As soon as they had dined, this Father John took the Merchant aside and soberly told him: 'Dear cousin, I know that you must be off to Bruges and I pray that God and St. Augustin speed and guide you! Please, dear cousin, take good care of yourself, watching carefully what you eat, particularly as hot as it has been these past few days. Farewell, cousin; God protect you from all cares! You know that if you ask anything of me, by day or night, anything that lies in my power to do for you, you need but say so, whatever it is, and it will be done just as you ask.

You and I have always spoken to each with complete honesty. Now, if I may be so bold, in this spirit of honesty, there is one other thing. I would ask you to lend me one hundred franks, just for a week or two, so that I can buy some animals I am charged to acquire in order to stock a place that my monastery owns. As God is my witness, it's too bad it's not your place!

I will not fail to pay you back on the date we agree upon, not by so much as twenty minutes, but I would ask that you keep this matter between the two of us, if I may, because I have to buy these animals before nightfall this very day.

And so I wish you a good journey, my dearest cousin, may God grant you good dealings and a pleasant trip.'

This noble Merchant gently answered right away, 'Oh my dear cousin, Father John, it is little enough that you ask of me. My money is your money anytime you ask for it and, what's more, not just my money but all that I own and possess is yours. Take anything you want; God forbid that you hold back with me!

But there is one thing, and you are fully aware of this, that for merchants like me our money is our plough. We have credit only so long as our reputation is good, and to be without money is not a laughing matter. Pay me back when you find it comfortable to do so; I am happy to do anything I can to make you happy.'

He went at once to fetch the hundred franks and hand them over privately to Father John. No one in the whole world knew of this loan, except for this Merchant and Father John. And so they had another drink, chatted, and walked about for their amusement until it was time for Father John to return to his abbey.

The next morning dawned and the merchant rode forth on his way toward Flanders, his apprentice as his guide, happy to lead him to Bruges. And there the merchant went successfully about his business, buying and bolstering his credit; he neither gambled any of his money away nor did he go dancing, but he behaved himself as is appropriate for a serious merchant. So, I will let him be about his business for now.

The Sunday after the merchant had begun his trip, Father John returned again to St. Denis, his crown and his beard all freshly shaved. In the whole household, from smallest servant on up, everyone was happy that Father John was back again. But to get to the point of my story: the beautiful wife agreed with Father John that his hundred franks should get him the entire night with her in his arms. And this agreement was speedily carried out. They enjoyed themselves that whole night through and then, when it was day, Father John went on his way, leaving the household behind with his jolly: 'Farewell! Have a good day!' No one there, nor anyone in the entire town, had any suspicion of Father John. So he went back to his abbey or wherever he went; I am done with him.

The Merchant, on the other hand, when the business fair was ended, began to make his way back to St. Denis, happy to see his wife and greeting her cheerfully, but he also told her that the merchandise he had bought was so expensive that he had to go to Paris at once to take out a loan. He had bound himself to pay twenty thousand golden shields, but he had certain friends in Paris who would make him loans, and with the money he himself had, he would be able to meet his obligations. Of course, the first thing he did when he came to Paris, because he enjoyed him and because of his affection for him, was to spend time with his friend, Father John. He did not ask him for the money owed, nor did he borrow any money from him; he was just happy to see him, to inquire if he was well, and to tell him of his business affairs — as good friends do. And, of course, Father John prepared a feast for him and was very happy to see him. His friend made sure to tell him how he had bought well and successfully, but that he now, in all candor, needed to borrow some money and then he would be just fine.

Father John said to him: 'You know how happy I am that you have returned safely from your trip, and you know that if I were rich, you should not have to worry about where to get the twenty thousand shields you need, especially as you so kindly just the other day lent me money when I needed it; and I am forever at your service and grateful to you, by God and by St. James. But to put all that behind us, I took the money back to our beloved lady, your wife, at home — precisely the same amount you lent me and paid it at your own table; she knows all about it, to be sure, and I have proof positive of her that I returned the money to her. But now, dear friend, you must give me leave to go, for our abbot needs to go on a trip and I must accompany him. My best greetings to your lovely wife, my own sweet niece, and fare you well, dearest cousin of mine, until we meet again.'

Our Merchant, a very wise and experienced man of the world, gained the credit he needed and paid the specific sums of gold that he owed to certain Lombard bankers, maintaining as he always did his good reputation. He then returned to his home, happy as a parrot. For he knew well that his estate was such that he was sure to make a thousand franks on his deal.

His wife met him with great joy at the gate to their estate, as was her custom from long ago, and they spent the entire night enjoying each other's bodies; for he was rich and totally debt free. At dawn, this merchant began anew to embrace his wife and kissed her face and made it very clear that he was not done with her. 'Enough, already,' she cried out, 'you've had enough!' But she returned his wanton playing again until at last the merchant said: 'I am a little angry with you, by God, even though it may upset you for me to raise it. Do you know what I'm talking about? I'm upset with you because it appears, God knows, you got involved in an arrangement Father John had with me. You should have warned me before I left that he had paid you one hundred franks in ready cash; for he thought himself ill-used when I spoke to him of having to borrow money; at last it seemed to me that way, judging by his appearance. But you must know, before God, our heavenly king, I never had in mind to ask him to repay a loan at any time. So I beg of you, my wife, that you never do such a thing again. Tell me anytime I am gone if any debtor has, in my absence, paid you, lest through your failure to do so I might ask him for something he has already paid.'

The wife was neither frightened nor caught off guard but boldly answered, without hesitation: 'By sweet Mary, I place all the blame on that false monk, Father John! I never gave him any tokens, that's for sure! He gave me a certain amount of gold, that's true. But, may his monkey's snout be damned, in the name of God, if I didn't believe that he had given me the money from you in honor of and to help me express our kinship, and also of course for the good time he has enjoyed here so often. But now I understand the difficulty he has placed me in, so I will answer directly and to the point.

You have far slower debtors than me! For I will pay you happily each and every day, and if ever I fail to do so, why, I am your wife, so charge all payment to my account. And that way you can always be assured that I will pay you as quickly as ever is possible. For, as God is my witness, I have not wasted a penny of this money but have used it all to appear beautiful for you, and I have used it well, honoring you always. And since I have used it so profitably by God, I say, let us not be angry with other but let us laugh and amuse ourselves. I will not pay any other way but only in your bed, where I pledge my luscious body to you, anytime, by God,. So forgive me, my one and only dearest spouse, turn to me and enjoy all this.'

The merchant, seeing that there was no other remedy and chiding her would be pure folly since what happened could not be changed, said: "Now, wife, all is indeed forgotten and forgiven, but I hope you will never be this generous again, as long as you live. Keep better charge of your goods; this I charge you with.' That is how my story ends; may God always ensure that we have enough credit to last us our whole lives."

Now our Host spoke: 'Well said, by *corpus dominus*![33] May you sail safely near the coast for many years to come, Sir noble master, noble mariner. May God give that Monk a thousand years of bad luck! Ha! I say to all men who will hear it: my fellows, be careful of japes such as this. Surely this Monk made a monkey of a man, and of his wife, also, by Saint Augustin! The lesson here is never to let a monkey enter your inn in the first place!'

Many of us seemed to wait for him to say more, as we did not understand just what he meant. But our Host remained silent for a moment, as if he had said too much, already. And that brief silence was filled by the Merchant on our pilgrimage.

---

[33] Body of the Lord,

"I could tell you plenty stories of weeping and sadness and betrayal and sorrow aplenty, as can many another man who has had the pleasure of wedded bliss visited upon him. I have no doubt about the truth of that."

He and the Host exchanged wry smiles and meaningful glances, and the Host did a low sweeping bow to the Merchant, before that worthy individual went on: "I have a wife who proves every day that she is the worst that one could ever have. For even if the devil himself were wedded to her I dare well swear to it that she would be more than his match. But what's the point of spelling out for you all the terrible things she does as a matter of rote every day? She is, in a word, the worst kind of shrew. Were I not already married, I swear to this assembled group, I would never be caught again in that trap. We married men live lives full of sorrow and care — ask anyone you know or run into, and I speak God's truth, by St. Thomas of India, at least for the majority — I say not all. God forbid that it should ever be so!"

He looked again at the Host and spoke: "Oh, fair Sir Host, I will admit that I have been married only these two months, no more, by God, and yet I am certain that a man who stays single his entire life, though others may stab him in the heart, will never be able to tell of as much suffering as I can recount of my wife's evils."

The Host seemed very sympathetic to the Merchant, patting him on the back and saying: "Now, my dear Merchant, may God bless and keep you. Since you seem to know so much about all that, please tell on and share what you know with the rest of us."

"I will gladly tell a tale. But of mine own sorrow, even though my heart is heavy, I will say nothing more."

The Merchant's Tale

"There once was a worthy knight in Lombardy, born in Pavia, and he lived there in great prosperity his entire life. He had been a single man for sixty years and enjoyed all the bodily delights of women whenever his desire moved him — just like many foolish men everywhere. And when he had passed his sixtieth year — whether it was for the sake of holiness or simply because of dotage, I am not certain — this knight took such a fancy to being a married man that he spent every waking minute trying to find a proper partner; and he prayed constantly to our Lord that he might be allowed to know the blissful life that can be found between a husband and wife, and to live forever under that holy bond with which God first bound man and woman. 'No other life,' he would say, 'is worth a bean, for wedlock is so easy and so pure that it is very paradise on earth.' This is the way everyone heard this old wise knight speaking about it.

And certainly, as eternally true as God is king, to take a wife is a glorious thing, particularly when a man is old and grey. Then is his wife the very fruit of his treasure; then he shall find a young, beautiful woman who can give him an heir, and he can lead his life in joy and comfort, whereas these single men know no song but 'alas,' as soon as they find adversity in love, which is nothing but childish vanity to begin with. For everyone knows that the lives of single men often are full of pain and woe; for they have built on shaky ground, and where they look for certainty, insecurity is all they find. Their lives are no different than those of the birds and beasts, full of freedom, with no boundaries, while married men in their estate live a blissful and ordered lives.

A married man's life abounds in joy and bliss, for who is more obedient than a wife? Who is as true and as attentive to a married man, whether sick or well, as is his mate? For she will not forsake him, whether he is well or not, loving and serving him tirelessly, though he lie bedridden till he dies.

And yet there are learned men who say this is not so, one of them being Theophrastus. Little does it matter that Theophrastus is lying when he says: 'Take no wife into your household just because you want to save some money. A faithful servant does more to keep down expenses than does your own wife, for she will claim that she is owed half of all you own. And if you fall sick, your friends, or a faithful servant will take much better care of you than she who has been waiting her whole life for the day when she gets everything you have. For if you take a wife into your home, the odds are that you will end up a cuckold.' Such stuff, and hundred times worse, does this man write, may God curse his bones!

But do not listen to such advice; ignore this Theophrastus and listen to me.

A wife is the very gift of God to a man; all other gifts, be they lands, fees, pasture — shared or held privately — are not really gifts; as the gifts of Fortune they will all pass on like shadows do upon a wall. Listen to me, as I say plainly a wife will endure and live forever in your home; by chance, wedded bliss may last longer than you expected."

"Truer words than these were never spoken," interjected our Host. "I know from my own experience that married life can last for a long, long time, and I myself can swear to that. But I don't understand what else you are saying. You seem to say both that marred life is bliss and that it is hell. God knows, I need no-one to teach me this, but which is it you are saying?"

"Listen but to what I say and to my tale," the Merchant responded, "and you shall know what I am saying.

Now, where was I , , , oh yes , , , marriage is one of the great sacraments. I consider anyone who does not have a wife to be damaged, for he lives without help and all alone — I am speaking, of course, of the people who are secular. And listen to why I am saying this — I don't say this lightly or without reason — woman was created to be man's helper. The Lord Almighty, after He made Adam, and saw how he was all alone, naked as a new-born, in His great goodness said: 'Let us now make a helper for this man, someone like himself.' And then He created Eve for him. Here may you see, and hereby is proven, that women are made to be men's helper and comfort, his earthly paradise and his pleasure. Women are so obedient and virtuous that, obviously, men and women live in unity. They are one flesh, and one flesh, it seems to me, has only one heart, the same in good times and in bad.

A wife? Oh, may the Virgin Mary bless me! How is it even possible for a married man to experience any adversity? As God is my witness, I have no explanation for that! No tongue can tell or heart imagine the bliss that exists between the two. If he be poor, why she helps him work; she keeps his goods and wastes never a bit of them; she likes the same things her husband likes and never dreams of saying 'no' when he says 'yes.' If he says 'do this,' she says only 'already done, sir.'

Oh, blissful state of precious marriage, you are so joyful and so virtuous and so recommended and approved by all that every man who has one should fall on his bare knees and thank God for sending him his wife — or else he should pray that God send him a wife to share the rest of his life. For then his life is rooted in security. He may never be deceived, it seems to me, if only he follows his wife's advice. In that case he can hold up his head with pride, for wives are ever true and always wise; and therefore, if you want to act like a wise man you must always do what your wife tells you to do. "

"Sir Host," interrupted the noble Wife of Bath, "I can see why you have been confused as to what the worthy Merchant is saying, but it seems to me that he is quite clear now and there can be no doubt about his slanderous attack on women, especially wives. He is mocking every good woman who ever lived and scurrilously lying about women and their goodness and wisdom."

"Is he indeed? It still seems to me that he is telling us all about the benefits of marriage."

"And so I am," the Merchant reclaimed his turn to tell his tale, frowning at the Wife. "Behold, how Jacob, as scholars tell us, following the good counsel of his mother Rebecca, bound the skin of the young goats about his neck in order to gain his blind father's blessing! Behold how Judith, as the story also tells us, through her wise counsel saved God's people and killed Holofernes while he was sleeping! Behold Abigail, whose sage advice saved her husband Nabal when he was about to be killed! Behold Esther, whose apt words delivered the people of God from suffering and her uncle Mordechai from being executed by her husband Assuere! This is why Seneca tells us that that there is nothing in the world more valuable than a humble wife."

"Humble, indeed," the Wife again broke in. "Now you can all see what he is saying. He wants women to stay in their place, and he tells us his examples of wise women who sacrificed themselves for men and then concludes that women are to be humble. You may fool some of these men here on our pilgrimage, but it takes more than this to hoodwink us women."

"Hoodwink, Madam?" answered the Merchant, smiling a thin smile at her. "Why, dear Lady, I am doing anything but hoodwinking. I am extolling the virtues of virtuous women and, I dare say, will continue to do so, if you but allow me to finish my story."

The Wife harrumphed and shook her head but, defeated for now, waved for the Merchant to continue. And he did.

"Many noble learned men agree with everything I am saying. Cato bids us to accept the chiding of a wife's tongue. She is to command, and you shall allow that; yet she will obey you for courtesy's sake. A wife is the keeper of the household, and that is why the sick man with no wife to keep his house can only wail and complain. I warn you, if you wish to act wisely, love your life well, as Christ loves His church. If you care for yourself you will love your wife. No man hates his own flesh, but tries to make it feel ever better, and therefore I tell you to cherish your wife or you will never prosper. Whatever men may say in joking or in their games, husband and wife are on the best path that people can find. They are knit together so well that no harm may separate them, particularly as far as the wife is concerned.

And that is why this January, whom I started to tell you about, in his time of old age, gave much thought to the rich life, the virtuous peace that is as sweet in marriage as honey. So, one day he sent for his friends to advise him on his intentions.

With a serious countenance he told them his story, saying: 'My friends, I am old and grey, and nearly, as God knows, on the brink of the grave. I believe that now is the time to think about the welfare of my soul. I know I have foolishly wasted my body, but I thank God for giving me the chance to change this!

I have decided to get married, and I want to do this as soon as possible — of course, to some sweet maid who is beautiful and young. I ask all of you now to help prepare for my marriage immediately, for I am in a great hurry. I will do what I can to find someone I can marry right away. But I have to assume that as there are many more of you than of me by myself, you will be more likely to find just the right alliance for me than I could on my own.

But I warn you of one thing, my dear friends, namely under no circumstances will I consider an old woman. She shall not be older than twenty, at most, because I like old fish and new flesh. Everybody knows that an old pike is better than a young, while tender veal is preferable to old.

I want no woman who is thirty or more years of age; I have no interest in bean stalks and dried forage. And these ancient widows, God knows, they are so practiced at deception and so good at mischief when they are not happy, that I would not have a moment of peace with one of them. Now much schooling produces much subtlety, and women are practically scholars of subtlety. But a man's hand may guide a fresh young thing, just as one can shape warm wax with one's hands.

And that is why I tell you again — and you should hear me clearly — that this is why I will have no old wife. I am certain that that if I had the bad luck of finding no pleasure in her, I should live my life in adultery and go straight to the devil when I die. Nor would I beget children from her! And I would rather mad dogs chewed me up than that my estate should fall into the hands of strangers. I am not in my dotage, and I'll tell you this much: I know full well why men should marry. I am not like those fools who know no more than my simplest servant nothing about marriage or why a man should marry.

A man who is unable to lead a chaste life should take a devoted wife and enjoy lawful procreation of children in honor of God and not just to have a paramour or someone to sleep with. And the couple should eschew lechery and pay their debt to each other when it is due.

Now this living together in chastity as do brother and sister, assisting each other's mischief, this, thank you very much, is not for me. For — and thanks be to God — I am not bragging to say that I am strong in limb and quite capable of performing as a man — I know exactly what I am capable of,'"

"That's the first thing you've said, Sir Merchant, that I can agree with," the Wife of Bath interrupted. "And I do so most heartily!"

The Merchant frowned, bowed sarcastically in the direction of the good Wife, and continued.

"As I was saying, the Merchant in my story told his assembled friends: 'I may be grey, but I am like a tree that blossoms before fruit grows on it; and we know that trees that blossom are neither dry nor dead. I feel grey only on top of my head; my heart and my limbs are all as green as laurel is throughout the year. So, now you have heard everything I intend to do, and I ask you all to agree, please, with what I am saying.'

Then some men there told various old stories about marriage; some blamed it and some praised it, but in the end, as is common in discussions, two of January's brothers, named Placebo and Justinius, fell into disagreement.

Placebo said: 'My dear brother January, you have no need, dear Lord of mine, to ask us assembled here for any advice, since you yourself, in your wisdom, have decided, based on your great prudence, to ignore Solomon's teaching: "Make all decisions based on advice, and you shall never have reason for regret." And, despite King Solomon's words, my own dear brother and lord, may God bring my soul to rest if I do not think your own counsel best.

For brother of mine, hear this now from me: I have been a man of the court for all of my life and, God knows, though I may be unworthy, I have much experience with many lords of very high degree and I have never disagreed with a single one of them. Truly, I have never said anything contrary to them, for I know full well that my lord always knows more than do I. I believe whatever he says to be right and just, and I will say the same as he does — or something just like what he said. Any advisor who serves a lord of high degree is a a great fool if he dares presume or even thinks that his advice is superior to his lord's.

Nay, lords are no fools, by my faith! You yourself have demonstrated here today such wisdom, so well-expressed and so complete, that I consent and affirm entirely all of your words and your opinion. By God, there is not a man in this town, or in all of Italy, for that matter, who could have said it better! Christ Himself could find no better advice than yours. And truly, by my father's kin, it is a bold act for any man advanced in age to take a young wife. But you have the heart of a young man, so jolly are you! Please do in this situation as you wish, for I am sure it will be for the best.'

Justinius, who had sat silently and listened, now spoke: 'January, dearest brother of mine, you have spoken; now listen to what I have to say. I advise you, by all that is holy, to take your time. Seneca, among many other wise things, said that a man ought to think carefully about whom he gives his lands or his animals. And since I ought to think long and hard about whom I give my possessions to, how much more should I consider carefully to whom I give dominion over my body forever.

I give you fair warning that it is no child's play to take a wife without careful consideration. A man should find out — this is my opinion — whether she is wise, sober, addicted to drink, proud, or in some other way a shrew; whether she be accustomed to scolding; if she is someone who will waste your property; whether she is rich or poor, or as easily angered as is a man. It is true that in this whole wide world no man will find someone who is perfect, neither man, nor beast, nor anything one can imagine; nevertheless, it ought to be sufficient in any woman if she has more virtues than vices — but all this takes time to determine.

God knows, I have shed many a private tear since I myself took a wife. More power to him who chooses the life of a married man; certainly I find in it but expense and care and duty, but no joy. And yet, God knows and my neighbors will testify to this, among women as a whole I have the most steadfast wife and the gentlest one they have ever met. But then, I am the only one who can know where my shoe squeezes my foot.

As far as I'm concerned, you can do whatever you want, but remember that you are a man of my age and whatever marriage you enter, particularly one with a young, beautiful wife, by the God who made water and earth and air, the youngest man among us here has his hands full if he tries to have his wife only to himself. Trust me, before three years have passed, your days of pleasing her will be over — by that I mean, your ability to satisfy her completely will be gone. There are a lot of duties required by a wife, and I can only hope that this does not end badly for you.'

'Fine' said January, 'are you done? Because I want to say: to hell with your Seneca and all your proverbs! I wouldn't give a bread-basket full of herbs for your learned comments. Men far wiser than you have agreed with my present intentions. What do you say, Placebo?'

'I say it is a cursed man indeed,' said he, 'who does not engage in matrimony, and that is a fact.'

With that, all rose, agreeing that he should be married to whom he chose and wherever he had a hankering."

"Oho," broke in the Wife of Bath, "I can see already how this is going to end. Could you at least tell a story that is less predictable and transparent? Ladies, help me out, here. Who doesn't know how this is going to end?"

"Well, I, for one, do not," the Host joined in. "I have no idea how this story is going to end."

"In that case," the Wife continued, "you are exactly what I thought you were and God help us all to be under your yardstick."

"I am not certain what you are saying," the Host answered her," but if it is what I think you are saying, you have said more than enough, and we should now let our friend the Merchant be about his business and tell his story. Go on, Sir Merchant, finish your tale. I can't wait to find out how it ends."

"And so I will," the Merchant said, smiling his thin smile, "I shall finish it right, just as it needs to be finished.

Every day from then on, January's spirit was totally engaged in indulging in his wild imagination and his constant thought of his impending marriage. His nights were filled with many a fair face and many a voluptuous shape passing before him, as if someone had placed a shiny, clear mirror in the common marketplace, where he could watch people pass by before his eyes. But he also began thinking about and evaluating the young girls who lived near him. He didn't know which one to linger over, for one had a beautiful face, another had a positive reputation for seriousness and a disposition that made everyone like her. Some were rich but had bad reputations.

Finally, his serious thoughts and his playful ones came together and he chose one girl in particular, purging all the rest from his heart. He chose her all on his own, because love is blind and cannot see what is right in front of it. And at night, when he was alone in his bed, he imagined in his heart and in his thoughts her fresh beauty and her tender age, her tiny waist, her long and slender arms, her wise bearing, her gentility, her womanly carriage and her seriousness. And when he had picked her, his decision was final and irrevocable, and he would consider no other.

Once he had made his choice, he thought every other man's wit so faulty that he could say nothing meaningful to oppose him; such was his fantasy. He hurriedly sent for his friends and asked them to do him the honor of attending him at once. He wanted to shorten their labor, one and all; there was no more need for them to ride about, searching, for he had decided where to place his affection.

Placebo and January returned, as did all of January's friends, and January began by asking them all a favor, and that was that none of them would disagree with him and argue with the decision he had made. He added that his decision was the will of God and would be the basis of all his future prosperity.

He told them there was a girl in that town whose beauty was widely the topic of conversation, though she came of an unimportant family. And that girl, he told them, was so young and beautiful that he had chosen her for his wife, to help him lead a life of pleasure and holiness. And he thanked God for her and for the bliss he would share with no one else. And he asked them all to take up his cause and make sure that he would succeed in his suit. For that, he told them, would put his soul at peace. He concluded: 'There is nothing to spoil my joy except for one thing that troubles my conscience, which I will acknowledge and share with all of you.

    I heard a long time ago, that no man may experience perfect bliss twice — that is to say, here on earth and in heaven also. Though a man may keep himself from the seven mortal sins and from every branch of that tree of sins, there is still such perfect felicity and such great peace and pleasure in marriage that I am afraid, at my old age, I shall lead a life so joyful, so wonderful, without any woe or strife, that I shall have my heaven here on earth. And since to enter heaven itself is only possible at an enormous price of tribulations and great penance, how should I, who is about to live in the utter pleasure that married men have with their wives, ever achieve that heavenly bliss in which I will live with Christ for eternity? This is my great fear, my two beloved brothers, and I need your help in resolving this issue.'

Justinius, upon hearing this folly, answered this silliness as appropriate, but he did not call on any authorities to bolster his argument because he wanted his answer to be short and to the point. He simply said: 'Sir, if there is no other obstacle than this, the Almighty may just work a miracle for you in His great mercy and make it possible for you to repent yourself of married life even before you complete the holy rights of Holy Mother Church that will introduce you to that married life you claim to be without strife whatsoever. I doubt that God showers more grace upon a married man to repent than He does on one who is single!

So, dear Sir, let me assure you by all that is holy: you have nothing to worry about. It's entirely possible that she just might be your purgatory. She may be the very instrument and whip of God, and your soul will skip up to heaven faster than an arrow leaves a bow. I hope to God that you shall learn that there is no such great felicity in marriage, nor ever more shall be, that it will rob you of your salvation, so long as you reply to the desires of your wife with temperance, as is proper and reasonable, and you pressure her not too amorously, and that you stay away from other sin.

I have told you all that I know, all that my limited wit can produce. Don't let my advice frighten you off, dear brother, but let us be done with all this.

If only you had listened to the Wife of Bath — who is close at hand — on this topic of marriage! She has described it well, in only a few words. May you fare well; God keep you in His grace.'"

We were all, especially the Wife of Bath, taken aback by these words coming from the mouth of the Merchant by way of Justinius. Or so it seemed to me. Nevertheless, confused as we were, no one said anything to interrupt him, and he continued, unabashed.

"At this, Justinius and his brother took their leave of January and of each other. They had seen the inevitable, so each did what he could to further the necessary agreements for this girl, May, to marry this January as quickly as possible. It would take far too long for me to describe every legal document and bond by which she was endowed with his property — or even to describe her rich outfit. But before long the day came that they went to the church to receive the holy sacrament. The priest appeared with his stole around his neck and bade her be like Sarah and Rebecca in wisdom and in faithfulness to her vows; and he said the usual prayers, and blessed them and asked God to bless them and secured them in the holy bonds of matrimony.

And the blissful couple sat down to feast with the other people on the dais. The place was filled with joy and happiness, with music and with the most delicious food that could be found in all of Italy. For their entertainment instruments were played with sounds more harmonious than Orpheus or Amphion of Thebes had ever produced. Each course was accompanied by music so lively that the trumpeter Joab had never heard the like nor Theodomas at the siege of Thebes, when that city was imperiled. Bacchus himself liberally poured the wine.

And Venus smiled upon all there, for January had become her knight, eager to express his desires both in his life as a free man and in marriage. And she, twirling her firebrand in her hand, danced before the feast and the entire company. And I say without hesitation that Hymen, who is the God of wedded bliss, never had seen such a happy groom in all his life. Hold your peace, you poet Martianus Capelus, who describes for us that joyful wedding of Philology and Mercury and of the songs sung by the Muses themselves! Your pen and your tongue are insufficient to do justice to this wedding.

When tender youth has married stooping old age the joy cannot be described in words. Try it out yourself — then you will know whether I have lied or told the truth.

But this was too much for the Wife of Bath, as she snorted loudly, raised herself in her saddle and proclaimed: "Sir Merchant, now I am totally confused by your words . . . they seem to wander about willfully, like the stream that meanders through the meadow near my house. Either such a marriage as you are telling us about is blissful or it is not. You seem to forget from moment to moment what you have just told us. Now you call January foolish — now you praise him for his wisdom in choosing such a young bride. I must ask you, finally, to say which it is. Is he as wise as Solomon or as foolish as Midas? I beg of you, make it clear!"

This outburst appeared to mirror the questions of others, as a number of pilgrims expressed their agreement.

But the Merchant was not troubled and simply answered: "Please be patient and allow my story to speak for itself."

"That is at it should be," the Host chimed in. "We do not require the glossing of a learned text. We have agreed to tell our stories, not to preach at one another. Please continue," he nodded to the Merchant, who nodded in return and did just that.

"At the wedding feast, May sat there with such a wonderful smile on her face that it was enchanting just to look at. Not even Queen Esther looked at King Assuer with such a look — so devout a look had May. I cannot do justice to her beauty, but this much I can say: she was true to her name, like a bright May morning, radiant with beauty and happiness. And January was transported each time he looked at her, and in his imagination he envisioned how he would ravage her in his arms that night, harder than ever Paris did Helen. But at the same time he worried that he would offend her then, and he thought: 'Alas, tender creature, I hope to God you can endure my passion. It is so sharp and keen that I fear you cannot sustain it. And God forbid that I apply all my might to you. I wish with all my heart though that it were already dark and that our night together would last forever. I wish all these people would go home.' And so he did what he could, subtly and within the boundaries of courtesy, to encourage everyone to leave the feast.

Finally, the last guests rose from their seats and those still remaining drank and danced a little faster and cast spices all around the house. Everyone was full of joy and bliss, all but a certain squire, named Damyan, who generally carved the lord's meat. He was so taken by the Lady May that the pain he was in nearly drove him mad. He was close to fainting and falling over where he stood, so sharply did Venus singe him with her torch when she was leading the dance. So he went quickly to bed, and I have no more to say of him right now, but I let him weep and mourn until the time comes when the beautiful May has pity on his pain.

Oh, you perilous fire that breeds in the straw of our beds! Oh, homegrown foe, that offers his service! Oh, servant traitor, false enemy within! Oh, you false adder that hides secretly in one's bosom. May God always protect us from you! Oh, January, in your drunken stupor of the pleasures of marriage, behold how your own squire Damyan, your sworn servant, makes plans to do evil unto you. God grant that you see the snake in your own home. For there is no plague worse in this world than is that homegrown enemy who spends all day in your presence.

The time has come when the sun has completed its daily ark across the sky and its body no longer hangs on the horizon in that latitude; night spreads his dark, rough mantel across the entire hemisphere. At last the celebrating troop has left the house of January, with thanks from all, and they ride home full of gusto, where they do the things they must do and, when the time comes, at last they also go to bed. And, of course, this impatient January wants nothing more than to go to bed himself; he downs great portions of the spiced wines of various kind meant to increase passion; and many other potions does he partake of, as he has learned from that cursed monk Constantinus Africanus, who has written all about them in his book *De coitu*.[34]

January has not skimped on anything he could possibly take, and now he begs his good friends: 'For the love of God, please leave my home, all of you, and soon, so you can make your way home.'

And they do as he asks them.

They have their final drink and the curtains are drawn.

The bride is brought to bed motionless as a stone and, as soon as the priest has blessed that bed, everyone has left the chamber, leaving old January to take young May, his paradise, his mate, in his arms; he holds her tight, kissing her over and over. But she cares little enough for his rough beard with its thick bristles

---

[34] *Liber de coitu—The Book on Intercourse.*

cutting into her soft skin like a dogfish, sharp as a briar — for he was all newly shaven in the current style, He rubs her hard on her tender face, saying: 'Alas, I must now trespass against you, my dear spouse, and offend you greatly, when the time comes that I climb on top of you. But remember,' he said, 'no workman worth his hire can work quickly and do his job well; my work will be done leisurely but perfectly. It does not matter how long we play, for we are bonded in true wedlock; and blessed be the yoke in which we cannot offend, for a man cannot sin with his wife, no matter what the two of them do together.'"

At this the Monk on our pilgrimage cleared his throat and interrupted the Merchant: "I must correct you there, Sir Merchant. It is not so that a man and wife can commit no sin. The law of Holy Mother Church tells us that they may engage in what you are referring to as their "work" only to the extent that they are seeking to create children of God and as long as they take no pleasure in the acts they perform. This is what the blessed Doctors of the Church teach us."

"What," countered the Merchant? "You say that a man and wife may have no pleasure in wedded bliss. Why, this is nonsense, and no God would forbid us from what He has given us to enjoy. After all, no one cuts himself with his own knife."

"And," the Wife of Bath once more entered the argument, "again I must agree with the Merchant. Why did God, as I have asked before, give us our things of joy if not to play with them and to use them as is proper in our own wedded bed?"

"Madam," the Monk bowed and answered, "I but share with you the teachings of Holy Mother Church."

"Well, truly, I thank you for that," continued the Merchant, "and it may be what the learned scholars say, those who also know many angels can dance on the head of a pin, but where I come from it is more commonly known what people do. Everyone I know believes I am speaking true, and so I will carry on. As I said, no man cuts himself with his own knife, and so our January explained to his young bride, May, that they could enjoy themselves as long as they wished, being now tied to each other in the bond of marriage instituted by God Himself.

And so he worked on her all through the night, and when the dawn rose in the east, he took a sop of fine claret wine and sat upright in his bed, loudly and clearly singing a morning song unmatched by any cock in the yard, and then he kissed his wife again and renewed their wanton pleasure. He was like a young colt, full of passion, and as full of playful talk as is a speckled magpie. The slack skin hanging from his neck shook while he was singing, so vigorously did he chant and croak.

God only knows what poor May was thinking all this time, faced with his scrawny neck as he sat upright in his nightshirt and nightcap. I know that she found his lovemaking not worth a bean. Then he said: 'Now I will rest; day has come and I need my sleep.' And he immediately fell asleep until past prime. And when he saw what time it was, he got up, as did the beautiful May, though she had to keep to her room until after the fourth day, as is the usage of good wives. For every worker sometime deserves rest, lest he not endure the term of his work. This is true for all living creatures, be they fish or bird, animal or human.

Now I must return to woeful Damyan, who, as I told you before, was languishing in love. If I could speak to him, I would tell him: 'O foolish Damyan, alas! Tell me this, if you can: how will you ever be able to tell properly your lady, that beautiful young May, about your love? She will surely turn you down. And if you say anything to her, she will reveal what you tell her. May God help you! I wish I had better news for you!'

This Damyan is burning up in the fire of Venus, so strongly does his desire torment him. He finally decides that he will risk everything, for he cannot continue any longer without doing something. So, he borrows pen and paper and writes all his sorrow down in a letter, a kind of lover's complaint or love song, written to his beautiful young Lady, May. He puts that letter in a silken purse that he wears at all times near his heart.

The moon, in Taurus on the day that January wed his beautiful young May, has now slid into Cancer, and May has stayed in her chambers as long as these nobles do — the rule is that a bride shall not eat in the common hall till day four, or day three, at least, and then she can feast from one noon to the next after the third day has passed. So now, the high Mass has been said and January and May, always as beautiful as a young spring day, have taken their seats in the hall again. And just then Damyan came to mind for this good man, this January, and he asked: 'By the Virgin Mary, how is it that Damyan is not attending to me? Is he not well, or what is keeping him from his duties?' His other squires, standing nearby, excused Damyan for his sickness, which prevented him from carrying out his duties — nothing else would keep him from service.

'I would think so,' said January. 'He is a noble squire, I can vouch for that! It would be a shame and terrible if he died. He is as smart, discreet and as able to keep a secret as is any man of his degree that I know, and on top of that he is quite manly and ever ready to serve, and he has all the makings of being a success. So once we have eaten I will visit him, along with May, to see how we can comfort him.' And everyone there gave him much credit for these words that, in his bounty and nobility, showed his interest in providing comfort for his sick squire — this was indeed noble.

'My Lady,' this January then said to May, 'do as I say. After dinner you and your ladies, when you are assembled in your hall, all shall go and see this Damyan and entertain him — he is a noble young man. And tell him that as soon as I have finished my nap I intend to visit him, and hurry with this because I will be waiting to sleep next to you in our bed.' And then he called to him a squire who was the hall marshal and discussed certain things with him and told him what he wanted him to do.

And this lovely May, along with her entourage of women, went straight away to see Damyan. She sat down by his bed and comforted him as gently as possible. Now this Damyan, when he saw his chance, secretly placed in her hand his purse and his letter in which he had written what he desired, sighing and moaning deeply, as if in pain the whole time. Now, under his breath, he speaks to her: 'Mercy, Sweet Lady! Do not let me be found out, for I am a dead man if this thing be known.' In one motion she hides the purse away in her bosom and is on her way — that's all I'm going to say, for now.

She returns to January and sits gently on the side of his bed, where he grabs and kisses her before he lies back and goes to sleep. Then May pretends that she has to go to that place where you know every human has to go now and then. There she reads the letter, tears it into small pieces, and deposits it in the privy.

Who starts to think and plan now, if not the lovely May, lying next to old January? As soon as he starts from sleep, startled awake by his own coughing, he asks May to take off all her clothes. He needs her to do him some pleasure, he says, and her clothes get in the way. Of course she accommodates him — whether her heart's in it or not. But lest the more squeamish here among us be angry at me, I dare not describe just what exactly he does to her — or whether she thought herself in paradise or in hell. I will simply leave them to do what they do — and that they do until the bell for evensong has wrung and they have to get up.

I don't know if it was destiny or chance, or heavenly powers or nature or the constellations above; whatever it was that the time was right. As the learned clerics tell us, for everything there is a time — if that includes seeking a married woman's love, I cannot say, but God Almighty, who knows that nothing happens without a reason, will determine all. Far be it from me to judge. The truth is that this young, beautiful May was so affected that day by the sight of sick young Damyan, that she was unable to drive away, no matter how hard she tried, the memory of his plea to be merciful to him. 'As God help me,' she thinks, 'I don't care about whomever this may make unhappy, for I know that I love him above all other beings in the world, even if he has no more than his shirt to his name.'

Behold, how quickly a noble heart can be moved!

And here you can see just how deeply the generosity of spirit runs in women when they consider things carefully. There may be some who are tyrant enough and have a heart of stone; they would have let him die rather than grant him their grace, rejoicing in their cruel pride, without knowing or caring that they had just killed a man."

Our Knight, who had been frowning off and on for some time now, listening more and more impatiently to the words of the Merchant, now spoke up: "Sir Merchant, I must object. Surely, we cannot call this love. No woman is so immediately smitten by the arrows of Cupid as to forget her wedding vows so quickly and agree to what you seem to be saying . . . . How can you call this love? . . . This is not love, for as shown in the tale I shared here with you but yesterday morning—"

"By the hair on the Virgin's holy chin," the Miller boldly interrupted, "your tale showed nothing but the silliness . . . the prattle so-called noble people spread about that we all know to be but straw and chaff. Real people do exactly what Damyan and May are about to do and don't give an old working horse's fart for what you call love."

"Come, come, now,' the Host commanded the Miller. "Stop this at once, you crude villain. This is no way to address a noble Knight or . . . any of us, in truth. Whatever you may believe, you have no right to speak this way or to correct anyone here. Enough!"

He turned to the Merchant and said: "Please finish your tale as best you can. I will attempt to stop any other interruptions."

That worthy pilgrim seemed to sneer a bit at the Miller — or was it the Knight? — as he returned to his tale, continuing again as if there had been no interruption.

"Our noble May, filled with pity, at once wrote a letter to Damyan in her own hand, in which she granted him her true love."

And he stressed these last words while he snuck in another brief look at the Knight.

"There now lacked only the time and the place in which she might slake his lust, for she was perfectly willing to do all he desired. And when she saw her chance, on a certain day, off to visit Damyan went young May, where she subtly thrust this letter under his pillow for him to read at his own leisure. She takes his hand in hers and holds it fervently but so secretly that no one notices, and bids him to be better soon; and then she goes to see January, who has called for her.

The next morning young Damyan rises afresh from his sickbed, leaving all sorrow behind. He combs his hair; he preens; he cleans up; he does everything that he thinks his lady wants and expects of him; and he is off to see January, fawning, like a dog trained for an archer. He is so pleasant to one and all (for slyness is everything; let him who can , , , be sly), that there is no one who has anything bad to say of him, and he stands completely in the full graces of his lady. But here is where I leave Damyan to go about his business, as I continue on with my story.

Some learned scholars believe that happiness is rooted in enjoying everything as much as we can. January, subscribing to this belief fully, makes sure he lives in total joy, but always appropriate to the honor of a noble knight. His home, his clothing — all are fit for a king, as much as his means allow. So, among many other things meant to demonstrate his high honor, he had a garden built, walled all about with stone — unlike anything I have ever seen anywhere else. I doubt that the author of the *Roman of the Rose*[35] could do justice to its beauty. Priapus[36] himself, though he is the god of gardens, could not fail to have been impressed by the beauty of this garden or of the well that was placed under the evergreen laurel. It was so beautiful that many a time the god Pluto, his queen Proserpina, as well as their entourage of fairies, danced and entertained themselves around that very same well — or so people say.

So much did old January take pleasure in walking there and delighting in this place that he allowed no one else to have the

---

[35] One of the most influential works of the western Middle Ages, the original *Romand de la Rose* (and its continuation by a second author) influenced and inspired many medieval poets who wrote about romantic love, including Chaucer.

[36] Greek god of fertility, frequently depicted with a giant, erect phallus.

key but himself. He always kept on his person his silver latchkey to the small wicker gate through which, when he felt like it, he let himself in. And when he felt like paying his debt to his wife in the summer, this is where the two of them would go privately, to do there in that garden such things as they could only do there. And this is how January and lovely May spent many a merry summer's day.

But worldly love lasts only so long, for January, as for every other creature that ever lived.

Oh, sudden chance! Oh, you unpredictable Fortune! Deceptive as the scorpion that flatters with your head as you are about to sting with your tail! Your tail is death, so full of venom! Oh, uncertain joy! Oh, sweet pleasurable venom! Oh, monster — so subtly can you make your gifts appear to be lasting to make fools of us all! Why have you deceived poor old January in this way after you seemed to make him your friend forever?

Suddenly you have taken away the sight in both his eyes and he is so grief-stricken that he wants to die.

Alas, this noble January, in the midst of all his wealth and his lust, has suddenly gone blind. He weeps and wails pitifully and feels more than ever the fire of jealousy lest his wife should be victim to some folly. That fire burns him so painfully that he wishes nothing more than that someone kill him and his wife together. For it is important to him that neither during his life nor after his death should she love again or be someone else's wife — he wants her to live out her life in the black habit of a widow, akin to the solitary turtledove who has lost his mate.

But as all things do, after a month or so, his sorrow began to ebb, for as he came to accept his blindness as permanent, he took his adversity more patiently. But his jealousy did not decrease. In fact, it was so strong that he would not allow his wife to ride or go anywhere, be it his hall or someone else's, nor any other place, not ever, without his hand on her at all times. This, of course, brought young May to tears quite regularly, for she was so deeply in love with Damyan that she thought her heart would break lest she have him — and soon.

For his part, poor young Damyan became the most sorrowful man ever, for never, neither night nor day, was he able to speak a single work to beautiful May, either about his feelings for her or of anything else without January hearing it — after all, his hand is on her always. But nevertheless, by notes back and forth and through secret signs that only they knew the meaning of, she was well aware of his goal and his intentions.

Oh, January, what good would it do you even if your sight was sharp enough for you to see ships sail off into the distance? For the blind may be deceived as easily as those who see.

Behold Argus, with his hundred eyes, with all his ability to scout things out and to see them clearly, was nevertheless deceived and, God knows, so are many more who think wisely that it is not so. You had best let go of that which you cannot see — I will say nothing more on this subject.

Now the beautiful May has imprinted in warm wax the latchkey that January kept for the small wicker gate to his garden, and Damyan, who knew exactly what May had in mind, secretly managed to make a copy of this key.

What else is there to say but that soon this key will be the source of some surprise, and you will hear all about it, if only you listen patiently.

Oh, noble Ovid, God knows you spoke truly when you told us that there is no trick that love will not discover, sooner or later, in some manner or way. You can see this in the story of Pyramus and Thisbe: though they were kept apart for a very long time, they finally got together, whispering through a wall that people thought no one would find a way around.

But now to our purpose: before eight days of July had passed, this January, through the urging of his wife, had caught so great an urge to find some pleasure in his garden for just the two of them that, like Solomon, he addressed his May one morning: 'Rise, my sweet wife, my own love, my noble lady! Listen to the song of the turtledove, my own sweet dove. Winter, with all of his wet rains, is past. Come now, with your dove's eyes and your breasts, sweeter than wine; for our garden is enclosed all about with stones; come with me, my pure white spouse. There can be no doubt but that you have wounded my very heart, oh, wife of mine. In all my life I have never known you to be blemished in any way! Come with me, and let us relish in our disport; for I choose you as my wife and as my only comfort.'

He wooed her with these old, tired words, but she had prearranged with Damyan that he should go before them with his latchkey. So this Damyan had opened the wicker gate and slipped in when no one could see or hear him and he was sitting quietly under a bush, waiting.

This January, blind as a stone, his hand on May, entered his beautiful garden, where he shut the wicker gate securely behind them. 'Now, my own wife,' he said, 'there is no one else here but you and I, and you are the creature that I love best. For by the God who sits above us in heaven, I would rather be stabbed with a knife than to offend you, my fair true wife!

As God is my witness, remember how I chose you, certainly not out of greed, of that there can be no doubt, but only for the love I felt for you. I am old and cannot see, so be true to me and I will tell you how you shall be the recipient of three things thereby: first, the love of Jesus; secondly, all the honor that can be yours; and thirdly, all that I own, towns and towers both. I give everything to you — draw up contracts any way you want — we shall do so tomorrow before the sun sets, as God may bring my soul to rest in bliss.

But now I pray you to kiss me and seal our covenant. And though I may be jealous, you cannot blame me. You are so deeply imprinted in my thoughts that when I think of your beauty and my unsuitable old age, even if I die, I may not for a moment be without you, for very love of you. Let no one doubt that. Now kiss me, wife, and let us enjoy this wonderful place.'

When the beautiful young May heard him speak like that, she pretended to weep a bit but then replied: 'You know that I too have a soul to save, as well as you, not to mention my personal honor and the tender flower of my womanhood which I devoted to you in that bond by which the priest tied my body to yours.

Therefore I will answer like this, by your leave, my lord, so very dear to me: I pray to God, by my own life, that the day may never dawn on which, like foul women do every day, I dishonor my kin or ruin my name by being false to you. Moreover, I pray that if I carry out such an offense, you strip me of my finery and put me in a sack so that you can drown me in the nearest river. I am a gentle woman and not just any wench — so how have I deserved that you speak to me like this? Is it not men who are most untrue, and is it not up to us women constantly to reprove you? Sometimes it seems that you have only one look on your face, and that is the one you use to reprove us when you speak of our unfaithfulness'.

Right about then she saw Damyan sitting in the bush. She began to cough and signaled to him to climb a tree there that was full of fruit. Up the tree he went, for he knew exactly what she had in mind and knew the signals she was sending him better than could January, her own mate. After all, she had told Damyan in a letter all about this and precisely what he was to do. And for now I let him sit in that pear tree while January and May merrily romp beneath it.

The day was bright and there was a nice breeze; Phoebus had sent his gold streams to please every flower with his warmth. It believe he was in Gemini at that time, not far from Cancer, so at the height of Jupiter's power. And it so happened, on that bright morning, that on the far side of this very garden, Pluto, the king of fairies, with many a lady in his entourage, was walking with his wife, the fair Proserpina, whom he had raped on Mt. Etna while she was gathering flowers in the meadow — you can read the full tale — of how he brought her home in his hellish cart — in the works of Claudian.

This King of Fairies sat down with her on a turf bench, fresh and green, and spoke these words to his Queen: 'Dear wife,' he said, 'no one can doubt that we experience every day the way women betray men, and I could tell ten hundred thousand stories all about your unfaithfulness and fickleness. Oh, wise Solomon, most wealthy among men, filled with wisdom and with worldly glory, it would be good for every man who has wit and reason to remember your words: "Among a thousand men I only found one who was good, but I found none at all among women." Thus speaks the king who knows all about your wickedness. And the author of the Apocalypse, it seems to me, rarely said anything positive about women. May a wild fire and a horrible infectious plague descend on your bodies before the sun sets!

You can't tell me that you don't see this honorable knight, about to be cuckolded by his own servant, just because he is blind and old. Behold where the lecher sits in the tree! Now, as I have the power, I will grant sight again to this old, blind, worthy knight, so that when his wife tries to betray him he shall know all her harlotry so that he can reprove her and other wicked women with it.'

'Shall you, indeed?' asked Proserpina. 'If that is what you plan to do, I swear upon my mother's soul that I shall make sure she knows just how to answer, as will all women after her, so that for their sake — though they be caught red-handed in guilt — they will know how to excuse themselves boldly and win out over those who accuse them. Not one of them shall die for lack of a good answer. Though a man see something with both his eyes, yet shall we women boldly put a good face on it, and weep and swear, and subtly correct you so that you men feel as stupid as a gaggle of geese.

I tire of your authorities! Enough with them! I have no doubt that this Jew, this Solomon, found many fools among us women. Even if he never found a single good woman, many other men have found plenty of women who are totally faithful, completely good and thoroughly virtuous. Just think of the ones who dwelt in the home of Jesus — they proved their constancy with martyrdom. There are many stories from the time of the Romans that tell of many a faithful wife, also.

But I beg you not to be upset with what I say — albeit Solomon claimed he could not find a single good woman. I ask you to take his true meaning, namely, that in the sovereign bounty of the Almighty there is neither male nor female, but only one God.

Aye, you make so much of this Solomon, when you should pay more attention to the one, true God.[37]

It is true that Solomon was rich and famous and that he built a temple, the House of God. But didn't he also build a temple to false gods? I can't think of anything worse than this. By God, as much as you want to gild his name, he was nevertheless a lecher and an idolater, and in his old age he turned away from God, and if God — as the good book tells us — had not spared him for the sake of his father, he should have lost all his realm right there.

I put no more value on a butterfly than I do on all the hateful things written about women. I am a woman, and so I feel that I have to speak up or else my very heart will swell up and break. For you yourself said that we are just chatterers and, as ever I hope to live my life, I will not cease, even if you call me discourteous, to attack those who want to do evil to us.'"

"Hear, Hear!" shouted the Wife of Bath, only to settle back in to her saddle again when the Host shushed her. The Merchant ignored her and continued.

"But Pluto answered his Queen: 'My Lady! I pray you be not angry with me, as well. Though you present a good argument, I swore an oath that I would restore January's sight, and so my word will stand. You know that, as I am a King, my word is my bond.'

'And I am the Queen of Fairey,' she said. 'She shall have her answer ready, I swear! But,' she took his arm, 'let us not speak of it any more. For in truth, I have had enough disagreement with you.'

Now let us turn back to January, who is in his garden with his beautiful May, singing much more merrily than any popinjay: 'I

---

[37] Medieval believers had no difficulty with fitting pagan gods into Christian theology. These gods are seen simply as precursors to Christ; allowing this pagan goddess, Proserpina, to exhort the pagan god, Pluto, to put his faith in the Christian God and to learn from the Bible.

love you the best and ever shall, and there shall be no one else'
By now they had gone far enough around the paths of the garden to return again to that pear tree in which Damyan was sitting, waiting, high among the green branches and leaves.

Now the beautiful May, so bright and shining, began to sigh and said: 'Alas, my tummy!' she complained to January. 'Dear husband! I don't care what else happens, but I must have one of those small green pears. Help me with this, for the love of Mary, Queen of Heaven. I can tell you that a woman in my condition can have so great a desire for this fruit that she might die if she is denied.'

'Alas, that I don't have a servant nearby that could climb up there. Alas! What a shame that I am blind.'

'Oh, dear sir, that is not a problem. I am well aware that you don't trust me, so I suggest that you embrace this tree with both your arms so that I can climb up high enough to reach the fruit, if only I can set my foot upon your back to start.'

'Of course; I shall do anything I can to help you; I would give the very blood from my heart.'

With that he stooped down and she climbed on his back, where she grabbed a branch above her, and up she went.

Now dear Ladies, I pray you not to be angry with me, for I am but a rude man who does not know fancy words — you must forgive me — but at once this Damyan pulled up her smock and thrust himself in.

Now when Pluto saw this great wrong, he suddenly restored full sight to January, allowing him to see as well as he ever had before. Of course, as soon as he regained his sight, January wanted to see but one thing and that was his lovely wife. So he cast both eyes up into the tree and saw immediately that Damyan had dressed his wife in such a manner that I dare not say it unless I wanted to speak most rudely. Now January at once started roaring and crying out as loud as does a mother when her child is about to die.

'Out! Help! Alas! Help me! What are you doing, you bold, nasty woman?'

But May was not flustered and she answered him calmly: 'Dear Sir! What is wrong with you? Please be patient and reasonable in your thoughts. It should be clear to you that I have this day restored your sight to you in both eyes, on peril of my soul! I shall not lie.

I was told that I could heal your eyes by doing this, and that there was nothing more likely to restore your sight than to struggle with a man up in a tree. God knows, I have done this with the best of intentions!'

'Struggle!' he sputtered. 'Struggle? Hell! Damn me, if it did not thrust it all the way in! May God in heaven reward you both with a shameful death! He fucked you! I saw it with mine own eyes! Hang me, if I didn't!'

'Then all I can say,' she answered calmly, 'is that the medicine didn't work. Because clearly, if you had your sight back, you would not say this to me. You have only partial sight, not nearly perfect enough to judge whether what you are seeing is real!'

'I see as well as I ever did, thanks be to God! And I swear that with both my eyes I saw him do you!'

'You are in a daze, dear husband.' She paused. 'So, this is the thanks I get for bringing back your sight! Alas, that ever I tried to do the right thing and be kind to you!'

To make a long story short, January was soon assuaged.

'O my dearest lady! Let's forget about all of it, then. Come down from the tree, sweetheart, and if I have misspoken, God help me, I deserve to be punished. But my father's soul, I could swear that I saw that Damyan having sex with you, and your smock all the way up over his chest!'

'Think what you will, dear Sir! But we all know that a man who has just awakened from sleep takes a while before he can see perfectly what is right in front of him; he does not see perfectly until he is fully awake. Just so is the case with a man who has been blind for some time — he cannot immediately see perfectly. His sight may not return to him completely until a day or two has passed.

Until your vision has settled down a while, you may be fooled by many things that you think you see. Be careful, I pray you, by the King of Heaven, for many men think they see something that is an entirely other thing than it seems to be. He who misconceives easily errs.'

And with that she leapt down from the tree.

Who is happy now but January? He kisses her and embraces her over and over and strokes her womb gently and leads her home to his palace.

Now good men, I hope you are all happy, for this is how the story of January ends.

May God and his Mother, Holy Mary, bless us always."

Not a few of the pilgrims found this story to be quite boorish, some of them saying that they had expected better from the Merchant. But others thought the story delightful — the Cook and the Tapister, the Pardoner and the Summoner, for example, were ecstatic and laughing for some time after the Merchant had finished. Indeed, the Haberdasher more than once pounded the Cook on the back, repeating as loudly as he was Abel to through his guffaws: "Th-th-thr-thrust it all the w-w-wway in, he did! All the w-w-w-way in!"

Our Host finally spoke up: "So! God have mercy on us all! I pray that God may keep such a wife far from me. Behold! What subtleties and deception women practice. They are as busy as bees, ever trying to deceive us foolish men. They always seem to want to leave the beaten path. The Merchant has told us a story that shows exactly that."

"What it has shown, Sir Host," the wife of Bath asserted, "is how foolish men can be and . . . that women can be more clever than any man who wishes nothing more than to have the best of a woman."

But the Host was not listening to her, following his own thoughts, as he paused and shook his head. "Of course I have a wife as true as steel, though she have little enough to brag about. But her tongue . . . oh, Lord . . . her tongue. It makes her a gossiping shrew, but that's the least of her many vices."

Abruptly, he stopped himself, looking around at the other pilgrims. "But I have said enough! I will stop there. Let all such things be water under the bridge."

Then he raised himself up in his saddle, now suddenly belligerent. "You want to know the truth?"

He paused, but then he continued in a softer voice, barely above a whisper, so only the pilgrims closest to him could hear. "I can tell you confidentially that I am very sorry to be tied to her. Hell, if I listed every one of her vices, I know some of you would truly think me foolish. And you know why? Somebody in this group would be sure to tell her all about it — I don't know who, and it doesn't matter since women delight in offering such wares at the public market. Lord knows I cannot do justice to all of her bad traits — so the best thing for me to do is to shut up."

The Wife, close enough to hear him, smiled broadly at the way he seemed to find it difficult to follow his own advice, especially when he had said so much, perhaps unintentionally.

The Host looked around, trying to find the next teller of stories, and his eye landed on the Clerk.

"Sir Clerk of Oxford, you ride along looking coy and being as quiet as a young maiden who is newly married, sitting at the dinner table with nothing to say. I have yet to hear a word from you — no doubt you are thinking about some sophistry, but as Solomon told us: 'to everything there is a season.' I don't know what's crept across your liver, but be of good cheer for a change, for God's sake; this is no time to study.

Tell us some worthwhile tale — I'm sure you've heard many a story at school.

You agreed to our plan, and I say it is now your turn to step up and tell a story, but for God's sake, no sermon. Please don't preach at us as do these Friars in Lent, beating us up to repent for old sins. But be careful that you don't let us fall asleep either while you're talking. Tell us some merry tale of adventures rather, and stay away from those philosophical terms, the rhetorical colors and those elaborate figures of speech. You can save those for when you need to show that you have mastered high style, as when you are writing for kings. Speak plainly to us, I pray, so that all of us rude men understand what you have to tell us."

This worthy clerk answered pleasantly enough: "Sir Host, you are the master here; you have the governance over all of us for now and I owe you obedience, at least as far as is reasonable. I will tell you a story which I learned from a clerk in Padua, proved great by his words and works, but dead now, nailed in his coffin. I pray that God will grant him eternal rest.

This man was known as Frances Petrarch, Poet Laureate, as he illuminated all of Italy with his rhetoric and his sweet poetry, just like Giovanni da Lignano did for philosophy and law and many other arts. But Death, who will not let us linger here, in the twinkling of an eye — or so it seems — has taken them both, and so we shall all one day die.

But to tell you more of this honorable man from whom I learned this tale, as I began to tell you, he did indeed practice the high style. Before he ventured into the body of the tale he began with a proem. In it, he described the Piedmond and the country of Saluzzo, telling us about the towering mountains of the Appenines that serve as the boundary of Western Lombardy, and particularly of Monviso Mountain, where the river Po springs from a small rivulet that is its beginning and source before it flows eastward, ever increasing its course to Emilia, Ferrare, and Venice.

Now I could share this proem with you, but it is entirely too long and, in my judgement, irrelevant to this story except as an introduction. Also, I will not imitate the high style of the Master but will tell it in a way that all here will understand.

I believe that this tale will more than answer the tale the Merchant told us, as it is the story of a virtuous wife who is true to her vows and suffers greatly in order to ever be a true wife." He nodded politely to the Knight, and then to the Wife of Bath, and began this tale.

The Clerk's Tale

"In the western part of Italy, at the foot of Monsivo, a once-active volcano, there is a lush plain, a region known as Saluzzo. Along with many beautiful sights, it is rich in produce and dotted with many a town and tower that date back to ancient times.

A long time ago, Walther, a Marquis in a long line of succession, was lord of that land, and all of his liege lords, whatever their status, were obedient to him. The Marquis enjoyed this delightful state year in and out. He was favored by Fortune, beloved and feared both by his lords and by the common folk. In terms of lineage, he was the noblest man in all of Lombardy — handsome, strong, young, and known for his honor and his courtesy. He was smart enough to govern the country successfully, except for one thing.

Now I fault him for this thing: rather than thinking ahead to the future, he spent all his time thinking about and living in the present, hawking and hunting everywhere. The rest he just let slide and, the worst of it: he was not interested in marriage, no matter what. And on that point, which his people were upset about, one day all of his advisors approached him and one of them — he was the wisest of the lot, and they thought he stood the best chance of expressing what they had to say most clearly and of having their lord understand them accurately — this wise man said to the Marquis, as follows.

'Oh, most noble Marquis, assured by your graciousness and bolstered by it, we dare to approach you this day to tell you what is troubling us. Accept in your great nobility, oh, Lord, what we with sorrowful heart now share with you, and let your ears not distain what we have to say to you. Albeit that I have no more to do with this matter than anyone else here, but in so much as you, our Lord, so dear, have always shown me favor and grace, I dare ask audience of you more than do others, Lord, that you may hear our request, although you, my Lord, can do whatever you wish.

There can be no doubt, oh, Lord, that we are so well pleased with all you do and all you have ever done, we could not possibly be happier — except for one thing, Lord. If it be your will, that you consider marriage, that would make your people the happiest ever. We ask that you bow your head under that blissful yoke of sovereignty rather than service, that people refer to as espousal or wedlock. Think, o Lord, as you so wisely do, how that our days pass in various ways and though we sleep or wake, roam about or ride, time is ever passing; it waits for no man. And though you are still in the budding flower of youth, time is always creeping up on us, quiet as a stone, and so it menaces every age and smites every estate; no one escapes it. And although we know that we shall all die, the specific date on which our death shall fall is unknown.

We ask that you, who have never refused us, please understand our intention, and choose, if you agree, a wife in the near future, the flower of nobility hereabouts, so that it is honorable to God and to you, as best we can judge. Deliver us from our constant fear and take a wife, for the sake of God. For were it to happen, God forbid, that your line should die out with your death and that some stranger should take over your heritage, that would be of great sorrow to those of us who should live to see it. This is why we pray that you marry, sooner rather than later.'

The meek prayer and the sorrowful faces of his people filled the heart of the Marquis with pity. 'My own dear people,' he said, 'you are asking me to do something which I have never planned to do. I have enjoyed a freedom which is found but seldom in marriage. Where I have been free, you are now asking me to enter into another's service and to place myself in bondage. Nevertheless, I understand your true intention and trust your judgment and ever have.

      Therefore, of my own free will I agree to marry as soon as possible.

But in so far as you have volunteered to help me find and choose a wife, I release you of that responsibility and absolve you of that offer. God knows that children are often unlike their worthy ancestors. Goodness comes entirely from God, not from the family that bore and raised people. I trust in the goodness of God, and in that spirit I entrust my marriage, my estate, and my welfare to Him; He may do with me as he pleases.'"

Here the Wife of Bath jumped in: "Wise words, worthy young clerk — you speak wisely here, and this tale promises to teach us something we can all learn from."

The Clerk merely bowed graciously before went on.

"The Marquis continued: 'So I beg you to leave it up to me to choose a wife by myself. It is a charge I happily take on and will endure.

But I beg of you, and I charge you, upon your lives, that no matter whom I choose for a wife, you will respect and honor her as long as she lives, in words and deeds, here and everywhere, as if she were an emperor's daughter.

In short, you must swear this: that you will not grumble at or question my choice, since it is at your request that I will lose my liberty. Thus, as ever I thrive, wherever my heart settles, that woman will I marry.

Unless you assent to this, we will never speak of this matter again.'

He settled on a date certain by which he would marry, reminding them again that he was doing all this at their request. They humbly fell on their knees, obediently and reverently, and thanked him, one and all, and then rode home, satisfied that they had achieved their goal. And the Marquis, on his part, at once commanded his people to start making plans for a wedding feast and gave appropriate charges to his close knights and squires. Of course they all did as he asked, joyfully doing their part to prepare for the celebration.

Not far from the sumptuous palace in which the Marquis was planning his marriage, on a lovely spot there was a village, and all its inhabitants made a living from the fields of the earth.

Among these generally poor people there lived a man who was considered by most to be the poorest of them all, but let's not forget how Almighty God sometimes sends his grace even into a crowded oxen stall. This man went by the name of Janicula, and he had a pretty, young daughter, who was named Griselda.

Now, if virtue is beauty, Griselda was one of the most beautiful people under the sun. She had been raised in poverty and never had so much as a self-indulgent thought. Far more often did she drink water from the well than wine from the barrel and, in her virtue, she knew labor far better than idling. And though she was of tender age, yet in the heart of her virginity there was ample maturity and steadfastness; and she treated her old poor father with great respect. She also took care of a few sheep in the fields, for she was never idle, from dawn to dusk. And she never came home without a few herbs or cabbages, which she shredded and cooked to sustain them. She slept on a bed that was hard rather than soft and, day-to-day, she filled her father's life with every obedience and diligence that a child may do in respecting a parent.

Many a time had the Marquis observed with his own eyes this poor creature, Griselda, when, by chance he saw her again while he was hunting. He did not consider her with wanton and lusty thoughts but quite seriously, noting her general demeanor and commending her womanliness in his heart. He was well aware of her virtue, which surpassed, even though she was so young, all others in attitude and in action. And though his people had no particular sensitivity for virtue, he himself considered very thoroughly her goodness and decided that if he were to marry, he would marry Griselda and no one else.

The day he had set for his wedding came and still no one knew whom he would marry. The people wondered and grumbled quietly among themselves: 'Will he, after all, not leave this path of vanity? Will he refuse, finally, to marry? Alas, alas, poor us! Why does he wish to deceive himself and us like this?' But in secret the Marquis had ordered the making of broaches and rings, set in gold and in azure, all for Griselda. And he knew what clothing to have made for her by measuring a woman of similar size; and he had all the other accouterments prepared that go into a state wedding.

It was well into the morning, about nine o'clock, and everything had been prepared in the palace for the big day — halls and chambers, all decorated appropriately. Outbuildings were crammed with the best food you could find in all of Italy, no matter how far you looked.

The royal Marquis was dressed for the occasion, and all the lords and ladies in his court were prepared for the festivities. The knights in his retinue, accompanied by lots of music and revelry, made their way to the village which I have already described to you. Griselda, totally unaware that all of this was meant for her, had gone to get water at the well. Now she hurried home because she too knew that this was the day on which the Marquis was to marry and, if possible, she wanted to see what there was to be seen. She thought: 'I will stand in the door with the other girls who are my friends and we will see the new Marquess, but to do that I have to hurry home to do all the chores I need to do as soon as possible and then I can behold her at my leisure if she passes here on her way to the castle.'

Suddenly, as she was about to cross the threshold into her home, the Marquis appeared and gently spoke to her. She set down the water pot right where she stood beside the threshold in the stall of an ox and fell on her knees, where she planned to stay until she had heard and marked carefully what his wishes were.

This Marquis most somberly asked this girl, who was equally serious: 'Where is your father, Griselda?' And with reverence and a most humble manner, she answered: 'Lord, he is right inside,' and without delay she went into the house and brought her father out to the Marquis. He took the old man by the hand and spoke to him privately: 'Janicula, I neither can nor wish to hide the desire of my heart any longer. If you agree, whatever happens, I wish to take your daughter from your household before I go today in order to be wed to her from this day until we both shall die. I know that you love me well and were born my faithful liege man, and I dare well say that whatever is my pleasure is yours also, and that is why I am making the point I have already made: namely whether you agree to my proposal and take me as your son-in-law.'

The old man was so astonished by this sudden development that he turned all red; he stood there, shaking and embarrassed; he could hardly speak, but finally he said: 'My wish is to do whatever you want. You are so dear a lord to me that I want to do all your liking; please govern this matter just as you wish.'

Here the worthy Wife of Bath interrupted again, but this time not to express her pleasure. All red in the face, nearly matching one of her petticoats, she exploded: "Great God! You have turned a corner and we find ourselves in the same old street, Sir Clerk. What began as a story promising to tell us all about real nobility has become the same old tale of women having to do as men please!"

The Clerk looked at the Wife with a bit of a frown but said nothing, for she continued.

"If they don't take us one way, they'll take us another! It's bad enough that she has to marry a man she has never met or known before, but he doesn't even ask her — he asks her father! And you,' she pointed at the Clerk, her finger shaking angrily, 'you . . . you pimple-faced sniveling Oxford drop–out, you have the nerve to tell this story in which a young girl is married off to a stranger and act as if it is any better than the story the Merchant told! Why, I ought to box your ears until there is nothing left of them — and don't think I can't!"

"Oh, madam," the Clerk answered her, still frowning but quite composed and not at all intimidated by the wrath of this woman. "I'm sorry if this story offends you. It is but a parable, a story meant to illustrate how an ideal wife acts and can be seen by all."

"Acts? Seen? This is not seen bur rather obscene, if you must know, and I have had enough!" the Wife sputtered, only to be interrupted by the Host.

"Madam! I beg of you! We all agreed to tell our stories, and you have told yours. Now let others tell theirs. I insist. I must insist!"

The Clerk, now with a sly little smile on his thin lips, bowed to the Wife, as much as his saddle would allow him to, and continued: "If you had but let me go a little further in my tale, Madam, you would have learned what is now to unfold. For the Marquis, in answer to Janicula's words, said: 'I thank you. Nevertheless, I want to have a private conversation in your chambers with just you and your daughter and me, and do you know why? For I want to ask her if it be her will to be my wife and to rule here after I am gone; and everything shall be discussed in your presence. I do not want to have this conversation without you in the room.'"

The Clerk looked pointedly at the Wife, waiting for a response, perhaps an apology, but she just snorted and stared off into the sky.

"Very well," the Clerk said, and then went on with his tale.

"So they went into the chambers to have these negotiations, as you shall hear in a moment, and as they did so, the people drew nearer the house and surrounded it and commented on how virtuous a household this was known to be and how attentively Griselda was known to manage for her father. But Griselda herself was astonished by all this, for she had never before witnessed such a sight.

She had never seen so many visitors surrounding her little house; she was not used to that and consequently she was all pale, but to make a long story short, these are the words the Marquis spoke in private to this demure, trustworthy, loyal young girl. 'Griselda,' he said, 'I hope it is clear to you that it is your father's pleasure and mine that you shall marry me, and this will stand, as I trust, if it be your will that it be so. But first I have certain conditions,' he continued, 'that, since it will be done very quickly, I must ask you to agree to, unless you need more time.

These then are the conditions: that you will always be happy to do whatever I ask of you, and that I can ask anything of you that seems best to me, whether you like it or not, and that you never grumble or complain about it, come day or night. And also that when I say "yes" you never say "no," neither by word or by a frown on your face. Swear to all this and I will here and now myself swear to our alliance."

Not knowing precisely what he meant, and shaking with fear, Griselda answered: 'My Lord, I am unsuitable and unworthy of this honor you offer me, but I will do just as you wish. And I hereby swear that I will never willingly, in deed or in thought, disobey you, and I swear this on my life, though I am loathe to die.'

The Clerk paused to take a small sip of wine, looking quite intentionally at the Wife and giving her a chance to speak, but she just snorted and waved her hands in the air as if to say: "I give up!" So he continued.

"Hearing this, the Marquis said: 'That will do, my Griselda,' and out the door he went, looking very serious, and she followed him and he introduced her to the people like this: 'This woman who stands here before you is my wife. I expect whoever loves and honors me to love and honor her; that is all I have to say!'

And because he did not want her to bring anything from her previous life with her, he ordered the women there to undress her right then and there. Of course they shrank back from even touching the old rags she was wearing, but nevertheless they managed to dress anew this beautiful girl from head to foot. They combed her hair that was hanging rather rudely and unkempt from her head, and they placed a crown on her head with jewels here and there, some small, some large. What else should I tell you of her array? The people scarcely recognized her in all her beauty because all these riches truly transformed her.

The Marquis betrothed her with a ring, brought just for that purpose. He put it on her finger and lifted her on a horse, snow-white and known for its gentle pace. Then, without further delay he took her to his palace, accompanied by the cheers of the joyful people along the way. And they spent the entire day celebrating until the sun began to descend.

Now to move this story along, let me say that God has favored the new Marquess with such grace that, each day, there were fewer and fewer signs that she had been born and raised in humble surroundings. She seemed to have come from an emperor's hall rather than a hut or an oxen stall. She became so beloved by and so much the favorite of everyone that folk who had known her from birth scarcely trusted their own memories — knowing that she was born the daughter of Janicula — for she appeared to be a wholly different creature than the one they had known.

Though she had always been virtuous, she now seemed to excel in moral qualities — she was so generous, so discreet and so wonderfully eloquent, so demure and so dignified, and she could so embrace people at their very core, that every person who beheld her lovely face fell in love with her. Her name was known not only in Saluzzo, the town itself, but spread throughout the region. The good that any single person saw in her was multiplied in word and passed on to others. The wonderful reputation of her generosity and her fame spread to such an extent that men and women, young and old, flocked to Saluzzo just to see her.

Thus, good fortune has allowed Walther to marry a lowly — nay, a royal — person and to live easily in God's peace in his home and well-honored. And because he had recognized real virtue hidden under low degree, he was considered to be a prudent man, something said only rarely of a ruler.

Griselda, by virtue of her homespun intelligence knew exactly how to carry out the duties of a wife, but she was also very good at addressing the common good — there was no discord, rancor, or heaviness in all that land that she could not appease and wisely bring to a good end. Even when her husband was away from the court now and then, if the nobles or anyone else was discontented, she would bring about atonement with her wisdom and her appropriate words and judgments of great equity — so much so that many thought she had been sent from heaven to save the people and to right their wrongs.

Not long after the wedding, she bore a daughter — even though she had rather brought forth a boy. The Marquis and all his followers were very happy about this for they knew that though a girl had come first, she could bear a boy, also, as the birth of the daughter showed that she was not barren.

Now, when this child had been nursing only a short time, it so happened, as occasionally it does, that this Marquis got such an overwhelming desire in his mind to test his wife, in order to know just how steadfast she was, that he was unable to get over his wish to test the limits of her obedience — he was determined, for no good reason, God knows, to cause his wife some dismay.

He had tested her enough before this, and he found her true every time. Some men call such behavior the sign of a subtle wit, but what need was there to tempt her, and to tempt her more grievously each time? As for me, I say that it ill befits someone to test a wife when there is no need to do so, merely putting her in anguish and making her afraid.

Nevertheless, the Marquis went ahead.

He came to her when she was lying all alone at night, and he was most somber, a troubled look on his face, when he asked her: 'Griselda, I trust that you have not forgotten that day I took you out of poverty and raised you up to this noble estate? Well, Griselda, the current nobility that I have placed you in, I trust, has not let anyone forget that I took you from a low, poor estate to put you in this state of well-being.

Now, no one can hear us but we two, but I need you to listen most carefully now to very word I say.

You yourself know how first you came here to this palace; it's not that long ago. And though you are very dear and beloved by me, you are not so for the nobles whom I rule. They are muttering that it is a great shame and unbecoming to obey you and let you be in charge of them, you who are born of low degree in a small village. And this murmuring has only increased since your daughter was born.

Now you understand that I value and must live with my people in peace and understanding; I cannot ignore the difficulties this matter raises. And so I must do with your daughter as is best, not as I wish to, but as my people want me to. And yet, God knows, I am most loathe to do this, and so I will not do this without your consent.

This then is what I require: that you agree with me in this matter, and you demonstrate now the obedience you swore to me in your village when I came to you on the day we were married.'

Griselda seemed unmoved by what she heard, for she did not say anything or show in any way that she was upset. She simply said: 'Lord, everything lies in your hands, and my child and I, with sincere obedience, are entirely yours, and you may make us flourish or make us die; we are yours, do with us as you will.'

"Nay, fie!" the Wife of Bath burst out. "This is too much. Surely he is up to no good with his new daughter — much less Griselda! I have had enough, and I hope everyone here has, too. What kind of mother would agree to this? No, by God! This is outrageous and ridiculous. I know no woman who would sacrifice her babe because her husband said so. This is nonsense!"

"Not so!" said the Host. "Nay, the nonsense is on your part. For you continue to interrupt our Clerk with your rude outbursts, and he is but telling us his story. So, peace, I command, and let him tell his tale."

"Hold, Sir Host!" the Clerk interjected. "I commend the worthy woman of Bath for listening so carefully to my tale. and I value her interjection. For truly, this is a monstrous husband who is testing his wife as no wife should be tested. I thank my noble fellow pilgrim for her observations and ask but to finish telling my tale."

"Indeed," the Wife answered, "I only hope then that the tale ends more pleasantly than this."

The Clerk bowed: "If you will but bear with me, and let me continue?"

He took the Wife's slight bow as acknowledgement and continued his tale.

"Griselda continued: 'So God save my soul, you can do nothing that will displease me, nor do I desire anything else nor do I fear to lose anything but you. This is the core of my heart and always will be. This will not change, no matter how much time passes, or even in death; none of this will change my feelings in any way.'

Happy indeed was the Marquis to hear her answer, even though he acted as if he were not; his face and his demeanor when he left that chamber were very somber. Immediately he called in a confidential servant of his, a kind of sergeant whom the Marquis had found to be devoted to him in various tasks, someone who could be counted on to execute bad things that no one else would do. The Marquis was certain that this man both loved and feared him and, as soon as he had heard his Lord's wishes, this man went to Griselda's chamber.

'Madam,' he said, 'you must forgive me, as I only do what I am ordered to do; you are wise to the ways of the world and you know that Lords' wishes may not be ignored. We can bemoan them and complain about them but, in the end, we must do as they command. So I will — there is no more to say. As I am commanded, I must take this baby from you.' With that, he took the child as if he felt nothing and acted as if he was going to slay it right then and there.

Griselda had to suffer and consent to it all, so she sat still as a lamb and let this cruel sergeant do what he was charged to do.

Griselda knew this man's reputation; suspicious was his face, unreliable his word, suspect what he was doing. Although Griselda was certain that he was about to slay this daughter she loved so much, she nevertheless wept not a single tear, conforming to everything the Marquis had sworn her to do.

But she did ask the sergeant, quite meekly, as he was a fellow human, could she kiss her baby one last time before it died? And he laid the tiny child in her arms, and she blessed the baby and soothed it and kissed it. And then she gently said to it: 'Farewell, my child! I shall never see you again, but since I have marked you with the holy cross of the Father Almighty — blessed may

His name be — Who died for us on the tree of the cross, I consign your soul to Him, little child, for you shall die this very night because of me.'

Now, I would think that it would have been very hard on a mere nurse to witness this, much less a mother, whom no one would blame for crying 'alas.' But so steadfast and consistent was Griselda that she endured this great adversity quietly and merely said to the sergeant: 'Here, take this innocent child and do as my Lord commands. But I ask one thing of you — that in your grace, though my Lord bid you not to, at least bury this little body someplace where the birds and beasts cannot tear it apart.' But he refused to acknowledge her plea in any way, and simply took the child and went on his way.

He then reported exactly Griselda's words and described her attitude, plainly and accurately to the Marquis. When he presented his dear daughter to that Lord, the Marquis felt a bit of regret but, nevertheless, he stuck to his purpose, as Lords do, when they do as they wish. He ordered the sergeant, upon pain of death, to wrap and bundle up the child very gently and secretly take it to Bologna. There the Marquis had a sister, the Duchess of Panico, and the servant was to deliver the baby to her and ask her to take care of this child and to bring it up in the ways of nobility. And he ordered him to tell her to tell no one whose child it was, no matter what.

The sergeant did as he was told, faithfully carrying out his orders.

Meanwhile we return to the Marquis, who was intent to find out if — by her attitude, her countenance or her words — Griselda might show a difference in how she felt, but he saw no such sign, as she was as kind and as steadfast a person as she had ever been. She was as happy, as humble, as active in serving him and as ever in love as she was with him before all this. No accidental sign of change nor of any adversity could be seen in her, and she never uttered her daughter's name, neither in remembrance of her nor in casual use.

"I must ask, Sir Clerk," the worthy Parson, silent until this moment, broke in. "What of the girl's disappearance? Did no one wonder what happened to the daughter of the Marquis? Surely her sudden absence was noted. How was this explained?"

"I compliment you on your question, good Sir Parson," the Clerk answered. "But, as you might have surmised from the way his people addressed him, no one would have dared to raise the question unless the Marquis himself made that possible. And he did not."

He bowed. "May I?"

"Of course," the Parson answered and resumed his normal silence.

"Four years passed," the Clerk continued, "before Griselda was with child again and, as God willed, she bore a boy child to Walther. This babe was very handsome, and not only the Marquis but everyone in the entire country was happy about this child and they thanked and praised God. But when this child was two years old and was no longer nursing, the Marquis happened to feel again the desire to test his wife, though there was no reason at all to do so.

But married men know no boundaries once they have found a patient victim.

'Wife,' this Marquis said, 'I have had to tell you once before how my people are not happy with our marriage, but it has gotten worse since my son was born. These murmurs slay my heart, my very will to go on, and soon they will totally destroy me. Now the people are saying: "When Walther dies, the blood of Janicula will succeed and be our Lord — such is our fate." My people say these things in terror and, as their Lord, I must take heed of such opinions even though they are not plainly spoken in my hearing. I want, above all, to live in peace, if at all possible, and therefore I find myself thinking that I ought to do with him as I did with his sister in the dark of night. Between you and me, I can only come to this one conclusion. And I must ask that you not inadvertently, of a sudden, cry out in your pain. I pray you to be extremely patient.'

'I have,' she answered, 'said this before and I ever shall: I want nothing but what you wish. I will not grieve — though my daughter and now my son — be slain, as you command. I have had nothing of these two children but first sickness and then after that sorrow and pain. But you are our Lord and master; do as you wish with what is yours; do not ask me for advice. As you know, I left all my clothing at my former home and put on the clothing that you gave me. In that same way I left behind, as well, my will and all my freedom. Therefore I pray you to please yourself; I will obey you in all. And you can be sure that if I could have known what you wished before you told me your desire, I would have carried it out completely. Now that I know your wish, I assent fully and firmly to your pleasure. What's more, if I thought for one moment that my death would please you, I would gladly choose to die right here and now, just to make you happy. For death is nothing compared to your love.'

And when this Marquis saw the constancy of his wife he cast down his eyes and wondered just how she was able to suffer what was happening with such a positive attitude. He left her with a most serious frown on his face, but in his heart he was most pleased.

Again the ugly sergeant came to her and, just as he had taken her daughter, or worse — if it is possible for human beings to be worse than this — he now takes her beautiful son. And she continued to bear it all with such patience that there was no appearance of sadness in her. She kissed her son and blessed him and again prayed the sergeant, if possible, that he might lay her little son's limbs, so delicate to see, in a grave deep enough so that the wild beasts and birds could not reach him. Again she received no answer from the sergeant — he went on his way as if nothing in all this bothered him but tenderly carried the baby boy to Bologna.

Now the Marquis found himself amazed, more and more, by her steadfastness, and if he had not been certain before that she loved her children perfectly, he would have thought that she suffered all this with a sad face because of some duplicity in her soul, some evil malice, or simple cruelty. But he was certain that next to him she loved her children more than anything in the world.

But now I want to ask the women here — has he not tested his wife sufficiently?

What else could a cruel husband come up with to prove a wife's faithfulness and loyalty, as he continued this cruelty or even worsened it?"

"Again, you would do better than to ask me," proclaimed the Wife of Bath. "For I would have him castrated and hanged by his remaining nether parts for but one of these acts, much less both. But then, I doubt that you wish to hear my opinion."

The other women on the pilgrimage, the Prioress and her Nun, said nothing, though the Nun seemed to want to say something, but a look from her superior sufficed to keep her silent. The Clerk, bowing deeply to the Prioress, waited for a moment, but nothing came from her but a short smile and a slight bow in return. So, he continued:

"Then be that as it may! We all know that there are people with a certain bee in their bonnets, who are incapable of stopping. They must stay the course as though tied to the stake, as they cannot cease to pursue their initial purpose.

Just so this Marquis could not stop testing his wife once he had begun. He watched to see whether by word or by facial expression her feelings for him were at all changed, but he never could find any sign of doubt in her. She was ever the same in herself and in her deportment as she had been, and this never altered. The older she became, the more true she was to him in love, if such a thing were possible, ever more attentive to him. And so it seemed that there was but one will shared by the two of them, for just as Walther preferred, so she agreed to all his desires. And, thanks be to God, all worked out for the best. She demonstrated just how a wife might avoid all worldly unrest if only she did just as her husband wished for her to do."

The Wife of Bath emitted a great scoff, but then she paused for a moment to frown before she asked: "Is that it? That's your story? It all worked out for the best? The best for whom? You promised a pleasant ending. This is an ending only your patient Griselda could find pleasant. You have earned no prize with this tale, Sir Clerk."

The Clerk managed a little smile I'm response and answered calmly: "But, dear Lady, I neither promised a pleasant ending, nor . . . is this the end. Be but a bit more like Griselda in her patience and you may yet feel differently about this story."

The Wife simply stared at him, mouth open, breathing angrily through the gap in her teeth. The Clerk took this for permission to continue.

"Over time, too, great scandal began to catch up with the Marquis. It was murmured commonly among the people that, because of his own cruel heart, and because he had wed a poor, common woman he had wickedly murdered both his children. Small wonder, because as far as anyone knew, there was no reason to think that they were anything but dead." The Clerk bowed to the Parson in silent acknowledgement of his erstwhile question, and then went on with his tale. "Because of this, whereas his people had loved him up to now, the scandal of this reputation meant that they now hated him. To be thought of as a murderer is a hateful thing.

Nevertheless, whether he actually harbored doubts or whether he was simply entertaining himself, Walther would not cease his cruelty: testing his wife was the only thing that mattered to him.

About the time his daughter would have been twelve years of age, he contacted the high court in Rome and asked them to construct papal bulls which would meet his needs. They were to say that the Pope himself, in order to appease Walther's people, wanted him to marry someone else whom he might desire. Actually it would be more accurate to say that he had papal bulls counterfeited, giving him permission to leave his first wife as if by dispensation of the Pope, in order to end the rancor and the discord between his people and himself. And, not surprisingly, the common people accepted as true everything they were told about this situation.

Personally, I have to think that her heart was filled with sorrow when Griselda first heard this latest news. But this humble creature, ever steadfast, no matter what, was quite disposed to endure this adversity of Fortune. She was ever prepared to accept Walther's desire and pleasure, because she had given him her heart and everything else that she had in the world.

Soon thereafter, if I am to tell this story properly, the Marquis secretly sent a letter off to Bologna. In this letter he explained all his intent to the Earl of Panico, who was married to his sister, and he asked him to send back again his two children, arrayed appropriately to their estate. And he charged him to do this without telling anyone, no matter who asked, whose children they were. Rather, he was to tell everyone that the girl was to be married to the Marquis of Saluzzo.

The Earl did just as he had been asked to do. On the appointed day he left for Saluzzo, with many a lord and lady in rich array, to accompany this girl there, her younger brother at her side. The beautiful young girl was clearly dressed for marriage, covered with translucent gems, and her handsome brother, who was seven years old, was dressed fittingly for such an occasion, as well.

Meanwhile, continuing his wicked practice, the Marquis arranged to address his patient wife before the assembled court, saying these blunt words: 'It is true, Griselda, that it has been convivial enough to have you as my wife because of your goodness, your loyalty and your obedience — certainly not because of your lineage and your wealth. But I have come to understand that great power, like mine, is accompanied by extreme requirements of obligations. In short, I may not act as freely as any common plowman can. My people, as well as the Pope, compel me and badger me day by day to take another wife, all to ease the rancor under my rule — of this there can be no doubt.

And so, I must inform you that my new wife is on her way here. I ask you to be strong of heart and to cede your place as my wife; take again the same dower you brought to me — this much

I grant you — and return to your father's house. No one experiences continuous prosperity and, with this in mind, I ask you to endure with an even temperament this turn of Fortune.'

As was her custom, Griselda answered with absolute patience: 'My Lord, I know and I have always known that there was no comparison between your magnificence and my poverty — no one doubts that. I have never thought myself worthy in any way to be your chambermaid, much less your wife. In this house, where you made me a lady — and for this I take God Almighty, Who makes my soul ever happy, as my witness — I never thought of myself as lady or as mistress of this household, but only as a humble servant of your Lordship, whom I always have and always shall hold above all other creatures.

But, truth to tell — and I know it is true because I have experienced it — old love will never again be the same as when it was first new. Please know, my dearest Lord, in no way, and even were I to die for it, never will I regret in a single word or deed that I gave my heart to you completely and permanently.

I thank God and you, that for such a long time, entirely of your beneficence, you maintained me in such high honor and nobility, something I was never worthy to be. And I pray that God may repay you appropriately for your generosity. There is nothing else to be said. I will gladly return to my father now and live with him until the end of my life. There I was raised from childhood and there I will lead my life until death, a widow clean in body, heart, and all.

As I gave my maidenhead to you and I am ever your faithful wife, God forbid that any other lord should take me to be his wife.

Furthermore, I pray that God, in His graciousness, grant you and your new wife all health and prosperity. I gladly yield to her this place, which once brought such joy to me. For since it is your pleasure, my Lord, who were once all my heart's rest, I shall go whenever you please.

My Lord, you remember that in my father's house you stripped me of those poor clothes which I was wearing and, in your graciousness, dressed me all new in rich array. I brought nothing else to you but my faith, my nakedness, and my maidenhead, and herewith I return to you again all the clothing you gave me, as well as your wedding ring — I restore to you all that is yours. I dare say that the rest of your jewels can readily be found in your chambers.

But since you offer me the opportunity to leave with the same dowry I brought with me — how could I possibly forget that it was only the clothes on my back . . . surely nothing fine to talk about . . . clothes I could hardly now find again — O, dear God . . . how gentle and kind you were in speech and action that day on which we married!

Naked I came out of my father's house, and naked must I return again to him; but yet I can only hope that it is not your intent that I leave your palace without even a smock. I know you would not do such a shameful thing as to have me expose the womb which bore your children, laid bare to the rest of the world. I hope you remember, my own Lord, so dear, that however unworthy I was, I was your wife. Therefore I pray you not to treat me as you would a worm by the side of the road. And in lieu of my maidenhead, which I brought to you and which I no longer have, that you grant me a smock — a smock as I once wore — that with such a smock I may cover the womb of her that once was your wife.

And with that I take my leave of you, my Lord, lest I overstay my welcome.'

Although the Marquis was able to choke out: 'You may keep the smock you have on now. It is yours to take with you,' he was scarcely able to control himself and had to leave, lest he show to all the sorrow and the pity that he felt for her.

But Griselda stripped down to her smock right then and there in front of all these lords and left the palace, bareheaded and barefooted, setting out for her father's house. Many people followed her, cursing Fortune along the way, but her eyes were tearless and she said not a word the whole way.

Her father, on the other hand, who had heard the news by now, roundly cursed the day and the moment that Nature brought him to life in this world. For, doubtless, the old man had always had his concerns about the marriage. He fully expected, in due time, whenever the Lord had had his lust fulfilled, that he would think it a degradation to his state to have married so lowly, and he would get rid of her as soon as he was tired of her.

Now he runs to meet his daughter as soon as the noise the people are making signal her coming and, weeping quietly, he covers her with her old coat, such as it is. But he would not allow it to touch her body, for the cloth was rude and was even older than the number of days she had been married.

Thus this flower of wifely patience went back to living with her father, this woman who showed to others neither by her words nor by her expression that she had been elsewhere for a time or that she might take offense at their new treatment of her. Judging by the look on her face, she had no recollection whatsoever of her high former state. Small wonder, for while she was in her state of nobility her spirit was ever full of humility. She never demonstrated a tender mouth, nor a delicate heart, nor pomp, nor the trappings of royalty, but always she was full of patient graciousness, discreet and without pride, ever honorable, and ever meek and humble toward her husband.

Men speak of the humility of Job — well-embellished by Clerks, mostly men. But I must say that though Clerks rarely praise the humility of women, no man I know can be as truly humble as can a woman, nor can a man be half as loyal as can a woman — at least, not that I have heard.

By the time the Earl of Panico arrived, the news of his trip spreading near and far, everyone had heard about the new Marquess he was bringing with him in such pomp and wealth that never before had human eye seen such noble array in all of West Lombardy. The Marquis, who had arranged everything, sent a message to Griselda before the Earl's arrival and asked he to come at once to the palace. And so she did, her heart humble and her face happy, without a single prideful thought. She knelt before him, greeting him most reverently and most appropriately.

He said to her, 'Griselda, it is my expressed will that this maiden, who will marry me, be received as royally tomorrow in my palace as possible, and that each and every person be treated appropriately to his state, in terms of seating and in service and high pleasure — all, as I can best provide. Sadly, I have no women capable of arranging the chambers as I want them to be, and so I want you to be in charge of all this. You know from the past just what I like. Although your own array is terrible and evil-looking, nevertheless I am counting on you to carry out your duty in this small way.'

She answered: 'Not only, dearest Lord, am I happy to do as you wish, but I myself desire to serve you and to please you however I may, forever and without waning. Not ever, in happy days and in sad — never shall the spirit inside my heart cease to love you best and with true feelings only.'

And at once she began to get the palace ready, setting tables and making beds. She took pains to have everything done right, telling the servants, in God's name, to hurry and to sweep quickly and to work speedily; and she, doing the most of them all, arranged every chamber and every hall.

The Earl of Panico arrived in the morning, bringing with him the two noble children entrusted to his care. People ran from everywhere to see them, so richly and beautifully arrayed, and quickly determined that indeed Walther was no fool for wanting to trade in his wife for what clearly was the better. The young maid was obviously more beautiful than Griselda and was, of course, much younger. Surely, the people said, Walther and this maid were bound to produce more beautiful and more gentile fruit because of her high lineage. Also, because her brother was so handsome in appearance, it was a pleasure for the people to see him, and now they commended their Lord for his actions.

Oh, you fickle people! So capricious and disloyal! Ever undiscerning and as unpredictable as a weather vane! You find delight in every new bauble and you wax and wane with your affection as does the moon. You are full of chatter, willing to pay good money for what you deem to be the most expensive trinket. Your judgment is false; your constancy is not to be relied on. Only a great fool would trust what you have to say!

This is what the serious people in that town said when they saw their fellows gawking in the street, happy and excited by the novelty of having a new lady in town to check out.

But I will mention no more of this and focus on Griselda instead, on her constancy and her productivity. She was intensely occupied in getting everything prepared for the feast. She was not ashamed of her poor clothing, even though it was crude and torn here and there, but she went most happily to the gate with the other folks to greet the new Marquess, and after that she went about her business. Cheerfully she greeted each of her Lord's guests, in precise concord with their degrees, and no one could fault her, even if they did wonder that someone dressed so poorly knew how to honor and reverence them so properly, but all they could do was to praise her prudence. The crowd could hear her commend most graciously the young maiden and also her brother, with all her heart, so well that no one could match her. But then, finally, when all these lords were seated for the feast, Walther called for her, though she was still busy arranging things in the hall.

'Griselda,' he said, continuing to treat her as had become his custom, 'how do you like my beautiful new wife?'

'I like her very much,' she answered, 'for, my Lord, in good faith, I never saw anyone more beautiful than she. I pray that God let her prosper, and I hope that He will send you both pleasure enough to last you a lifetime.' She paused: "But I must beseech you, my Lord, to do one thing I dare ask of you. I must warn you lest you harass this tender maiden or torment her as you did me, for she has been raised more tenderly and, in my opinion, she could not take the adversity the same way as could a person raised in poverty.'

And when Walther observed again her patience, her happy countenance, and lack of malice, he was struck with how he had so wickedly offended her. Ever had she been as constant as is a wall, always operating out of her innocence. And now this scoundrel of a Marquis began to change his heart, to feel pity for her because of her wifely loyalty.

'Griselda, my love,' he said, 'I have tested your faithfulness and your goodness and I now know it to be enough. I want you never again to be afraid or to be treated badly. You have been tried as much as any woman who ever was arrayed in great estate or harmed by extreme poverty, and I am well convinced of your loyalty and steadfastness, my wife.'

And with that he took her in his arms and kissed her.

But in her amazement, she did not comprehend this. It was as if she had not heard a thing he had said. I believe that until she was able to emerge from her astonishment, she was afraid that she was living in a dream.

'Griselda,' Walther continued, 'by the High God Who died for us, you are my wife; I will never have another, nor never had another, as God save me. This young woman, who you thought was going to be my wife, is your daughter. This young man beside her is my son and shall be my heir — of that I have made certain. You bore them faithfully in your body and they have been kept secretly all these years at Bologna. Take the two of them to you again, for now you may see that you have lost neither of your two children.'

And then he turned to all assembled there. "You people who have spoken ill of me, I want you to know that I did not do any of this out of cruelty nor out of malice but simply to test your steadfastness — I never had any intent to kill my own children, God forbid, but simply to keep them where they lived secretly and quietly until I could be certain of your intent and your will.'

When Griselda heard this, in her joy she fell down in a dead faint, but awakening from her swoon she called her children to her and held them, weeping pitifully, embracing them and kissing them tenderly. Like a true mother, she bathed them in the salty tears that washed her own face and her hair. Oh, how pitiful it was to see her swooning and to hear her humble voice now!

'Oh, Lord my God, I thank you with all my heart that you have saved my beloved children! I could die right here and now and it would not matter since I am firm in Your love and in Your grace, with no fear of death now or when my spirit leaves me. Oh, tender, oh, dear, oh, young children of mine! Your sorrowful mother thought all this time that cruel hounds or some foul vermin had eaten you. But God, in His mercy, and your benevolent father tenderly have kept you alive and well.' Again she swooned down to the ground but held so tightly to her two children that when she embraced them they were able to free themselves only with great difficulty. Many a tear ran down many a sober face that day among those who stood beside her. They could scarcely stand being near her, she was crying so piteously.

Walther comforted her, now that he had put an end to her sorrow, and she stood, disconcerted from all she had experienced, while everyone made joy and feast for her until she had again caught her composure. Now Walther treated her so well that it was a pleasure to see the happiness between the two of them, together again at last.

The ladies there, when they saw that it was time, took her back into her chambers and stripped off her crude clothing. When they returned with her into the hall, she was arrayed in a shining golden robe with a crown on her head and many jewels, and then she was honored as was appropriate and right.

And so this pitiful day had a glorious end, for every man and woman there did their best to spend the day in mirth and revelry until the stars shone bright in the night sky, for this feast was more solemn in every man's sight and more costly than had been the celebration of their marriage.

Griselda and Walther lived many years in great prosperity, in perfect concord and constant peace. Walther successfully married his daughter to a lord who was one of the worthiest in all Italy; and he kept his wife's father in peace and rest at his court until his soul left his body. Walther's son eventually succeeded him peacefully, fortunate in marriage and without the need to test his wife as had his father.

The world is not so strong anymore as it was in olden times, and that is why the great poet has told this story.

Now I did not tell this story so that wives should follow Griselda's model of humility, for it is unlikely they will succeed, even if they tried to do so. But I told it so that every man, no matter what his state in life, should be constant in adversity, as Griselda was; and that is why Petrarch told this story in the high style he used in writing it."

"If that is why you told it," commented the Wife, "why was it not about a man being tested?"

The Clerk continued as if the Wife had not posed this question.

"As this woman was so patient with a mortal man, well might we all receive graciously whatever God sends to us; for it is very reasonable that He tests what He has created. But He tempts not those who are saved. As St. James tells us, if you read his epistle, He tests people every day, of that there is no doubt. For our own good He allows us to be beaten by the sharp scourges of adversity in many ways — not to know what we will do, for He has known from all eternity, before we were born, what we would do. But because His governance is for our best always, let us live in virtuous patience.

And one more thing, before I end, Lords, if you will allow me. As I have already stated: it would be very difficult nowadays to find in any town two or three Griseldas; for if they were put to such tests, what appears to be gold is nowadays so often brass that, though the coin be beautiful to look at, it will burst into pieces rather than bend.

So, now, hear this, for the love of the Wife of Bath." He nodded a low bow in her direction— I could not tell whether he was mocking her or not. "May God keep her and all like her in high mastery, else it were a pity.

I will, in all sincerity, now sing for you a song, fresh and new, for your delight, I hope. May you leave negative thoughts behind as you listen to it:

Griselda and her patience are long gone,
Both buried together in Italy.
And because of that I shout out in open audience
That no married man be so foolish as to test
His wife's loyalty in the hope of finding another Griselda
For he shall certainly fail in this.

Oh, noble wives, full of great prudence,
don't let humility nail down your tongue,
and don't let any clerk to have opportunity
to write a story about you of such marvelous
patience and kindness as Griselda displayed.
Let rather Chivache[38] swallow you into her entrails!

Better to follow the example of Echo,[39] who cannot keep silent,
but ever answers in reply.
Don't be made a fool because of your innocence
but sharply take control.
Imprint this lesson well in your mind
so that it may help everyone when needed.

You arch-wives, stand ready to defend yourselves,
Strong as a great camel.
Don't allow men to offend you!
And you, slight women, feeble in battle,
Be as vicious as a tiger in far-off India,
And wag your tongues as fast as a mill. This I advise you.

Nor be you afraid of them; do not pay them attention;
For though your husband be armed in mail,
The words of your crabbed eloquence
Shall pierce his breast and his neck guard.
I advise you to bind him with jealousy
And you shall then make him shudder like a quail.

If you are beautiful, when other folk are around
Make the most of your face and appearance;

---

[38] A legendary cow, — ever lean, because her only sustenance is patient wives.

[39] In Greek mythology, Echo was cursed for speaking too much. Her punishment was to she her own voice, being left merely with the ability to echo what others said.

If you are foolish, spend freely so that
You have more friends when you are in trouble.
Be of good cheer, as light as the leaves on a linden tree,
And let your man care and weep and wail."

Our worthy Host, when the Clerk had finished his song, swore loudly: "By God's bones, I would give a barrel of ale if my wife at home had heard this story just now! This is a gentle tale for our time. As for me, you know how I feel; whatever will not be, let it go."

But the Wife of Bath was not satisfied: "What, pray tell, are you saying, Sir Clerk? Such confusing advice you leave us with! After hearing this story, no woman in her right mind knows what you are advising her to do. It's beyond me, why you tell this story and then exhort us not to emulate Griselda! Go back to your school and read some more books and keep your mouth shut, because you know nothing of the world, and all you do know is claptrap and boulder dash! Why I never!"

"And never you shall, Madam!" the Clerk concurred.

The Host chimed in: "Never, indeed you shall!" And looking around for the next story teller, he was pre-empted by the Tapister, who now volunteered. "I think I have a story that is just right for this moment."

The Tapister's Tale

"As you all know, I am a weaver and, I might add, a maker — and a lover — a great lover of small rugs" — at this the Carpenter gave him a mighty shove, nearly knocking him from his horse — "fine, fine, I will behave myself, and, as I was saying, a maker of tapestries great and small — large enough to cover a wall and small enough to serve as a decorative hanging. My tapestries are known far and wide, and they grace the homes of numerous nobles and many a wealthy merchant. They can be used to cover and make warm great walls as easily as they will warm, and heat up, I dare say, the most intimate parts of — all right, all right, I know; I will keep a civil tongue.

We all heard our Merchant's story about a sly, lecherous wife who betrayed her foolish husband, and then our learned Clerk's tale about a most submissive wife who — I think he said, doesn't exist in the real world. But she did all her husband asked her to do and, in the end, was rewarded with all she could ever hope for. So much for deceptive and submissive wives. Whether these stories explained anything or not, I'm not sure, but I don't want to talk about the kinds of wives there are but to explain why women are the way they are in the first place."

The Wife of Bath interrupted: "Oh, pinch me . . . I'm afraid I have been transported to Paradise . . . where there's yet another man who will explain women to us. I am all ears and simply cannot wait to hear this."

"Madam," the Tapister responded, "whether you are all ears or all eyes or all teeth or all, whatever all you may be, you shall nevertheless hear a story that any man here can attest to as God's truth."

The Wife just rolled her eyes and waved at the Tapister, as if to say — go on, already — surely I have heard worse.

And go on he did.

"This is a short story that will give you much food for thought. And I will begin by saying that this tale contains some things not in the good book as we all know it. But if you think about the stories we learn in that book you must admit that there are some things that no scholar has tried to explain to us common folk. And this story does not explain all of them either, but it does tell us something about women, as I have told you, that I guarantee will not only match your experience but will each you something, also.

So, in the first days after God had created the earth, He watched Adam roam about the place with all the other creatures, the animals and the birds, and He soon realized that Adam, while seemingly happy and content, was alone and needed a companion of some kind, someone who was more like him than the creatures that surrounded him. And so God cast a deep sleep upon Adam and, while he was sleeping, God took out one of Adam's ribs to use as the beginning of this companion. And as He was turning this bone over in His hands and musing just what this creature should be — enough like Adam to be a proper companion, but not so much like him that they were identical — a bushy-tailed dog that had been playing at God's feet, suddenly snatched the bone out of His hands and dashed off with it. Now as God had no intention of putting Adam to sleep again so he could take another of his ribs and start all over — in fact, concerned that this would cripple Adam and make him useless, He went off in pursuit of this dog.

You may be wondering where this all happened, and I can tell you that it was somewhere near the shores of the Red Sea, where the creation of the world took place to start with.

So, God being faster than anything else — when He chose to be — soon caught up with the dog and grabbed him by his bushy tail. But the dog pulled free, leaving that tail behind in God's hand. The dog kept running until it came to the sea, where, without hesitation, it jumped in and eventually came out on shore — maybe somewhere in Egypt, tailless but still in possession of

Adam's rib. Don't ask me what finally happened to that rib — the story I heard did not say, and so I cannot tell you. Maybe it's buried somewhere in the sands of Egypt. Maybe the dog chewed it up. I simply don't know.

But back to my story. When God realized that the dog had escaped and all He had was his tail, He had to decide what to do next. He was not about to take another rib from Adam, but he did have the dog's bushy tail and so, He decided to make the best of a bad situation. He simply said, as does the priest in the Mass to this day: 'Hocus pocus,'[40] and immediately the dog's bushy tail turned into Eve.

Oh, I know, this is not the story the good book tells us, but it explains a lot, don't you think? If Eve had been made from Adam's rib, would women not be much more reasonable and understanding, as men are? Instead, they nag and complain all day long, just like a dog grabs hold of a bone and worries it until there's nothing left. It makes much more sense that woman was created from a dog's tail, as she never stops grumbling and growling about things, no matter how good they seem to be — just the way a dog's tail is constantly wagging, and none of us know what it means. I know this is not told to us in the books we know, and I would not know of it either, had I not heard it from a stranger I once met, who was from a distant land. But this is how we learn the truth, from those who have travelled the world and have real explanations for what we do not understand.

But to continue. You all know that Adam and Eve had two sons, that much the good book tells us — and also that they were named Cain and Abel. So, as we are told, those two sons were making their sacrifices to God — they did that in the old days, as the book tells us. People were supposed to give to God the best of

---

[40] Illiterate worshippers who heard Mass in the Middle Ages misunderstood the Latin words said by the priest at the transubstantiation (*hoc est corpus meus*, meaning "this is my body") as "hocus pocus," quickly making that phrase synonymous with the idea of magic.

whatever they had: animals or grain or whatever — to sacrifice the best to thank God for all He had given them. So, one of those sons — I don't remember for sure which one — I think maybe it was Abel — he sacrificed one of his sheep and the other — that must have been Cain, then — he was burning some of his grain as his sacrifice. But it had been damp, or maybe, it wasn't his best grain? I don't know, but we are told that the smoke didn't rise to the sky and that was a sign that God was displeased by the sacrifice.

They didn't know much in those days, and so they didn't know for sure why the smoke did not rise, but Cain knew that he had not burned his best grain — that what he sacrificed was old and damp and probably rotten, and he guessed that it had not pleased God. And when he saw the smoke just hanging over his sacrifice and not rising up to the sky the way it was supposed to, while at the same time the smoke from Abel's burning sheep shot straight up to the sky — that was a thing of beauty to see, the way the smoke rose up instead of hanging in a dreary cloud over his foul grain. Anyway, Cain got very angry. And since he could not take it out on God, he decided to punish his brother, instead. So, in his anger at God, he hit his brother with a shovel, when Abel wasn't looking, and before he knew it, his brother was dead.

You can imagine how upset Adam and Eve were then, but there was nothing to be done. Cain had killed his brother and that was that. So, time passed and eventually Cain had some children, and one of them he named Seth. Now the good book does not tell us who his wife was, or where she came from. She had to have been his sister, right? Well, the book also does not tell us whether Adam and Eve had any daughters or where his sons would have found women to marry. It's just more of what it leaves us in the dark about, and that you might never have thought about except for my story, with which, as you can see I am filling in holes for you with the tale that the stranger shared with me when he was buying some of my best tapestries. To tell you the truth, he told me these stories to reward me additionally for the quality of my fine work.

And this is what he told me, which — as I have said — will explain much to you, if you will only listen to it. Cain had three sons, but Adam and Eve had one daughter.

The bible does not tell us about her, but my friend did.

She was, of course the aunt of the three boys, but because there was no one else, this was the only woman they could marry. But how were three men to marry one woman, aunt or not? Well, they all prayed to God to help them solve this problem — all this took place, of course, long after God had sent them from the Garden of Eden because Adam had eaten the forbidden fruit. You may ask where this garden was, or even where they were. And I will tell you — not where the garden was, but it must have been not too far from there — how far could they have travelled in those days? So, they were still somewhere near the Red Sea when this took place, and that is also where I was when my foreign friend told me all this happened. So, as I said, they prayed, imploring God to help them in some way as it would have been very unfair for only one of them to have a wife and the other two to go without. And remember that God had made Eve as Adam's companion so, obviously, His plan was for men to have mates — as we can see, just by looking around us, still today. Of course, I must admit, that He may not have thought this through enough to supply women for the sons of Adam and Eve.

So, you say, Cain could have had some daughters, but then brothers and sisters would have had to marry each other, and that — I think we can all agree — would have been even worse than nephews marrying their aunt. That's bad enough, I say.

Be that as it may, God heard their prayers, and He said to Adam and Eve: 'I will help you but, for this to happen, you must lock up your daughter overnight in a shed, along with a dog and a pig.' Now Eve thought this was very strange, but God reminded her that He had made all the creatures and therefore they were all good and, besides, He was God, and He knew better, and she would simply have to trust Him. So, she did, and she and Adam did as God had told them to do, and they locked up their daughter in a shed, along with a dog and a pig they selected for this purpose — whatever that purpose was. God knows, they did not know. Aha, that's funny: God knows — because He did. Get it? No matter.

The three in the shed fell into a deep sleep but, when Adam and Eve opened the door in the morning, out came three beautiful young women. Everyone was delighted because now there were three wives for three husbands and, soon, the three young women married the three sons of Cain and started their individual households. Now, if you think about it, you must realize that because there were very few people alive at the time, Adam had what we would now call a considerable estate — he owned much land, So, when Adam divided up everything he owned, the three sons of Cain were wealthy, with no masters except themselves, and each of the couples quickly settled into their new prosperous lives.

It was the custom in those days — as it is still today in some parts of the world — that parents paid a formal visit to their newly-married children's houses shortly after the wedding. In this case, the duty fell to Adam and Eve, even though Cain's sons were really their grandsons, but there weren't that many people around yet, so everybody had to pitch in. And so, Adam and Eve visited the homes of their grandsons and their new wives. And when they got to the first house, Eve asked her grandson, among other things, how he liked his wife — whether he was satisfied with her. And he answered: 'On the whole, mother, she suits me well. She's a good-looking woman and she keeps a very clean house.' But Eve responded: 'It sounds to me as if there is something else — something you are not happy about." And the grandson answered: " Well, yes, I am generally happy, but my wife snaps and snarls at me with harsh words when I least expect it. And she's also often grouchy — very hard to please. I don't know what to do exactly to please her and she makes little effort to humor me.'

This, of course, made it clear to Adam and Eve that this first grandson's spouse was the one who had been turned from a dog into a woman.

They went on to visit the second son and, this time, Adam asked him: 'So how are you getting on with your new wife?' The grandson answered: 'I am happy with her in most things. She is peaceful and patient, but the house is a mess. She does nothing to clean it up or to tidy things. I think she's a little lazy; she prefers being idle to doing her work, and she loves to talk to the neighbors — she's always gossiping with the people living around us.'

Now, if you're paying attention, you are wondering where these neighbors came from. After all, there weren't any other people besides Cain and his children. And that is another one of those points that the good book doesn't bother to explain, and here, I must admit, the man who told me this story was no help, either. Nevertheless, in this story, the second grandson's wife is said to be a first-class gossip with her friends, spending all her time talking to the neighbors, whoever they were and wherever they came from — leaving her husband to clean the house and to take care of all the mess.

Whatever the explanation, the grandson's answer made it clear to Adam and Eve that his wife was the pig who had been turned into a woman. And, so when they went to visit the third grandson and his wife, and they asked him whether he as satisfied with his new wife, they were not surprised at his answer: 'Oh, yes, dear grandparents of mine. I am indeed. She's so sweet and well-spoken and always does everything she can to please me and to make my life wonderful. She never barks at me and she keeps a sparkling clean house — there's never a mess of any kind. I would say, that she's as fine a woman as you are, dear grandmother!'

Well, the story tells us that this is all it took for Adam and Eve to know that this was indeed their daughter.

Now, once again, you may ask yourself, did they not know she was their daughter just by looking at her. But I think we are supposed to assume that the three women all looked alike, or this is still another piece of the story that we are not expected to ask questions about. Of course that's the way it is with a lot of religion — all those mysteries that we're just supposed to take on faith, you know, like the Holy Trinity and the Virgin birth and all that stuff that doesn't — with my apologies to all the religious folks here among us — well, that doesn't make sense when you think about it. I mean, I've never understood how the priest's *hocus pocus* turns bread and wine into the body and blood of our Savior. We've still got time on this pilgrimage for the learned holy priests and nuns among us to explain some things to us unlettered folk.

Maybe — and I wouldn't say it's not — that's the way religion's supposed to work — I don't know — but there's God's boat full of things we don't know and aren't even supposed to know, according to some people. So, I don't know and I really can't tell you more. I've told you this story I know about the early days of humans and maybe I've explained some things that were never before explained properly — at least, in the stories I have heard and have been told by priests and clerks.

But, more importantly, I have also told you a story that explains why women — well, most women — act the way they do — why some snap at their husbands and why others are slovenly. And I am quite sure that every man here with us can recognize women he knows in my story, and I hope this explains some things that you have maybe all wondered about for a long time.

That's all I have to say."

When the Tapister finished his story some of the pilgrims, especially the men, nodded in approval and agreed that they had heard a very enjoyable tale, But the Wife of Bath just shook her head and frowned, as she had probably heard some version of this story before and knew that it was futile to say anything about it.

Our Host, who had been reluctant to let the Tapister tell his story to begin with, found the story quite pleasing, much to his surprise, and he said as much: "Well, Sir Tapister, I must admit that you have told quite a good story. I know I can see my wife in this story very easily, and I don't mean the third wife.' He laughed heartily at his own little joke. 'But now, let's move along and let me find someone who shall tell another tale — as enjoyable as the last." With that he looked around at the pilgrims and then, most courteously, as if he were speaking to a meek young maiden, he said: "My Lady Prioress, with your permission, as long as I am sure you take no offense, I would ask that you share with us a story now, if this is your pleasure. Will you be so kind as to favor us, my Lady?"

"Most gladly," she answered, returning the Host's bow ever so slightly. "But I know only holy stories, tales of saints and of good deeds done by holy people seeking to do God's will. And, if I am to tell a story, I will begin with the holy prayers we say at matins every day: 'Oh, God, our God, how marvelous is Your name and its presence in all our world. Your Glory and Your Name are honored not only by men of nobility everywhere, but even by the mouths of babes sustained by Your bounty, spreading Your praises even as they suckle at their mother's breasts.'

This prayer will give me the strength to undertake the telling of my story in Your praise and in praise of the pure lily who bore You but will remain virgin evermore. She did so not in the vain hope of increasing Your Honor, for she herself is the glory and the root of all Your bounty and, second only to her son, the salvation of our souls.

Oh, Mother Mary; oh, Virgin Mother pure; oh, fiery bush of Moses, ever burning yet never burnt! Through your humility may the Holy Spirit, Who filled you with everlasting virtue when he first took refuge in your heart, conception of the Father's wisdom — may He help me now to tell my story with proper reverence.

Lady, to whose generosity, to whose magnificence, to whose virtues and deep humility no human knowledge can do justice, forever, as we pray to you, you go before us in your graciousness and bless us with the light of our prayer that guides us unerringly to your son, so dear. My ability to call forth your great worthiness, oh, blissful Queen, is so lacking, that I cannot sustain the weight of it, but am like a newborn infant who can scarcely express any words at all — so limited am I — and this is why I pray for you to guide my song that I shall here sing of you."

And so she began her tale.

The Prioress's Tale

"In a great city in Asia, there was an enclave of Jews, sanctioned by a lord of that area for their skill at practicing their foul usury — a trade that creates villainous profits and is abhorrent to Christ and any of His followers.[41] Now, people could ride or walk through this area, for it was ungated and open at both ends. Just outside this place there was a Christian school with many Christian children who learned, year by year, Christian doctrine as it was practiced there; in other words, they learned to sing and to read as children do in their early years.

Among these children was the son of a widow; this little schoolboy, seven years of age, attended school every day and, as he was instructed, he was accustomed to kneel down along the way to recite his *Ave Maria*[42] whenever he saw the image of the Virgin. This little boy had been taught by his mother to worship our blissful Lady, Christ's mother most dear, and he never failed to do so, as he was a wonderful child who wanted to do nothing more than spend his day learning.

But before I continue, I must tell you that every time I remember this story I feel like I am in the presence of St. Nicholas, known and venerated for his great devotion to Christ as a child.

One day, as this little child sat in school, learning from his primer, he heard other children singing antiphonal hymns, particularly the *Alma redemptoris*.[43] He drew nearer to that sound

---

[41] Lending money at interest was unlawful for Christians. But Christian rulers and nobles were quite content to borrow money from Jews, accruing debts that were all too often "repaid" by massacring or banishing the lenders and their communities.

[42] Latin for "Hail, Mary," a very popular prayer and the basis for the Rosary.

[43] *Alma redemptoris mater* — "O nourishing Mother of the Redeemer."

and listened carefully to the words and melody, until he himself had memorized all he could hear. Of course he had no idea what the Latin words meant, as he was of such a young and tender age. But one day he asked one of his fellow students to explain the song, to tell him what it was about. He asked this in all humility, on his knees before his fellow student. This older boy answered him: 'I have been told that this song was written in honor of our most gracious Lady and to beseech her to help us and comfort us when we die. That is all I can tell you about it, for I don't know very much grammar.'

'So then this song is written in reverence of the mother of Christ?' asked the young boy. 'In that case, I will spend all of my energy learning the whole thing by heart before Christmas has passed, even if it means that I am beaten three times an hour for neglecting my primer; I will learn this song to honor Our Lady!' Every day after that, his friend taught the boy privately on the way home until he knew it by heart, and from that day on, he sang it, word for word, in keeping with the melody — twice a day, on the way to school and on the way home, he sang it, all for the glory of the Virgin.

As I said, this little boy sang the song loudly and joyfully, on his way through the Jewish part of town, as he went to and from school. His heart was pierced so sweetly by his devotion that he was not able to help himself but to pray to Mary in this manner.

Now, our ancient and first enemy, that serpent Satan, who makes his home in the hearts of Jews, swelled up and said to them: 'Oh, you people of Judaism, alas! Is this something you find acceptable, that this child shall walk where you live and sing like this, just as he feels like it, totally against the spirit of your own law?' And from that moment on the Jews conspired to take this innocent's life.

They hired a killer who lived in an alley there and, as this child passed by his place, this cursed Jew grabbed him, held him down, slit his throat, and then threw the body in a near-by pit. No, I say, not just a pit but a privy that these Jews used to purge their very entrails. Oh, cursed people, all new Herods, what good will your evil action do you? Murder will out, surely; of that there is no doubt and, in this case, it will spread the honor of God, as this innocent blood calls out to the very heavens about the damnable deed that you have committed.

Oh, little martyr, forever virgin, you may now sing, for all eternity in the train of the white celestial Lamb, of which the great evangelist, Saint John, wrote on Pathmos that they who, when they were flesh and blood and knew not woman, now dance forever before the Lamb, singing a song ever new.

This poor widow, the little boy's mother, waits the entire night through for her child to come home, but he does not return. And so, as soon as daylight comes, her face pale with fear and her mind full of worry, she seeks him at school and everywhere else, learning finally that he was last seen in the Jewish quarter. Her breast filled with the fear only a mother can feel, half out of her mind, she searches every place where her child might possibly be found, praying every step of the way for help from Christ's mother, so meek and kind, until at last she looks for him among the cursed Jews.

She inquires, praying pitifully, of every Jew that lived in that area, whether her child passed that way, and they all answer 'No.' But in His grace, Jesus put into her thoughts to cry out for her son near that very space where he had been thrown into the privy.

Oh, Great God, who proclaims His glory through the mouths of innocents, behold here Your power, as this jewel of chastity, this emerald, this bright ruby of martyrdom, lying there with his throat cut from side to side, suddenly began to sing *Alma redemptoris*, so loudly that the streets ring with it.

The Christians all around wondered at this and immediately sent for the Magistrate, who came without delay, praising God, who is the King of Heaven, and also his mother, the honor of all mankind. As soon as the Magistrate arrived, he commanded the Jews to be bound. And with pitiful lamentations, the child, continuing throughout to sing his song, was taken up and carried, in a great procession, unto a near-by abbey, his mother swooning next to his body. Those present were scarcely able to separate this new Rachel from her son's death bier. The provost at once had all the Jews that knew of this murder tortured and executed in the most shameful manner. He was not about to allow such wickedness to go unpunished: 'Those who deserve evil shall have evil.' He had them drawn by wild horses and, by law, after that, they did hang.

Meanwhile this innocent child lay upon his bier before the main altar for the duration of the Mass, after which, the abbot and his convent prepared the body for burial. And when they sprinkled him with holy water, this child again loudly sang: *O Alma redemptoris mater*! The abbot, a holy man, as monks are known to be — or, certainly, ought to be — began to entreat the child, saying: 'Dearest boy, I beseech you, in the name of the Holy Trinity, tell me why you sing like this even though we can all see that your throat has been cut.' And the child answered: 'My throat is indeed cut to the very neck bone, and it is true that I should have died some time ago. But because Jesus Christ, as you will find in holy books, wants His glory to continue and to be remembered, as well as the worship of His dear mother, I am still able to sing *O Alma* this loudly and clearly.

In life I always loved the wellspring of all mercy, Christ's dear Mother, as well as I could, and when it was time for my life to end she came to me and asked me to sing this very anthem as I was dying — as you have heard me do — and when I was finished singing it seemed to me that she laid a seed on my tongue. And this is why I am still singing and will continue in honor of that blissful gracious Maiden until that seed is taken from my tongue. Before my end she said to me: "My dear child, I will take you with me when the grain is removed from your tongue. Do not be afraid; I will not forsake you."

Then this holy monk, this abbot I mentioned, took the grain from the boy's tongue and the lad immediately and gently gave up his spirit. And seeing this miracle, the abbot, with tears trickling down like rain, fell face down, flat on the ground, and lay as still as if he had been tied up. The entire convent also fell down on the pavement, weeping and calling upon the dear

Mother of Christ until they rose and left, taking with them this martyr from his bier. They enclosed his little body in a tomb of clear marble, where he is to this day and will be until the day when we may meet the Lord!

Oh, young Hugh of Lincoln, slain thus by accursed Jews, as is well known, for it happened not too long ago, pray for us through all eternity, for us unreliable sinful folk, so that the merciful God, in his great mercy, multiply His mercy on us, for the sake of His blessed mother, Mary. Amen."

When the Prioress had finished this miraculous tale, everyone on the pilgrimage who had heard her was so somber that it was something to behold, until our Host began to joke again. It was then that he looked at me for the first time and said: "So, what kind of man are you? Every time I see you, you're staring at the ground as if you are hunting rabbits. Draw closer and try to put a smile on your face. Come on, now, the rest of you, let him through. He needs his space, for he is round in shape like I am. You look like a lively little doll for some woman to embrace, with your small, slender face."

He turned to the group: "He looks a bit like he comes from another world, don't you think? This one, who seems not ever to say a word to anyone else." Then he turned back to me: "So, as other folks have told their stories, now it's your turn to tell us something to entertain us, and I urge you to begin."

"Sir Host," I answered him. "I hope you will not be disappointed because I know no other story except this one poem I learned a long time ago."

"That will do, I am sure" he said, and then, to the other pilgrims: "Looking at him, I think then that we will hear something excellent, if I am any kind of judge."

And this is how I began my poem about Sir Thopas.

The Narrator's Tale of Sir Thopas

"This is Part One:

Listen, My Lords, with good intent,
And I will tell you, as is well-meant,
Of mirth and of solace,
About a Knight who was quite a fair gent,
Both in battle and in tournament:
His name was Sir Thopas.

Born was he in a far country,
In Flanders, off beyond the sea;
At Poperyng. In that place
    His father was a gentleman,
And the Lord he was of that country —
As was ordained in God's grace.

Sir Thopas was a doughty swain,[44]
White was his face as porcelain
His lips, red as a rose;
His complexion was deep red in grain
And I will tell you, most certain,
He had a handsome nose.

His hair, his beard were like saffron
    Hanging to his belt all down;
    His shoes of leather Cordovan.
    Made in Bruges were his hose so brown,
    His cloak of famous silk renown,

---

[44] "hearty fellow," although *swain* usually means a rustic rather than a noble.

That cost a lot for a Genovese man.

He could hunt after wild deer
And ride after hawks with his peer,
A grey goshawk[45] on his hand.
On top of that he was a good archer,
And he had in wrestling nary a peer
Wherever there was a ram in the land.[46]

Many many maids, bright in bower,
Mourned after him as their paramour
When they were better off sleeping;
But he was chaste and no lecher
And sweet as is the dog-rose fair
That bears the wild rose hips.

And it happened on a day,
In truth, as I well tell you may,
Sir Thopas went out for a ride.
He climbs upon his steed all grey,
And in his hand his lance so gay,
A long sword by his side.

He spurs his steed through a forest fair
Which has many a wild beast in its lair,
Indeed, both bucks and hare.
And as he spurs both north and east
I tell you now, he felt, at the least,
A sad, sad, most sorry care.

All about him spring herbs large and small;

---

[45] A bird of prey; a type of hawk used in the hunt.

[46] Wrestling contests, for which the prize was frequently a ram, were usually engaged in only by peasants, never by nobles or knights.

Some are licorice, some are caterwall,[47]
As well as many a wild clove.
Also nutmeg to put into ale,
Whether it be fresh or stale,
Or to put into a chest to improve.

Then birds sang -- none can say nay --
The sparrow hawk and the popinjay,
So that it was a joy to hear.
The thrushcocks also made their lay
As did the wood pigeon out on the spray
Singing out full loud and clear.

Sir Thopas then fell into such love longing,
When he heard of the birds all this singing,
And spurred his steed madly through the wood.
His fair steed his spurs were so pricking,
Sweating that one could its wet sides ring,
So covered were they all with blood.

Sir Thopas finally so weary was,
From spurring along in the thick grass,
So fierce was his courage,
That he laid down in that same place,
To give his steed some needed solace
And also have good forage.

'Oh, blessed Mary, may we blessed be;
What is wrong that such a love ails me
And binds me up so sore?
I dreamed the whole night through, by God,
That an elf-queen shall my lover be
And sleep under my cloak, forever more.

---

[47] A plant prized for its odor.

An elf-queen I will love, iwis,[48]
For in this world no woman there is
Worthy to be my mate in town.
All other women will I forsake
And to an elf-queen I will me take
Through every dale and down.'

Into his saddle he climbs anon,
Pricking his horse over fence and stone,
An Elfin queen to see.
Until he had ridden so far and gone
That he found, as in a faint or swoon,
The country of Fairy—
Tis a country to which no none,
Neither woman nor child, dare ride or be gone.

And suddenly there was a great giant
Who went by the name of Sir Oliphant,
A perilous man, indeed.
He said: 'Young man, by Termagaunt,[49]
Unless you spur right out of my haunt
I will slay you at once with my mace.
For here the Queen of Fairy,
With music of harps and pipes,
Lives in this very place.'

The young Knight said, 'As well as I can be,
Tomorrow I will meet with thee,
When I come here in my armor.
And then I hope, as I pray,
You shall with my small lance so gay

---

[48] Middle English for "surely" or "definitely"; derived from "I know"; the equivalent of German *gewiss*.

[49] A figure commonly thought to be a Saracen god.

Pay for your insults sore.
I will pierce your throat, come what may,
Before we have passed the prime of day,
For here you will be slain.'

Then Thopas pulled back fully fast,
For the giant great stones at him cast,
That came from his mighty sling.
But safely escaped young Sir Thopas,
Entirely through God's good grace,
And through his gracious bearing.

Now listen, My Lords, to my tale,
Far merrier than a nightingale,
For now I will with renown,
Tell how Sir Thopas, without fail,
Spurred his steed home over hill and dale,
And has returned to his home town.

His merry men commanded he
To gladden him with mirth and glee,
For he must prepare to go fight
A giant whose heads number three,
For the love of a lady and the nobility
Of her that shone so bright.

'Do accompany me,' he said, 'my minstrels,
And story-tellers, tell tales
Now, as I am arming,
Of romances that are about royals
About popes and about cardinals
And also about love-longing.'

They served him first some sweet wine
In a cup very fine
And full of spice,

And gingerbread that was also fine
With licorice and cinnamon
With sugar sweet and nice.

Next he put on a white layer
Of cloth that was made so fine and clear,
Breeches as well as a shirt.
Over that shirt a jacket of fine leather
And on top of that a chain-mail shirt
To protect his heart from being hurt.

And over that his fine armor deft
Was carefully made with Jewish craft;
Very strong it was of heft.
And on top of that his coat of arms
As white as if made of lily flower;
All this for combat then was left.

His shield was made of gold so red
And on it was a wild boar's head,
A carbuncle[50] on its side;
And there he swore, on his ale and his bread,
That soon the giant would be dead,
No matter the time or tide.

His greaves[51] were made of leather fine,
The sheath for his sword of ivory refined,
His helmet of brass most bright;
His saddle, too, of ivory dearly won;
His bridle shone like the sun,
Or perhaps as the moon light.

---

[50] A red gem; thought, by some, to possess miraculous healing powers.

[51] Armor worn on the front of the leg.

His spear was made of wood of cypress;
It betokened war and nothing of peace.
The head was very sharply ground
His horse was all dappled with gray.
It ambles well along the way,
Very softly and round in the land.

Behold, My Lords, Part I is at an end.
But I am happy to tell more of it
If that is what you want.

And here I begin Part Two:

Now hold your mouths, for charity,
All you knights and ladies free,
And listen only to my tale
Of battle and of chivalry above,
And also of ladies deeply in love;
Soon I will all of you tell.

People speak of romances worthy of prize
Of the beloved Horn and of Ypotise,
Of Bevis of Hampton and of Sir Gee,
Of Sir Lybeaus and of Pleyndamour[52]
But Sir Thopas, he is the flour
Of all royal chivalry.

He climbed up on his good steed
And went on his way, in adventure to lead,
Sparkling like the flame in a fire so warm.
Upon his helmet there was a tower
And therein was stuck a lily flour —
May God protect his body from harm.

---

[52] A list of heroes from popular romances and tales of the time.

And because he was a knight adventurous
He refused to sleep in any house,
But lay covered only by his hood.
His shining helmet was his pillow
And next to him grazed his steed
On the finest herb so good.

He himself drank water from a well,
As did the Knight Sir Perceval,
Who was so worthy in armor,
Until on a certain day —"

"Stop! No more of this, for the sake of bleeding Jesus," the Host, who had apparently had enough, interrupted me. "Your utter stupidity is wearing me out, so that, as the Good Lord is my witness, your worthless drivel is making my ears bleed. I can only pray that the devil take these rhymes; as near as I can tell, you are spouting pure dog shit."

"What do you mean?" I asked. "Why do you stop me from telling my tale when you have let everybody else tell his? I am doing the best I can."

"God help me," the Host answered, "let me put this as simply as I can. In a word, your rhyming has less value than a turd. You're just wasting our time. Of all this is not clear enough, let me be as plain as possible plain, Sir! Stop! No more of these rhymes, if that is what you call them. Enough is enough!" He shook his head several times, as if to clear out cobwebs. Then he seemed to have an idea. "Here — let me suggest this — maybe you can tell us something else. Do you know something in real verse, or maybe something in prose — something — anything at all that will be somewhat entertaining or maybe teach us something new."

"I would be happy to, by the sweet wood of Christ. And I think I have just what you are looking for. I do know a little thing in prose that, if I am not mistaken, you might like better. Of course, if you don't like this, either, I just don't know. In that case, you are just too picky," I said. "This is a moral story, very virtuous, although — in my time —- I have heard it told by various people in various ways."

The Host made a gesture with his hands to indicate that he was willing to go along with this new proposal, and so I began.

The Tale of Melibee

"As we all know. each Evangelist that tells us about Jesus Christ's suffering does not tell the exact same story as the other Evangelists do. Nevertheless, the effect of what they say is true and the same as the one made by their fellows, even if they differ in the telling. When they describe the Lord's passion, some say more about one thing and others say less about another. I'm talking about Mark, Matthew, Luke and John, who all finally make the same point.

And so, my Lords, I beg of you, that if you find me telling the story differently, in that I rely more on proverbs than you have heard before when someone else told this little story, it is just to drive home the point the story makes. And even though I may not use the same precise words as you heard in the past, please don't blame me, for you shall hear no difference in any way from the point of this story which I have in mind, as I tell this merry little tale. So, listen to my story and allow me to tell it from beginning to end.

There was once a young, powerful, wealthy man by the name of Melibee. With his wife, Prudence, he had a daughter, Sofia.

One day Melibee went out for his entertainment, leaving his wife and daughter at home, safely behind locked doors. Three of his avowed enemies, however, entered the house through upstairs windows, where they severely beat Melibee's wife and afflicted Sofia's body with five mortal wounds on her feet, hands, ears, nose and mouth — leaving her for dead.

When Melibee returned to this havoc, he tore his clothes in grief, shrieking as if mad. Prudence did everything she could to persuade him to stop, but he only got worse. After a time, she said: 'My Lord, please do not act so foolishly. A wise man would not weep like this. By the grace of God, your daughter will recover. And even if she were dead right now, you should not destroy yourself over such as loss. After all, Seneca told us: "The wise man does not mourn inordinately the death of his children.

Indeed, he suffers that just as patiently as he awaits his own end."'

Melibee retorted: 'How can you ask a man suffering like this to stop crying? Jesus Christ Himself wept at the death of his friend, Lazarus.'

Prudence responded: 'I am well aware that people who mourn are not forbidden to weep. The Apostle Paul wrote to the Romans: "You shall rejoice with those who are joyful and weep with those who mourn." Appropriate weeping is allowed, but excessive weeping is not. What is appropriate is spelled out for us by Seneca: "When your friend dies, let your eyes neither overflow with tears nor be too dry. Though tears well up in your eyes, do not let them fall; and when you have lost one friend, make the effort to find another. That is smarter than weeping for your lost friend, since that will change nothing." Be governed by wisdom, and put sorrow out of your heart. Remember Ecclesiastes: "A happy man lives comfortably into old age, but a heart filled with mourning dries out one's bones." Solomon tells us that sorrow damages the heart in the same way as moths destroy our clothes and worms the trees. We must accept the death of our children just as we do the loss of our temporal goods. Remember ever-patient Job who, after countless trials, even after he had lost his children and everything he owned, said: "The Lord giveth and the Lord taketh away; let it be done according to the will of the Lord. Blessed be the name of the Lord."'

Melibee answered her: 'You speak truth and so your words have merit. But truly, my heart is so overwhelmed by this sorrow that I am lost.'

'Listen to me,' answered Prudence. 'Call together your true friends, as well as your wise family members. Lay out your situation and listen to their advice and then act according to their judgment. Solomon says: "If you do something on good advice you shall never have regrets."'

So, based on the good counsel of Prudence, Melibee called together a great many people, including surgeons, physicians, old folk and young, even some of his past enemies with whom he now seemed to be reconciled, as well as neighbors who honored him — out of fear, rather than respect. The group also included numerous flatterers and clever, experienced lawyers.

Pitiful Melibee made his case but, even though he was seeking advice, it was evident that he was angry and eager to avenge himself by making war on his enemies. A surgeon, thought to be wise by profession and common consent, was the first to respond: 'Sire, as befits surgeons who treat all and may do no harm — who care for both opponents in a fight after they have wounded one another — it is not consistent with our practice to foster conflict or to take sides. We will work day and night to heal your perilously wounded daughter, so that — if it be God's will — she will be completely well as soon as possible.'

The physicians agreed, adding that just as illness is cured by its opposite, so do men heal war by vengeance.

His envious neighbors, his false friends, and the flatterers pretended to weep, and greatly praised Melibee's power, might, wealth and friends, diminishing the might of his adversaries and saying plainly that he should avenge himself on his foes in war.

Then a respected lawyer spoke: 'My Lords, the reason we are assembled in this place is very sad and grave, both because great wrongs and much evil has been carried out and because of the severe damages that may result in due time because of the wealth and power of the two parties involved. Hence a bad decision in this case would be very dangerous.

Wherefore, Melibee, this is our considered opinion: first, we advise you, above all, to be very careful, ever on the lookout for anyone who might endanger you; second, we advise you to keep enough armed men in your house to protect you and your goods. But we do not deem it wise at this time to start a war or to avenge yourself hastily. We need time and space to deliberate before reaching a final conclusion. As the well-known proverb tells us: "He that judges hastily will soon have regrets." People deem wise that judge who understands quickly but is slow to reach judgment.

Even though delay is troubling, it is nevertheless not a bad thing in making decisions or in taking vengeance, so long as it is sufficient and reasonable. Such example was given to us by our Lord, Jesus Christ, when the woman taken in adultery was brought before Him; although He knew what he would answer, He did not want to provide it immediately — He needed time to deliberate, and so He wrote on the ground, not once, but twice. This is why we request time for deliberation, after which we shall, by the grace of God, counsel you well.'

Now, full of scorn for these old, wise men, the young people entered the fray, shouting for war! They argued noisily that just as the iron must be struck while hot so must men right wrongs while they are fresh and new.

Then an old wise man asked for silence: 'My Lords,' he said, 'many shout for war without knowing what war really is. When it is fresh, war has so large and wide an entrance that anyone can enter, but it is impossible to anticipate how it will all end. For truly, when a war is begun, many a child as yet unborn is destined for death as a young man, or he lives his life in sorrow until he dies a wretched death. Thus, wise counsel and thorough deliberation must precede any war.'

But he was interrupted rudely and told to be quiet, demonstrating that he who preaches to those who do not listen simply annoys them with his sermon. Ecclesiastes tells us: "music annoys those who weep"; by that he meant that it is as useful to address those who are annoyed by your speech as it is to sing to the weeping.

So the wise man sat down again. For Solomon says: "Do not speak when you have no audience."

There were also many who counseled Melibee privately, saying one thing in his ear but publicly saying the opposite.

Melibee quickly decided that he was being counseled to make war immediately ; so, he agreed and confirmed their decision. But Lady Prudence now most humbly spoke: 'My Lord, I dare to beseech you most sincerely not to rush into anything without first listening to me. For Peter Alfonse says: "If you wait to requite those who either do you good or harm you, your friends will abide, and your enemies will fear you longer." The proverb says, "he hurries well who wisely can wait" and, "there can be no profit in ill-advised haste."'

Melibee answered her: 'Know that, for many reasons, I have no intention of following your advice. Surely, everyone would take me for a fool if, on your counsel, I were to go against what has been decided and affirmed by so many wise men. Secondly, I believe that all women are evil and no good comes from them. For, "among a thousand men," says Solomon, "I have found one good man, but I have never found even one good woman." In addition, if I were governed by your counsel, it would surely seem, God forbid, that I have given up mastery to you! Ecclesiastes tells us: "if the wife have mastery, she will destroy her husband," and Solomon says "never, ever, give up power to your wife or to your child, or to your friend, for it is far better that children ask you for what they need than that you are their whim." Also, if I were to follow your advice, I could not possibly keep secrets from going public.'

Prudence politely and patiently listened to her husband and then, with his permission, spoke: 'My Lord, your first argument may be easily answered, for it is not foolish to change a decision when the situation has changed, or when something seems to be other than what it was before. Even if you had sworn or promised to do something and then failed to do so for a good reason, no one would accuse you of lying or of breaking your oath. For it is written that "a wise man loses nothing by making a better decision." And even if what you are doing is established and ordained by many, many people, you need not carry it out unless you want to. Truth is more likely to be found in a few wise and reasonable people than in a mob where everyone is yelling and foolishly shouting.

As to your claim that all women are evil, with all due respect, if you despise all women, remember that "he who despises all, offends all." And Seneca tells us that, 'the wise man despises no one but will gladly, without pride, share whatever he knows with everyone. And that which he does not yet know he is not ashamed to learn from those lesser than himself." And, Sire, it is easy to show that there have been many good women. For surely, if all women were evil, our Lord Jesus Christ would never have stooped to being born of a woman. Not to mention that because of women's goodness, our Lord Jesus Christ, when He had risen, appeared to a woman rather than to His Apostles. And just because Solomon says that he never found a good woman does not mean that all women are evil. For, although he failed to find a good woman, many other men have found many women to be good and true."

Here, the Miller unleashed so a great fart that it roused most, if not all, the pilgrims — to the unbounded delight of the Cook, who joined in with: "That's the right response to this awful, boring tale." He turned to me: "You promised a 'little' thing, but the only thing that's little about this . . . is . . . ." His thought died for lack of a fitting comparison. But this did not stop the Miller: "I have just let you know what I think of this tale, and I can only hope that it will soon vanish in the air as did my . . . comment." He laughed uproariously at his own jest, as did the Cook and a few others, while the Host hastened to my defense: "Oh, come now. Surely we must not engage in such childish behavior. This . . . I do not know what to call you, Sir . . . . This . . . elf . . . with my apologies" — he nodded at me with a slight bow — "must be allowed to tell his tale without further such boorish interruptions. It is clearly a moral tale and one we can all learn from."

While I was privately quite amused by this situation, I pretended to be deeply offended, pursing my lips and huffing and puffing for a bit before I settled down to continue my tale, returning the Host's bow to make clear my appreciation for his intervention.

"As I was saying: Lady Prudence suggested that the true meaning of Solomon's words was simply that he found no woman who was perfect. As she put it: we all know that no one is perfect save God alone, as He Himself records in His gospels. For there is no creature so good but that he lacks something of the perfection of God, his maker. As to your fear that if you were governed by my counsel it would give me mastery and lordship over yourself — Sire, with all due respect, that is not so. For if it were true that a man should be counseled only by those who have lordship and mastery over him, there would be little counsel indeed. For a man who asks for counsel still has free choice to follow or ignore it. To your argument that women's chattering can obscure what they don't know, and that they cannot hide what they do know — Sire, these things are said of wicked women who are chatterers.

There is a saying based on such women, namely, that there are three things that drive good men from their homes: smoke, leaking rain, and wicked wives. And of such women Solomon says that "it were better to live in the desert than with women who are debauched." But, by your leave, Sir, that is not who I am. Many times have you tested and found true my deep silence and my enormous patience. You know from experience how well I can hide and conceal things that should be kept secret or hidden.

And finally, as to your fifth reason, that women make use of bad counsel to control men, God knows that this argument is not applicable here. For, clearly, at this moment, you seek counsel to do wrong, and if you wish to do wrong and your wife restrains this evil goal and wins by reason and good counsel, she should surely be praised rather than blamed. This is how you should understand the philosopher who tells you that "by means of evil counsel women are victorious over their husbands."

And whereas you blame all women and their arguments, I shall show you by multiple examples that many women have been — and continue to be — quite good and that their counsel is beneficial. There are men who have said that women's counsel is either too expensive or totally worthless. But even if many women are evil and their counsel is vile and worthless, there have also been many good women, discreet and wise in their counsel. Through the good advice of Rebecca, his mother, Jacob won the blessing of his father Isaac, as well as rule over his brothers. Through her good advice Judith delivered her city of Bethulie from the siege and destruction of Olofernus. Abigail delivered her husband Nabal from death at the hand of King David, as she appeased the King's anger with her good counsel. Also, Esther, by her good counsel, greatly benefited the people of God in the reign of King Ahasuerus. There is a wealth of stories about the good counsel provided by women.

Moreover, when our Lord had created Adam, our forefather, He said: "It is not good for man to be alone; let us make him a helper like himself." Here you can see that if women and their counsel were evil, our Lord God would never have created them nor called them the helper of man but rather the confusion of man. And as a clerk once told us: "What is better than gold? Jasper. And what is better than jasper? Wisdom. And what is better than wisdom? Woman. And what is better than a good woman? Nothing." So, Sire, you may see that many women, as well as their counsel, have been good.

Therefore, Sire, if you will trust my counsel, I shall restore your daughter to you whole and sound. And also I will make sure you emerge from all this with honor.'

Melibee agreed: 'I can see that the words of Solomon are true. He says: "words spoken prudently and correctly are honeycombs, for they provide sweetness to the soul and health to the body." My dear wife, because of your sweet words and because I have tested and proven your great wisdom and truthfulness in the past, I will now be governed by your counsel in all things.'

'Now, Sire," said Lady Prudence, 'since you promise to be governed by my counsel, let me begin by teaching you how to choose good counsel. First, you must meekly beseech the high God to be your counselor, and you must make yourself ready to receive His counsel and comfort, as we are taught by Thobias: "Bless the Lord at all times, pray that he direct your way, and ensure that all of your counsel be in Him forevermore." St James says: "If any of you have need of wisdom, ask God." And only after that shall you follow your own best thoughts about what is most useful. And you must drive from your heart three destructive things: anger, covetousness, and haste.

No man deciding the best thing to do may operate out of anger. First, anyone filled with anger believes that he can do things he is actually incapable of. Second, someone who is angry cannot make good decisions; and anyone who cannot make good decisions cannot give good advice. Third, a man who is angry, Seneca tells us, is capable only of saying hurtful things, and his vicious words stir up others to become angry, too.

You must also drive covetousness out of your heart, for the apostle tells us that it is the root of all evil. A covetous man can neither think nor judge because he can think only of that which he covets. And he will never gain that, for the richer he is, the more he wants.

Finally, Sire, you must not act in haste; you cannot make the right decision based on a sudden thought, but you must reflect on it fully. For, as you know from the common proverb: "he who judges quickly, regrets quickly." Sire, you know that you do not always feel the same way about everything; surely in one moment one thing seems the best, while in another it is the opposite.

When you have thought long and hard and have, after thorough deliberation, decided what is best to do, then I strongly advise you not to tell anyone. Do not betray your thoughts unless you are certain that doing so shall be best. Ecclesiastes says: "Neither to your enemy nor to your friend shall you uncover either your secrets or your mistakes, for they will listen to you and look and seem supportive in your presence but scorn you when you are gone." Another clerk tells us "that you will rarely find anyone who can keep secrets," and the good book tells us that, "As long as you keep your thoughts to yourself, you keep them imprisoned, but when you share them with another, he holds you in his trap." And that is why you are better off if you keep your thoughts to yourself than to ask someone to keep your secrets. For Seneca asks, "if you are not able to keep your own thoughts secret, how can you ask anyone else to do so?"

But should you determine that sharing your thoughts will make things better, then do so in this manner.

First, do not let on whether you prefer peace or war, or this over that, and do not uncover your will or your intention. You can be sure that these counselors are generally flatterers — I mean the counselors to your great lords, for they make certain that they are always saying pleasant things, consistent with the lords' desires, rather than words that are true and useful. And that is why we say that unless it be his own, the wealthy man rarely has good counsel.

Next, seek out only those of your old friends who have been most true, wise, and proven in counseling and seek their advice. Solomon says that "as a man's heart delights in flavors that are sweet, so does the counsel of true friends provide sweetness for the soul." He also says that "there is nothing equal to a true friend; neither gold nor silver are equal to the good will of a true friend." And that "a true friend is the best defense; he who enjoys that has found a great treasure." Always seek the counsel of old friends who are experienced and have proven themselves with good counsel. For the good book tells us that "in old men there is wisdom, and time contains prudence—"

But now the Shipman broke in with a loud voice: "May your Prudence go straight to the devil in hell — straight, without one more word of endless blathering about wherefore and how and when and whatever in God's bloody name you want to yammer on about."

He turned to the Host: "If this is not worse than the first story with which this godforsaken nome pummeled our ears and imperiled our wits, I have never crossed the seas in a storm. By the High God above, this has to stop — now! I am so bored by all this back and forth, by what Solomon or Seneca or Ecclesiastes or the good book or some other knowitall said a thousand years ago. Seneca said this and somebody else said that and Godonlyknowswho said the other, and I say I am near cutting my own throat." He looked around and saw several pilgrims nodding assent. "And, what's more, by the bleeding feet of Jesus,

I say also that there are many here who would do the same, lest they have to listen to more of this turdheap being shoved up our asses by this, this—"

"Indeed, Sir Shipman," the Knight cut him off. "I must heartily disagree. This is a wonderful parable of how we should all be guided by prudence, and all that goes into making a good decision based on appropriate counsel. Surely we can all benefit from exercising more prudence."

"Prudence?" The Shipman retorted. "Prudence, my ass! If I hear one more word about prudence, I am likely to relieve myself of the breakfast I enjoyed earlier today. To hell with your prudence and your parables. This fellow must either tell us something less boring or he must sop babbling on. I can't take any more of it."

Now the Tapister joined in. "The Shipman is right, damn it all. This is awful, this drivel about prudence and endless arguing about whether or not to kill those who would kill us and then this unbearable woman's endless quibbling about how to find good counsel. May such stories and the people who tell them all go to the devil in the same handcart. I know for a fact that the devil would enjoy this more than do I." He looked around. "Am I right?"

The Man of Laws ostentatiously cleared his throat, waited for what was more or less silence, and then — looking at me — intoned: "My dear Sir . . . I don't rightly know your . . . what it is you do or your status . . . but I do know this: if you wish to teach us all something useful, you might be better served by embellishing less and stripping your story down somewhat. In my experience, I have found that audiences are more receptive to ideas expressed briefly and succinctly than enveloped in clouds of less relevant adornments." He gave me a condescending smile. "I believe this is what some of our companion pilgrims are trying to tell you."

Now the Host interjected, knowing that he was once again losing control of our troop and of everything we had agreed to before our journey began. "Need I remind you," and he looked around sternly at the company, "that all of you assented to hearing a story from each of your fellows before our pilgrimage comes to a close, and that this — yes, I will admit that he is somewhat strange — but nevertheless, he is entitled to tell his story, especially since I myself stopped him in his first effort."

He paused. "I believe he is doing the best he can."

No one said anything.

"So then," he continued, ever more sure of himself, "let us abide by our agreement."

Turning to me, he offered: "Go on then, continue."

"It may seem," I meekly offered, "as if all these details are unnecessary but, I think, if you will hear me out, you will see that it all ends with good winning out over evil, as it must."

"Fine and good," answered the Host. "But you would be wise to consider the objections you have heard and grace us with more corn and less chaff. Nevertheless, you have been interrupted often enough, and I believe you are telling us a story all should hear. So, continue now, and let us have no more interruptions."

"I thank you, Sir Host, and Sir Knight, for your gracious efforts to let me finish. And finish I will. I know but one way to tell this story, and I am telling it just so.

Where was I? Oh yes, about choosing counselors wisely. Very well — let me continue with the invaluable words of Lady Prudence to her spouse, Melibee.

She told him: 'At first, share your thoughts with only a few, but eventually you can tell more people, as needed. But always make sure that your counselors have the three qualities that I have identified before: that they be true, wise, and greatly experienced. And never accept the counsel of one advisor alone, for there are times when you should seek the counsel of many. Solomon says: "Things end best when there are many counselors."

Now that I have told you whom to seek out as counselors, let me teach you whose counsel to avoid. First, don't listen to fools; as Solomon says, "do not take a fool's counsel, for he can counsel only out of his own desires and whims." And the good book tells us that "the essence of a fool is this: he assumes the worst about others and the best about himself."

You must also avoid the counsel of those who flatter you rather than tell you the truth. That is why Cicero says 'that among all the traps of friendship, the worst is flattery." So, avoid and fear flatterers most. The good book tells us "rather to fear and flee the sweet words of flattering praisers than the sharp words of friends who speak the truth." Solomon says "that the words of a flatterer are traps to catch the innocent," and that "he who says sweet and pleasant things to his friend is simply laying a snare before his feet with which to catch him." And that is why Cicero says: "neither listen to flattery nor pay attention to words that flatter." And Cato adds: "be well advised and avoid the sweet words of flattery."

In addition, you have to avoid the counsel of long-time enemies with whom you have become reconciled. The book says that "no man returns unscathed into the graces of an old enemy." And Aesop advises "not to trust anyone with whom you have formerly been at war or have fought against; and do not share your thoughts with them." And Seneca tells us why: "Where there has been much fire over a long period of time, some warmth will remain." That is why Solomon says: "never trust an old enemy." For surely, though your enemy is reconciled with you and pretends to be humble and bow down to you, do not trust him. For he is certainly feigning humility more for his own welfare than because he loves you, as he thinks his deceptive face is giving him the victory that he could not achieve over you by confrontation. Peter Alfonse teaches us: "Do not seek the company of your old enemies, for whatever good you do them they will pervert into wickedness."

You must also avoid the counsel of your servants and those who treat you with great reverence, for they are likely doing this more out of fear than love. That is why the philosopher says: "No man is true to someone he fears." And Cicero says that "no great emperor will endure unless his people love him more than they fear him."

You must also avoid the counsel of drunkards, for they can keep no secrets. As Solomon tells us: "There is no privacy among drunkards."

You must, furthermore, be suspicious of the advice you receive from those who tell you one thing in private and say another in public. For Cassidorus says: "It is trickery to do one thing in public and the opposite in private." Similarly, you must question the counsel of those who are evil. For the good book says that "the counsel of evil folks is always fraudulent." And David tells us that a happy man is one who has not followed the advice of scoundrels.'

"And I say," the Miller interrupted rudely, nearly pulling me off my horse as he grabbed my sleeve to keep from falling down himself, "I say, and I say this without proper or false or counsel of any kind because my ears are counseling me to do so — no benefit of Seneca or Solomon or Cicero or anyone else — I say, by Christ's hairy arms, stop! No more of this. You drone on about the perils of choosing bad counsel, but what about the peril to our ears? When, on God's green earth, will this end? By the sweaty brow of sweet Jesus, have we not heard enough of this cat piss?" He turned to the other pilgrims. "When will the time come for this . . . this butcher of words to stop killing us with his words? By God Almighty, did we not ask him kindly to tell a simple story without all these authorities, and has he done as we asked? No! I say, no! He has not! And he has not changed anything since last he promised to."

"Sadly, I must agree with this Miller," the Clerk joined in. "In justice, this is more than we should have to listen to. We did not agree to be killed by boredom when we said we would pass the time on this journey by telling tales." He shook his head in a way that bespoke helpless confusion and looked around for agreement.

There was now general murmuring, rising to a level that made it very difficult to make out individual opinions, as pilgrims began to speak for and against my continuing with my tale, with the Host attempting futilely to restore order. Some hearty curses, as well as objections to those same curses, filled the air, as chaos threatened to descend on our once-so-merry group. Our Host seemed at a loss.

Finally, the Man of Laws gained the upper hand, or should I say, the upper voice, for he managed to quiet the group enough so that all could hear: "Peace, peace my fellow pilgrims." He waited until everyone was silent, even though the impatience of many was palpable. "We have been here before, my companions on this blessed journey."

The Prioress crossed herself most piously and kissed the cross on her chest.

The Man of Laws continued. "Let us remind ourselves of what we agreed to and . . . perhaps . . . what we need to agree to! First, I remind you all that we agreed solemnly in a manner equivalent to a legal contract to certain rules we would follow on this journey. And . . ." here he quieted a new outbreak of objections with his outstretched arm. "And . . . and . . . like it or not, each of us has the right to tell a tale of . . . our own . . . choosing, and the rest must all listen, whether it be a tale to our liking or not."

More murmuring and muttering.

"Yes, yes, that is why we agreed to have an impartial judge decide at the very end . . . at the end, I say . . . of our journey, after each of us has told a tale . . . a tale, as I said, of our own choosing . . . who among us will have told the best story. In other words," he paused for dramatic effect, "in other words . . . the time to judge these tales has not yet come. It will come when we reach our journey's end and our esteemed Host will, as our oral contract demands, make and announce to all of us, his decision as to the best story."

He paused again, this time to general silence.

"That time, however, has not yet come. Therefore it behooves us all to honor the terms of our agreement and to let everyone," he looked rather condescendingly at me, "everyone, I say, no matter what the tale, or the quality of story-telling, have his time at the table, so to speak, in order to tell the story he wishes to share." He looked around at everyone. "This is a matter of solemn agreement, and it must be honored."

The Host ostentatiously cleared this throat several times. "Indeed," he announced, looking around imperiously. "Indeed, it is so, as our noble Man of Laws has reminded us. The time for judgment is yet to come, and it is judgment reserved, as you all agreed," he looked around once more, "to me . . . and to me alone," his voice strengthened, filled with increasing importance and conviction. "And so, since this is not the time for judgment but the time for telling tales, I will ask our noble . . . our noble . . ." (as did the Man of Laws, our Host still does not know what to call me), ". . . our worthy . . . story-teller . . . to continue and to complete his tale, with all due consideration for the . . . the . . . the objections that have been voiced heretofore." He looked at the Man of Laws, as if for approval, and then bowed to me. "Please continue . . . Master."

I glanced down at the ground for a moment, to compose myself, before I looked up and said: "And so I thank you all, for your kind forbearance. My tale will soon come to an end." Here a smattering of applause could be heard from scattered pilgrims, overridden by the MIller's objection: "Not bleeding soon enough!"

But now I was the one not to be deterred, especially after all that had just been said. "Indeed, it is coming to an end . . . as is appropriate to it. For I am telling it the only way I can, and so I will."

But some of my fellow pilgrims were not appeased.

"We've heard you say that before," the Tapister challenged me.

I was uncertain as to my answer to this point, but then a most unlikely voice was heard, that of the Nun's Priest. He spoke calmly but firmly: "I must agree with the learned Lawyer that we have all agreed to tell . . . and to listen to a story told by each of us. I am most grateful to my good friend here for telling us this story of great virtue and . . . and . . . prudence, and," he paused, as if to think of precisely the words he needed for what he was going to say next, "and . . . we are doing that, have been doing that."

Again, he paused before continuing. "On the other hand, and with due deference to you, Sir," he bowed in my direction, "it seems to me that we also . . . each of us . . . has the responsibility to tell a story that . . . that . . . whose purpose, whose point is not lost in the telling. For," and now he spoke rapidly, as if he had suddenly discovered what he wished to say, "why tell a story that we all do not enjoy? Surely we will stop listening, and then all will have been lost."

The ensuing silence was ended by the Clerk: "The worthy Priest speaks wisely and well. And if I may follow up the learned Lawyer's words about our contract — a contract has two sides to it: that which is promised by one side and that which is expected and seemingly agreed to by the other. Our contract, it seems to me, besides the agreement for each of us to tell a story, also includes implicitly that we expect to hear stories we can listen to. I would therefore argue that there is a middle ground here, on which we come together to tell — and to listen to — stories that are told as well as possible and received similarly. In that vein, then, may I suggest that our worthy story teller listen to the objections of his fellow pilgrims and tell the story more . . . sparsely, perhaps, with fewer quotes from authorities . . . and, perhaps, fewer examples, but still keeping the substance? As our Host suggested earlier: more corn and less chaff?"

Silence, while the pilgrims thought over what the Clerk had offered.

Then the Lawyer answered: "I find that what our young Clerk has said here to be a wise and cogent recommendation for honoring what I spoke of as a contract."

Now many of the pilgrims were looking at me, waiting for a response. But the Host spoke first.

"My friend," he addressed me, somewhat as one might address an unruly school boy, "what do you say to this? Can you tell your story in a somewhat shorter manner?"

"Perhaps," the Clerk chimed in, "with fewer quotes, or even — dare I say — none, from the authorities?"

Secretly, I was somewhat relieved, for I must admit that I had been telling the endless story of Melibee and Prudence mostly to get even with the Host for cutting off my first tale. I felt now that my purpose had been fulfilled, and so I agreed, far more joyfully in my hearty of hearts, than I wanted the pilgrims to note.

"Very well," I said, as seriously as I could, trying to find the balance between being properly offended and appropriately appeased. "I have heard your objections and, even though I still believe there is only one way to tell this story as it must be told, I will attempt to cut it shorter but yet make the point it has for us."

There was general murmur of assent and I finally had the chance to finish.

"I believe I was at the point in the story where Prudence advises Melibee on whose counsel not to take. And she advises him to avoid the counsel of the young, for it is not seasoned. But now I will try to be less long-winded and tell you only what matters. I will serve up," I bowed to the Clerk and then to the Host, "only the corn and not the chaff."

And so I continued, careful not to use more words than needed.

"Prudence said: 'Now, Sire, I will teach you how to determine the value of advice according to the doctrine of Tullius, who tells us that he who gives false advice" — and here I interrupted myself — "my sincere apologies. Old habits are difficult to break and I was, indeed, falling into my old habit, trying to tell the tale as I believe it should be told . . . but I will endeavor to honor your pleas and my promise — and not do so again.

Where was I, oh yes, Prudence was teaching Melibee how to determine the value of advice offered him by others.

She said to her husband: 'In this process, you must tell the truth and assess the value of the advice and its potential consequences, as well as its feasibility. A man may change his purpose and his counsel when necessary or because it may cause damage, for counsel immutable under any conditions is wicked.'

Melibee now spoke: 'Please tell me how you feel about the counselors that we have chosen in our current situation.'

'My Lord,' she said, 'I must tell you that your counsel in this matter is merely a series of foolish decisions. You have erred first in how you assembled your counselors. You have called on too many, and they have been the wrong people. Moreover you have fallen victim to anger, covetousness and haste, and you showed your counselors your inclination to war and vengeance. You have made no distinction between counselors, and then you simply yielded to those greatest in number.'

'I have clearly erred, but I am now prepared to do just as you tell me to.

'Let me ask you how you understood the advice of the physicians?'

'I understood them to say that just as I was injured, so should I injure in return!'

'Oh my,' said Lady Prudence, 'how easily we turns things to meet our own desire and pleasure. The physicians told you that good and evil are contraries, not that one heals the other. How did you understand the advice of the old, wise men and the men of law that you should protect yourself and your home.'

'I should fortify my house with high towers.'

'Alas, high towers are usually signs of pride — you were really advised to fortify and strengthen yourself. As for the advice you got from all the rest, who are not your true friends, you must ignore it and understand what I now tell you.

You were attacked by the world, the flesh, and the devil, and you do not have legal standing to avenge yourself of any of them. You have allowed them to enter your heart through the windows of your body because you have insufficiently defended yourself against their assaults and temptations.

In short, you have let the seven deadly sins enter your body through your five senses.'

'But how, if you are right, is anyone ever to avenge himself properly?'

'If you want to avenge yourself on your enemies, find the judge with jurisdiction over them, and he will punish them according to the law.'

'Ah, since Fortune has supported me from birth I will rely on her, with God's help, to help me ease my shame.'

'Nay, nay! Do not rely on Fortune, for she is neither steadfast nor stable. Since you seek vengeance, and you don't want it done according to the law and by a judge, you must rely on the Sovereign Judge that avenges all evil and wrongs.'

'But if I do not avenge myself, I invite everyone to do more evil to me.'

'Avenging evils must be left to judges, but let us assume that you are in a position to avenge yourself. Your enemies have the advantage on you and, for now, the best thing is to be patient and accept what is.'

"Patience may be a sign of perfection, but I cannot rest until I have avenged myself, even if my revenge is excessive.'

Lady Prudence shook her head: 'Vengeance must never be excessive. A man must be temperate in his self-defense and, as God is my witness, you know very well that you now wish only to get even, and you have no intention of being temperate.'

'It is no great mystery that I am angry and impatient, but I am wealthier and more powerful than my enemies!'

'Yes, and there is nothing wrong with wealth and its proper use, which is to be neither niggardly nor to spend too freely. But, in maintaining your goods, you must keep in your heart God, conscience and reputation, and you must not go to war for the sake of riches. Victory in battle proceeds from the will and the hand of the Almighty. And since no man can be so certain of his virtue that he knows God will give him victory, every man should greatly dread initiating a war.'

'If war is not an acceptable conclusion, what is the alternative?'

'Peace, the greatest and most excellent thing in the world.'

'You know very well that my enemies have started all this and have no interest in peace. Are you suggesting that I go and humble myself and bow down to them and ask for mercy? For that, by God, would destroy any reputation I have.'

'Sire, I care for your honor and your profit as I do for my own, and I do not counsel that you seek out your enemies to make peace. Rather, begin by making peace between yourself and God, and then God will send your enemies to you, ready to do your will and all you command. In the meantime, let me speak to your enemies in private; once I know their will, I can counsel you more effectively.'

Melibee agreed to this, and Lady Prudence sent for his enemies and showed them the great benefits of peace and the harmful results of war. They were so taken by her wise words that they agreed to a reconciliation and placed themselves at her will, admitting that they had gravely and immeasurably offended Melibee and were ready to make amends.

Melibee was most pleased to hear this, so Lady Prudence sent for his kin and his true friends and asked them to give their advice and consent as to the best way to proceed. And, when they had heard everything and had examined what Lady Prudence had said in great detail and with much deliberation, their advice was to seek peace. Soon Melibee's foes came before him to admit their wrongs and to beg his mercy. Melibee graciously received their oaths and pledges and assigned a certain day on which they were to receive and accept his judgment and sentence.

He then told Lady Prudence that he planned to take all their possessions and to exile them forever.

But she said: 'This would indeed be a cruel and unreasonable sentence. I implore you not to do that, so that people can praise you for your pity and mercy and so that you will have no regrets.'

Melibee's heart began to incline to the will of his wife, and he assented to her counsel, and when his enemies returned, he said to them: 'Even though you have acted badly and done me wrong, inasmuch as I have witnessed your great humility, sorrow and repentance, I am moved to be gracious and merciful. Therefore I receive you back into my good graces and forgive you completely all the evils you have committed against me and mine. I now understand that if we repent ourselves of the sins and guilt which we have earned in the sight of our Lord God, in His generosity and mercy He will forgive all of them and bring us to the bliss that is everlasting.'

Amen."

Now when I had finished telling this story of Melibee and Prudence, the Tapister said loudly: "Praise be to God above. It is finally finished. We can only thank all the angels and saints and our mother Mary that we have heard the last of this Melibee and his chattering wife."

"Amen" could be heard from various pilgrims, but the Host interrupted them: "Thank God, indeed, for this wonderful story of Melibee and the graciousness of his wife, the Lady Prudence. On my Christian faith, and by the precious corpse of St. Madrian, I would gladly give a barrel of ale if only Goodlief, my own wife, had heard it! For she knows nothing of such patience as this Melibee's wife possessed.

God's aching feet — when I beat my servants she brings me bigger clubs and shouts: 'Kill these dogs, all of them, and break every bone they have.' And if one of my neighbors fails to bow to her at church or be so foolish as to get in her way, she shakes her first in my face and yells at me: 'Weakling! Coward! Avenge your wife! By God's body, I'll take your knife and you can have my distaff and go spin!' She starts up like that in the morning and finishes only late at night: 'What shame that I was ever born — to marry such a pantywaist, a cowardly ape bested by any other man who comes along! You will never stand up for your wife!'

Unless I want to spend every day in fights, this is the way I must live. I have no choice but to get the hell out of my own house — else I am done — unless I want to go around like a wild lion, like an idiot. I just know that one day she'll get me to kill one of my neighbors and then, God knows what! I am a dangerous man when you put a knife in my hand, even though I am afraid to take this woman on — she is formidably strong, if truth be told. Anybody who does her wrong or crosses her will learn that soon enough!"

He paused, composed himself and continued: "But I've said enough — let's move on."

He looked around as if to remind himself which pilgrim had already spoken and which had not.

"My Lord Monk, rouse yourself — your turn to tell a tale. You can see we're near Rochester already. Look lively now and don't hold up our game. But as I think about it, I realize that I don't even know your name. What shall I call you? My Lord Sir John, or Sir Thomas, or maybe Sir Albon? Pray tell, on your father's good name, what holy order do you belong to?"

Whether the Monk was preparing to answer or not, we will never know, for our Host went on with a barrage of comments.

"By God, your skin is white enough! It must be an excellent pasture where you feed. You don't strike me as a penitent friar or a cloistered. I'll bet you hold some important office — maybe you're in charge of the sacred vessels or the wine cellar for, by my father's soul, I'll be damned if you're not in charge of everything where you live."

The Monk seemed to squirm a bit in his saddle, but the Host was just hitting his stride.

"You don't strike me as a common cloisterer or novice, but a master of some sort, well-schooled and clever. On top of that you've got quite the build and the body, and you're handsome enough! I can only hope to God that whoever first brought you to the religious life gets his proper punishment!"

Here the Host looked around and winked at some of the pilgrims before turning back to the Monk.

"You could have been some cock, screwing your fair share of willing hens. If you had devoted yourself as much to satisfying your lust in breeding as you have the goods for it, you would have fathered many a newborn by now! What a shame that you and your brawny muscles are all covered by that great cloak!"

Another wink to the rest of us.

"May God strike me, but if I were the pope, not only you but every man — I don't care how tonsured he might be — should, for the welfare of the world, be married. The Church has kept to itself the very flower of manhood, and we laymen are no more than shrimp. Weak trees cannot help but produce scrawny offshoots. This is why our children are so sickly and feeble that they themselves can barely make more babies."

By now he was riding right next to the Monk, poking that worthy cleric in the ribs as if they had been great pals.

"So our wives will want to try out priests like you because you strapping clerics might just be better at making the payments of Venus than are the rest of us. God knows you don't pay with counterfeit coin!"

He laughed loudly at his own joke and settled back in his saddle.

"But don't be bothered by my banter, my Lord; I'm just having fun with you. Of course,' he paused and inspected the Monk from under his scrunched up brows, "it happens that silly words sometimes contain a great truth!"

The worthy Monk took it all in stride. He did not smile or show any other emotion, but answered: "I'll do my best, as it is appropriate, to tell you a story, or two, or three.

And if you choose to listen, I will tell you about the life of Saint Edward . . . or . . . first, let me tell you some tragedies, of which I have a hundred in my cell. By tragedy I mean a story, usually found in books about ancient times, of someone who has achieved great prosperity but falls from this great height into misery and ends terribly. They are traditionally told in poetic lines of six feet, known formally as hexameter, but many have also been passed down to us in prose and in meters of various kinds — but enough of that.

Now listen, if you want to hear me, but first I must ask one thing from you: if I don't tell these stories of popes, emperors and kings in chronological order, or according to the time in which they lived, but tell some before and some after they should be told — as they come into my memory — just blame my lack of knowledge."

Without waiting for an answer, he began.

The Monk's Tale

"Through these tragedies I lament the woes of those who reached high status but fell, with nothing to save them from their adversity. They demonstrate for a fact that when Fortune forsakes us no man can change her mind. My advice is: do not count on lasting prosperity, but learn from these tried and true examples.

I will begin with Lucifer, though he was an angel rather than a man. We know that Fortune cannot harm an angel; nevertheless, this angel fell from high status because of his sin and was condemned to hell, where he remains. Oh, Lucifer, brightest of all angels, now you are Satan, never able to leave the misery into which you have fallen.

Behold Adam, created in the fields of Damascus by God's own hand, not begotten of man's unclean sperm — and ruler of all paradise, except for one single tree. No human man has ever had as high a status as Adam until he was exiled from his well-being to labor, hell and misfortune — all because of his own bad judgment.

Behold Samson! His birth announced by an angel, he was consecrated to God and extraordinarily noble — until he lost his sight. There was never another as strong or as hardy, but he shared his secret with his wife and ended up killing himself in misery. Samson was a noble, all-powerful champion who, unarmed, with his bare hands, killed a lion he met on the way to his wedding. His false, unfaithful wife knew how to please him until he shared with her his secret, and then she betrayed Samson to his enemies and left him for another. In his wrath, Sampson tied three hundred foxes together and set them on fire with a burning torch tied to each tail. Then he let them loose to burn the fields of corn, all the olive groves and the vineyards in that land.

With no weapon other than the jawbone of an ass, Sampson killed one thousand men in combat. After that, so thirsty that he was about to perish, he prayed to God to show him mercy and send him something to drink, lest he die. And out of the jawbone, completely dry, sprang a well, of which he drank his fill. Thus, as the Book of Judges tells us, God came to his aid.

One night, by sheer force of strength this mighty Samson pulled up the gates of the city of Gaza, despite all the Philistines, and carried them high up on a hill for everyone to see. Oh, noble, all-powerful Samson, beloved and dear, had you not shared your secret with a woman, you would have had no peer in all the world.

Having received a divine message, Samson never drank hard liquor or wine, nor did he ever cut his hair, for that is where all his strength lay. He governed Israel for a full twenty years, but all would end in misery because a woman brought him to an unhappy end. He told his lover, Delilah, that the source of his strength was his uncut hair, and she deceived him and sold him out to his enemies. One day, while he lay sleeping with his head in her lap, she cut his hair and let his enemies in on his secrets. Finding him like this, they tied him up and blinded him.

While he still had his hair, there were no ropes strong enough to bind him, but now he is imprisoned in a cave and forced to grind corn with a mill stone. Oh, noble Samson, strongest of men; Oh, erstwhile judge, in all your glory and wealth! Now you may well weep with your sightless eyes, bewailing your descent into wretchedness.

Let me tell you about his end. One day his enemies held a great feast and made him play the fool before them in a magnificent temple. But finally, Sampson launched a terrifying assault on them, for he grasped two of the pillars and pulled the entire building down, killing himself and all his enemies. Three thousand bodies lay under that rubble. But that is all I will say of Samson, whose story is proof, cold and plain, that if men want important secrets to be kept secret, they should not tell their wives.

The works of Hercules, sovereign conqueror, speak loudly of his greatness. For at the peak of his strength, he was the best. He killed and skinned a lion; made meaningless the boasts of the

Centaurs; slew those cruel birds of prey, the Harpies; stole golden apples from a dragon; drew out Cerberus, the hound of hell; killed the cruel tyrant, Busirus, and forced his horse to eat his flesh and bone; slew the fiery venomous serpent; broke one of the two horns of Achelous; killed Cacus in a stone cave, as well as the mighty giant Antheus, and the wild boar; and carried the heavens on his shoulders. Never did a man kill more monsters. He was known throughout the world for his strength and his great virtue, and he went everywhere. He was so strong that no man could stop him. Trophee tells us that he set pillars as boundaries at both ends of the world.

Hercules had a lover, Dianira, beautiful as May, and history tells us that she sent him a shirt, newly fashioned and beautiful. Alas, this shirt — alas, indeed — was so cleverly saturated with venom that before he had worn it for half a day it made all his flesh fall from his bones. And when he saw no way out, he had himself buried in hot coals because he did not want to die of poison. This, then, is how the worthy, mighty Hercules died.

Who can then ever trust Fortune over time? He who involves himself in this dangerous world is often laid low before he knows what happened. Wise is the man who knows himself! Beware! When Fortune chooses to deceive she waits to overthrow a man in some way he would least expect.

One can hardly do justice to King Nebuchadnezzar's mighty throne, invaluable treasures, glorious scepter or royal majesty. Twice he conquered the city of Jerusalem and took away with him the vessels of the temple. His sovereignty was on display at Babylon, seat of his glory and delight. He castrated the most beautiful royal children of Israel and made them his servants. The wisest of these Israelites was Daniel, for he could explain the dreams of kings. He had no equal throughout Babylonia in this.

In his pride, Nebuchadnezzar had a statue made of gold, sixty cubits long and seven across, and commanded everyone to bow down and revere it; those who refused were burned in a fiery furnace of red. But Daniel and two of his companions would not adore this idol. This King of Kings was proud and arrogant, sure that God, in all His power, could not relieve him of his estate. But suddenly he lost all his dignity and began to act like an animal — like an ox, he ate hay and lay down in the rain; for a time, he lived with the wild beasts. Like an eagle, he grew feathers instead of hair and his nails were like a bird's claws until God, in due time, released him and returned his wit. Then, weeping, he thanked God and spent his life in fear of doing anything wrong or trespassing again. And from then until he was laid on his bier, he knew that God was full of might and grace.

Balthasar, son and successor of Nebuchadnezzar, apparently learned nothing from his father, for he too was a proud idolator. But Fortune cast him down, and there he lay as his kingdom suddenly fell apart. He organized a feast for his lords and encouraged them to enjoy themselves, and then he told his officials: 'Go and bring out the vessels that my father in his prosperity took from the temple in Jerusalem, and let us thank our high gods for what our fathers left us, as is right.' His wives, his lords, and his concubines all drank their fill of various wines from these noble vessels. But then the king saw a hand, writing these words on the wall: '*Mane, techel, phares,*' but no one knew what these words meant, except Daniel, who told this King: 'God gave your father glory and honor, power, treasure and income, but he was proud and did not fear God, so God sent him much wretchedness and took his kingdom from him. He was cast out of human company and lived with the animals until he came to understand that our Lord has power over every rule and creature. Then God had compassion on him and restored his person and his rule.

You, his son, are also proud and believe the same things he did; and thus you rebel against God. Therefore, great pain is coming your way. This hand that wrote on the wall was sent by God to tell you that your rule is at an end and your kingdom will be divided between the Medians and the Persians.'

And that very night the King was slain and Darius succeeded him, even though he had neither right nor legal claim on the kingdom. From all this, my Lords, you should learn that there is no certainty in lordship, for when Fortune chooses to forsake a man she will take away his rule, his riches, and his friends.

Zenoboam, the Queen of Palmyra, descended from Persian royalty, was such an outstanding warrior and so fierce that no man surpassed her in fortitude, in lineage, or in worthiness. I do not say that she was the most beautiful woman ever, but her appearance could not be improved. She shunned the company of women from childhood and chose instead to spend her time in the woods, spilling the blood of many a hart with her long arrows. She was so speedy that they could not escape her and, when she was older, she killed lions and leopards and ripped apart bears. She knew where to find the dens of wild beasts, spent many a night in the mountains, and beat any young man in wrestling.

She kept her maidenhead from all men, refusing to bind herself to anyone. But finally, after a long time, her friends got her to marry Odenathus. They were very similar in interest, living happily and faithfully — except for one thing. She wanted to have a child, but she would lie with him only one time. When this act did not produce a child, she allowed him to lie with her again, but only once in forty weeks. No matter whether Odenathus was happy with this arrangement, he got no more from her, for she believed the it was lechery and shame for women when men played with them. Eventually she had two sons by Odenathus, and she raised them to be virtuous and learned.

As I said, in all the world you could find no more honorable creature, wiser or more measured, so unbeatable in war, so courteous, or elegant. Her clothing was covered entirely in precious stones and gold, she neglected hunting for no one, loved to learn all she could from books about how to spend her life virtuously. She and her husband conquered many lands in the East and many a fair city that had allegiance to Rome, and no enemies ever managed to escape them while Odenathus lived. After his death, she held the reins by herself and made alliances with many foes, spending her time riding and entertaining herself. No one was courageous enough to fight her in open field.

Her two sons, Hermanno and Thymalao, were arrayed like kings, heirs to all their father had ruled. But since Fortune's sweetness is always tainted with bitterness, this mighty queen's time was limited. Fortune soon made her fall from royal ruler to misfortune and wretchedness. When the governance of Rome fell into the hands of Aurelius, he and his legions moved toward Zenobia and, in short order, made her flee, caught her and her two children, and conquered her country. Aurelius showed off her chariot, covered with gold and precious stones. He forced the queen to walk before it, golden chains hanging from her neck, crowned as a queen and dressed in clothes dazzling with precious stones. Alas, Fortune! She who once was the terror of kings and emperors is now the object of ridicule by common people; she who once wore a helmet in the midst of violent battle and by force won strong towns and towers, must now wear woman's wear on her head; and she who once held a scepter of flowers must now wield a distaff to pay for her keep.

Oh, noble, worthy Pedro, glory of Spain, held up so high in majesty by Fortune! Indeed, men should bewail your pitiful death! Your brother betrayed you and killed you with his own hand, succeeding to your reign and all your possessions. He whose banner was marked with a field of snow and a black eagle fashioned this cursedness and this sin. A traitor from Brittany, just like Charlemagne's Oliver, he was corrupted by greed and brought this king to such a plight.

Another noble Pedro, King of Cyprus, conquered by Alexander the Great, was slain by his own men for his great chivalry, as he slept in his bed before dawn. Thus does Fortune turn and control her wheel, bringing men from joy into sorrow.

Great Bernabo Visconti, god of delight and scourge of Lombardy, what high status had you achieved before your own brother's son, double-allied with you as nephew and son-in-law, left you to die in his prison!

No tongue can do justice to the suffering the Earl Ugolino of Pisa underwent in that tower tower where he, along with his three little children (the oldest barely five years of age), was imprisoned. Alas, Fortune, you were most cruel to place these birds in such a cage.

Ugolino was condemned to die in this prison, with barely any food or drink, because Roger, Bishop of Pisa, had falsely accused him. And then, one day, the jailor, who usually brought food, shut the prison gates permanently. Ugolino heard it and said 'Alas that I was ever born!' And his three year old son asked him: 'Father, when will the jailer bring our soup? Do you have a scrap of bread anywhere? I am so hungry that I cannot sleep. I wish to God that I could fall asleep forever, for then I would not feel this hunger in my belly.' For a few days this child cried like this, until the time came when he lay down in his father's embrace, said: 'Father, father, I must die now!' and left this world that same day. And when the father, in his sorrow, began to bite his own arms, his remaining children thought he was doing so out of hunger rather and begged him: 'Father, eat your fill of our flesh, that you gave us.' Soon enough they and the mighty Earl of Pisa were all dead, for Fortune separated them from their high status.

Though Nero was as evil as any fiend living in hell, the entire world was subject to him. His clothing was beaded from top to bottom with rubies, sapphires and white pearls, and there was never an emperor more pleasure-seeking, more pompous of display or more prideful than he. He never wore the same clothes twice and, when he wanted entertainment, he had golden nets with which to fish the Tiber. All his desires were turned into law, and Fortune obeyed him as his friend. He burned Rome for his pleasure; he killed senators just to hear them weep; he slept with his sister, killed his brother and slit open his mother's womb to see where he had been conceived. He shed not a single tear for her but said only: 'She was a beautiful woman.' Then he ordered some wine and had a drink.

In his youth, Nero had a virtuous tutor who made sure no vices mastered his charge. But that did not last. When Seneca tried to tell him that "an emperor has to be courteous and hate tyranny," Nero forced him to slit his wrists and bleed out in a bath.

But then Fortune turned on Nero, thinking to herself: 'By God, I am silly to keep in such high status a man so filled with vice. I will cast him from his throne when he least expects it.' And so, the people revolted against him because of his wickedness. He fled the palace and knocked on the doors of those he thought to be his allies, but all the doors remained shut against him. He nearly lost his mind for fear, knowing that the common people were looking for him. In his terror he ran into a garden to hide. There he found two men sitting by a great, red, flaming fire, and he asked them to kill him and cut off his head so that his dead body would not be mutilated. But he ended up killing himself in his despair, and Fortune was simply amused.

Never did a king have a captain like Holofernes, who subjected more people, or was more powerful in the field of battle, or more presumptuous, or more famous. And Fortune kissed him most lecherously, leading him here and there, until he suddenly lost his head. People were in terror of him not only for fear of losing wealth or freedom, but also because he forced people to renounce their own beliefs. 'Nebuchadnezzar is your only God,' he proclaimed. No one dared challenge him, except Joachim, a priest in Bethulia. But death came to the drunk Holofernes one night, while he was sleeping in his bed within an enormous tent. For all his pomp and power, Judith, a woman, cut off his head and escaped with it.

What has not already been said about the royal majesty of King Anthiochus, of his pride or his evil deeds? For much of his life he had no equal, but then he fell from great prosperity and died, wretchedly, on a hillside. Fortune had encouraged him to think he could reach the stars, weigh the mountains, and restrain the oceans' floods.

But he hated, above all, God's people, and he wanted to destroy them in torment and pain. He killed the generals Nicanor and Timotheus and ordered his chariot to be prepared for an attack on Jerusalem. But so hard did God smite him for his wickedness with an invisible but incurable wound that his pain was intolerable. Nevertheless, he ordered his men to prepare for battle, but suddenly God made him fall from his chariot so hard that his limbs and skin were shredded and he was unable to walk or ride a horse but had to be carried around in a chair. Then evil worms inhabited his body and he smelled so unbearably that none of the people who nursed him could stand his stink. Finally he knew that God was the lord of all, because this robber, this murderer, starved on a hillside in all his stink and pain.

Everyone has heard of Alexander the Great and how those he did not overcome by force were happy to seek accord with him because of his reputation. No other conqueror can be compared to him, for the entire world quivered before him in terror. He was the epitome of knighthood and nobility, and Fortune made him the heir of her honor. He loved wine, women and honor in arms. He conquered Darius and a hundred thousand more kings, princes, dukes, and bold earls, and the world was his as far as a man can ride. No one can do justice to his chivalry. The son of Philip of Macedonia, Alexander ruled for a mere twelve years. Then Fortune, without a single tear, allowed the six of dice to turn into a one, and he was poisoned by his own people. Oh, Alexander, you had the entire world under your control — and yet it seemed not to be enough. How courageous was your exemplary knighthood! Alas, who can withstand false Fortune and poison?

Julius Caesar rose from humble birth to royal majesty, through intelligence, courage and hard work, and he eventually won the entire West, and made all other countries the tributary of Rome. He was the Emperor of Rome until Fortune turned on him. Oh, mighty Caesar, who conquered the entire Orient by capturing and killing Pompey the Great, your father-in-law, the foremost chivalric knight of the East. Allow me to mourn for a moment this mighty Pompey, whose head was brought to you, noble Caesar, to win your favor. Pompey, too, was brought to such an end by Fortune!

Julius Caesar returned to Rome in triumph, his head covered with laurel, but eventually Brutus and Cassius conspired against him. As was his custom, Caesar went to the Capitol, only to be slain by false Brutus and his other foes. But so manly was this Julius in his heart and so committed to decorum that, despite the pain of his fatal wounds, he threw his mantle over his hips so no man should see his private parts and shame him. Fortune suddenly turned from friend to foe. One must always keep an eye on her — just consider all these mighty emperors.

Even thought he was able to intimidate Cyrus the Great, Croesus, once king of Lydia, too, was captured and led to the stake to be burned, until such a rain came down from the sky that the fire was abated, and he made his escape. He could not wait to start another war, certain that with Fortune so clearly smiling down on him his enemies could not harm him. He relied strongly on a dream that guaranteed his revenge. It seemed to him that he was high in a tree where Jupiter was washing his body, front and back, and Phoebus brought him a beautiful towel to dry himself. His daughter explained the dream in this way: 'The tree represent the gallows, and Jupiter portends snow and rain, and Phoebus, with his clean towel, represents the rays of the sun. It is clear that you, dear father, shall be hanged, but the rain will wash you and the sun will dry you.' He should have been warned by these words but, despite his royalty, Croesus was hanged.

As you can see, tragedies clearly warn us that Fortune will always attack proud rulers when they are most unaware. Just when men trust her, she betrays them, covering her bright face with a cloud."

"Good Sir" interrupted the Knight. "No more of this, I pray you! Though what you say is true enough — I agree — and no doubt there is much more, but a little tragedy goes a long way. I, personally, find all this to be very stressful, indeed, to keep hearing about people who were enjoying great wealth and comfort and then suffered a mighty fall! This is the opposite of joy and solace, as when a man has been in great poverty and climbs from that to become fortunate and then to remain prosperous. Something like that is a joy to hear, it seems to me, and it would be good to tell such tales. But I'm afraid that I have heard my fill of these horrible stories that end only in grief and sorrow and death. Surely you can speak of better things than these!"

"Yes, indeed," chimed in the Host, "by St. Paul's bells, I must agree. You are absolutely right, Sir Knight! This Monk is merely making noise! He rails on about how Fortune covers . . . God only knows what . . . with clouds. And then he goes on and on and on about what he calls tragedies — as we have all heard him and, by God's knees, it is nothing more than crying over spilled milk. We cannot undo what has happened and complaining about it won't make it better. Besides, as you say, most worthy Knight, it is most distressing to keep hearing about sad things."

He turned back to the Monk: "Sir Monk! Please, I beg of you, stop this, as God may bless you! Your story annoys everyone here." He looked around for assurance and was emboldened by several nodding heads. "Talk like this is not worth a butterfly because it is neither entertaining nor fun.

So, Sir Monk, by name of Lord Peter, I beg you most heartily to share something different with us. For, to tell you the truth, if it were not for the tinkling of the bells that hang from your bridle on both sides, by the heavenly King above, I should have fallen asleep by now, no matter how deep the mud through which we have ridden. If that had happened, why, all your tragedies would not have been remembered — their telling in vain. For surely the clerks are right when they say that a man who has no audience makes his point to no one. And I know for sure, from experience, that the meaning of something leaves its mark on me when a thing is said well. So, Sir, I beg you, why don't you tell us a story about hunting?"

The Monk answered firmly and without hesitation: "No! I have no interest in this game. Let somebody else talk — I have said what I am going to say!"

Our Host accepted this answer, shrugged his shoulders and turned to the Nun's Priest, addressing him boldly and quite rudely: "Hey — you — Priest — come here. Come over here, Sir John! Tell us something to make us all happy. I see you ride a pretty bad nag, but that's no reason to be unhappy. So what if your horse is both lean and foul? If he serves your needs, who gives a red beet? So long as you are happy on the inside — that's all that counts!"

The Nun's Priest answered: "Yes, indeed, Sir. Yes, Sir Host, you are exactly right. For unless I be merry, I will indeed suffer the consequences." And he immediately began to tell his story, this gentle Priest, this good man, Sir John — as follows here.

The Nun's Priest's Tale

"Once upon a time there was a poor elderly widow, whose small cottage sat in a pleasant valley, beside a grove of trees. This widow, whose story this is, was a model of patience who led a very simple life ever since she had last been a wife; she had few possession and almost no income. Through careful management of what God sent her way she provided for herself and her two daughters. She possessed only three large sows, three cows, and one sheep — named Malle. Sooty were her bedchamber and her hall, where she ate many of her meager meals; she had no need for rich sauces, nor did she taste dainty morsels on her tongue, as her diet was dictated by what she could afford. She was never the victim of over-indulgence, as her moderate diet and the daily exercise of her work kept her healthy, and she was satisfied with what she had. She was not prevented from dancing by gout, nor did apoplexy make her head shake, as she never drank wine — red or white. Her dinner table was usually decorated in white and black: milk and brown bread, of which she had plenty, some bacon and now and then an egg or two, for she was a kind of dairy woman.

Her yard, bordered with sticks and a dry ditch, was home to a cock by the name of Chauntecleer, who had no peer in crowing in all the land. Merrier was his voice than the organ you can hear in church on Mass days, and the timing of his crowing was more accurate than any clock or timepiece in an abbey. Nature told him exactly when each hour was struck in town, and when the sun had risen fifteen degrees nothing could prevent his crowing. His comb was redder than the finest coral, notched as if it were a castle wall; black was his beak, shining like jet, and his legs and toes were azure in color. Whiter than a lily were his nails and his complexion was like burnished gold. Seven hens were at his command, there to satisfy every desire of this noble cock. They were his sisters and his lovers both, and their coloring wonderfully matched his. And the fairest one of these by the coloring of her throat was the lovely maid, Pertelot. She was courtly, discreet, gracious and sociable, and she carried herself so attractively from the time she was a mere seven days old that she had securely locked away Chauntecleer's heart. He loved her and therefore all was well with him. Such a joy it was to hear him sing in harmony with the sweet sun rising in the spring: 'My love has gone to the country.' For this was a time, it seems, when animals and birds had the gift of speech.

One day then, at dawn, as Chauntecleer was perched on his roost in the henhouse, surrounded by his wives, the fair Pertelot next to him, he began to groan loudly, as a man does when he is troubled deeply by a dream. When Pertelot heard him carrying on like this, she was frightened and said to him: 'Dearest heart, what is troubling you that you groan like this? You are usually such a good sleeper! Fie, for shame!'

'Madam, please, do not take it amiss. By God, I dreamed just now of such trouble that my heart is still pounding. Now, by the victor over the cross, help me interpret my dream correctly and keep my soul from a foul prison! In my dream I was roaming up and down in our yard when, suddenly, I saw a dog-like beast that clearly wanted to seize my body and kill me. He was between red and yellow in color, and his tail and both his ears had black tips, unlike the rest of his fur. He had a small snout and his eyes glowed red. Every time I remember him, I still feel like I am going to die of fright! This is what caused my groaning.'

'For shame!' she cried. "Fie on you, you coward! As God is my witness, now you have lost my heart and all my love! By my faith, I cannot love a coward! Rest assured that no matter what women say, we all want husbands who are brave, wise and generous — and able to keep a secret — we want no miser or fool or one afraid of a weapon or a boaster, I swear to God! How dare you tell your love, without shame, that you are afraid of anything? Although you have a beard you seem nevertheless not to be a real man. Good God! Are you going to tell me that you are afraid of dreams?

As God is my witness, dreams are nothing but fantasy. They are brought on by eating too much, often by fumes in the stomach and by misbalanced or excessive humors. Clearly your dream last night is caused by too much red bile — I am sure — because red bile makes people fear arrows in their sleep and imagine red flames, or red beasts that want to bite them, or conflict, or dogs — small and large — just as melancholy humor causes many men suddenly to cry out in their sleep because they are being chased by black bears or black bulls, even black devils who want to grab them. I could also tell you of the other humors that fill many a man's sleep with terror, but I won't do that right now.

Didn't that wise man, Cato, admonish us to "pay no attention to dreams"? Now, Sire, when we get down from these perches, for God's sake, take a laxative. On peril of my soul and of my very life, I am advising you to do what's best — far be it from me to lie to you — purge yourself both of your choler and of your depression. You can't do this soon enough and, because we have no apothecary near us, I myself will teach you about herbs that will help and benefit you. I will find them right here in our own yard, herbs which have the natural properties to clean you out above and below.

For the very love of God, don't forget that you are quite choleric by nature. Even when the sun is at the height of its ascension you never find yourself filled with hot humors. And when you do, I'm willing to bet a groat that you are likely to be suffering from a recurring fever or an ague. For a day or two, you need to partake of digestives that kill worms, or take your laxatives made of laurel, or century, or maybe hell-bore — which grow right here — of caper-spurge, or shamus, or ivy, all right there in various parts of our lovely garden. You can pick them just where they grow and eat them on the spot. Be happy, husband of mine, for the sake of your father's family! All I can tell you is not to be afraid of dreams!'

'Madame,' he answered her, 'with all due deference to your high learning, as well as to Lord Cato, whose wisdom is acknowledged by all — though he did indeed tell us not to be afraid because of our dreams — as God is my witness, you can find many old books written by people of even greater authority than was Cato — God grant me salvation — who make precisely the opposite point; these men know very well by their own experience that dreams predict the joys as well as the sorrows that will happen to people in their lives. There can be no disagreement about this; it is proven every day.

One of the greatest authors ever known to man tells the story of two well-intentioned fellows on pilgrimage, who came to a town so crammed full of people and so limited in lodging that they could not find even a simple cottage to house them both. Since they had no choice but to sleep in two different places for that night, they parted company and each of them went off to his host and took his lodging where he had found room. While one of them slept in a stall in a remote corner of a yard kept for plow-pulling oxen, his friend was lodged quite comfortably, whether by luck or by good fortune — which we know governs us all equally.

And, long before dawn, this second man dreamed, in his bed, as he was sleeping, that his companion was calling him, saying: 'Alas, I will be murdered this very night right here in this ox-stall. Help me now, dear brother, for if you do not come here at once, I will surely die.'

This man was startled from his sleep by fear but, awakened, he simply turned over and went back to sleep, thinking his dream to be nothing more than fantasy. He had this same dream twice, but then, when it came a third time, his friend seemed to say: 'Now I have been murdered, as you can see by my bloody wounds, so deep and wide. If you get up early in the morning and go to the west gate of the town, you will see there a cart full of dung in which my body is hidden. Make sure the driver is arrested, as I was killed for my money, and that is the truth!' With his pitiful pale face, he also described in detail how he was killed and, sure enough, that dream turned out to be entirely true. In the morning, when that man went hurriedly to the yard where his friend had been staying and called out for him, there was no answer. But the owner of the yard told him: 'Sire, your friend left town at the crack of dawn.'

Now suspicious because of his dream, he went to the west gate of the town, where, just as his dream had foretold, he found a dung cart bound for a dung yard, and it looked just like the one the dead man described in the dream. With a heavy heart this man began to cry out for revenge and justice for his companion: 'My friend was murdered this very night, and he lies in this cart, face up, with gaping mouth. I publicly call on the ministers of justice in charge of this town to come at once and to behold, alas, my dead friend.' What more is there to say about this story? The people assembled and turned over the cart and found, in the middle of the dung, the dead man, recently murdered.

Oh, blissful God,' Chauntecleer continued, 'so just and faithful to us, look how you ensure that murder will always be found out. It will out — we see this every day — murder is so disgusting and abominable to God, who is so just and reasonable, that He will not allow it to be hidden away, even if it takes a year, or two, or three. Murder will out — of that I am certain! In this case the ministers of that town arrested the cart driver on the spot and tortured him and the ox-yard keeper until they finally acknowledged their wickedness; then they were hanged by the neck until dead.

Here you can see that dreams should be paid attention to — but there's more. In that same book I read — in fact, in the following chapter — about two men who, for whatever reasons, wanted to sail across the sea to a distant country, but they were delayed by an opposing wind, which made them wait in a splendid city that was situated on that harbor. But one day, by late tide, the wind had begun to change, blowing now in the direction that served their purpose. Happily did they go to their beds that night, prepared to set sail at dawn.

But listen to this!

One of the men experienced something amazing in his sleep, as he had a memorable dream shortly before the sun was to rise. It seemed to him that a man who was standing by his bed told him not to sail that day: 'If you leave tomorrow, you will drown. That's all I have to say.' When the man woke up he told his friend about his dream, begging him not to undertake the voyage — at least, not to leave that day. But his friend laughed at him and scorned his advice. 'No dream will frighten me enough not to do what I have planned. I give no credence at all to your dreams, for dreams are but fantasies and trickery. People are always dreaming about owls and apes and other bewildering things — they dream of things that never were and never will be. But I can see that you intend to stay here and foolishly waste our tide and, God knows, I feel bad, but all I can say to you is: good day!'

So he took his leave and went on his way. Now, I don't know the details but before he had completed half of his journey, there was a mishap and suddenly the bottom of the ship was torn apart and sank deep into the water, all in view of the other ships that were close by, sailing in the same direction.

And so, my beautiful Pertelot, so dear to me, from these old stories you can learn that we ignore our dreams and their meanings at our own peril, and I say to you that I have no doubt but that frightening dreams should not be ignored.

I remember reading about the life of Saint Cenhelm, son of Cenwulf, the noble king of Mercia. As we all know, he was murdered, but he had a dream in which he vividly foresaw his own murder. His nurse interpreted his dream for him completely, warning him to avoid places and people who might have treasonous intentions. But he was merely seven years old and had little enough reason to pay attention to dreams — so pure was his heart. By God, I would give my shirt for you to have read this story, as I have.

I say clearly to you, Lady Pertelot, that Macrobeius, who wrote of the dream that the noble Scipio had in Africa, attests to the truthfulness of dreams and says that they are warnings about things experienced by men only later. In addition, I would ask you to consider carefully whether Daniel, in the Old Testament, gave credence to dreams. Also, read about Joseph and you will see that sometimes dreams — I do not say all dreams — contain warnings of what will happen in the future.

Remember the king of Egypt, Lord Pharaoh, and his Baker and his Butler, who all thought that dreams have no significance. If you examine the histories of many other realms you will come across many wondrous stories about dreams. Didn't Croesus, the king of Lydia, dream that he was sitting in a tree, which portended that he would be hanged? What about Andromecha, the wife of Hector, who dreamed the night before it happened that Hector would lose his life if he went into battle that day? She warned him, but to no avail; he went to fight anyway and was soon slain by Achilles. But that story would take too long to tell, and I have little time, as it is almost day.

Let me say this, in brief: I am certain that I am facing some adversity, just as foretold in this dream. And let me say also, right now, that I don't believe in laxatives because I know well that they are poisons. I do not care one whit for them, and I curse them!

But enough of this; as God knows me, let's talk about something more enjoyable, Lady Pertelot, something with which God has blessed me greatly. For when I see your beautiful face and how it is so scarlet red around your eyes, it makes me lose all fear of dying. There's great truth in the Latin proverb: *In principio, mulier est hominis confusio,"* the meaning of which is: "Woman is man's joy and all his bliss."[53] For when I feel your soft body beside me in the night, even if I cannot mount you then because our perch is too narrow, alas, it brings me so much joy and solace that I defy dreams of any kind.'

And with that he and all his hens fluttered down from their perch because it was now day, and he called them together with his clucking to enjoy the corn he found in the yard. Then he acted like a royal prince, afraid no more. By prime, he had embraced

---

[53] Chauntecleer, either intentionally or because he does not know better, mistranslates this Latin phrase, which actually says that women are the source of all confusion for men.

Pertelot with his wings twenty times and copulated with her each time. He looked like a grim lion as he roamed up and down on his toes, for he deigned not to set foot on ground. He clucked whenever he found pieces of corn, and his wives all ran to him then. So, I will leave Chauntecleer to his feed for now — royal as any prince in his hall — and tell about the adventure that is about to happen to him.

When March — the month in which God first created man and the world began, — had ended, and thirty-two days more had passed since then, one day Chauntecleer, in his full pride, was roaming about the yard with his seven wives by his side. When he cast up his eyes at the bright sun — which had by then spent twenty-one degrees or more in the sign of Taurus — this cock knew naturally, and not because someone had taught him, that it was prime, and so he crowed loudly and blissfully.

He announced: 'I can see that the sun has now climbed up the sky as much as forty-one degrees and more. Listen to how these happy birds are singing, Lady Pertelot, bliss of my world, and see how the new flowers spring from the ground! They raise my spirit and bring comfort to my heart.'

But, as all things in this world end in woe, suddenly a terrible thing happened. God knows that worldly pleasure is fleeting, and a skilled writer could do justice to this point in some chronicle penned for the appropriate sovereign ruler. But now, let every wise man listen carefully to me, for I swear that this story is as true as anything found in the story of Lancelot de Lake, a tale held in high esteem by women.[54] But let me return to my point.

A sly and evil fox, all red but with black-tipped ears and tail, that had made its home in a nearby grove for three years now, had, the night before — all as foreseen by God — broken through the hedge protecting the yard in which the handsome Chauntecleer and his wives were want to roam. This fox was quietly hiding among the cabbages well into the morning, waiting

---

[54] Lancelot was regularly the hero in many romances, which are, of course, total fiction.

until the time was right for him to attack Chauntecleer, as murderers do when they lie in wait to kill someone.

Oh, false murderer, skulking in your den! Oh, modern day Judas! Today's Ganelon! False deceiver, you Greek Synon, who brought Troy to such devastation! Oh, poor Chauntecleer, cursed be the morning on which you flew down from your perch! You were fully warned in your dreams that this day would be perilous for you but, according to scholars, whatever God foresees must necessarily happen.

Ask any serious student and he'll tell you that this is a matter of great disputation and disagreement — and has been for thousands of thinkers. I am in no position to separate the wheat from the chaff in this regard, as have the sainted Doctor of the Church Augustin, or Boethius or Bishop Bradwardyne — whether God's divine foreknowledge compels me to do a certain thing (I use "compel" rather than "necessitates"), or whether, if I have been given free choice I can do or not do a certain thing, even though God knew exactly what I would do — long before I was even born. Or, if God's foreknowledge constrains nothing and consists only of inferential necessity.

Only, let's not fret over such questions. My tale is simply about a cock, as you can tell, who — to his sorrow — took the advice of his wife to strut around without a care in the garden on the day about which he dreamed — as I have already told you. Women's advice is often fatal; it was the advice of a woman that first brought us into woe and forced Adam to leave Paradise where he had been completely happy and totally peaceful.

But lest I offend someone without meaning to, if I place fault on women's advice, pay no attention to that — it is only meant playfully. You should read writers who explore such ideas, and then you can hear what they say about women. Remember that what you hear from me are the words of the cock rather than mine own — I personally can divine nothing negative about women.

Lady Pertelot, in all her beauty, lay there with all her sisters, relishing the warm sand while the noble Chauntecleer crowed more merrily than the mermaids in the sea (we have it on the word of Physiologus that they sing well and happily). And as he was following a butterfly in the cabbage with his eyes, he noticed this fox, lying there, close to the ground. He suddenly lost all interest in crowing, abruptly jumping up and down like a man terrorized to his very core, shouting loudly all the while: "Cock! Cock!" For it is natural that an animal knows its enemy and will flee from it as soon as it lays eyes on that predator, even if it has never before seen that creature.

The instant Chauntecleer noticed the fox he wanted to flee, but the fox reassured him: 'Noble sir! Alas, where are you going? Are you afraid of me, your friend? Surely I would be no better than Satan if I were to injure you or do you any harm! I am not here to spy on your secrets; to tell you the truth, I am here for only one thing: to hear you sing. I find your voice to be as beautiful as that of any angel in heaven. On top of that, your singing expresses more feeling than ever did Boethius, or anyone else who has ever sung.

My Lord your father — may God bless his soul — as well as your mother, in all her gentility, both added greatly to my own personal fulfillment when they came to my home. And I want nothing more than your delight. When people talk about singing I always say that as long as I have enjoyed eyesight I swear that I have never heard any man sing as did your father at dawn. Truly, his singing always came directly from the heart. And in order to make his voice most powerful, he would strain himself so that both his eyes were closed, and his cry would ring out with him on his tiptoes, his neck stretched narrowly and long. And he was so prudent that no man, no matter where, could surpass him in song or in wisdom. I have had the chance to read, in *Lord Burnel, the Ass,* the verses about the cock who received a blow from a priest's son on his leg when he was young and naive but then, in return, made the priest lose his benefice. But this cannot compare to your father's wisdom and discretion, or his cleverness. So, please, Sir, for charity's sake, sing now and let us see whether you are the equal of your father."

Duped by these words, Chauntecleer began to beat his wings, like a man who cannot tell that he is being duped, so taken was he by this flattery.

Alas, my Lords, there is many a false flatterer in your courts, and you find them more pleasing, by my faith, than those who speak the truth to you. Read Ecclesiastes about flatterers: beware, my Lords, of their treachery!

Standing as tall as possible on his tiptoes, Chauntecleer stretched out his neck, closed his eyes and began to crow loudly. And Sir Russell, the fox, jumped up, caught the rooster by the neck, and was off to the woods, the cock flailing on his back, with no one around to pursue him.

Oh, Destiny, you cannot be avoided! Alas that Chauntecleer ever left his perch! Alas that his wife paid no attention to dreams! And, of course, you can one sure that all of this mishap occurred on a Friday.[55]

Oh, Geoffrey,[56] dear sovereign master, who complained so powerfully about the death of the noble King Richard, slain by an arrow, why do I now lack your skill and your learning to chide Friday forcefully, as you did? For, in fact, he was killed on a Friday. If I had the ability, I would lament properly Chauntecleer's fear and his pains.

All I can do is swear to you that the clamor made by all the hens in the yard when they saw their lord and master's plight was not matched by the cries and lamentation of the women at the fall of Troy when Pyrrhus caught King Priam by the beard and killed him with the edge of his sword, as we learn in the *Aeneid*. But above all this din could be heard the shrieks of Lady Pertelot, far louder than Hasdrubal's wife when her husband lost his life and the Romans burned Carthage. That woman was so filled with

---

[55] Fridays were thought to be the day on which bad things tended to happen (narrowed by us to Friday the 13th). It was supposedly the day of the week on which — among others — Julius Caesar, Richard the Lionheart, and Jesus Christ, Himself, all died.

[56] Geoffrey of Vinsauf, not Chaucer.

torment and rage that the devoted heart caused her to run intentionally into the fire and burn to death.

Oh, you sorrowful hens, shrieking like the senators' wives when Nero burned the city of Rome, killing all their husbands. And Nero did all that without an ounce of guilt. But let me return to my story.

This blessed widow and her two daughters heard all the commotion and the laments coming from their hens, ran out of their abode and saw the fox streaking toward the woods — the cock flopping about on his back. Now they joined in, crying: 'Out! Out! Help and alas! Look! Look out! It's a fox!' They, and many men with staves now chased after them. There went Collie, the dog, and Talbot and Gerland, and Malkyn, distaff still in her hand; now cows and calves, even pigs, terrorized by the barking dogs and the shouting men and women, all running until they thought their hearts would burst. They were screaming like the fiends of hell; ducks were quacking as if they were being chased to be slaughtered; in terror the geese flew over the tree tops; the bees fled their hive, so hideous was the noise — Oh, Lord, God, bless me! — surely Jack Straw[57] and his mob, chasing Flemings down, never produced half as much noise as was made this day in the chasing of one fox. There were brass trumpets and boxwood horns and ivory, and they were blowing on them — there was so much shrieking and huffing and puffing that the sky seemed to be falling.

Now, good people, listen to this: behold how Fortune turns upside down so suddenly all the hopes and pride of her enemy! This cock on the fox's back finally overcame his fear enough to speak to the fox: 'Sir, if I were you, so God help me, I would turn to those chasing me and shout at them: "Go home, you prideful knaves, all of you — may the plague take you! For now I have reached the woods and, in spite of all of you, the cock will stay here with me. I will eat him up, by God, and I can't wait!"'

---

[57] One of the leaders of the Peasant's Revolt in 1381.

Without thinking, the fox answered: 'You're right! I'll do exactly that!' But the moment he opened his mouth to speak, the cock nimbly slipped from his jaws and flew high up into a nearby tree. And when the fox saw that the cock had escaped, he lamented: 'Alas, Chauntecleer, alas! Indeed I have mistreated you in as much as I frightened you when I grabbed you and took you out of your yard. But you must know, Sir, that I did it with all the best intentions. Come on down from that tree and I'll explain everything to you. So God help me, I will tell you the truth of it!'

'Nay, never,' the cock answered. 'Then we would both be cursed! And I would deserve to be cursed, my blood and my bones, if you tricked me more than once. Make me sing with my eyes closed when I should be paying attention? He who intentionally closes his eyes when he should be looking — may God never let him prosper!'

'You are right,' the fox said, 'may God damn him who lacks so much discretion and control of himself that he jabbers when he should keep his mouth shut!'

So, you can see what happens when you are reckless and negligent and trust flattery!

But one last word to those of you who think this a foolish tale, all about a fox or a cock and hen. Seek out the moral, my good people, for St. Paul says that everything written is put down for us to learn. So, take the fruit and leave the chaff behind. And so, Good Lord, if it be Your will, as my master says, make us all good and bring us to His high bliss! Amen."

"Well, damn my eyes, Sir Priest," our Host burst forth, "if I don't hope that God blesses your ass and both your stones. What a fun story you've told us about this cock, Chauntecleer! If I have ever spoken truth, I must say that if you were not a priest you would make quite a rooster yourself! If you have as much passion as you seem to have muscle, it would take lots of hens to satisfy you, it seems to me — more than seven time seventeen."

He turned to the assembled pilgrims: "Look at the muscles on this gentle priest — look at that neck — and what a chest he has! Damn! He looks around at the world like a hunting hawk with those piercing eyes. He certainly has no need to be made up with the red dye we import from Portugal. No sir! No indeed!"

And, turning again to the Nun's Priest: "I'll be the first to admit that I don't get it — you working for a nun!" He shook his head in amazement before he went on: "All I can say is" — and here he bowed and tipped his hat to him — "that I hope good things may happen to you for sharing this wonderful story with us."

Once more, he shook his head, still pondering what he could not understand, but then, remembering that he had to call on someone else, he took a moment to collect himself and look around, and finally his eyes landed on the Carpenter.

"You, my dear master Carpenter," he said, "you seem like a reasonable man, someone who can tell us a worthy and worthwhile story. What about it? Are you ready to share a tale with us? God knows we have heard some profitable tales as well as some none of us probably wish we had ever heard. Well?"

The Carpenter smiled, straightened himself up on his horse, and answered: "Indeed, Master Host. I will be happy to do so."

The Carpenter's Tale

"Before I begin with my tale, let me apologize for the behavior of some of my companions and fellow guild members from our beloved city of York. God knows I have tried to prepare them for this journey and to teach them how they are to act in such illustrious company, and yet — to my deep disappointment — my brothers in trade and commerce have not all demonstrated the behavior expected of us as we take the name of York out into the country and this pilgrimage." His fellow guild members reacted to his apology as one might expect. The Tapister and the Weaver were simply too much in their cups even to notice; the Dyer looked down, slightly ashamed, but not for long; and the Haberdasher waited until the Carpenter was no longer looking at him and then stuck out his tongue at him and made a gross gesture.

The Carpenter continued.

"I am a carpenter by trade and proud of it for, without craftsmen like us, especially carpenters, much of the world's story would be very different. Our very own Lord and Savior, Jesus Christ, was a carpenter and the son of a carpenter. O, blessed Saint Joseph, patron saint of carpenters and the model for all Christian carpenters, how much we all have to learn from you."

He crossed himself and looked around again at some of his compatriots, but none of them seemed particularly touched by his words. "I was blessed in particular, when my parents not only named me Joseph, but apprenticed me to the best carpenter in York, from whom I learned this magnificent trade and acquired the excellent skills that I now practice for the good of all, day by day."

Once again, he crossed himself.

"I was even more blessed by God and the angels above to marry a woman named Mary and, if I do say so myself, we have tried to live like the holy family, on the same holy principles we have learned from Joseph and Mary in the good book."

He looked around again, as if waiting for approval or applause but, when there was no response, he went on. "Although God, in his goodness, has not seen fit to give us any sons, my wife and I have been blessed with six daughters, praise be to the Almighty, whose names are inscribed on this cross I carry on my chest — carved by my own hand."

He piously kissed the cross and held it up for all to see.

"Now, I think you will all agree that the craft I practice has a long and glorious history and is much blessed by God and acknowledged in the good book and in stories that have been handed down to us over many generations and from many countries in the world. After all, none of us would be here today were it not for that great and holy carpenter, Noah, who was instructed by God Himself in how to build the ark that saved all mankind when the Lord was angry enough with sinful men to flood all He had created. But He spoke to Noah and told him just how to construct the ark that saved the beasts of the field and Noah's family. And who could forget the Greek Epeius, skilled artisan that he was, who built a mighty wooden horse that was used by the Greeks to overcome the great city of Troy by the stealth and cunning that allowed them to hide their soldiers in the belly of the horse — to burn, pillage and destroy that great city once they had entered through the city gates in their wooden structure.

Although many wonderful, stories could be told about any number of skilled artisans and their deeds, my story is about none of these examples that show the importance of carpentry to us all; rather it is a story about a great craftsman and carpenter who lived in ancient times and was known as Daedalus. I am no scholar, but I have been told that his name meant 'someone who works cunningly,' and certainly he was able to build anything, including labyrinths, wooden animals, and wings that enabled him to fly.

This Daedalus was born in Athens, a descendant — on his father's side, as well as his mother's — of kings, although in some stories his father was the greek god Hephaestus and it was this heritage that enabled him to build anything people desired and some things they could not even imagine. He created statues from any material available, made so well that people thought they were alive. There is a story that tells of the great hero Hercules, mightiest of men, who saw a statue of himself — that Daedalus had crafted — in a threatening stance and reacted as if he were really being attacked by it, smashing it with his club because he felt endangered. Of course, when he realized what he had done, he was quite embarrassed and apologized profusely to the gifted artisan who had represented him so well in wood that he thought this effigy could harm him. Daedalus was able to make such pieces because he knew how to make the body look as if it moved freely, as human bodies do. He also made faces with realistic features, like eyes with all the parts human eyes have.

He is often called an architect and a sculptor, but we must never forget that at the heart of all he did was carpentry. We are told that he had a nephew, called Calos, his sister's son, who was apprenticed in his workshop, and some said that this Calos was even more talented than was his uncle. Sadly, Daedalus could not tolerate such talk and threw his nephew to his death, off a hill in Athens. The mother of Calos killed herself in grief, and Daedalus was banished from the city, eventually finding his way to Crete. There he was welcomed with open arms and soon became a favorite of King Minos, who put Daedalus in charge of the upkeep and maintenance of everything in his palace.

While King Minos was at war with Athens, Scylla, the daughter of his opposing king, fell deeply in love with him, even betraying her father and her own people in order to be with Minos — but that's a whole other story that has little to do with my tale of the great craftsman, Daedalus. What matters about it is that when Minos rejected her, she became very angry and cursed him — although I do not know what exactly her curse was. His wife, Pasiphae, also put a curse on Minos, because he was constantly unfaithful to her. Finally, she betrayed him in return, but this was not by her own choice, as you will see. The curse Pasiphae had put on Minos was that when he slept with other women he would fill them not with new life but with death: scorpions, snakes, and other vile, deadly creatures.

It is important to know that Minos had asked for the aid of the Greek god of the oceans, Poseidon, to help him conquer Crete. Poseidon did — sending Minos a beautiful white bull as a a sign of his favor — and Minos was victorious over Crete. Of course, Poseidon expected Minos to sacrifice the bull to him, but Minos liked the bull too much to do so. Poseidon became very angry at this and punished Minos by putting a spell on his wife Pasiphae so that she would fall in love with this very bull. Although it seems unlikely to us, Pasiphae fell so completely for the white bull that she spent day and night trying to find a way to mate with him. What matters to my story is that Pasiphae was able to act on her passion with the bull only because of the skills of Daedalus — whom I have not forgotten in all of this, for he is the center of my tale.

She knew how skilled Daedalus was in all things, and so she asked him to build something that would allow her to satisfy her lust for this animal. Well, you can imagine that even for the Greeks, such a thing was outrageous but, after he had collected himself and seen that she was, indeed serious, Daedalus used his considerable imagination and even greater skills to construct a cow from wood, wrapped with cowhide. It was so well-done that it looked completely life-like, and anyone seeing this miracle would think this was a living, breathing animal. The wooden cow was hollow, so Pasiphae could climb into it to have her way with the bull, to whom this creature would have appeared to be just another cow with which to mate.

So Pasiphae entered the cow and was wheeled out into a field where, as any bull would, the white bull mated with the wooden cow, or rather, with Pasiphae, inside the wooden cow. Happily, this sated her lust for the bull forever, but unhappily, the bull had impregnated her. The issue of this unnatural union was a male child who was named Asterion but would become known as the Minotaur, part man and part bull. As an infant, he was nursed by Pasiphae and roamed about freely, but as he grew into adulthood, he became increasingly moody and dangerous, and it was necessary to restrain him. Once again, Daedalus was called upon to solve this problem, so he built an enormous, elaborate maze underneath the palace, and here the Minotaur reigned supreme. And Minos also made use of the labyrinth to imprison enemies who, he knew, would eventually be disposed of by the Minotaur.

For the Minotaur, the maze served two purposes: no one could easily find the Minotaur to ogle or bother him in some way, and the Minotaur could not find his way out of the maze, so cleverly was the labyrinth constructed. The Minotaur was eventually killed by Theseus but, again, that is a long story and not the one I am here to tell you.

My story ends sadly, with the death of this gifted carpenter and, more unfortunately, the death of his son, as well. But it was not a failure of his skills that led to the death of his son, rather the foolishness of young Icarus, who abused the wonderful invention built by his father.

Daedalus had several children, of whom Icarus was the best known. A time came when King Minos had decided that his life-long friend and ally Daedalus had become his enemy. It was then that Minos confined him, along with Icarus — some say, in a tower, and others say, in the very labyrinth Daedalus had built. The story I believe is that father and son were imprisoned in the labyrinth. Now Daedalus knew that his maze was too intricate even for him to escape in the way one might normally try to gain freedom: finding a way through and out of the maze. He also knew that even if, against all odds, they managed to discover an exit, the landscape of Crete was such that they would never be able to reach a boat or a ship before the guards stationed along the shore would recapture them.

He determined that the only way out was by air. But the ability to fly was reserved for birds. So Daedalus carefully studied those creatures and finally built —out of wax, and wood, string and feathers — a pair of wings for his son and another for himself. He strapped these wings to his body and learned how to fly, and then did the same with his son, teaching him how to manipulate the wings so that he could fly anywhere he wanted to. But he warned his son adamantly that he was to fly neither too high, where the heat from the sun would melt the wax and cause the wings to fall apart — or too low, too near the sea water, which would soak the wings and make them too heavy to sustain their bearer — either extreme leading to death. Icarus, of course, said that he fully understood, and he waited impatiently for the time he and his father would take to the sky and escape their imprisonment.

The time came when Daedalus decided to attempt their escape, and he and his son took wing and rose into the sky like giant birds, escaping the bonds of the ground and leaving their jail behind. Soon they were flying over the various islands that they knew well, and everything was going as planned. But young Icarus was so delighted with his ability to fly that he began to soar higher and higher, eventually getting so close to the sun that the wax holding his wings together began to melt and, inevitably, he plummeted down to the water and drowned. All his father could do was to look on and weep, as he cursed the impetuousness of youth and mourned the demise of his son, the son who he himself called the best thing he had ever made. Small comfort it would have been to him to know that to this day that part of the ocean is called the Icarian Sea.

While Daedalus lived for many more years and invented and constructed countless other amazing things over the course of his lifetime, he mourned the death of his son — at his own hand, or so he was known to say — every day thereafter.

As you can see, Daedalus was the greatest of craftsmen, the first practitioner of carpentry — with the exception of blessed Saint Joseph, of course — so skilled in its arts that he could build anything. There can be no question about his importance and the importance of carpentry from ancient times all the way to today. Despite the foolish Carpenter in the story told by the Miller, carpentry is a craft to be proud of, for it is the noblest of professions, as is shown by this illustrious history.

This is my tale; I hope you are happy to have heard it."

The Host seemed pleased indeed by this tale, saying: "My dear Carpenter, you have done well. I have learned much from your story and I bless you and your craft, for you have shown both it and yourself to be the font of many skills."

"O yes," interrupted the Weaver, drunk enough to illustrate his very craft by the way he was weaving in his saddle but seemingly still in good control of his tongue, "my friend Joseph is an upright man, but his is not the only craft that has a long historical pedigree and is the subject of many tales in ancient times. My own craft, weaving fine cloth, has been known for as long as carpentry, I dare say, and I have a tale to tell you that will show just that."

The Host, seeing that there would be no way to prevent the Weaver from having his way, rolled his eyes and gave in.

"As you will then, Ralph the Weaver," he agreed. "Tell your tale and make it interesting, if you please."

"That I will — that I will," the Weaver replied and began, after a hearty pull from the wine skin he had been working all day.

The Weaver's Tale

"I am but a humble weaver of cloth and not a great story teller but I will do my best to tell you a tale that honors my trade and my fellow weavers. The great Roman poet Ovid tells us of many things in his books and, though I cannot read, I have heard some of these stories more often than others because they relate to my honored trade. This particular tale, found in the writings of Ovid, shows, once again, just how important weaving is for all of us and always has been.

Although weaving is itself a kind of story-telling, it has often also been accompanied by story-telling. Who can deny that he greatest story tellers are really weavers, for do they not weave together the threads of stories to form new stories, just as the threads of various colors are woven together to create new tapestries, new stories in cloth? After all, is it not the poets and the scholars who tell us about the colors of rhetoric? This is no accident but speaks to the importance of weaving and of the technical terms of weaving that also shape old and new stories. As I said, Ovid tells us this story about weaving and about great weavers in our past, and I will attempt in my own poor way to do justice to it and weave it with and for you.

It begins at a time when the gods were bored — oh yes, even the gods can become bored, sitting around and telling stories to one another just to while away the time. On one such occasion, the goddess Minerva herself, listening to various stories, was deeply moved by the Aonian Muses' songs and their anger and pain, and heard with pity and with particular attention the story of Arethus, naked, running for her honor from the lustful Alpheus, unequal in strength, without hope, praying to Diana for help — who then threw out a cloud to cover her, and she eventually turned into water.

Minerva heard and even appreciated the indignation that story recounts, but it also made her feel things different from those the other gods may have felt. After all, even if we sit in one place and hear someone tell one story to all of us, each of us there is probably hearing a somewhat different story than the person next to us. On this day, it appears that Minerva heard something other than her fellow gods heard. For this story made her ask herself, privately, of course: 'Praising these women is one thing; it's just fine — but why am I not being praised? Where is the praise for me and my divine powers? Am I to be ignored like this without doing anything about it?' Thinking further about the ways she felt slighted, she soon settled on one particular slight she felt more deeply than others. It was the case that she had been hearing more and more from the other gods and from her servants about Arachne, a woman in Maeonia, who was as famous for her abilities in spinning and weaving as she was for absolutely refusing to give Minerva any credit for her craft or her skill.

Now Arachne was a young woman, a girl, really, famous neither because of where or to whom she was born, nor because her family deserved great repute or fame. She was famous because of the great skill she showed — a skill she came by, at least in part, because of her family tradition. Her father was Idmon of Colophon, a man who had acquired a considerable reputation of his own for his skill in dying wool a kind of purple that was the envy of the world, using the materials of a Phocacean shell known as murex. Arachne's mother had died when Arachne was very young, and Arachne had grown up in the modest home and workshop of her father. Idmon, in the little village whose name I have told you. I do know that Arachne was not very old by the time she had achieved considerable fame as a weaver.

People came from everywhere to admire her work and to learn from her, and that included the nymphs who lived on the vine-covered slopes of the mountains near and far and those who dwelt in the waves of the waters all around. Not only were Arachne's finished products a joy to see but many came just to watch her at work — work, no, this was not work. It was art, pure and simple, and she was the artist miraculously fusing threads of many colors to merge before their eyes into ethereal beauty. It was clear to see that her work was divinely inspired, whether she was winding the rough yarn into a ball she could work with, or working the materials with her graceful fingers, repeatedly teasing out the small clouds of wool to where they were drawn into long threads she manipulated to do her magic. Finally, she gracefully twirled the thin spindle so it shone in the light before beginning to embroider the work with the various needles she used so effectively.

But, to the chagrin — and, eventually, the ire — of Minerva, she always made a point of denying divine inspiration or intervention, bristling at the idea that she needed a heavenly mentor to do what she did. She believed herself above the fray, merely saying, when she was pressed: 'all are welcome to compete with me; I will concede the prize to whoever produces something more beautiful than do I.'

Having resented Arachne and stewed about her for a very long time, mighty Minerva finally had enough of all this, and she decided to end it. She appeared in the doorway of Arachne's workshop disguised as an old woman, grey-haired, leaning on a cane to support her seemingly aged legs as she limped in and asked if she could sit and rest for a while. Arachne was nice enough to her but did not pay her any further attention, continuing the work she was doing at her loom. The old woman watched a bit and then engaged the girl in conversation: 'You know, when you are young, you think little of old age or of the wisdom that comes with age. But that does not mean that age has nothing to offer.'

Arachne nodded somewhat indifferently, paying much more attention to whirling her shuttle than to the old woman. But the goddess was not to be denied and continued: 'I ask that you listen to me and that you learn from my advice.' Again Arachne nodded and Minerva continued. 'I tell you there is nothing wrong with seeking to be famous for your skill at weaving but, at the same time, do not forget the goddess and do not try to out-do her.'

This time Arachne did not nod in agreement.

'It is not too late, dear girl,' Minerva pressed her case, 'to ask the goddess for forgiveness for your pride; ask humbly and she will forgive you, my dear girl. Please do not persist in the foolish pride of youth.'

But Arachne's limited patience for the advice coming from this old woman was coming to an end. Her dismissive scowl showed her increasing anger; certainly she was too proud to give in to such words. Finally, she interrupted her weaving, clearly irate at the words of the disguised goddess. She slowly put down her shuttle and rose, so that she looked down at the old woman seated there.

Angered enough to have ceased working on her wonderful tapestry, she restrained herself no longer, saying forcefully to Pallas Minerva, disguised as an old woman: 'You, old crone, you dare come here to my house, weak-minded and worn down by tiresome age, before life has totally destroyed you — you dare come to me to say these things. But I have some advice for you: If you have a daughter-in-law, or if you have a daughter, share your advice with them. I don't need your wisdom — I have enough of my own. It seems that you come here because no one else ever listens to your advice. Well, I agree with all the others: you have no advice for me.'

She paused before she finished what she wanted to say: 'If the goddess is so concerned with me why does she not come to me herself to tell me these things? Better yet, let her come here and compete with me, and let our work speak for itself. I would welcome such a contest and am prepared for it at any time.'

Of course this was more than the goddess could bear. She jumped up, throwing off her disguise, appearing in all her glory and power as Pallas Minerva.

'Behold! She is here!' her Olympian voice suddenly echoed in the room and throughout as she towered over the hapless girl. At once, all those gathered in the workshop fell on their knees and worshipped her. All, that is, except Arachne, who was unmoved, unafraid, although she turned somewhat red before becoming very pale. But basically unfazed by the sudden appearance of the goddess, she smiled a thin smile and held up her shuttle to show that she was quite willing to take on a contest with anyone, including a goddess, eager to win what, alas, would certainly not be a prize to her liking.

And without further words the contest begins, as Arachne quickly strips her loom of the beautiful tapestry she is making and prepares it anew, while the goddess quickly sets up her loom also, in another part of that room.

Now each stretches her yarns over the frames of the looms and, as was the custom in those days, the frames are fastened to the cross-beams; then the warp threads are held apart while the thread of the weft is slipped between them. Their nimble fingers insert, again and again, with lightning speed the pointed shuttles they have readied. They draw them through the warp, regularly pushing the weft into place, supported by the notched teeth of the comb that moves with great agility from row to row.

The two weavers work swiftly, their clothes bunched tightly under their breasts, skillfully using their arms, their efforts not labor but rather a joy to witness. Behold how the startling shreds of purple change the cloth, fading off eventually into lighter shades. See how the hues of the threads touching each other appear to be the same but those distant from them are vividly different. The famous ancient poet describes with wonder how the tapestries mimic the very sky, lit by the sun with glorious rainbows, shining with thousands of separate hues. So wonderful are they, that our poor eyes fail to discern the changes from one color to the next, but the hints of gold tell anew the ancient tales spun freshly into the cloth, to be remembered forever.

Minerva's canvas shows an argument that she herself waged with Neptune on the Martian hills, where the court of Areropagus hosted the hotly-fought debate for the rights to the city and to its name. She weaves into the landscape the other gods with their easily-recognizable attributes that identify the twelve on their thrones, Jupiter in the center, presiding with all his majesty. Neptune stands, poised to strike through the stone that spews forth unceasingly the water symbolizing his claim to the city.

Minerva herself appears in full armor, wielding a shield, with sharp spear and helmet, a breast-plate protecting her chest and throat. A mighty olive tree, pale but laden with fruit, springs from the spot she has struck with her spear, and Victory floats over the scene, governing all.

But not content with this, Minerva adds a vibrant contest in each of the corners, glorious in color and filled with miniature characters. These depict for her human rival just what prize she should expect to win should she succeed in her daring challenge. The first corner shows Mount Rhode and Mount Haemus, two peaks — once human, now icy — who dared to reach for the divine. In the second we see how Juno turned the queen of the pygmies, who dared to compete with her, into a crane, who is then forced to attack her own people. The third depicts Antigone, metamorphosed into a white stork, clattering in her misery to Juno after her failed contest with the divine queen. And the fourth shows Cinyras, weeping bitterly as he clasps the frozen steps of the temple that were once the arms and legs of his daughters. But, in the end, Minerva surrounds her tapestry with the olive wreaths of peace, the branches of her very own tree.

Not to be outdone, the girl of Maeonia begins with Europa, riding on the waves of the waters that take her away, deceived by the bull on which she rides as she bids farewell to her companions — all so vivid that there seems to be a living bull and real waves. Arachne presses the point by adding Asterie, struggling beneath the eagle, and Leda overpowered by the swan. She depicts Jupiter in repeated seductions of human women: as a satyr impregnating Antiope with twins; in the form of Amphytrion, so that he can sleep with Alcmena; seducing Danaë in the form of a golden shower; and taking advantage of Aegina in the form of a flame, Mnemosyne as a shepherd, and Proserpine as a spotted snake. She adds mighty Neptune, first, as the pawing bull lusting for Canace, begetting the Aloidae in the form of Enipeus; then, having his way with Theophane in the form of a ram; now beguiling Demeter, the golden mother of the cornfields, as a horse; now seducing Medusa, the snake-haired mother of

Pegasus, in the form of a bird; and lastly, deceiving Melantho as a dolphin. Each of these she depicts in their symbolic time and space. She adds Phoebus looking like a countryman, then with the wings of a hawk, now in a lion's skin and now as a shepherd deceiving Isse, daughter of Macareus. Finally, there is Bacchus, tricking Erigone with disappearing grapes, and Saturn begetting Chiron in the form of a horse. She encircles all of this with a narrow border of flowers intertwined with ivy.

Not the goddess of Envy, not even Minerva herself, could find any fault with the work of Arachne. Angered by the perfection of her human competitor's work, the golden-haired weaver goddess, in her rage, furiously ripped up Arachne's tapestry that so graphically showed the evils committed by gods. Then, firmly grasping her shuttle of boxwood, she forcefully struck Arachne in the face and forehead, three times, four times, cruelly inflicting unspeakable agony.

So terrible was the girl's pain that she knew not what else to do but, despairing, she turned various strands of her yarn into a noose that she slipped around her own neck. But Minerva, perhaps in a moment of divine pity, lifted her by that noose, saying: 'You want to hang? Fine, hang! But live on, as well, both in your own infamy and in your descendants, from now unto the end of time.' Abruptly she dropped the dead girl, sprinkled her with the deadly magical herb of Hecate and disappeared in a cloud. But the pitiful Arachne was left to writhe on the floor, her hair falling away in clusters, her nose and eyes shrinking up, her entire head becoming smaller and smaller and her whole body becoming tinier and tinier. In the end her elegant fingers became spindly legs on the sides of her body, which had turned into mostly belly, and she became a spider, weaving her eternal web from out of her very self.

This, then, is a story of how the ancient gods punished pride, even justifiable pride by a great weaver. They wanted humans to know that they dare not compete with the divine, no matter how gifted they may be.

But, perhaps like Minerva herself to start with, I also heard a different story than the one the teller perhaps meant to relate.

For me this is a story about how ordinary humans can challenge and even outdo the wonders of nature all around us, even though they are gifted to us by our eternally generous creator. Rater than acknowledge the grandeur of Arachne's artistry, Minerva could no nothing more than destroy it, alongside the powerless young woman who dared challenge — and perhaps bested — her, the goddess.

But we are fortunate to trust in a Christian God who does not punish us for daring to imitate or equal Him. Oh, I know, we cannot equal His creation, but I have seen the work of weavers and other artisans that surely transports its fortunate viewers into experiencing divine beauty. Arachne's tapestry may be lost to us but not her story, which reminds us not only of the extraordinary work she produced but inspires all those of us who continue to ply our — and her — trade today, following in her footsteps, rewarded and appreciated properly or not."

With that, the Weaver concluded his tale to murmurs of admiration by some and words of puzzlement from others about what he was saying in his final words.

But the speculation was cut off abruptly by the Host.

"Behold, we are about to enter Sittingbourne, a fitting place to stop for the night, to refresh ourselves, and to prepare for tomorrow's culmination of our journey to the sacred shrine of the Holy Martyr in Canterbury. I have arranged for us to stay at The Three Crowns, a jolly inn belonging to an old friend of mine, who is awaiting our arrival and ready to welcome us, one and all."

This announcement was met with various expressions of relief, joy, and even a prayer or two of thanksgiving, as we prepared to dine and rest ourselves from our ride of the day — much longer than the first but, thankfully, leaving us with a shorter journey for the third and final day of our pilgrimage.

I don't know how my companions slept, but I spent a dreamless night, unusual for me, and was fully prepared to ride out the next morning, as we all gathered on our horses in the inn's courtyard.

It seemed clear that our Host intended to regain control of the story-telling on this third and last day of our pilgrimage, as he gathered us to say: "My fellow pilgrims, one and all. Many of us have now told their tales, but there are still some to be told. In order to ensure that we all have the opportunity to tell a story on the way to Canterbury, I will make certain today that those from whom we have not yet heard, get their turn before it is too late. And so, to begin this orderly process we must all willingly participate in this day, I call upon our worthy Physician to begin our last day's telling of tales."

Perhaps it was too early for our drinking companions to object, or perhaps they were too tired from another late night, or perhaps our troop had finally settled into the order we had all agreed upon in Southwerk — whatever the reason, no one objected, the Physician cleared this throat several times, and we departed our inn on the way to our pilgrimage's end.

The Physician's Tale

"The Roman historian, Livy, tells us that there once was a noble knight, by name of Virginius, known to be honorable and worthy of admiration, a man with much wealth and many friends.

He and his wife had only one child, a daughter, who was more beautiful than any woman you have ever seen. Trying to outdo herself, Nature showered her with so many outstanding qualities that she seemed to be making a statement: 'Behold how I, Nature, when I choose to do so, can shape and adorn a creature! Who can possibly match my results? Not Pygmalion, no matter how long he might chisel and hammer, sculpt or paint; I dare well say that Appelles or Zeuxis would waste their time if they were presumptuous enough to attempt to imitate me. For He who is the first cause of all has appointed me to be His chief deputy, charged with making and adorning all earthly creatures, just as I please. Everything under the moon that waxes and wanes is under my control — though I ask nothing in return for what I do. My Lord in Heaven and I are in full agreement on this, and I made this young woman in praise of God, as I do all others of my works, no matter their color or their shape.' This, it seems to me, is how Nature might speak about this perfect creature.

This maid, in whom Nature took such delight, was fourteen years old, and Nature, with the same white with which she decorates the lily and the same red with which she tints the rose, adorned this noble creature even before she was born, for her coloring was as perfect as could be. And the Sun itself dyed her bountiful hair to be like the streams of his burnished heat.

But if her beauty was unmatched, her virtue exceeded her appearance by a thousand times. There was nothing lacking in her of any praiseworthy quality, especially morality. She was chaste in spirit and in body, her virginity flowering in humility and abstinence, as she always acted moderately and patiently, ever appropriate in how she carried herself and how she dressed. Her speech was always discrete, and though she might have been as wise as Pallas Athena, I can attest that she conversed ever womanly and plainly; she never relied on affected expressions to make herself look intelligent, for her speech was always appropriate to who she was, and everything she uttered was meant to increase virtue and gentility.

She was as modest as a maid should be, constant in her thoughts, and always keeping busy lest she fall into laziness. Bacchus had no access to her tongue for, as we all know, the combination of wine and youth increases desire the same way oil or grease fans the flames of a fire. And, entirely of her own accord, she pretended many a time to be ill so that she could avoid companions who were likely to act foolishly at feasts, celebrations and dances — occasions of flirting.

People say that such events make children grow up too quickly, making them precocious and bold — something that is very dangerous and always has been. Let her learn boldness soon enough when she becomes a wife.

And you governesses who have had the daughters of noble men in your charge, I hope you are not offended by what I say. You must know that you had the jurisdiction over the daughters of lords with only two possibilities: either you ensured chastity or, in your weakness, you failed. You know the old dance well enough and have yourself sworn off such misconduct forever — well, then, for the sake of Our Lord, Jesus Christ, make sure at the cost of your own salvation that you never stop teaching virtuous ways to your charges!

A venison poacher who has given up his thieving ways and his greed for deer is the best warden for a forest full of game. So, carry out your duty — you can do it well if you but choose. Be careful not to give in to vice, lest your evil intentions damn you to hell for all eternity — for whoever gives in is surely betraying all that is good. And remember what I say to you here: the very worst imaginable of all betrayals is the betrayal of innocence.

You fathers and mothers, also, if you have children, one or more, you bear the responsibility to protect them so long as they are under your care. Be vigilant, lest they perish because of the example of how you yourselves live or because you fail to chastise them properly. For I tell you with certainty that you will pay the price for everything they do. When the shepherd is weak and negligent the wolf tears rends many a sheep and lamb. Let this one example be sufficient for you — for I will now return to my tale.

The young maid about whom I am telling you kept herself so well that she needed no supervision; she was so prudent and good that other maidens, who observed how she lived, could read, as if in a book, everything that makes a maiden virtuous. Consequently she became so well known everywhere, both for her beauty and for her virtuous behavior, that everyone who valued virtue in all the land praised her.

But not Envy, who is jealous of other people's well-being and delighted by their sorrow and misery. This we are told by St. Augustin.

One day this maid went to visit a temple with her mother, the way young girls do. Now there was a judge in the town who was the governor of that region, and it so happened that he saw her and at once came to a decision as she passed by. So struck was he by the beauty of this maid, that his heart and mood were altered completely, and he said to himself: 'I don't care who stands in the way — this is a maid I must have!'

And now the devil entered his heart and led him to think that he could win her over to his purposes by trickery. He was reasonably sure that he could not succeed by force or by bribery, for she had powerful friends and besides, she was so firm in her own beliefs that he knew for certain that he could not persuade her to sin willingly. So, after some thought, he sent for a scoundrel in the town that he knew was clever and ruthless. And this judge privately told the fellow his story and made him promise to keep it to himself, for if he told anyone he would lose his head. And when the scoundrel had agreed to the cursed deed the judge proposed, the judge was very pleased and rewarded the villain with precious and valuable gifts.

They soon had constructed their scheme in all details, and had decided point by point just how this lechery should be achieved — as you shall be told in just a moment. The wicked judge, named Apius (this was really his name, because this is no fiction but a well-known historical event — certainly the point it makes is valid — there can be no doubt about that), this evil judge ensured that his lust would be sated as soon as possible. For the moment, he sent his hired scoundrel, Claudius, home. But soon thereafter, as the story tells us, this false judge sat in his court, as was his custom, and passed judgment on various cases. Then, suddenly this false Claudius appeared in great haste before the judge to say: 'Lord, if it be your will, I ask that you grant me justice in this charge which I bring against Virginius. And if he denies it, I am prepared to prove it through witnesses who will support the charge stated here.'

The judge answered: 'I cannot pass final sentence in this case without the presence of Virginius. Let him be called, and I will then gladly hear your case. You will have justice and not be wronged in this court.'

Virginius appeared to hear what the judge had to say to him and was faced immediately with the cursed charge about which I will now tell you the details.

'Your poor servant, Claudius, hereby shows you, my dear Sir Apius, how a knight by the name of Virginius, against all right and justice, holds my servant against my will — my legal slave, stolen from my house under the cover of dark one night when she was very young. I will prove this by means of witnesses, lest you have any doubt. Whatever he may say, my Lord, mighty judge, she is not his daughter; so I beg of you, give me back my servant, if it be your will.' Behold, such was the charge brought against Virginius.

Virginius quickly looked this scoundrel up and down before telling his side of the story. He was fully prepared to prove what he was saying as a knight would do, and then, with numerous witnesses to disprove everything his opponent had said. But this cursed judge would not delay matters; he would hear no further from Virginius or his witnesses. Instead, he immediately passed judgment — which was:

"I rule that this fellow should have his servant returned to him at once. You, Virginius, shall not hold her in your house any longer. Produce her at once and let her be placed under our guardianship. The fellow shall have his servant returned — this I grant.'

Now when this worthy knight Virginius realizes that he must, according to the sentence of this judge Apius, perforce, give over his daughter to this judge to live a life of lechery, he goes home immediately and sits down in his hall where he summons his beloved daughter, his face dead as cold ashes as he considers her lovely face. Though he feels a father's pity like a stake through his heart, he will not be deterred from his purpose.

'Daughter,' he addresses her. 'My dearest Virginia, there are only two options available to you: either death or dishonor. Alas, that I was ever born! For never have you deserved to die by the sword or knife. Oh, dear daughter, ender of my life, which I have raised with such care and pleasure that you were never absent from my mind! Oh, daughter, my final sorrow as you are the final joy of my life; oh, jewel of chastity, you must accept your death with grace, as this is my decision. Not in hate, but in love, must you die! My own woeful hand must smite off your head. Alas, that Apius ever laid eyes on you! For he has falsely made his judgement against you today.'

And he told her everything about the case, as you have already heard — there is no need to rehearse it again.

'Oh, mercy, dearest father,' then said this maid, embracing his neck with both her arms, as she had done so often, with tears bursting from her eyes. She wept: 'Good father, must I then die? Is there no other way, no other remedy?'

'Alas, no, dearest daughter, there is not!'

'In that case, you must give me a few moments to prepare for my death. Did not Jephtha grant his daughter a little time, alas, to prepare before he slew her? And God knows, her only sin was to be the first to run out to meet her father and to welcome him with great joy.' And then she fainted but, recovering from her swoon, she rose and said to her father: 'Blessed be God that I shall die a virgin! Now give me death lest I suffer dishonor. In the name of God, do as you will with your child!'

And then, before she fainted anew, she begged him more than once to be gentle with his sword. Her father, his heart and thought heavy with sorrow, cut off her head, clutched it by the top, and went at once to present it to the judge who was still sitting in his court. And when the judge saw him with his grisly tribute, so the story tells us, he immediately ordered Virginius to be executed, but just then a thousand people burst in to the court to save the knight, moved by pity and sadness for him, knowing that a false judgment had been passed.

The people had been suspicious of the whole thing, because of the way in which Claudius had brought this case, and they knew that it was done with the collaboration of Apius — his lechery was well known. That is why they immediately apprehended this Apius and cast him into a dungeon, where he ended up killing himself. And Claudius, the accomplice of Apius in all this, was condemned to be hanged high in a tree. As for Virginius, they asked for mercy's sake that he be exiled, to avoid his certain execution. All others who had been involved in this entire wickedness were hanged, more or less.

Here then you can see how sin is rewarded. Be careful, for no one knows when or how — or how painfully — God may strike him. The trembling worm of conscience will acknowledge a life of wickedness, however secret it may be, even if only one man and God know about it. He can be a learned man or an unlettered one — he cannot know how soon he will have reason to fear. And so I pray that you take this advice: forsake sin lest sin cause you to be forsaken."

The Wife of Bath, who had been shaking her head and clucking like a chicken in disgust during the latter parts of the story told by the Physician, now burst out: "Oh, may God bless me always, my dear Sir Physician, if this is not a most horrendous tale! Is this the best you can do to start out our last day's journey so early in the morning — with such a tale? First you lecture us on our responsibilities to care for those who are innocent, and then you tell us this preposterous tale about people who behave like none of us, and nobody I know, would act. Surely you cannot believe, Sir Physician, learned man though you must be, that your story teaches us the value of virginity! You cannot believe that the horrible death this maiden suffered was better than the loss of what made her a maiden, do you? Surely, as a professed healer of human ails you could tell a tale more inclined to foster our health and well-being, instead of this . . . this . . . stain on parenthood and blind ignorance!"

The Physician was about to answer her, but not before the Host intervened, cursing and swearing as if he had gone mad — but not in support of the Wife or her comments— showing again that the Weaver's observations about the story we each hear were more valid than they might at first appear to be..

"Damn me to hell, by the blood of Christ and the nails that bound Him to His wooden cross, if this was not a false scoundrel and villainous judge! I pray to the high God above that judges and lawyers like that be rewarded with as shameful a death as possible. May they rot in hell!" He paused for a moment. "In any case, this blessed young maiden is dead. Alas, alas, that she had to pay for her beauty with such a great price!" He shook his head in wonder and pity at Virginia's fate, but the Wife of Bath was not at all pleased by his observations.

"What?" she shouted at him shrilly. "Now it's her fault for being beautiful? Can a woman not be beautiful without being killed for it? How dare you say this was the cost of her beauty!"

The Host was unabashed by this outburst. "I have said it before, and I will say it again: you can see every day that the bounty of Nature and the gifts of Fortune lead many a person to an early and pitiful end. I have no doubt but that her beauty was the direct cause of her death. And for this I pity her. Alas, that she had no choice but to die so horribly!"

The Wife could do nothing but sputter. The Host continued without another glance at her, now addressing the Physician:

"Truly, my own sweet master, you have told a great truth here. All too often do these gifts of which I speak cause our downfall — certainly they earn us more harm than good — alas! You have told us a pitiful tale, indeed.

But, be that as it may, it's all water under the bridge now. Lord knows, you are a deserving man, and I pray that God preserve you, along with your tools for divining our piss and being able to tell whether we are healthy or no. May the Lord almighty bless those potions you first learned about from ancient healers, as well as every container that keeps your medicines. May God Himself and the Blessed Virgin bless and keep them all! So may I prosper, but you're a fine specimen of a man, aren't you! You speak to us like any powerful bishop might do!"

The Physician's odd look in response made the Host ponder.

"What? Did I say something wrong? I'll admit that I may not use the right words and certainly don't know all the right technical terms for everything you do. I do know though that your very presence makes my heart pound faster to where I feel almost as if I'm going to have some kind of attack right here and now. By the dusty bones of Christ! But I feel for sure like I need some medicine or maybe a quick drink of a hearty, strong ale, or maybe to hear a happier story to make up for the one of this poor maiden, for whom my heart is so filled with pity!"

He laughed loudly and then noticed the Pardoner, whom he addressed with a bit of a leer and a sudden exaggerated lisp: "Now, my thweet little friend, you, Pardoner, why don't you tell uth a good joke or a thstory about a prank, or thomething entertaining?"

"By Saint Runyon," the Pardoner answered at once, ignoring whatever the Host had in mind in speaking to him as he had. "I'm delighted to do just that! But first things first! Here, in the shade of this tavern, I must enjoy a big drink — and have a hunk of this good bread."

But his response was met with a shared outcry from several of his fellow pilgrims. "No, no — don't let him tell one of his bawdy stories! Make him tell a moral tale — one that will teach us something worth knowing — and then we will gladly listen to him."

"Of course," he responded, "happy to serve! But I need a moment and another good drink to think of something you will all like." And he did indeed take another mighty quaff from his wineskin and broadly wiped his mouth with his sleeve. Obviously enjoying the audience he had been given, he looked around, winked broadly, and proclaimed: "My valued fellow pilgrims! Whenever I have the opportunity to preach in churches, I make sure that I do so loudly and impressively, my voice ringing out like a mighty bell; after all, I know everything I am going to say by heart, from much practice, and I have only one message, and it is always the same: *Radix malorum est Cupiditas*.[58]

I like to begin by letting everybody know where I come from, and then I show all the bulls[59] I have — and I have many! First — for self-protection — I hold up the seal of the local bishop on my license to sell pardons, so that no one — priest or clerk — will be tempted to disturb me in doing Christ's holy work. And then I tell my stories, all the while holding up the bulls I possess from popes and cardinals, patriarchs and bishops. I sprinkle in a few words of Latin now and then — like saffron, to season my sermon and inspire devotion."

He took several large bites of his bread and washed that down with a big pull on his wine sack.

"Then I parade before them my beautiful glass cases crammed full of rags and bones — and make sure that everyone believes them to be holy relics. For example, I have, mounted in brass, a shoulder bone of what I proclaim to be some holy Jew's sheep. I hold this up for all to see and I say: 'My good people, listen closely to what I am about to tell you. If you place this bone in your well and then, when your cow or your calf or sheep

---

[58] Greed is the root of all evil.

[59] An edict issued by a pope, named after the "bulla" or leaden seal that authenticated it.

or your oxen are bitten by a venomous serpent, simply take water from that well and wash the beast's tongue with it — it will be healed instantaneously. Not to mention that any of your sheep that drink the water from this well will be healed at once of any pustules or scabs they may have. But that's not all: if the good man who owns these beasts will make sure to take a good drink from this well once a week, early, before the cock crows — just as that holy Jew taught us — that man's live stock and all his possessions shall increase and multiply.

Have I mentioned that this sacred bone heals jealousy? Even if a man is deep in a jealous rage, put some of the water into his soup and he will never again distrust his wife, though he is face to face with proof of her misdeeds — even if she has been with some priest . . . or two . . . or three." He paused to give us all another exaggerated wink.

"I have here also a mitten, as you can see, which has the wonderful quality of multiplying the crops of any man who wears it when he is sowing — be it wheat or oats — so long as he has faithfully given me his pennies or silver coins."

More bread and wine.

"But, my good men and women, I must warn you of one thing: God forbid that there be any man in this congregation that has sinned so grievously that he is too ashamed to confess and be forgiven, or if there be any woman here, young or old, who has been unfaithful to her husband — for neither of these will be granted the grace or the ability to take advantage of the wonderful relics I have here. But the rest of you, those who are not guilty of these grievous faults, are free to join me up here. So, in God's name, make your offering, and I will absolve you by the authority vested in me by these many bulls.'

By using this simple trick I have earned an easy hundred marks[60] each and every year since I first became a pardoner. I stand there in the pulpit, just like any cleric would, and preach to the ignorant folks before me just as I told you — plus, I have a

---

[60] Quite a large income, easily in six figures in dollars in our time.

hundred other tricks I use to gull them. I like to stretch out my neck so I can nod to the people I am addressing, both east and west, the way a dove sitting in its barn is likely to do. My hands and my tongue both move so fast that it is a joy to see me at work. I preach only about greed and its many evils, and that is how I free them up to give their pennies — to me.

I seek only to get rich — I have no interest in making people less sinful. As far as I'm concerned, their souls can go pick blackberries when it's time for them be buried. We all know that many a sermon springs from evil intentions — whether it be to please certain folks or to flatter some, or to gain advancement by being hypocritical, or to fuel the pride of the preacher, or perhaps even out of hate. If I dare not take on directly someone who has wronged me or my friends, why, I will sting him instead with the sharpness of my tongue in my sermon. That way he cannot avoid my slander. I will not mention him by name but everyone will know exactly who I am talking about by subtle hints and the ways I have of identifying him. This is how I get even with those who attack us pardoners — I spit out my venom under the guise of holiness, appearing to be pious and truthful."

Between bites of his bread and drafts of his wine, he grinned unabashedly at the Host.

"I can describe my intention in a few words, for I preach only about greed. And that is why my theme is still, and always was, *Radix malorum est Cupiditas*. Yes, I preach against the same vice I practice, namely avarice. And even though I myself may be guilty of that sin, that is how I persuade others to turn away from it and to repent most deeply. Of course that is not my primary goal, because everything I say is motivated by my own avarice. So, then, that is clear enough.

I always provide many examples from old stories — stories of long ago — because ignorant people love these old tales; they can understand and remember them well. Don't think for a moment, while I am preaching and earning gold and silver for what I have to say that I have any intention of choosing to live in poverty! Not a chance! That was never my plan. My goal is to preach and beg in lots of countries; I have no interest in making a living by weaving baskets or by begging for a pittance or two. I do not plan to follow in the footsteps of the apostles. Rather, I want to have money, wool, cheese and wheat, whether I get them from the poorest page or the most poverty-stricken widow in the village — what do I care if her children starve — so long as I can drink the sweet blood of the grape and have a jolly baud in every town.

But listen, ladies and gentlemen, for my conclusion: you want me to tell a tale, now that I have had my fill of food and drink and, by God, I hope to tell you something that you will have no reason to dislike. I may be a wicked, evil man myself, but I can still tell a moral tale — I do it all the time to make my living."

There was considerable rumbling among the pilgrims at this. But the Pardoner now clearly felt that he was in control of the conversation. "Alright, alright! Keep it down. Here goes — the beginning of my story."

The Pardoner's Tale

"There once was a group of youngsters in Flanders, who foolishly squandered their time in taverns and brothels, occupied with gambling and debauchery. They danced and rolled their dice day and night, accompanied by harps, lutes and guitars; and they ate and drank way too much, thereby making their sacrifice to the devil in his very own temple through their horrible excesses. Their oaths were so horrible and damnable that people shuddered when they heard them. With their behavior they tore and ripped the body of our lord Jesus Christ — they must have thought that the Jews had not done enough of that — and they laughed as they watched each other sin. They were surrounded by slim, shapely dancing girls, more young girls selling fruit, musicians with their harps, prostitutes and various peddlers — all of them devil's servants whose purpose was to kindle and nurture the flames of lechery, immediate neighbor of gluttony. The blessed bible makes it clear that lechery has its roots in wine and drunkenness.

Behold, how the drunk Lot — totally against nature — unwittingly slept with his two daughters; so drunk was he that he didn't know what he was doing.

Herod, so interested in the story he heard from the Magi, sated with food and wine at his own table, gave the command to kill John the Baptist, who had done nothing wrong.

Seneca speaks absolute truth when he says that he can find no difference between a man who is insane and one who is drunk, except that madness in a scoundrel lasts longer than does drunkenness.

Oh, cursed Gluttony, you are the first cause of our ruination. We were damned because of you, first and foremost, until Christ paid the price to save us with His own blood.

In short, behold the immeasurable price that has been paid out to make up for this cursed evil!

All the world was corrupted because of gluttony.

There can be no doubt but that our father Adam, along with his wife, was driven from Paradise into perpetual sorrow, to work and labor every day, because of that vice. For, as far as I know, Adam remained in Paradise as long as he held to his fast — only when he ate of the forbidden fruit on that tree was he immediately cast out into sadness and suffering.

Oh, Gluttony, we are right to accuse you! Alas, if a man only knew how much evil comes from excess and gluttony, he would be much more careful about all he eats when he sits at the table.

Alas, our little throat and our mouth desirous of tasty things — they make us move heaven and earth, go east, west, north and south on land, air and water, just to get one extra morsel of tasty food or drink!

Saint Paul knows well how to write of this: 'Food is for the belly and the belly for food, but both will be destroyed by God.' It is bad enough to say it, by my faith, but far worse to do it: to drink so much of the white and the red that, by his cursed excess, a man turns his throat into a veritable privy.

In tears the Apostle sorrowfully tells us: 'Many walk among you of whom I have said — I weep as I pronounce this with pitiful voice — to be enemies of Christ's cross, and because their belly is their god, their end is death.' Oh, belly, stinking bag, full of dung and corruption, the sound of either end of you is foul! How much work and money goes into feeding you! How these cooks pound and strain and grind! They do the opposite of what the priest does at holy mass, as they turn reality into appearance, all to fulfill our greedy desire. They knock the marrow out of bones, because they wouldn't think of throwing away anything that might go through the gullet, soft and sweet. For people's delight they make sauces of the spices found in leaves and bark, and roots — only to increase appetite. But the truth is that anyone who pursues such delicacies is already dead, even while he lives embroiled in those vices.

Wine is a lecherous thing, and drunkenness is filled with quarrel and misery. Oh, man who is drunk, your face is disfigured, your breath is sour, and you are disgusting to embrace; your nose sounds as if you are saying, over and over: 'Samson, Samson!' And yet, God knows, Samson never drank wine. You crash to the ground like a stuck pig; you lose control of your tongue and all self-respect, because drunkenness is the true grave of a man's wit and his discretion.

A man controlled by drink cannot keep a secret — there can be no doubt. So, stay away from the white and the red, specifically from the white wine of Lepe that is for sale in Fish Street and Cheapside. This Spanish wine subtly creeps into other wines growing next to it and that results in such vapors that when a man has had three cups and thinks he is home in Cheapside, he finds himself to be in Spain, in the actual town of Lepe, rather than in La Rochelle or any other town in Bordeaux, and that is when he sounds as if he is saying 'Samson, Samson.'

But if there is one thing I need you to hear, gentlemen, note, I pray you, that all the great deeds, truly, and the victories recounted in the Old Testament were carried out by men who practiced abstinence and relied upon prayer to our one, true, all-powerful God. If you don't believe me, just look in the Bible — it's there as clear as day.

Remember that Atilla, the great conqueror, died in his sleep, dishonored and shamed, bleeding from his nose — all because he was drunk. A leader of men should always be sober. And above all, don't forget the command given to Lamuel — not Samuel, but Lamuel, I say — read the Bible and there you will find advice specifically about giving wine to those who are to mete out justice. Well, enough of this; it has to suffice.

And now that I have addressed gluttony, I must take on gambling. Dicing is the mother of all lies, of deceit, of cursed perjury, of blasphemy, of manslaughter and of waste — both property and time — not to mention that it undercuts and dishonors anyone who has the reputation of being a common gambler. And the higher his status is, the more unfortunate he is thought to be. A prince who gambles in his policy or in rule is, by common opinion, despised by others.

Stilbo, a wise and honored ambassador, was sent from Sparta to Corinth to craft an alliance. When he arrived, it so happened, just by chance, that he found all the greatest people in that country playing at dice. This persuaded him to get away from there as quickly as possible, to report: 'I am not about to be dishonored in a place like that, nor will I go down in infamy as the person who allied you with gamblers. You can send other wise ambassadors if you like but, by my reputation, I should rather die than to ally you with gamblers. For you, who are known for your honor shall not ally yourself with gamblers, neither by my intent nor by any treaty I have made.' Thus spoke this wise thinker.

And don't forget the King of Persia who scornfully sent to King Demetrius, as the story goes, a pair of gold dice because that king was known as a gambler — hence his reputation and his honor were considered to be null and worthless. There are plenty of other honorable things lords may do to while away the time.

Now let me say a word or two about frequent and false oaths, as we read about them in old books. Constant cursing is a horrible thing, and false oaths are even worse. Matthew tells us that God Almighty forbade swearing altogether, and the holy prophet Jeremiah says of swearing specifically: 'You shall keep your oaths well and never lie, keeping them in truth and righteousness.' But idle swearing is simply wicked. Remember how in the first tablet of God Almighty's ten commandments, the second commandment is: 'Do not take my name idly or in vain.' Note that he forbids such cursing before he mentions murder or many other evil acts.

I say that this is intentional, and this is how it is meant. If you understand the commandments of God, then you must admit that this was his second one. Moreover, I can assure you that the house of anyone who curses outrageously will never be without retribution. 'By God's precious heart,' or 'by His nails,' and 'by the blood of Christ in the Abbey of Hales, come seven and not your five and three,' or 'by God's arms, if you cheat me, this dagger will find its way through your heart.' The fruits of these damned bones are false oaths, anger, deception and murder. Now, for the love of Christ, Who died for us, stop your cursing, both great oaths and small.

And with that, Lords, I will begin my tale.

The three revelers I want to tell you about were sitting and drinking in a tavern long before prime and, as they sat, they heard a bell tinkle before a dead body that was being carried to its grave. So one of these three called to his servant, 'Go quickly and ask whose body is passing by here; and see to it that you tell us his name accurately.'

"Sir,' said the boy, 'no need to do that. I was told a couple of hours before you came here. He was, sorry to say, an old pal of yours who was suddenly slain last night as he was drinking, just sitting there on his bench. Along came a devious thief, whom men call Death, who is going all around the countryside killing people, and he split your friend's heart in two with his spear and went on his way without another word. During this plague he has killed a thousand or more. But, Sir, before you face him, I think you would do well to be prepared for such an enemy. You must at all times be ready to meet him — that is what my mother taught me, and that's all I have to say.'

'By the Virgin,' added the innkeeper, 'the young man is telling you the truth — a little more than a mile from here he killed every man, woman, child, worker and servant in a large village. As far as I know, that's where he lives. It's only smart to be careful with him, because he can do great damage to a man.'

'By God's arms,' proclaimed this reveler, 'is it really that dangerous to meet up with him? I swear right here, by God's blessed bones, that I will seek him out on every street and path. Listen, my friends,' he said to his two companions, 'we three should be together in this. Let us swear eternal brotherhood to one another and, together, we will kill this false traitor Death. By God's eternal honor, this villain who slays so many others shall be slain before the sun goes down.'

Th three of them pledged to live and die for one another as though each was the other's brother. And they got up, in their drunken rage, and headed toward that village that the innkeeper had mentioned. They swore many a grisly oath along the way, ripping and tearing the body of Christ at each step, swearing that if they got their hands on him, death would surely die!

Before they had gone a half mile, just as they were climbing over a stile in a fence, they ran into a poor old man. He greeted them politely: 'Now, my Lords, God protect you!'

The proudest of the three revelers answered; 'What now, fellow, bad luck to you! Why are you all wrapped up like this, except for your face? And how do you come to live to such an old age?'

The old man looked him in the face and said: 'Because I can find no one, though I walk all the way to India, either in a city or in a village, willing to exchange his youth for my old age, I am condemned to this, my dotage, for as long as it is God's will. Alas, Death himself does not want my life. And so I wander, restless wretch that I am, knocking on the ground — which is the entrance to my mother — with my staff, from morning to night. I plead with her: 'Dear Mother, please let me in! Look how I am wasting away, my flesh, my blood, my skin. Alas, when will my bones finally at peace? Dear Mother, why won't you let me exchange the chest of all my valuables resting in my chamber all these years for a simple haircloth in which to wrap my body?' But she refuses to do that kindness to me still, though my face be pale and wrinkled.

But young Sir, you do yourself no honor by speaking so churlishly to an old man who has done nothing wrong in word or deed. You can read it for yourself in the sacred scriptures: "You should stand in the presence of an old man with white hair upon his head." This is why I advise you not to harm an old man now, no more than you would want others to abuse you when you reach old age, if you live so long. And may God be with you, wherever you are going! I myself must be on my way to where I am bound.'

'No way, you old scoundrel!' said one of the other gamblers. 'By God, you will not leave so easily! You will not get away from us so lightly, by St. John! Just now you were talking about this traitor Death who is going around the countryside killing all our friends. As you are obviously his spy, I swear to you by God and the holy sacrament, that unless you tell us where he can be found, you will pay dearly! You are clearly in cahoots with him in his killing of us young people, you false thief!'

'Very well, young Sirs, if you are indeed so intent on finding Death, turn into this crooked path, at the end of which there is a grove of trees where I left him, as God is my witness, under a tree, because that is where he lives. Despite your boasts, he will not hide from you. See that oak? That's where you will find him. May the God who redeemed all mankind save and remedy you!'

As soon as the old man had said this, the three revelers ran as fast as they could toward the tree and, when they got there, they came upon what seemed to them nearly eight bushels of florins — beautiful, round, gold coins. No longer did they think about Death then, for they were so happy to see the treasure they had found, those shiny, beautiful, gold coins, that all they could think to do was to sit down and admire this precious horde.

The worst of the three spoke first: 'Listen to me, my brothers; even though I spend my time joking around and gambling, I am quite smart. Fortune has gifted us with this treasure so that we can live forever in happiness and pleasure and, by God's boundless dignity, as easily as it came to us, so we should spend it. Which one of us had any idea when the day began that it would end so well? And if we could carry this gold from this place home to my house — or to yours — for there can be no doubt but that it belongs to us — we would be in seventh heaven.

But we cannot get away with that during daylight. People will think that we are nothing but thieves and hang us for this, our own treasure. No, these riches must be carried away in the dark of night, as cleverly and as secretly as we can manage it.

So I suggest that the three of us draw lots to see which of us shall run into town — and that without delay — and surreptitiously acquire some bread and wine, while the other two guard and keep from public notice our fortune, and if he gets back in good time, we will, after dark, agree on where it is best to take it.' So, one of them held straws in his fist, and each one drew and it so happened that the lot fell on the youngest among them, who immediately went off to town to carry out their plan.

But as soon as he had gone, one of the two remaining said to the other: 'Well you know that you are my sworn brother, and I have something to propose that will benefit you. We both know that our friend has left us here with lots and lots of gold that we agreed to divide among the three of us. Bit if I can devise a plan whereby just the two of us would be able to split it, would you consider that to be the act of a friend?' The other one answered: 'I don't see how that could happen. He knows the two of us are here with the gold, so what can we do? What shall we tell him?'

'If you can keep it between us,' said the first scoundrel, 'I will tell you in a few words what we can do to bring this about.'

'Of course,' the other one said, 'I swear to pledge myself not to betray you .'

'In that case, you know that there are two of us, and two of us together are stronger than one alone. As soon as he comes back, act as if you want to wrestle with him, and I will stab him in the side while you hold him, and then, even as you are struggling with him, you stab him, too, and then all this gold will be divided, my dear friend, between the two of us. And we can entertain ourselves fully just as we want to and gamble whenever we feel like it.'

Meanwhile, the youngest of them, who had gone to town, kept thinking about the beauty of those dazzling, new, gold florins. 'O Lord, he thought, 'wouldn't it be wonderful it I could keep the entire treasure for myself! There isn't a man living anywhere under the throne of the Almighty that should live as happily a life as I would then!' And at last our enemy, Satan, put it in his thoughts to buy poison with which to kill his two companions. You can be sure that the evil one found him to be pliable and easily brought to his ruin. Now fully intent on killing his companions — untroubled by any second thought — he quickly found the local apothecary in that town, and he asked him to sell him some poison to kill his rats, as well as the weasel that had moved into his yard and, as he told the apothecary, was killing all his fowl. He was set on getting rid of this vermin that destroyed his property under cover of dark.

The apothecary assured him: 'You shall have something that, as God may save my soul, is so powerful that there is no creature in all the world that shall not die after eating or drinking something that has been treated with this concoction, even if it were only a grain of corn. Whoever consumes any of this poison will die and in less time than it takes to walk a mile — that is how powerful and violent it is.'

So this cursed young man, carrying the poison in a box, happened to run into someone in the street who was able to give him three large bottles. He poured the poison into two of them, keeping the third clean of the poison for his own drink, as he expected that he would need the whole night to carry the gold to safety. As soon as he had filled all three bottle with wine, this reveler, may he have ill fortune, returned again to his two companions.

No reason to make a short story longer than it need be! Just as they had planned his killing, they swiftly carried it out, and when this was done, the one said to the other: 'Good, let's sit and drink and enjoy ourselves for a while before we bury his body.' And it so happened that he took one of the two bottles with the poison and he and his buddy shared the wine, and so the two of them died also.

I am certain that Avicenna never wrote in any set of rules or in one of his writings about more signs of poisoning than these two wretches showed by the time they died. And this was the end of these two killers and their false poisoner, as well.

Oh, cursed sin of all cursedness!

Oh, villainous murder, oh, wickedness!

Oh, gluttony, lechery and dice!

You evil and intentional blasphemer of Christ with your habit of cursing and your pride!

Alas, mankind, how can you be so false and unkind to your creator, who made you from nothing and redeemed you with His precious blood, alas?

Now, good men, may God forgive you all your trespasses and keep you from the sin of greed. All of you can be saved by my sacred pardons, if only you bring me your offerings in gold coins or silver — I will take anything — silver brooches, spoons, rings — and bow your head under this holy bull! Come up, you wives, offer up your wool. I will enter your names here in my rolls at once and you shall be able to enter the bliss of heaven! With my great power, I absolve you — those of you who make your offering — so that you will once again be as clean and as pure as the day you were born.

Gentlemen, this is how I preach!

And may Jesus Christ, the healer of our souls, grant that you receive His pardon — that is best of all — far be it from me to deceive you!

But — sirs — I did forget to say one thing in my tale.

I have here in my bag relics and pardons that rival those offered by any man in England, given to me directly by the hand of the pope. If any of you are moved with devotion and right now wish to make your offering and receive my absolution, come to me at once, without delay. and kneel before me meekly to receive your pardon. Or you can receive more pardons if you like, as you wend your way on this pilgrimage, all nice and new, if, after every mile or so, you offer up your nobles or pennies, tested and true, more with each mile that we pass. You should be most honored to have with you a pardoner who is able to absolve each and every one of you as you ride through the countryside, no matter what adventures you may experience along the way. Who knows? One or two of you may fall off your horses and break your necks. But think about how fortunate you are that I happened to join your company — someone who can absolve you of sins great and small when your soul passes from your body."

He looked around at us all and then continued.

"It seems to me that our Host should be the one to begin, because he is more befouled with sin than anyone. So, come forth, Sir Host, and be the first to make an offering. You can kiss each of my relics for no more than merely a groat. Go on and open your purse!"

"Not on your life!" the Host answered. "You are asking me to take the curse of Christ upon me. Stop it already — nothing like that is going to happen; you can have my oath on it. You want me to kiss your stinking underpants, while you have me believe that it is the relic of a saint, though it is stained with what comes from your asshole. No, by the cross Saint Helen found, I'd rather have your balls in my hand instead of some relic or even some reliquary. In fact, that gives me an idea: let's cut them off and I'll help you carry them, and then we can find a shrine for them in some hog's turd. What do you say to that?"

The Pardoner was so angry at the Host's response that he was speechless, unable to say one word in return.

But the Host, who had now had enough, turned to the rest of the pilgrims and said: "Alright, enough of that game. I am tired of it. I refuse to get involved with anyone who is that angry."

But when he saw most people laughing at what had just transpired, the Knight spoke up: "I believe we have had enough, indeed. No more, please." He bowed lightly to the red-faced Pardoner and said: "Sir Pardoner, be happy and don't let this bother you any more." And turning to the Host, he continued: "And you, Sir Host, for whom I feel great affection, I ask that you forget all this and give the Pardoner the kiss of peace. And you, Pardoner, I ask that you join our Host and, as we have till now, let us all laugh and joke with one another."

And indeed, only a little surly, the two kissed one another and we went on our way.

But the Host had to pick another pilgrim to tell a story and so, as we rode on, he looked around and saw the Squire in a friendly conversation with the Franklin. He called out: 'Squire, you, young sir, come over here and, if you've a mind to, perhaps you'll tell us a love story. Surely you know as much about that subject as any man here."

"I doubt that, Sir Host," he answered, "but I'll do my best to tell you a story. Far be it from me to foil your will — I will tell a tale. But, please, forgive me if I do not do it justice. I mean to do my best. So, here goes."

The Squire's Tale

"In the land of the Mongols, in Tsarev, there lived a king whose war with Russia ended the life of many a brave man. This noble king's name was Genghis Khan, and there was no more excellent ruler at that time anywhere. He had every royal quality, and he faithfully kept the laws of the religion he was born into. He was bold, wise and wealthy, merciful and equally just to all, true to his word, kind and honorable, courageous and reliable, young, active, strong, and as eager in arms as any of his knights. He was a handsome young man, favored by Fortune, and so constant in his behavior that he was without equal.

This noble king had two sons with his wife, Elpheta; the oldest was named Algarsif and the other was called Cambalo. This worthy king also had a daughter, his youngest child, and her name was Canacee. Sadly, I am neither eloquent nor skilled enough to do justice to her beauty — I dare not even attempt such a thing. My English is just not up to it. It would require a master of rhetoric, expert in all the colors of that art, adequately to describe every aspect of her.

I am not such, and I must speak merely as I am able to.

So this Genghis Khan, of whom I have been telling you, had worn the crown for twenty years and, on the Ides of March, as he did each year, he let his birthday be proclaimed throughout his city of Tsarev. Phoebus, the sun, was cheery and bright, near to his high point in the face of Mars and preparing for the house of Aries — the very embodiment of a choleric humor. Because the weather was so pleasant and warm, the birds, spurred on by the shining sun, the season and the new greening of spring, sang loudly, in the full blush of emotion. In fear no longer of the biting, cold sword of winter, they seemed to luxuriate in the warm spring.

Genghis Khan sat high in his palace on his throne, wearing his royal vestments, his crown on his head, reigning over a feast so ceremonial and abundant that there has never been one like it in the whole world. If I tried to tell you all the details, it would take me a long summer's day, but there is no need to describe every course or the order in which they were served. So I will not describe their strange sauces, or the decorative swans, or the herons native to that land. We are told by old, well-travelled knights, that in that country they love food that we in our country wouldn't prize highly.

Of course, no one can describe everything.

So I will not hold you up, since it is past prime already and there is no benefit in telling you all this, for it will only slow down the story. So I will return to what I was saying before.

After the third course had been served, with the king sitting there in all his splendor, listening to the beautiful music of his minstrels playing while he ate, suddenly there rode into the hall a knight on a brass horse, a large shiny mirror in his hand, a golden ring on his thumb, a naked sword hanging from his belt — and he rode right up to the high table. The hall was suddenly totally silent, as everyone marveled at this sight.

The strange knight, who had appeared so unexpectedly, was — aside from his uncovered head — dressed entirely in exquisite, full armor, and he greeted in proper order the king and queen and all the lords sitting in that hall, with such great respect in his words and appearance, that Gawain, known for his courtesy, though he were to reappear magically here, could not have improved on a single word. When the knight reached the high table, he delivered his message flawlessly, in a manly voice and in the formal manner of his country. And to make even better what he had to say, his demeanor matched his words, just as taught by those who teach the art of oratory. And though I cannot do justice to his style or reach so high a standard, I will do what I can: this is the gist of what he said, as well as I can remember it.

'On this solemn day I bring you greetings from the King of Arabia and India, who sends his best wishes and asks you, in acknowledgement of this day, to accept from my hand — ever at your service — this horse made entirely of brass. It can, in one complete day — that is, twenty-four hours — bear your body anywhere you wish to go. It can be anywhere you wish, dry or wet, without any harm whatsoever to you, through foul weather or fair. Or if you desire to fly as high in the air as an eagle soaring through the sky, this same steed will carry you — you need simply turn a pin on it — with no danger to you, until you arrive at the place you want to go to — and back again, whether you rest or fall asleep on his back. The man who made this created many such ingenious things. He observed numerous astral configurations, and he understood the subtleties of all their controlling forces.

Behold also this mirror in my hand. It has the power to show you whether adversity will befall your kingdom or yourself, and it will let you know who is your friend and who is your foe. In addition, if any lovely lady has her heart set on a man of any kind, she shall witness his betrayal if he be false, she can see who his new love is, and she will know clearly everything he is doing in secret, as there is nothing he can hide. Aware of the sensuous summers you enjoy here, my Lord has sent this mirror to your wonderful daughter, the Lady Canacee — as well as a ring I will also tell you about .

This ring has wonderful powers: if your daughter wants to wear it on her thumb or carry it in her purse, there is no bird that flies under the heavens whose speech she will not understand, knowing the meaning clearly and plainly. Moreover, she will not only be able to answer that bird in his language, but she will know every plant that grows in the ground and whom it might heal, no matter how deep or wide the wounds.

Finally, this naked sword that hangs from my belt has the ability to cut straight through the armor — were it as thick as a mighty oak — of any man you smite with it. And whomever you wound with this sword's stroke will never be healed until you decide, in your kindness, to strike the wound again with the flat side of this sword. Then he will be whole again. This is the absolute truth — I tell you no lie. It will never fail you, for as long as you possess it.'

As soon as this knight had finished with his message, he rode his horse back out of the hall and got down, leaving it in the center of the courtyard, still as a stone, shining like the sun. The knight himself was led to a room, where his armor was taken off and he was fed.

The sword and the mirror gifts were taken by officials assigned to do so and stored in a high tower. The ring was solemnly presented to Canacee, right there at the table. But, to tell you the truth, the brass horse could not be moved, standing in place as if it were fastened to the ground. No matter what pulleys or machines equipped with windlasses they might have applied, they would have been unable to move it. And do you know why? They did not know the trick. And so they had to leave it there in place until the knight taught them what it took to move it, as you will hear later.

The courtyard was crowded with people moving around to get a look at the horse standing there, so high, broad and long, so well-proportioned and powerful as any great steed that might have come from Lombardy. At the same time it had all the best qualities of a horse, including the alert eyes of a gentle Apulian charger. Truly, neither nature nor human skill could have improved it in any way — so everyone agreed. But the most amazing thing was that a horse like this, made entirely of brass, could move the way it did. All the people there said this was true magic.

Of course, various onlookers offered multiple explanations, with as many theories as there were heads. There was so much murmuring, it sounded as if a swarm of bees had been let loose in that courtyard. Arguments were rich with imagination. Some called on old poems, such as the myth of Pegasus, the winged horse that could fly. Other old stories were brought up, also, like the one about the Trojan horse, fashioned by Synon, that brought that city to its destruction. One bystander even said: 'I am deathly afraid that it is filled with armed men who want to conquer our city. It would be good if everyone knew that.' Another whispered secretly to his friend: 'He is wrong, because this is really an illusion like those conjured up by magicians performing at great feasts.' So they went back and forth with their various theories, the way unsophisticated people often do when faced with something made more cleverly than their ignorance will let them comprehend. And we all know that they usually end up with the wrong conclusion.

There were others who puzzled about the mirror that had been carried up to the high tower — how in the world it could show such things. They were answered by those saying that it was perfectly normal but relied on various angles and clever reflections — there had been one like it in Rome. Alhazen and Vitello, and Aristotle were mentioned as having written of strange mirrors and perspectives — so said some who had heard of their books.

Still others wondered about the sword that supposedly could pierce anything, and they brought up King Telephus and Achilles, who had a wondrous spear that could both wound and heal, just as could that sword. They discussed certain ways to temper metal and the chemicals that might be used to accomplish that — mysterious for many, certainly for me.

And there were those who spoke about Canacee's ring, agreeing that none of them had ever heard of a ring with such amazing powers, remembering that Moses and King Solomon supposedly were versed in similar artifice. Some spoke their piece and moved on. Others conjectured that it was a wondrous thing shaped from ashes of fern, even though it was neither glass nor such ashes. Perhaps it was the product of skills lost long ago. Most finally ceased their yapping and wondering, except those who mused deeply about the causes of thunder, or ebb and flood tides, and spiders webs, and fog, and any number of things we don't really understand. So they yammered on and considered and supposed until the king finally rose from feasting.

By this time Phoebus, the sun, had passed the meridian angle and the royal beast, the gentle Lion, was still ascending with his star Aldiran. Genghis Khan proceeded to his Presence Chamber, led by the loud music of his minstrels playing various instruments so beautifully that it was heavenly to hear. Behold the lusty children of Venus dancing all about, as that divine lady, positioned in Pisces, beamed down on her followers.

Once this noble king has taken his throne, the foreign knight was summoned and allowed to dance with Canacee. This was the beginning of such revelry and delight that it could never have been brought about by just anyone. If you want to enjoy such a festivity it has to be arranged by someone who knows Love and his service and is as charming and passionate as May itself.

Who could possibly do justice to these dances unfamiliar to us, the voluptuous exchange of glances, the subtle looks and smiles — disguised, lest jealous men notice them? No one, except Lancelot, and he is long dead. So I will pass over all this sensuality. I will say no more about it and will simply let these people enjoy themselves until it is time to dress for supper.

In the midst of all this music, the steward ordered the spice cakes and wine to be served, and the ushers and squires carried out the orders immediately. After the guests ate and drank their fill, they were off to the temple, as is only right, and once the service was completed, they spent the rest of the day feasting. What need is there to describe all that was available to them? Everybody knows that the feast of a king has plenty for the highest and the lowest among us, with more delicacies than I even know of.

Once supper had been finished, this noble king, surrounded by the crowd of lords and ladies, went to see his brass steed. I have already told you about the excitement generated by this horse fashioned from brass. It was unlike anything since the siege of Troy, an earlier time when people also tried to make sense of a strange horse. The king had no choice but to ask the knight again for an explanation of the qualities and powers of this steed, as well as the secret to controlling it.

As soon as the knight put his hand on the bridle, this horse began to trip and dance. The knight explained: 'Sire, it is simple.

When you want to ride somewhere you need merely turn a pin in his ear, about which I will tell you — and only you. Then you tell the horse the name of the place or the country where you wish to go, and when you get there and decide you want to stop, tell him to descend and turn another pin that controls all the elements of the machine. He will descend at once, just as you bid, and will stay there as long as you do. Though all the world conspire to the contrary, he will not move from that spot or be transported. If you wish him to leave from somewhere, just turn this pin and he will disappear from everyone else's sight — to reappear, be it day or night, when you decide to call him again in the way that I will tell you when we two are alone. So, you can ride him anytime you want to, as that is all there is to it.'

When the king had learned everything he needed to know from this knight and had committed it to memory, he was happy and delighted. While he joined in again with the reveling of his lords and ladies, the horse's bridle was taken to the high tower to be kept there with the precious royal jewels. The horse disappeared from sight — I don't know how it was done. And I have no more to say about it. So, I leave this Genghis Khan in joy and happiness, feasting with his court until the dawn,

This is the end of part one of my tale."

The Squire took a sip from his wineskin before he continued.

"And this is how part two of my story begins.

Sleep, the steward of digestion, crept up on the Court and nudged them toward the rest that much drink and effort call for. Yawning, the king — who had a sanguine disposition — kissed his followers goodnight and told them that it was time to get some sleep. 'Treat your blood well, for it is nature's friend,' he fittingly advised them as they retreated to their rest, tired, and drowsy, knowing that it was time.

I will make no effort to chronicle their dreams — their heads were filled with alcoholic fumes, causing fantasies that make little sense. They slept well into the morning, for the most part, but not Canacee, a moderate person, as women should be. She had taken leave of her father in the early evening to go to her rest because she did not want to be pale or look unfit for the celebrations the next day. The ancient ring and the mirror excited her so much that her complexion must have changed twenty times after she awoke. She had even had a vision in her sleep caused by these precious objects. She called on her lady-in-waiting even before dawn and told her that she was ready to get up.

Now this old woman, known to be wise, as was her mistress, asked her: 'But Madame, where are you off to so early, while everyone else is still asleep?'

'I am not sleepy, and I just want to get up and go for a walk.'

Her governess then awoke the rest of her women and, some ten or twelve strong, they got up with their beautiful mistress Canacee, who was as ruddy and bright as the young sun when it has passed four degrees in Aries, no higher than that by the time she was ready to go out. Dressed appropriately for the season she walked about lightly and enjoyed herself with her ladies, as they followed a path in the park.

The fog rising up from the ground made the sun seem reddish and huge, so fair a sight that it, and the singing birds, the morning, and the season itself were all delightful. But imagine Canacee's surprise when she suddenly understood exactly what the birds were singing and what they intended.

As she was walking along, there was a falcon sitting high overhead in a tree that was all dried out and white as chalk. And the falcon began to cry out in a very sad tone that resonated throughout the forest. She had beaten herself so woefully with her own wings that she was all covered with blood, and it ran red, all down the trunk of the tree. And she kept wailing and shrieking, stabbing herself over and over with her own beak — it was sad enough to make a tiger or any beast in the wild weep along with her out of pity. If I am to do justice to this falcon, no man alive anywhere has ever heard shrieking from a falcon so beautiful in plumage or noble in shape. She seemed to be a peregrine falcon from a distant land and, as she stood on that branch, she fainted now and then for loss of blood, nearly falling from the tree.

Because the fair princess Canacee was wearing the quaint ring, she was able to understand everything any bird might say in its own language, as well as to answer it, also in its language. What she heard this falcon to be saying made her nearly die of sorrow. So she quickly approached the trunk of the tree, looking pitifully at this falcon all the time, and held wide her apron, for she knew that the falcon must fall from its perch the next time she fainted from loss of blood. Canacee stood there for a while and then addressed the falcon, just as you shall hear.

'If it's possible for you to tell me, what is the reason you are suffering like this? Are you grieving a death or a lost love? For I know well that these are things that bring such woe to a noble heart, causing more sadness than any other grief can. Seeing you destroy yourself tells me that either anger or fear have made you treat yourself so cruelly, since I cannot see anyone pursuing you. For the love of God, spare yourself as, surely, this cannot make things better! West or east, I have never seen neither bird nor beast that treated herself so badly. I feel such great compassion for you that you are killing me with your sorrow. For the sake of the Almighty, please come down from your high perch and, as I am a true daughter of a king, if I can know the cause of your illness, and if it is in my ability, I will heal it before the sun sets again, so help me the God of all. Surely I can find the right plants to salve your heart!'

The falcon only increased its pitiful shrieking, finally falling down from its branch and lying motionless on the ground, as still as a stone. Gently, Canacee took her in her lap, where she eventually awakened from her swoon. As soon as was revived from her faint, she immediately began to speak in her hawk language: 'As everyone can see, it is proven every day, both in practice and by word of our authorities, that pity is quickly felt by a noble heart, with compassion for the sharp pain of others — noble hearts display nobility. My beautiful Canacee, I see clearly the compassion you feel for my distress, for Nature has imbued you with the essence of true feminine graciousness. So, while I have the time and the opportunity, I will share with you my plight, not in the hope of feeling better but to be one with your heart and to let others learn from my example — for the same reasons as the lion chases its cub.'

While the falcon spoke so movingly of her sorrow, Canacee wept as if she were going to turn completely into water, but the falcon begged her to stop but then began, with a heavy sigh, to tell her story.

'From the day I was born — alas, that fateful day — I was nurtured so tenderly on that grey marble rock that I had not a worry in the world until I was able to fly high in the sky on my own. Close to where I grew up there lived a male falcon who seemed the epitome of all nobility but was really filled with betrayal and deception, all under the cover of a gentle appearance. So much did he seem to reflect the very color of truth, so pleasant was he, so cleverly did he deceive that no one could suspect his deception. That is how well he cloaked his awful true colors with lovely hues. Like a snake hides among beautiful flowers, biding its time to strike, just so did this hypocrite of the god of love carry out his duties and his practices, while his actions and appearance seemed totally in accord with noble love.

You know how on a tomb there is a beautiful sculpture on top but underneath that is the rotting corpse — this is a precise equivalent of this hypocrite. And this is what let him carry out his intent that — except for the evil one himself — no one truly knew. He had wept and lamented for so long and pretended to be in service to me for so many years that my heart, ever true, was filled with pity for him. All unaware of his absolute evil, I was fearful that he would die, based on his oaths and his assurances. So I finally granted him my love — upon one condition: that he would forever maintain my honor and reputation, both privately and publicly. Because I thought he deserved it, I gave him my entire heart and all my feelings and forever exchanged my heart for his.

This was, of course, known only to God and to him, otherwise I would never have said yes. But the saying has been true for a long time and is so still now: "A thief does not think like an honest man." And now he could see that I had granted him my love completely, just as I have told you, and given him my ever faithful heart, just as he had sworn to give his heart to me. So, this deceitful tiger fell on his knees with such deep humility, with such high reverence and, by his appearance, with such noble manners, overcome with such joy, or so it seemed, that not even Jason and the Trojan Paris could have imitated his artful arguments. Jason, you ask? Yes, Jason, for surely no other man since Lambeth, the first man to be in love with two women at one time, none of these or anyone else since humans were first born — no one, by even a twenty-thousandth part — nay, none were worthy of undoing his sandals as far as their duplicity in pretense goes — no one has betrayed anyone so absolutely as he did me.

His manner toward any lady — no matter how smart — was heavenly to behold, so well could he disguise and manipulate all things, both by his words and by his looks. And because of the faithfulness I thought was in his heart, if anything bothered him or hurt him, be it ever so slight, and I became aware of it, I felt as if Death himself was ripping me apart. And so, before long, as happens, my will was the agent of his will; by that I mean that my will obeyed his will in all things — as far as is reasonable — but always maintaining the boundaries of my honor. I have never loved anything more — or even as much — as him and, as God is my witness, I never will, again.

My believing only the best about him continued for a year or two. But then things were such that Fortune required him to depart from the place we called home. Certainly, I was grief-stricken; words cannot do justice to how I felt. I can say this without hesitation: it taught me what death must feel like. No one can imagine the pain I experienced. So the day came when he took his leave, so sorrowfully that I was sure he felt the same pain I did, by his expression and by the way he spoke. Of course I believed him to be faithful and I was sure that he would return in a short while. As often happens, the reason for his leaving was a matter of honor, and so I made a virtue of necessity and bore it well, since there was no choice. As best as I was able to, I hid my pain from him and took his hand, with St. John as my witness, and said: "Don't forget that I am yours, always! Remain to me as I have been to you and ever shall!" There is no point in recounting what he said to me. Who could have said it all better than he — and who could have acted worse?

When he had said all he had to say he was off. You may be familiar with the saying: "When you eat with a friend, bring a very long spoon." He was on his way, and he followed that path until he arrived where he was meant to go. Whenever he rested, I suspect he was thinking of this saying: "Returning to one's own kind makes the heart happy." Men say this, I think.

It is the nature of men always to be looking for something new, just as caged birds do. Even if you pay attention to their needs day and night, and keep the straw in that cage fresh and smooth as silk, and feed them sugar, honey, bread and milk, yet, no sooner is the cage left open, than birds will kick over their cup and fly off to the woods to eat worms — so interested in something different are they and so in love with novelties of any kind — they are not bound by the nobility of blood.

And this is exactly how my peregrine falcon acted. Though nobly born, well-formed and happy, good-looking and humble and free, he happened to see a kite, a scavenger bird, flying by, and he immediately fell in love with this kite, and all his love for me disappeared.

Thus is he now unfaithful, and the kite holds him in her service and I am lost, without remedy.'

And with that this falcon began to cry anew and fainted again in Canacee's lap.

She and all her women were filled with sorrow for the pain of this hawk, but they did not know how to help her. Canacee took the falcon home with her and bound all the wounds she had inflicted on herself. She could do little more than dig up herbs and make fresh potions from healing herbs in order to salve the wounded hawk. She worked at this from dawn to dusk, making a cage by the head of her bed and covering it with blue velvet as a sign of all women's solidarity. On the outside the pen was painted green, the color of unfaithful birds, be they small or large, hawk or owl. And there were magpies painted on there, as well, for they chide and cry out defiance all day long.

Now I leave Canacee with her hawk; I say nothing else of her ring until we have reason to tell how, through the efforts of Cambalo, this falcon regained her love, fully repentant, as the story tells us and as I will recount later. For now I will halt in this part of the story in order to tell you of adventures and battles without equal — they are so marvelous.

I will begin with Genghis Khan, who conquered many cities in his time. After that I will tell you more about Algarsif, his son, and how he won Theodora to be his wife, enduring many perils for her sake and successful, ultimately, because of the brass steed. And after that I will tell you more of Cambalo who jousts with Canacee's two brothers in order to win her hand. And I will begin again where I leave off, as this is the end of part two of my tale."

The Squire seemed deeply moved by his own tale; he sighed, wiped his brow and enjoyed another draft of wine.

"So,' he continued, 'Apollo drove his chariot so high in the sky that the house of the god named Mercury, the sly—"

"Oh, I think not," interrupted the Host. 'It seems to me that we have heard our fill of birds and of their keepers. I must ask you, my dear Squire—"

But here the Host was interrupted by the Franklin, who addressed him: "Sir Host," he cleared this throat loudly, "I must say something here in response to the wonderful story of foreign lands and strange customs the Squire has shared with us." The Host looked perplexed, but the Franklin simply turned to the Squire, bowed, and said: "Ah, my dear, dear Squire. In faith, you have acquitted yourself well and ably. I can only praise your wit and the manner in which you have told this story."

The Squire was taken aback at the interruption, and sputtered: "What? I do not understand. There is much more to tell."

"I am certain of that," the Franklin assuaged him and gently patted him on the arm. "But there is only so much time and we have a number of stories yet to hear."

The Squire frowned, but the Franklin politely continued: "Indeed, I am most impressed, young Sir. Considering your youth, to speak so feelingly and so beautifully? I salute you, Sir." By now the Squire seemed to feel somewhat better and he allowed himself a small smile at the Franklin's words of praise.

"Well," he began, but the Franklin was not finished: "Nay, nay, good young Sir, you have done your duty and you have carried it out as well — no, did I say, as well? By my mother's grave, I meant to say better, much better than anyone could expect."

The Squire seemed very happy to hear this, but the Franklin had more ingratiating to do.

"I will go to the grave proclaiming to the world that there is no one here, young Sir, who is your equal in eloquence, no matter how long any of us will live. May God give you good fortune — you deserve it — and may He bless you with the grace to persevere in your virtues. I can't remember when I enjoyed listening to anyone as much as I have this day."

He paused for a moment, looking down wistfully, but then continued.

"I have a son about your age, and I swear by the Trinity, I would give twenty pounds worth of real estate — even if it had just been deeded to me freely — if he were ever to become a man of your great discretion. I say that wealth is meaningless compared to virtue. How often I have had to rebuke my son — and will, no doubt be required to do so again — for he seems not at all interested in living an honorable life. He would rather spend his time gambling and spending his money foolishly, losing everything he has been given. And God knows he would rather spend time talking to an ignorant page than conversing with a noble knight who could teach him something of nobility."

"Your nobility be damned," answered the Host. "But since you have begun to talk already, why don't you continue. You know that each of you has agreed to tell a tale or two or break your word, and you —as I'm sure you know — have not yet shared with us a tale."

"I know that very well, Sir," said the Franklin. "I pray that you do not think the less of me for having a few words to say to this young gentleman. I am not quite done."

"Oh, by Christ's bleeding toes, quit wasting our time and tell us your tale."

"Alright, then, gladly will I tell my story to you, Sir Host, and to these other worthy pilgrims. With your permission," he bowed low to the Squire, who answered him with an appreciative nod. "And at the wish of our worthy Host," now he bowed, considerably less deeply, to our Host, "I will do as asked. God knows, I want no disagreements with you, doing my best, as my wits allow, to do your will. I pray to the Almighty that you will find what I have to say pleasing — for then I can be sure that it is good enough."

He bowed again to the Host, who seemed happy enough about this response. Then the Franklin began his tale.

The Franklin's Tale

"In days of yore, the ancient, noble Britains told tales about various adventures and they rhymed them in their Breton language and sang them, accompanied by their instruments, or sometimes they just read them for entertainment. I remember one of those tales, and I will tell it to you as best I can.

But ladies and gentlemen, because I am a simple, uneducated man, I ask you even before I begin, to excuse my rough speech. Certainly I never had the opportunity to learn rhetoric, so my speech is plain and unadorned. I have never slept on Mount Parnassus, where the sacred muses live, nor have I studied Marcus Tullius Cicero. As I live and die, I know only the colors we see in the fields, or those used in dying or painting; the colors of rhetoric are foreign to me. I do not resonate with such matters. Nevertheless, if you listen, you shall hear my tale.

In Armorica, also known as Brittany, there once lived a knight who was in love with a lady and did his best to serve her as best he could. He went to lots of trouble and did great things for this lady all in an effort to win her hand. She was the most beautiful woman you can imagine and she came from such great nobility that the knight hardly dared, for fear of rejection, tell her of his woe, his pain, and all his distress. But finally, because of his worthiness and his meek homage to her, she felt such pity for all he had suffered that she privately agreed to take him as her husband and her lord, to the degree that husbands govern their wives. And, in order to enjoy the greatest bliss possible in their lives together, of his own free will he gave her his word as a knight that never, ever, day or night, would he assume power over her against her will, or ever show any jealousy. He would obey her and do as she wished in everything, as lovers do with their ladies, so long as he appeared to be in charge in public — that much he required, lest he be shamed in the eyes of the world.

She thanked him most graciously, saying: 'Sir, since your nobility compels you to offer me such free rein, I pray to God that I will never be the cause of conflict or strife between us. Please know that I will always be your humble, faithful wife until the day my heart stops beating — on that you have my word.' And so they were both content and at peace.

Now, dear sirs, I know one thing that is certain: that those who wish to be lasting friends must be willing to do each other's bidding. Contrary to what you have heard in other tales on this pilgrimage, love cannot be compelled by control. When control arrives, the God of Love immediately unfurls his wings and, farewell — he is gone! Love must be as free as a spirit.

By nature women seek freedom rather than being penned in like slaves. And, to tell the truth, so do men. He who is most patient in love always holds the advantage. There can be no doubt but that patience is a great virtue for, as scholars tell us, it achieves things that stubbornness will never gain. Every word from one's mouth cannot be to correct or complain. You must learn to accept suffering or, as God is my witness, you will know suffering, whether you wish to or not.

Everyone in the world, at one time or another, does or says the wrong thing. Whether it be anger, sickness or one's humors, a change in humors, wine or grief — any or all of these cause us, too often, to do or say something we should not. We simply cannot atone for every wrong we commit. Anyone experienced in governance knows that an act of wrong-doing must be followed by restraint.

And this is why this wise and worthy knight promised patience to his wife — to live peacefully — and she just as wisely swore to him that she would never demonstrate a flaw in her behavior.

Here is an example of a wise and respectful agreement that allows her to accept him both as her servant and her lord: servant in love and lord in marriage. And this is how he was both lord and servant. Servant? Nay —- superior in lordship. For he has both his lady and his love — unquestionably his lady but also his wife, all of it under the law of love.

When he had been blessed with this good fortune, he brought his wife, to his home, not far from Penmarch, and there they lived, blissfully and comfortably.

Only someone who has been married can know the joy, the ease, the prosperous life that exists between husband and wife. The two of whom I speak here lived in this blissful state for a year or more until one day, this knight whom I have been telling you about — whose name was Arveragus of Kayrudd — decided to go to England, also called Brittany in those days, for a year or two, to make his name by carrying out daring deeds. His heart was completely set on such an adventure and, as the book tells us, he was not to be prevented from his quest.

Now I will let this Arveragus go about his business and tell you more of Dorigen, his wife, who loves her husband with all of her heart. In his absence she weeps and sighs as noble wives do when they feel sad. She grieves, stays awake, wails, fasts and laments. She misses him so much that nothing in the whole wide world matters to her. Her friends, who knew how she suffered, comforted her as best they could. Day and night, they preached to her that she was surely killing herself, all for no reason. And, doing all they could, they tried to provide her with every comfort possible in their effort to help her cope with her sadness.

Now everyone knows that, given enough time, you can chip away at a rock until some figure is engraved in it. Thus, they comforted her long enough so that finally, hope and reason carved some consolation on her. She could not continue for much longer in such passionate sorrow, and so it began slowly to assuage.

Nevertheless, if it had not been for the letters Arveragus thoughtfully sent her, assuring her that he was well and that he would return soon, her sorrow would surely have slain her.

When her friends noticed that her sorrow had somewhat lessened, they begged her, on bended knee, for the sake of God, to join them in their social activities in order to drive away the remaining dark thoughts she was harboring. And finally, seeing that it was for the best, she gave in.

It so happened that her castle was located near the ocean, high above the water, and she and her friends enjoyed taking walks along the paths that were there; and on those walks she saw many boats and barges sailing to wherever they were off to. But this only added to her sadness, for it made her think: 'Alas, is there no ship, as far as I can see on this shore, that will bring my Lord home to me? That would heal my heart of all this bitter pain I am feeling.'

One day she was sitting near the water, thinking, and she happened to look at the bay littered with jagged, black rocks. These dangerous barriers filled her with fear and frightened her so much that she could not stand. She sat on the grass, sadly beholding the sea, sighing, with a heart cold as ice, saying: 'Eternal God, in Your divine providence You govern the world, and You create everything for a reason, so we are told. But dear God, why have you made such useless things as these grisly, evil, black rocks that seem to be simply foul chaos rather than another fair piece of your creation? For nowhere, south or north — no, neither east nor west, as far as I can see — do they seem to be of any use to man, bird or beast. They do nothing but cause trouble.

Do You not see, oh Lord, how they simply destroy Your people? They have killed a hundred thousand men, now all forgotten. Do you not recall that man was so important a part of your creation that You made us in Your own image and likeness? I would think You had more love for us than that! Why do You employ such means to destroy us — such means that do no earthly good but are simply destructive? I know that scholars will say, as they always do, that it is all for the best — that You have Your reasons — and that it is not meant for me to know them.

But I always end up with the same conclusion: that there is one God who causes the wind to blow but who must also protect my lord! I suppose I must leave the argument to the scholars. But I wish to God that, for my love's sake, all these black rocks were sunk into darkest hell.'

She cried many sad tears, but this is all she was ever able to think or say.

When her friends noticed that walking along the sea, rather than being a comfort, had become unpleasant for her, they found other places to entertain her and themselves. They took her to rivers and springs and other delightful places where they danced and played chess and backgammon.

One day, they spent the entire day, from morning on, in a nearby garden, which they had provisioned with food and drink and everything else they needed. It was the sixth morning in May — and May itself had painted this garden full of beautiful leaves and flowers by means of his sweet showers. The garden had furthermore been so artfully arranged by the skill of gardeners, that there never was another garden so beautiful, unless perhaps it was Eden itself. The sweet odors of the flowers and the beauty of the place would have brightened the heart of anyone ever born, unless they were enthralled by sickness or too much sadness — so gorgeous and pleasant was this place.

After they had eaten their meal they began to dance and sing, but not Dorigen, whose sadness and lamenting lingered because the man who was at once her husband and her love was not there dancing before her. But there was nothing else to do — she must put aside her sorrow and bide her time for now.

Among those whom Dorigen could see dancing before her was a squire, more attractive and dressed more jauntily than, I swear, is the very month of May. He sang and danced in a manner far superior to that of anyone else there or of any man since the beginning of the world. On top of that, if we were to describe him, he was one of the most handsome men alive — young, muscular, quite virtuous and rich, wise, well-liked and held in great esteem. And, if I am going to tell you everything — in a word — unbeknownst to Dorigen, this lusty squire, named Aurelius, was a servant of Venus and had been in love with Dorigen for the better part of two years or more without, of course, ever being courageous enough to tell her how he felt.

All that time he had been suffering in silence, in despair, daring to speak of it only with words of general, unspecified sorrow in his songs. That is how he could share with the world that he was in love and that his love was not returned.

He produced many songs, ballads, lays, laments, and roundels, all about how he could not tell his beloved of the pain he was suffering. All he could do was to languish like the furies do in hell, for surely he would die, as did Echo, who could not declare her love for Narcissus. He could not express his secret in any way other than you have heard me say here, except that at dances, where young people sometimes are able to exhibit their feelings, he occasionally looked at her like a man asking for grace from a lady. But she knew nothing of his interest in her.

Nevertheless, one day in May he happened to be strolling next to her and, as he was a man of worth and honor and had known her for a long time, they fell into conversation. And Aurelius used this occasion, little by little, to begin to uncover how he felt and, when he thought the time was right, he said to her: 'Madam, by the God who made this world, if I, Aurelius, had thought that there was a chance that it would make you happy, I would have accompanied your husband, that day when he left to cross the sea — never to return. I know that offering you my service is in vain and that the only reward I can hope for is a broken heart. But Madam, I beg of you, by all that is holy, have mercy on my sharp pain, for with a single word you can slay me or save my life. Here, at your feet, I pray to God to be buried! I cannot say anything else except that you have mercy on me, my love, lest I die.'

She looked at him with astonishment and asked: 'Is what you are saying to me here really true? Never before this moment had I had any idea how you felt. But now, Aurelius, now that I know your desire, I say to you that by the God who gave me spirit and breathed life into me, I shall never be an unfaithful wife, in word or in deed, as long as I draw breath. I will forever be his with whom I am one. Take this as my final answer to your plea.'

But then, in ironic jest, she added: 'I'll tell you what, Aurelius. Now that I have heard your poignant lament, I will — so God help me — agree to be your love on the day on which you get rid of all the rocks, stone by stone, that now line the coast of Brittany and let neither ship nor boat pass through them with safety. I say to you that when you have cleared the entire coast of these rocks, so that no stone can be seen, that day I will love you best of any man. This I swear to you, by all that is holy to me.'

He asked: 'Is that it? There is nothing else that will let you to be benevolent to me?'

'No, indeed! Never! By the God who made me. For I know full well that this can never happen. So, let this folly leave your head and heart forever. What joy is there in a man's life if he loves the wife of another man, who can have her body whenever he likes?'

Hearing her response, Aurelius could do nothing but sigh heavily. After some time, he finally uttered: 'Madam, we both know this is impossible! So I have no alternative but to die a horrible, painful death!'

And with that he turned away and went off by himself.

Now Dorigen was joined by her friends, who knew nothing of what had just happened, and they roamed up and down the garden paths, reveling and enjoying themselves the rest of the day, until the sun went down. The horizon stole the sun's light — in other words, it was night — and so they all went their way, feeling good after their day together.

But not poor wretched Aurelius, alas! He returned home, feeling his sorrowful heart grew cold in his body, fearing that his death was now inevitable. Kneeling, he held his arms up to the heavens to say his sad prayers. Nearly insane with sorrow, he barely knew what he was saying, but with a pitiful heart he began his lament to the gods, starting with the sun.

'Apollo, god and lord of every plant, herb, tree and flower, who gives, as you are inclined, each of them their time and season, depending on your variable position in the sky. Lord Phoebus, cast your merciful sight on your wretched Aurelius, who is so miserably lost. Behold, oh Lord, that without malice my lady has ordered my death unless, in your graciousness, you show some pity to my dying heart. I know for certain that, other than my lady herself, you are the only one who can aid me, if you so wish. Help me now to devise how I may find help.

Your blissful sister, the shining Luna, chief goddess and queen of the ocean — even though Neptune rules the seas, she is still empress over him — as you know, her desire is to be kindled and lit by your fire, which is why she ever obeys you. Just so do the oceans naturally obey her, as she is their goddess both in the sea water and in rivers, one and all. And so, Lord Phoebus, this is my request — perform this miracle or break my heart — the next time the sun and moon are set in opposition, in the sign of Leo, ask her to create such an enormous tide that it will cover the highest rocks in Armorica by at least five fathoms. And ask her to let this tide endure for two years. Then I will be able to say to my lady: 'Behold, just as you requested, so it has been done: the rocks are gone.'

Lord Phoebus, work this miracle for me. Ask the Lady Luna not to go any faster in her cycle than you do for two years, meaning that she shall always be at full moon, making the spring floods last day and night. Ask her to sink every rock down into her own dark regions under the ground, where Pluto lives, for unless she does this to help me win my dear lady in this manner, I shall never ever enjoy the hand of my beloved. To show my gratitude, I promise to walk barefoot all the way to her temple at Delphi. Oh, Lord Phoebus, behold these tears on my cheeks and have some compassion for my pain.'

And as soon as he had finished this, he fainted dead away and lay, as if in a trance, for a very long time.

He was finally found and picked up by his brother — who knew all about his suffering — and carried him to bed. And here, in this torment and condition, I will leave this wretched creature for now. Whether he lives or dies — the choice is his.

Now Arveragus, the flower of chivalry — along with other worthy men — has returned home, healthy and with great honor.

How blissful you are now, Dorigen, to embrace again your husband, this handsome knight, this worthy man of arms who loves you like the beating of his own heart.

He has no reason in the world to suspect that any man has spoken of love to his wife while he was away — of that he has no fear. He gives no thought to such things, dancing, jousting and being carefree. And so, I leave these two to live in joy and bliss and return to telling of the love-sick Aurelius.

Two years and longer poor Aurelius suffered in his sick bed as if tormented by the furies of hell, without comfort all this time, except what his brother, a scholar, was able to do for him. Although that individual knew all about this situation and the pain, he dared not whisper a word of it to anyone else. He kept it locked in his heart, more secretly than ever did Pamphilus his feelings for Galathee. His chest was outwardly unmarked, showing nothing, but just beneath the surface there lodged the arrow of his brother's pain, right in his heart. And we need no reminder that it is most dangerous to perform surgery on a wound healed only on the surface, for the arrow is still there, barely hidden.

When he was alone, this brother wept and lamented until, one day, he remembered something from his days as a student in Orleans, France. Young students are always seeking out arcane arts wherever they can find them and, this certain day, he remembered seeing a book about natural magic lying on the desk of one of his fellow students — who was a student of law but was interested in other things, as well. That book was all about the workings of the twenty-eight astrological houses of the moon and other such foolishness that we no longer pay attention to — for Holy Mother Church protects us from letting such illusions embed themselves in us.

When he thought of this book, his heart began to dance in his chest, as he said to himself: 'This is how my brother shall be cured! Because I know for certain that there are skills by means of which people create all kinds of illusions, such as those brought about by these crafty magicians. Many times have I been told how at great celebrations these illusionists have made water fill the hall, with boats rowing up and down; or they make it seem as if a grim lion has come into the hall; they can make flowers grow in a vast field; or vines, laden with grapes, white and red; or even a whole castle built of lyme and stone. And then, with a snap of their fingers, they made it all disappear again, and it was all gone.

So I am thinking that if I can find one of my school friends in Orleans, one who knows about these mansions of the moon — or other natural magic — he can make my brother win his beloved. I am sure there are scholars who can make it seem that all the black rocks of Brittany are gone from the sight of men, letting ships come and go as they please, and he can easily make such an illusion last a week or two. This will allow my brother to ease his pain, for she must then keep her word — otherwise he can at the very least disgrace her!'

To make a long story short — he went in at once to his brother's sick bed and persuaded him to get up and accompany him to Orleans. And they immediately prepared to go there in hopes of having his care lessened.

When they had almost reached that city — they were within a furlong or two — they ran into a young scholar walking all alone, and he politely greeted them in Latin — and then he amazed them by saying: 'I know why you have come here to Orleans.' And before they could take another step, he told them exactly why they had made the journey and what they were looking for.

When the scholar from Brittany asked him about friends whom he had known in the old days, the stranger told him that they were all dead, causing him to weep many a tear.

Aurelius and his brother got down from their horses and accompanied the magician to his home, where they were made comfortable. No food or drink that might please them was lacking. Neither Aurelius nor his brother had ever seen a house as well arranged as this one.

Before they went in to supper, their host showed them forests, parks full of wild deer, the biggest antlered stags anyone had ever seen, a hundred of them pursued and slain by packs of hounds, some with arrow wounds bleeding copiously. And when the deer disappeared, they saw falconers at a beautiful river where they had slain heron. Then Aurelius witnessed knights jousting in a field and, after that, his host brought him great pleasure when he showed his lady dancing, and then — as it seemed to him —Aurelius himself dancing with her. And when this magician, who was creating all of this, thought it was time, he clapped his hands and — farewell — everything they had seen vanished. And all this time that they were watching these marvelous sights they had never left the house, sitting in the magician's study, where he kept his books and where, aside from the three of them, there was no one else present.

The magician called his squire and asked him: 'Is our supper ready yet? It's been nearly an hour, I would say, since I asked you to prepare it, when these worthy gentlemen and I retired to my study where I keep my books.'

'Sire,' replied the squire, 'it is ready for you whenever you like, even as we speak.'

'In that case, we should go in to supper; after all, lovers need their rest.'

And after they had eaten, they began to discuss what this magician's fee would be to remove all the rocks off Brittany's coast, from the Gironde to the mouth of the Seine.

The magician explained how difficult it would be and swore to them, in the end, as God was his witness, that he would accept no less than a thousand pounds and would not do it for anything less than that.[61]

His heart filled with joy, Aurelius answered without hesitation: 'To hell with a thousand pounds! I would give this wide world, which people say is round, if it were mine to give. We are in complete agreement; we have a bargain! And you have my solemn word that you will be paid in full! But look to it that

---

[61] An enormous amount of money; perhaps as much as a million dollars today.

neither lack of diligence nor laziness keep us here in this place any later than tomorrow.'

'Indeed,' said the magician, 'take my word in return, as my pledge of good will.'

When the time came, Aurelius went off to his bed and slept soundly through most of the night, for now, because of his efforts and his newfound hope, his sorrowful heart enjoyed a respite from his suffering.

In the morning, after dawn, they immediately set out for Brittany, Aurelius riding next to this magician until they got to where they wanted to go. And, as these old books recorded, this was in the cold, frosty season of December.

The sun, which at its high point of the year shone like burnished gold with its bright streams of light, had by now grown old and was grayish silver in color. And of late it rested in the house of Capricorn, it seems to me, a pale shadow of its real glory. Bitter frost, along with sleet and freezing rain, had destroyed everything green in the yard, and two-faced Janus was sitting by his fire, drinking wine from his bugle horn, looking forward to enjoying the roast of wild boar when every lively man shouts: 'Noel!'

Aurelius did all he could to make the magician feel good and be happy, urging him to do his best to rescue him from his misery, lest he end it all with the slice of a sword.

For his part, this clever scholar felt such pity for Aurelius that he worked as speedily as he could, night and day, looking for the right time to work his magic — that is, to create his illusion, to create the appearance or to conjure it up — I am unfamiliar with the exact terms of astrology. In short, he intended to make it look to the lady, and to anyone else, like the rocks on the shore of Brittany had disappeared.

Finally the time came to work his tricks and this evil of cursed superstition. He consulted his properly adjusted Tolletanian tables and took into account everything: the years, the dates, the correct charts, the proportions, the distances, the relevant angles, the planetary movements — all he needed to work the equations he relied on. And by his calculations related to the eighth sphere he knew precisely how far the star Alnath was pushed into the head of Aries, normally in the ninth sphere. In other words, he took into appropriate account everything related to working his magic.

When he had determined the position of the moon, everything followed in proportion: when the moon would rise, in which sign, and all that was related to it. He was certain of the moon's position, based on his calculations, and consequently all of the related activities that pagans relied on in those days to create illusions and questionable practices. He did all this as quickly as he could, and by his magic the rocks seemed to be gone for a week or two.

Aurelius, still in despair as to whether he would ever have his love or whether it would all end badly, had been waiting for this miracle night and day. As soon as he saw no more obstacles in the water, that the rocks were not visible, he fell on his knees before the magician and said: 'I, Aurelius, worthless wretch that I am, thank you, my lord, and my lady Venus, who have brought solace to my cares.' He immediately made his way to the temple where he knew he would find his lady, and when he saw his chance, right there, he greeted his sovereign lady in all humility, his heart beating out of his chest.

'My one true lady,' said this sorrowful man, 'the person I am at once most afraid of and most dearly love as best I am able to — whom I am most loathe to displease of all the people in the world — I suffer with such love for you that I will surely die here at once at your feet, unless I share with you my misery and my hopes. There is no doubt that if I cannot share my pain I will die — with no fault of your own, you slay me with this hopeless pain.

And even though you do not care whether I live or die, you must now take care not to break your word. Change your heart — for the sake of the high God above — lest you end my life because of my love for you. Madam, you well know what you promised — not that I have the right to challenge anything about you, my sovereign lady, in your graciousness — but in a garden not far from here, in that very place, you know what you promised me.

You pledged yourself most faithfully to love me best — God knows you said those words even though I am unworthy of your love. So I have to say this to you now, Madame, more for the sake of your honor than to save my own life.

I have done exactly what you asked me to and, if you are so inclined, you can go and see for yourself. Then you can do whatever you wish, but keep in mind your promise, as I wait for you, alive or dead. Whether I live or die lies totally in your hands — but there can be no doubt that the rocks are gone.'

With that he bowed and took his leave, while she stood there, turned to pale stone, without a drop of blood left in her face. Never in her life had she imagined that this would occur. 'Alas,' she said, 'that such a thing could happen to me! Never did I imagine even the slightest possibility that such a monstrous change, such an unbelievable occurrence, could ever take place! Surely this is against any natural law or process!'

Dazed and petrified by fear, this sorrowful and distraught creature made her way home. For a day or two all she could do was to weep and wail, fainting so often that it was a pity to see. She told no one what it was about, her face pale and marked with sorrow, lamenting secretly: 'Alas, Fortune, to you and to you alone can I complain about my fate. Without my knowledge, you have locked me in your unyielding chains, and I can see only two options: death or dishonor. I must choose one of them. And if I have to choose, I would rather give up my life than to have my body be shamed, or to know that I have been unfaithful, or to lose my reputation. Surely my debt will be paid in full with my death. After all, have not many noble wives or maidens killed themselves in history — alas — rather than have their bodies be violated?

And many, many stories bear witness to this. When thirty tyrants, filled with wickedness, had killed Phidon of Athens at a feast, they ordered his daughters to be arrested and brought before them in shame, all naked, to fulfill their foul delight, and they made them dance on the pavement in their fathers' blood — may the curses of God cause them eternal misery! But these pitiful maidens, filled with fear, rather than lose their maidenheads, as the books tell us, covertly jumped into a well and drowned themselves.

The men of Messene demanded fifty Spartan virgins on which to sate their lechery. But every one of those maidens chose to die rather than allow her maidenhead to be taken by force. So then, why should I fear death? Behold the tyrant Aristoclides, who loved a maiden named Stymphalides. The night her father was slain, she went straight to the temple of Diana and grasped the image of the goddess tightly with both hands, refusing to let it go, and they were unable to separate her from that image until they had killed her.

If simple maidens have such resolve, to die rather than to be defiled by men's foul lust, it seems to me that a wife should be the foremost to slay herself rather than be defiled. What shall I say about the widow of Hasdrubales, who took her own life in Carthage? When she saw that the Romans had conquered her city, she willingly entered the fire with her children, choosing to die rather than letting the Romans carry out their wickedness on them. And did not Lucretia kill herself, sad though it was, in Rome, when she was raped by Tarquin, because she could not live bereft of her good name? Remember the seven virgins of Miletus, who killed themselves in fear and woe rather than be raped by Gauls. I can think of a thousand stories or more about such situations. When Habradus was killed, did not his beloved wife also kill herself, letting her blood flow into the deep, open wound of her husband, saying: 'This is the least I can do to ensure that they will not be able to defile my body?

I do not need to cite more examples of women who ended their own lives rather than be defiled by men. I can conclude only that it is better for me to choose death over defilement. I will either remain faithful to Arveragus or somehow kill myself, as did the beloved daughter of Democion to avoid being dishonored.

Oh, Scedasus, how sad it is to read about the death of your daughter, alas, for she too ended her own life in a case like this. Just as sad, or even more so, is it to read about the Theban maiden who killed herself because of Nichanor, for the same reason. And there was another Theban maiden who did likewise — she atoned for her rape with her life.

What shall I say about the wife of Nocerates, who took her life in the same dire situation? How faithful to him was the beloved of Alcibiades, choosing to die rather than to allow his body to be unburied! What a marvelous wife Alcestes was! What does Homer tell us about the noble Penelope but that everyone in Greece was aware of her chastity? We all know what was written of Laodamia, who, when Protheselaus was killed at Troy, chose not to outlive her husband by a single day. I can say the same of the noble Portia, unable to live without Brutus, to whom she had given her whole heart. All the lands of heathendom honor that perfect wife Arthemesie. Oh, Queen Teuta, your wifely chastity may well be a mirror for all wives. And we can say the same of Bilia, Rhodogune and Valeria.'

Dorigen spent several days lamenting in this manner, contemplating her imminent death. Arveragus, this worthy knight, found her like this and immediately asked her why she was weeping so pitifully, but all she could do was to weep even more sadly: 'What a pity,' she sobbed, 'that ever I was born!'

She explained: 'thus did I promise' and 'thus did I swear" — and told him everything just as I have already described it — there is no reason to tell it all again.

But this husband, just smiled and spoke to her most gently: 'Is that all, Dorigen — just this and no more?'

"Oh Lord, as God is my witness, is this not enough? God forbid, but this is more than too much!'

'Oh, come now, wife! Let sleeping dogs lie. It seems to me that we should be able to solve this problem before the day is out. By my honor, you shall keep your word! As God, in His wisdom, may be merciful to me, I would rather be stabbed with a knife for the true love I feel for you than have you break your word! Truth is the most important and most valuable thing we can honor!'

But then, unable to control his emotions, he burst into tears: 'Of course I must solemnly forbid you, on pain of death, that ever, as long as you draw breath, you mention a word of all this to anyone else! For my part, I will bear my suffering privately as best I can! You, on the other hand, are not to show how you are feeling in public, lest people get suspicious or surmise what is happening.'

Then Arveragus called a Squire and a Maid: 'I want you to accompany Dorigen and bring her to a certain place she is going now.' The three of them took their leave and went on their way. Of course the servants did not know why they were going with Dorigen, for Arveragus had no intention of letting anyone else in on his secret.

Now, there may be some among you listening to me," he looked around and nodded slightly at the Wife of Bath, who merely scowled back at him, "who think Arveragus is a fool, and you believe that he is risking his wife's welfare. But before you shed too many tears for her, listen to the end of the story. Things may work out better for Dorigen than you think — so, hold off your judgement until you have heard all of it.

But this Aurelius, who was so in love with Dorigen, happened to run into her in the middle of town, right in the busiest street, as she was on her way to meet him in that garden, as arranged. He was also on his way to the garden, for he had been watching her carefully to know whenever she left her house to go anywhere. So they met, whether it was by accident or fate, and he greeted her happily, inquiring where she was going. And she answered, half mad, as she was: 'I am going to the garden to do what my husband told me to do — to keep my word — more's the pity!'

Her answer and her demeanor stunned Aurelius and made him feel great compassion for her and for her sorrow, and he was taken aback by the decision of this worthy knight, Arveragus, to insist that his wife keep her word — so much did he loathe the idea that she should break her promise. And the more Aurelius thought about it, the more pity did he feel deep in his heart for Dorigen. Weighing all sides of the issue, he finally decided that he would rather give up his lust than to be such a churl as to break all the expectations of gentility and nobility.

And so, in short, he said this: 'Madame, please tell your husband and lord Arveragus that seeing your deep distress and considering his amazingly noble response to you, that he would rather be dishonored — and what a pity that would be — than having you break your word to me, I, for my part would rather suffer for the rest of my life than to harm, in any way, the love you two share. Therefore, Madam, I release you from every bond and every pledge you have made to me, ever, in your life, and I swear on my honor that I shall never accuse you of not keeping your word.

And with that I take my leave of the most faithful and best wife that I have ever or will ever know, as long as I live. I can only hope that every wife will remember what happened to you, my most noble lady, Dorigen, and be most careful of the promises she makes! And, let no one forget that a Squire can act as nobly as can a Knight!'

Dorigen fell on her bare knees to thank him and then returned at once to her husband to report everything that Aurelius had said, word for word. You can be sure that he was so happy then that I do not have the words to do justice to it. So, then what more is there to say about that, except that Arveragus and Dorigen led the rest of their lives in sovereign bliss, without a single moment of strife between them. He treated her like a queen and she was always faithful to him. That is all I have to tell you about this happy couple.

"By the bent knees of the Virgin—" the Wife of Bath interrupted. But the Franklin ignored her and continued.

"I am not yet finished," he explained. "All me to complete my tale as I heard it . . . .

Meanwhile, Aurelius, who has gotten nothing for all that money he committed to pay, is cursing the moment that he was brought into the world. 'Alas, how stupid of me, agreeing to pay 1,000 pounds in refined gold to this philosopher! What in the world shall I do? I can only imagine that this is the end of me. I will have to sell everything I have and be a beggar; I cannot stay here and bring shame on my family. I must try to adjust this agreement. Hopeless though it may seem, I will have to ask this magician whether I can pay it back in installments, year by year, little by little. If he agrees, I will forever be beholden to him. But I have to keep my word — I will not be a liar.'

With a heavy heart he empties his coffers and brings all his gold to pay the philosopher, maybe half of what he owes, beseeching him to be so noble as to give him time to pay the rest: 'My noble Master, I can say that I have always been faithful to my agreements, without exception. And you can count on it that my debt to you will be paid in full, whatever it takes, even if it means that I have to beg for money, wearing only rags. But, if you will agree to carry my debt, based on my solemn oath, and extend my payments for two or three years, I can repay it all. Otherwise I will have to sell my inheritance — that is all I have to say.'

When this Philosopher heard these words, he somberly asked: 'Did I not keep my covenant with you?'

'Indeed you did, totally and truly.'

"And have you not had your lady as you desired?'

"No, no,' he shook his head sadly and sighed in deep sorrow.

"And why not? Tell me, so I may understand this.'

Sadly, Aurelius told him the story just as you have heard it — no need to tell it again — and concluded with: 'Arveragus, in all his nobility, would rather die in sorrow and misery than have his wife break her word.' He also told him about Dorigen's suffering and just how abhorrent it was to her to be a wicked wife — that she would have rather given up her own life, and that she had made her pledge in all innocence because she had never heard of making things seem what they were not. 'All of that made me feel such great pity for her that I sent her back to her husband unconditionally just as he had sent her to me unconditionally. That is the sum total of it; there is no more to say.'

Then this Philosopher answered: 'My dear brother, each of you acted nobly, one to the other. You are a Squire and he is a Knight, but God, in his blissful power, forbid that a Scholar cannot be just as noble as any of you; do not doubt that!

Sir, I hereby release you from your entire debt of 1,000 pounds — as if you had just now sprouted out of the ground and I had never before laid eyes on you. For, Sir, I will not take a single penny from you for everything I did, nor for all the effort I put into it. You paid for me to eat well while I was there — that is enough. Farewell and a good day to you!' With that he got on his horse and went on his way.

So, gentlemen, I must put the question to you now, and I hereby ask you: who in this story acted most nobly? What do you think? Tell me now, before we go any further on our pilgrimage. That is all I have; my story is ended."

The silence that followed was finally broken by the Host, who said: "All I can say is that for someone who claims not to know the colors of rhetoric, you certainly threw a bucket of multi-colored paints at us in telling your story. Now I am pondering your question about who is the most noble, but damn me if I know."

The Clerk cleared his throat and pronounced: "This tale had a neat twist, or should I say, a series of twists, but is it really the story you meant to tell? Is the question you ask us to answer really who is the most noble, or is it who got away with the most?"

The Franklin was somewhat disconcerted by this question and asked: "Sir Clerk, I do not know what you mean. Surely everyone who had a choice to make acted nobly in this tale, bringing about the best resolution of the problem."

"Oh, come now," the Wife of Bath chimed in. "Still another tale about a woman who is placed in an impossible situation by the men around her — this time, by outright trickery and the devil's own works." She crossed herself and continued to mutter, but softly.

"If truth be told," the Clerk continued, with a slight bow to the Wife," it's not just the woman who is put in jeopardy — the men are, too — and this, I believe, is the point our noble Franklin wishes to make: that everybody solves each layer of the problem nobly, perhaps each more nobly than the last — demonstrating that each and every person can be noble or act gently. And, of course, you are right, Madam, in what you say about the woman. For she unwittingly, and foolishly — I might add — brings about this dilemma which really involved only her, and which her husband solves rather without thinking of her experience at all, considering only his own reputation and not at all hers. Of course, their marriage is based on deception to begin with, and he, in the spirit of continuing that deception, does not keep the agreement he made to begin with."

"What do you mean, Sir?" questioned the Franklin, a bit agitated by now. "Deception. The marriage based on deception? "How does he not keep his agreement?"

This stirred the Wife back into action: "Oh, I know exactly how he breaks his agreement!"

"Do us all the honor," slyly said the Clerk, smirking and bowing low in his saddle to the Wife this time.

"As I heard the agreement," she went on, "it was that the wife would be in charge in the marriage — yet, when faced with this dilemma, she leaves the decision up to the husband, and it is he who condemns her to sleep with the other man." The Clerk smiled more broadly. She continued: "If they were true to their agreement, she herself would have made the decision, and her decision, fool that she was, was to kill herself rather than have a sample of another — what appears to me, tasty, young — man. What really happens here is clearly that the husband makes the decision for her, and it is based entirely on his concern about his own supposed honor. And not only does he command his poor wife to sleep with her lover, but he also forbids her to show any of her true emotions about doing something she dreads doing.'

"And," the Clerk hastily added, "in making this decision, his reasoning is terribly flawed, for he makes this decision to save his honor, but how can he maintain his honor if the honor of his wife is so besmirched? His wife will have slept with another man! Where is the honor in that, for either of them?" Now he was warming to his argument. "I fear our noble fellow pilgrim, the Franklin, has tried to pull the wool over our eyes and sought to make this story — which does not to manage it at all — to knit together courtly love and marriage. He tries to persuade us by ending his tale —a did our noble companion, the Knight — with a sort of *demand d'amour*. But, instead of asking who loves the woman more, he is asking us to decide who acted more nobly in this matter because he seems to believe that there is a series of noble actions in this story, when, in fact, it is a series of deceptions by people who really have little choice!"

"Little choice," blustered the Franklin now, "little choice? I beg your pardon, sir, but they do indeed have choice!"

"I will argue only about one, then, rather than take each one in turn, which I could easily do. However, the one most glaring is the young lover himself. Let me put it to you this way, my dear Franklin: he is relieved of his debt by the magician because he was not actually able to satisfy his lust — and that is clearly what was at stake here: his lust — meeting this lady for a trist, for nothing is said to make us believe that he will — or can — remain with her or will love her for the rest of their lives together. Clearly the Knight expects her to return to him after she has slept with the Squire, no?"

He paused to let this question sink in, but there was no answer from the Franklin. Then he continued, pressing his point: "Ah, you have no answer for this question! Then allow me to ask how he would have paid the magician the enormous sum of 1,000 pounds had he slaked his desire for the lady's body successfully?"

"That is not at all the point of my story, sir! And I even warned you all not to judge Arveragus too harshly or too soon."

"Of course you did — precisely because it is not the point of the story you wish for us to hear, but it is nevertheless the actual point. Yours is a story of deception piled on deception. Let me ask you this: were the rocks in the water really gone or did it just seem as if they were gone? Aren't rocks not visible to sailors far more dangerous than rocks that they can see? It seems in your story — a story full of 'seems' — that were they just covered over, making them far more likely to be a danger to the husband than before."

The Clerk now seemed to have really reached the heart of his argument, but the Knight interceded. "Tut, tut, my fellows pilgrims. Let us not spoil our enjoyment of these stories with too much worrying about the point, but let us rather enjoy each other's company and continue on our way."

The Host, who seemed rather befuddled by the entire exchange, quickly concurred. "Indeed, Sir Knight, you speak wisely, and I agree. We should not spend our time arguing about this or that story, or even whether our noble friend the Franklin, who pretends not to know the colors of rhetoric, has proven himself a very master with them."

Now the Dyer entered in: "Yes, indeed, Sir Host. I must agree with you. But I must also say, if I may, that this matter of colors is rather of great interest to me, and it makes me want to tell a story about real colors, not those imposed on language or how we use rhetorical colors most effectively by rule."

The Host seemed relieved by this unexpected help and quickly answered: "Very well, Sir Dyer. This is a good time to hear from you and to listen to your story — a story of colors, you say. By your appearance you look to be an expert in this matter, so I am all ears."

And, while the Clerk had to be satisfied with matters as they stood, the Dyer — in all his colorful glory — settled in his saddle and told his story.

The Dyer's Tale

"I believe we can all agree that color is the spice of all beauty in the world our God has created, just as I know that all of us here remember how, just a short time ago, we celebrated Easter with eggs decorated in many beautiful colors, our own clothes dipped in the fresh hues of springtime and of new life. I make no secret of what I do and, indeed, celebrate that I am fortunate enough to be able to create and add to the glorious colors of Nature every day, with everything I do. I am a proud dyer of cloth, someone who makes pleasing all those beautiful clothes you are wearing."

He bowed particularly in the direction of the Wife from Bath. "Without my trade, you would go about in drab, boring fabrics that would all look the same, and the world would be a much less colorful and joyful place.

As I said, I make no secret of what I do – and I couldn't, as my hands and my very face would give me away. But I wear the marks of my trade gladly because my trade is much more important than you might think. Color is the first thing the Almighty created when He said: 'Let there be light.' He might as well have said: 'Let there be color,' for without color all that light would illuminate nothing worth seeing. It is the color that makes the light worthwhile, for without it we would all be living in a world so drab that we would have no reason to be in it or to relish anything about its appearance.

Now I am here to tell you a story about colors, for colors make the world go round, and have since the beginning, in the Garden of Eden. When God created Paradise, He made a place full of color, for without color we could not distinguish one thing from another — all would be the same. Think of the colors of the different animals in the world, the various plants, the birds of the air, the people who make our lives interesting. Imagine how we could possibly tell each other apart without color. Indeed, it is a gift that helps us know who everyone is: for we know that kings wear purple and ladies of the night are festooned in yellow, and when we see a monk it is the color of his habit that tells us not only that he is a monk but what kind of monk he is. And surely, it is no accident that learned rhetoricians rely on the colors of rhetoric as other pilgrims have reminded us, to give life to everything they teach us, to make what they tell us become memorable, and to give us the knowledge and the beauty with which their colors fill us.

Now I could tell you an old story about a misshapen troll who could spin straw into gold and you might say, but that is not a story about color. Indeed it is, for how do we know when we see gold if not for the wonderful color that marks it and distinguishes it from silver or lesser metals? And what is it that attracts us to gold? What makes it so valuable? Of course the metal has certain properties that make it malleable and useful in many different ways, but I tell you that it is the color alone that we find so charming, that keeps us enthralled, and that finally makes it so valuable. Ask any lady of great wealth, or actually any woman you know, why she loves gold bracelets. Surely it is not because they are malleable or useful — no, it is because they are beautiful and because they enhance beauty by being beautiful, by adding their luster to the grace of the lady's finger, or arm, or neck. Why do alchemists spend all their time trying to turn baser metals into gold and silver? Greed, yes, of course, but are they not compelled by the beauty of gold and silver in themselves? We may not all be enthralled by wealth, but we are all dazzled and enchanted by the beauty of gold and silver, rubies and lapus lazili, and all sort of other precious stones —— beauty that invites and beckons and charms, as do so many colors.

Today, I could tell you the story of two star-crossed young lovers from warring families. They could not be kept from each other by parental commands, by walls, or by any force on earth. You may ask what this story has to do with color, but you will see the crucial role that is played in this ancient tale by the colors red and white — for white is a color, too, as our fellow pilgrims, the venerable Nun or the worthy Friar, can tell us, for they are known by their habits. And red? Why red is the color of blood, the very thing that keeps us all alive and that determines in the end whether we are healthy or ill. Nay, even our very temperament is determined by blood and the hues of other bodily fluids on which we rely.

Earlier in our journey to the beloved saint's shrine, the learned Man of Laws complained that Chaucer has told all the great stories already in one place or another, and this story to which I have already referred is another one that poet, too, has told. In brief, this is how he told it in his stories about good women in the past.

It seems that once there were two noble families who lived in ancient Babylon. And, as is often the case in great cities, then and now, the dwellings of these families were separated only by a common stone wall. One of the families had a handsome son, named Pyramus; the other, a beautiful daughter whose name was Thisbe. Now it would not have been unusual for these two young people to be joined in marriage, except that their fathers would never have agreed to that, for each was so angry with the other that none of their friends could assuage the fiery wrath that they held for each other. But the two young people fell in love and, as is often the case, their forbidden love grew hotter than any emotions that could have been kindled intentionally by their warring fathers.

It so happened that the wall between their homes had a chink in it that ran from top to bottom, a rift that could only be seen if one looked very closely — a rift that the young lovers had, of course, espied. So, through this chink the two often spoke to one another in gentle tones, sharing words of love quietly and in secret. This is how they deceived those who would keep them apart, often cursing the very wall that served as an obstacle to them. They would share their desire to be together and kiss the cold stones keeping them apart. This went on until, one day, having secretly pledged their hearts to one another, they determined to steal away that very night in order to meet at an agreed-upon time at the grave of King Ninus, who was buried under a mulberry tree they both knew.

It seemed to Thisbe that the sunset on that day could not come soon enough and, as soon as the sun had dropped beneath the horizon, without a word to anyone, she covered her face so as not to be recognized and made her way out of her home to the appointed place. But, as fate would have it, suddenly she saw a wild lioness coming out of the near-by woods, all red with the bloody remains of a beast she had killed there. The lioness was thirsty and meant to quench her thirst at a well located near the grave. At this sight, the terrified Thisbe ran quickly to a nearby cave that she found by the light of the moon, accidentally dropping and leaving behind the pure white shawl that she had used earlier to disguise herself. When the lioness had drunk her fill, she prowled about the well and, coming across Thisbe's white shawl, began to shred it with the sharp teeth in her blood-red maw and then dropped it as she returned to the woods.

When, shortly thereafter, Pyramus arrived, he could see the tracks of the lioness, and a feeling of dread arose in him. When he found the torn, white shawl, he began at once to bewail his fate: 'Alas, the day I was born! How can I ask forgiveness of Thisbe, since I am the one responsible for her death? What was I thinking, to ask a woman to go to a place like this in the dark of night? And how could I be so slow? Are two lovers to be slain on one night? May the wild beast that shredded this shawl do the same to me!' He kissed and drenched the bloody white shawl with his tears, warning it that it would soon hold his red blood as well as that of Thisbe. And with that he thrust a sword into his chest so that the blood poured from him like water from a conduit, his scarlet river of life spurting onto the white berries of the nearby mulberry.

In the meantime, Thisbe worried that Pyramus might think her false not to have appeared there, so she returned from the cave to the grave, only to discover the bloody body of Pyramus. How she wept and bewailed the bleeding body of her lover, covering herself with his precious red blood. She called to him and he looked upon her with his dying glance. Then Thisbe saw her white and red shawl and his sword, and she keened: 'I will follow you, my dear Pyramus, as I am the cause of your death. I pray only that our wretched fathers, who would not allow our unity in life, let us share one grave in death.' And with that she drove the sword into her heart, her blood joining his in turning red the white berries of the mulberry tree.

With this short legend the ancient poets explained the colors of mulberry tree berries, as many of their stories served to explain the hues of plants and other living things. But this well-known account depicting the importance of colors is not what I wish to share with you today. The tale I want to tell you now is yet another story of how color can be the difference between life and death. We are close to reaching our final goal and I—"

"Listen, Simkin, or whatever your name is," the Host broke in, "I am still in charge of this pilgrimage — I need not remind you that you all agreed — and it is not up to you, Sir Dyer, or anyone, besides me, to decide who has told a story and who hasn't and, more importantly, whose turn it is to tell one."

"Well, then," the Miller asked, "has he told his story or hasn't he? I say he has!" Looking around the group, he blared: "Who's with me on this. Who then agrees that this Dyer has told his story? Come on, now!"

There was a bit of grumbling from a few of the pilgrims, but little else. And then the Knight spoke: "Peace! Peace! We did agree, as our Host reminds us, to be governed by him. So, we should let him decide."

"Pigs balls!" erupted the Miller. "Our 'Sir Host' can't decide if the turd he sees in the road is an apple or horse shit! Someone else needs to decide!"

At this, more of the pilgrims began murmuring, most because they were unhappy with the Miller. Then the Man of Law's voice rose above the general rumble: "Our Knight has spoken truly. We did indeed agree and, though some of us may be unhappy with this or that of the Host's decisions, we yielded him the governance, and we must abide by it."

"My bleeding ass!" the Miller said loud enough for those close to him to hear, but then he remained silent.

The Host ignored the Miller's final comment, cleared his throat loudly and, bowing in the general direction of the Man of Law's and the Knight, riding next to one another, proclaimed: "I thank you, kind Sirs!" He waited a moment, for effect, and then continued: "It is then my decision that the Dyer has not yet told his story, and he may continue. Go on then, Helfrich, and tell the story you mean to tell. But be quick about it, as we are getting ever closer to the blessed city of Canterbury."

Helfrich, who seemed unbothered by all the fuss, smiled, bowed to the Host and did continue, much as if he had not been interrupted.

"Thank you, thanks to all. I will tell my story, although you, Sir Host, must know, that haste makes waste. So, I will shorten this ancient story that some of you may have heard before but perhaps without realizing that it is color that decides the fates of those of whom it tells. Many who know this story believe that it is simply the adventurous tale of a famous warrior and his lover, but they do not realize how important color is to the outcome of this narrative. Trust me that my telling will make that clear. I will indeed shorten the story and give up certain of the colors of the rainbow that the best rhetoric is filled with, but I will keep the main points of the tale.

Now, if all I wanted to do — and if I had the time — was to tell you an adventure tale, I would tell you how the hero of my story was born to a lovely lady named Blancheflour, who had fallen in love with a noble by the name of Rivalen, whom she had nursed back to health from certain death. Our hero's birth, sadly, came at the cost of his dear mother's life, and he was then raised by a good-hearted servant and his wife, and he grew into an accomplished young knight. I would also tell you how this young hero, kidnapped by pirates, was brought by fate back to the court of his mother's brother, the ruler of Cornwall, whom he so impressed with his many skills that he became his favorite. Imagine then, this ruler's joy when Rivalen returned to his court and revealed that the young man was none other than the king's nephew. I would tell you of the many adventures our hero underwent, culminating finally in his saving his uncle's kingdom by slaying a dragon but being seemingly fatally wounded in doing so.

By now, some of you have realized that I am referring to the initial parts of the story of Tristan and Isolde, which I will now continue at the point at which Tristan is nursed back to health by the lovely Isolde, who is, of course, the young wife of Tristan's uncle, King Mark. As did his father before him, so Tristan, too, falls in love with the noble woman who returns him to health. Unfortunately, Isolde is married to his uncle, to whom she is faithful until she and Tristan unwittingly drink a love potion meant for Mark and Isolde.

Now, the handsome Tristan and the beautiful Isolde are deeply in love but do not wish to hurt King Mark. For some time they manage to keep secret their affair, an affair King Mark is only too happy to ignore as long as he can. This includes various accusations and subterfuges, of which I will tell you only one.

It seems that Mark's advisors convince him that Isolde needs to prove her faithfulness. So they arrange for a trial by fire on an island. Isolde secretly tells Tristan to be at the shore disguised as a monk, his identity hidden by the cowl of his robes. When Isolde's boat arrives, Isolde asks the monk to carry her to shore, lest she get her feet wet. The disguised Tristan pretends to stumble and then falls in such a way that Isolde lands on him, straddling him with her legs. Then, when the time comes for Isolde to take an oath that she is faithful to Mark, she swears: "I have had no man between my legs, save my husband and this pious monk, who carried me to shore from the boat. If this is not true, may the fire through which I am about to pass burn my flesh until I am dead." This is, of course, a valid oath, and she passes the trial by fire unharmed.

Nevertheless, in due time, the evidence of the love affair between Tristan and Isolde becomes undeniable and even Mark must acknowledge it. He forgives Isolde and takes her back, but he does not follow the counsel of his advisors who insist that Tristan be executed for his long-time treasonous affair with their queen. Unable to kill his nephew Tristan — whom he cares for deeply and who, by now, has saved his kingdom numerous times — Mark merely banishes him from the kingdom for all time. Tristan, still a relatively young man, continues to have many adventures in many lands, proving himself again and again to be the greatest hero in his time.

Indeed, having accepted the fact that he can never be with Isolde again, he marries — really only as a favor to a friend, the friend's sister, who is also named Isolde, but Isolde of the White Hands. Ever faithful to his original Isolde, he refuses to consummate this union, even though he continues to be married to Isolde of the White Hands — never forgetting his love for the original, his only beloved, Isolde. Finally, in one of his many battles, he is wounded with a poisonous spear, and the wound festers and brings him close to death. It is clear that the only person who can heal this fatal wound is his one, true and first love, Isolde.

So Tristan sends a messenger to Isolde in far-off Cornwall, along with a ring — originally given to him by this Isolde — that will prove to her that the message comes from him. He tells the messenger that if Isolde hears his plea for help and is returning with the messenger, his ship is to be trimmed with a white sail, signifying her presence; If, on the other hand, she has not returned to him, they are to hoist a black sail, instead.

When Tristan's Isolde sees the ring, she recognizes it, of course, and immediately sets out to return to Tristan. In the meantime, Tristan's health continues to deteriorate, and the only thing that keeps him alive is his hope that Isolde will come back to him. When the messenger's ship finally enters the harbor, clearly flying a white sail, Isolde of the White Hands, who is with Tristan in the castle tower, is the first to see it. Tristan, made aware of the ship, feebly asks her whether the sail on the ship is white or black, and his wife answers that it is black. When he hears this news, Tristan's will to live fails him; he turns his face to the wall and breathes his final breath.

By the time Isolde reaches the castle, Tristan's followers are already mourning for him. Isolde rushes to Tristan's bed, but it is too late. In her grief she lies down beside her love, her lips closing on his, and, with her arms around him, she also dies of grief. The two lovers are buried in a single grave, from which — in one night — sprout two trees, their branches growing together to form one growth. The trees grow buds which are fiery red in color and which remain that way to this day.

This is the end of my story of these two lovers, who died needlessly because of a lie about color. You can see, from this story, that color is essential and can even be a matter of life and death. And those of us who bring color to the world should never be looked down upon but should be treated as important and necessary members of our communities."

The Dyer fell silent, as did the pilgrims, a few of whom had never heard his story before and were pondering this tale of undying love and of the role that colors played in it. But it was not long before the Host cleared his throat and said: "That was a tale rich in the colors of rhetoric and of your trade, Sir Dyer. But let us move on, for time does not stand still. Let us discover our next story-teller." And once again the Host looked around, searching for a pilgrim who had yet to tell a tale, and this time his eyes landed on the Nun who accompanied the Prioress and her priest.

"My worthy ancient lady Nun," he addressed her. "We are nearing Canterbury and have some tales yet to be told. One of them is yours. Would you be so gracious now, as to share with us the wisdom you have no doubt acquired over the many years of your life."

The companion of the Prioress looked hard at the Host and spoke.

"Sir Host, I need not be reminded of the many years God above has allowed me to live on this earth in His service. The aches in my bones and the groans my body sends forth on a regular basis are reminder enough — may God thank you for your troubles. Nevertheless, I will most gladly share with you a holy tale that, I can only hope, makes up for some of the licentious, lecherous and otherwise despicable stories we have been subjected to."

Some of our drunken and churlish companions chuckled conspiratorily and muttered low objections of various kinds, while the Nun waited imperiously — certainly without being fazed — for all to quiet down, and then she began.

The Second Nun's Tale

"It is no secret that we all, each and every one of us, must be ever vigilant and wholeheartedly eschew the vicar and nurse of vice, that porter at the gate of delights, that we, in our English tongue, call Idleness.. Rather, we should do our all to overcome her with her enemy, that is, proper Enterprise, lest the evil one take us captive through our own wicked inactivity. He, who is constantly lying in wait to ensnare us with his thousand devious traps — as soon as he sees that we are idle, he is able to catch us easily by grasping the hem of our garment, without us being at all aware that we have been caught.

We have good reason to work and to avoid being idle. And even if we had no reason to fear the end of life, reason alone tells us, without a doubt, that idleness is foul laziness that produces nothing. Sloth keeps us on a short leash that only lets us sleep, eat and drink, devouring everything that the labor of others has given us.

And so, to keep us from any idleness, that can cause such terrible chaos, I will do my faithful and true best, here and now, to share this translated story of the glorious life and the suffering of her who was covered with garlands of roses and lilies — of course I mean you, Saint Cecilia, virgin and martyr.

As I begin my story, I invoke your help, Mother Mary, the flower of all virginity, about whom Bernard wrote so beautifully. I ask you, who brings comfort to the wretched, to inspire me as I recount the death of the virgin whose worthiness merited eternal life and victory over the devil, as you will hear when I recount her life and death. Oh, Virgin and Mother, daughter of thine own Son, wellspring of mercy, cure of sinful souls, whom God chose — in His goodness — as His home. You who are most humble even as you are raised up above all creatures, you so ennoble our very nature that the Creator of all did not distain from clothing

His own Son in flesh and blood. He who is peace and love eternal, the Lord and Ruler of the triune universe, forever praised by earth, sea and the heavens, took on human form within the blissful cloister of your womb. And you, unblemished virgin, gave birth from your own body — remaining pure virgin — to the Maker of every living being. In you is contained all magnificence, along with mercy, goodness, and such compassion that you, the very sun of excellence, not only provide succor to those who pray to you but many times, simply out of your own bounty and generosity, you anticipate their needs and heal men even before they seek your help.

Help me now, oh, meek and lovely blissful Virgin, help this banished exile in this bitter desert; remember the Canaanite woman who said that dogs may eat the crumbs that fall from their master's table; and even though I, unworthy child of Eve, am full of sin, accept my faith. And since faith without works is dead, grant me the time and the ability to turn away from all that is most dark. Thou, who art so lovely and full of grace, be thou my advocate in that high place where Hosannah is sung constantly, without end, thou, Mother of Christ, sweet daughter of Anne. With your light, illuminate my imprisoned soul, pressed down by the corruption of my body and by the weight of earthly desire and false affection. Oh, haven of refuge, oh, salvation of all who are in sorrow and stress, help me now as I turn to my work at hand."

"Is she going to pray or tell us a story," the Miller could be heard, loudly asking the Cook as he nudged him familiarly.

"By the Virgin she so deeply loves, I hope a story cannot be far off," the Cook answered.

The ancient Nun crossed herself several tines and look imploringly to the heavens, but then continued.

'I will not be put off by louts and whoremongers but will tell my tale of the blessed Saint Cecilia as best I can. Of course, I beg all of you who wish to hear my tale to forgive me for failing to embroider it with great cleverness; I share the words and the meaning of him who observed and wrote down this story out of reverence for the saint, and I beg all of you here to improve the work I offer you.

To start with, I believe that it is important to consider the name of Saint Cecilia, as it is handed down to us in stories. In English it means 'Lily of Heaven,' because of the purity of her virginity, or possibly the white of her honesty, and the green of her conscience and of her spotless reputation — all of which combined to make her name 'Lily.'[62] For some, Cecilia means 'the blind path,' for she did her teaching by good example. For others, as I find it written here and there, it is a combination of 'heaven' and 'lia,' where symbolically 'heaven' represents holiness and 'lia" her constant activity. Cecilia may also mean 'the absence of blindness' because of the great light she shed by her wisdom and her exemplary goodness. Or else, behold, the name of this virgin derives from 'heaven' and 'leos,' for which, properly, people refer to her as 'the heaven of people,' example of every good and wise work that is done. For 'leos' means 'people' in English and, just as people can see the paths of the sun, moon, and stars, so spiritual people can see in this delightful virgin the bounty of faith, the brightness of wisdom and the shiny excellence of good works. And just as philosophers tell us that the heavens move constantly, are round and always on fire, just so was the beautiful Cecelia always moving and busy with good works, round and whole in strong perseverance, and ever burning brightly with charity.

So, now that I have told you all the things her name means, I can begin my tale.

As the story is handed down to us, this bright virgin, Cecelia, came from a noble Roman family and was raised from her cradle in the faith of Christ, at all times bearing His gospel in her mind. Books tell us that never for a single moment did she cease loving

---

[62] The Second Nun here provides popular, if inaccurate, associations for the name "Cecelia," which seems to derive from "caecus," the Latin word for blind. In the liturgy practiced in the Middle Ages, white is associated with innocence and joy, while green represents hope.

and fearing God or praying that He keep and protect her maidenhead. And when the time came that this maiden was to marry a young man — named Valerian — and the day arrived for the wedding, she was completely devout and humble, but courageous, as she wore a hair shirt under her beautifully-fitted golden robe. And while the organ played, she sang to God in her heart: 'Oh. Lord, I offer my soul as well as my body, unblemished, lest I be damned.' And driven by her love for Him who died for us on a cross, she fasted every second and third day, praying constantly.

The night came when she must go to bed with her husband, as is customary, but when they were alone, she said this to him: 'Oh, my sweet and dearly beloved husband, I have a secret that I will tell you if you want to know it, but you must swear never to betray it.'

Of course Valerian swore that nothing would ever persuade him to share her secret with anyone, and then she said to him: 'There is an angel who loves me and in his love protects my body, waking or sleeping. If it seems to him, God forbid, that you touch me or love me impurely, he will slay you immediately, as soon as you act, and you will die in your youth. But if you love chastely, he will love you for your purity as he does me and will shine his joy upon you.'

Now Valerian, who wished to be in accord with God, answered: 'If I am to believe you, show me that angel, and if he is truly an angel, I will do exactly what you have asked me to do, but if turns out that you love another man, I swear that I will kill you both with my own sword.'

Cecilia answered him: 'If you want to see the angel you must place your trust in Christ and be baptized. Go to the Appian Way and, after three miles, say to the poor people that you will meet there precisely what I tell you. Tell them that I, Cecelia, sent you to see that good man, Urban the Elder, for a private reason but with good intentions. And when you see blessed Urban, tell him what I told you to say. And after he has rid you of all sin, you will see that angel before you depart there.'

Valerian went to that place and, just as he had been told, he found the holy man, Urban, among the catacombs. Without delay, he delivered his message to Urban and that holy man threw up his arms in delight. With tears in his eyes, he said: 'Almighty Lord, Jesus Christ, sower of chaste advice, shepherd of us all, take into your heart the fruit of this seed of chastity that You have sown in Cecelia. Behold how like a busy bee without guile, Your servant Cecelia ever serves You. See how she has sent here to You this fierce lion of a husband to be as meek as any lamb.'

And at once an old man dressed in white appeared, and he held a book in his hands that had letters of gold. This old man stood before Valerian, and when he saw him, the terrified Valerian fell down before him. But the old man raised him up and began to read from his book: 'Lord, God of faith, you are the unequaled ruler of Christendom and Father of all, above all, and over all, everywhere.' These words were written there in gold. When he had read them the old man asked: 'Do you believe these things? Yes or no?' Valerian answered: 'I believe every word! Truer beliefs than these, I dare day, no one on earth can have!' Then the old man disappeared — Valerian did not know where — and Pope Urban baptized Valerian on the spot.

When Valerian returned home, he found Cecelia in her chamber and, standing next to her was an angel, holding in his hands two crowns, one of roses and one of lilies, and — as I understand it — he gave one to Cecelia and the other to Valerian, her spouse. The angel said: 'Always guard these crowns with your clean body and pure thought. I have brought them to you from paradise, and you can be sure that they will never rot or lose their sweet odor. No one else in this wide world will be able to see them unless he is chaste and hates evil. As for you, Valerian, because you listened so quickly to good counsel, tell me what you desire and it shall be granted.' Valerian said; 'I have a brother whom I love more than anyone else. I ask that he be given the grace to know the truth, just as I have.' The angel responded; 'God is pleased by your request, and both of you shall enter His blissful feast with the palm of martyrdom.'

Later, after the angel had finished speaking, Valerian's brother Tiburtius came there. And when he savored the odor spread by the roses and lilies, he began to wonder out loud: 'Where in the world does the sweet odor of roses and lilies that I smell here come from at this time of the year? Even if I held them in my hands, the odor could not be more powerful — this sweet smell that has pierced my heart has completely changed me.'

Valerian answered: 'We have two shining crowns, snow white and rose red, that your eyes are unable to see, but you can smell them because of my prayer for you. You will also see them, dear brother, if you are willing to accept and to believe the truth, without delay.'

'Are you really saying this to me or am I hearing this in a dream?'

'In dreams is where we have been up to now, my brother, trust me! But now we can live in truth for the first time.'

'But how do you know this? In what way have you come to that?'

'I will tell you. The angel of the Lord has told me the truth, and you can also know it if you will renounce your idols and — above all — be chaste.'

Saint Ambrose, the worthy Doctor of the Church, solemnly tells us in his preface to the Mass: 'To gain the palm of martyrdom, Saint Cecelia, filled with God's gift, gave up the world and all she had. Witness the confessions of Tiburtius and Valerian, who received from God's bounty two sweet-smelling crowns delivered to them by His angels. That blessed virgin brought these men to heavenly bliss, showing the world the value of chaste love.'

Then Cecelia showed Tiburtius — plain and simple — that all idols are but foolish and deaf, charging him to leave them behind.

Tiburtius was convinced: 'Unless I lie, I must say that only a beast would not believe you.' And when she heard this she kissed his chest and was very happy that he could hear the truth.

This lovely maiden then said: 'This day I declare you to be my brother. Behold, just as I became your brother's wife through Christ's love, so I take you now to be my brother, since you have disowned these idols. Go now with your brother and be baptized and cleansed so that you too, as did your brother, may see the angel.'

Tiburtius asked Valerian: 'Dear brother, where are we going? Whom are we to see?'

'Whom are we to see? Come with me joyfully and I will take you to Pope Urban.'

'To see Urban? My brother, is that where you plan to take me? That would be quite remarkable! You cannot mean that Urban who has been condemned to death multiple times and hides out here and there without daring to stick out his head? If he is discovered, people will burn him at the stake as soon as he is found, and we will burn alongside him if we are in his company. And while we spend our time seeking this God of yours who is hidden away in some secret heaven, in this world will we be burned alive!'

Cecilia boldly responded: 'It would make sense for people to fear losing this life, my dear brother, if this were the only life there is and there were no other. But there is a better life in another place about which the Son of God told us, in His grace, and it can never be lost, you can be sure of that. That Son's Father is the Creator of all men, and He made all of us for a reason. There is no doubt but that the Holy Ghost, who proceeds from the Father, has endowed us all with a soul. When He was here on earth, by His words and miracles the Son of God made it clear that there is another life for us after this.'

Tiburtius asked: 'My dear sister, have you not professed that there is only one God, ever constant? How are you now bearing witness to three of them?'

She said: 'Let me explain before you go. Just as every man has three mental faculties — memory, imagination and judgment — just so are there three persons within one God.' And she proceeded to teach him about the coming of Christ and of His suffering. She recounted the many details of His passion and how God's Son was in this world to earn salvation for humans who were shackled in the chains of sin and dreadful care.'

And when she had finished, he went off in good faith to see Pope Urban.

Urban thanked God and, with a light and happy heart, baptized Tiburtius and perfected his learning, making him God's knight. And Tiburtius was rewarded with such grace that every day after that he saw before him the angel of God, and any favor he asked of God was granted at once from that day on.

It would be impossible to count all the miracles Jesus worked through the three of them but, after some time, to make a long story short, the Roman officers of the law captured them and brought them before the prefect, Almache, who questioned them. Hearing their answers, he ordered them to go to the statue of Jupiter, with these instructions: 'It is my sentence that whoever refuses to sacrifice to Jupiter shall lose his head.'

So these three martyrs of whom I have been telling you were taken by an officer named Maximus and his soldiers and led forth, with Maximus himself weeping for pity at their plight. But after listening to the teachings of these saints, Maximus led them away, with their tormentors' permission, to his own home where, before the day was out, they had persuaded their tormentors and Maximus and all his servants to leave their false faith and to trust only in God. Before night fell, Cecelia had brought in priests to baptize them all, and when the dawn came Cecelia, ever faithful, said to them: 'Now then, my dearly beloved Knights of Christ, cast all works of darkness from your lives and put on the armor of light. Truly, you have won a great battle and your course has been run — you have kept the faith. You have earned the crown of everlasting life. The true judge, whom you have served, shall reward you with this, as you have earned it.' And when she had said this to them, they were taken away to make a sacrifice to Jupiter.

Now when Valerian and Tiburtius were brought to that place — to come quickly to the conclusion — they would neither burn incense nor make sacrifice; they simply knelt down in humility and true devotion. They both lost their heads in that place, but their souls went straight to the King of Grace.

Maximus, who witnessed this, his heart filled with pity, told everyone that he saw their souls rise upward toward heaven, surrounded by angels transparent with light. His words converted many a person who heard them, and that is why Almache had him beaten to death with a whip enforced with lead. Cecelia took his body and gently buried him next to Tiburtius and Valerian in the cemetery, under one headstone. But then Almache ordered his officers to take Cecelia and bring her into his presence to sacrifice and burn incense to Jupiter. But these men who had been converted by her true teachings, simply wept and recounted what they had learned from her, shouting louder and louder: 'Christ, Son of God, is the one true and equal God, served so well by His true servants. So say we all with one voice, before we die.'

Hearing about this, Almache ordered Cecelia to appear before him so he could ask her: 'What kind of woman are you?'

'I am born a noble woman.'

"I ask you, at your own peril, what your religion is and what you believe.'

'You have asked your question badly, for you want two answers to one question. That was an ignorant question.'

'Why do you answer me so rudely?'

'Why? Because my conscience and my faith are pure.'

"Are you then not afraid of all the power I wield?'

'I have no fear of your power. I say that a mortal man's power is no more than a bladder filled with air. All its boasts are blown up with the prick of a needle.'

'You were wrong to begin with — yet, you persevere in your error. Do you not know that our mighty and noble princes have decreed that every Christian shall be punished unless he denies his faith but will go free if he just renounces it!'

'Your princes are wrong — as are your nobles — and your sentence makes us guilty, but it is false. You know very well that we are innocent of wrongdoing, and just because we do reverence to Christ, as we are Christians, you charge us with a crime and make us criminals. But we who have taken on this virtuous name may not deny it.'

'Alright, you have a choice: make sacrifice to Jupiter or deny your Christianity —either act will set you free.'

The holy blissful martyr, Cecelia, just laughed, and said: 'Oh, my dear judge, you are so confused by your foolishness — do you really want me to renounce my innocence so that I may be guilty? Behold how this judge dissembles here in public court. He glares and raves as if he has lost his mind.'

"Miserable wretch. Have you any idea of just how powerful I am? Have not your own rulers granted me the power and the authority over the life and death of the citizenry? How dare you speak so boldly to me?'

"I am merely telling the truth. I do not speak in pride; in fact, we hate this deadly sin of pride. But if you are not afraid to hear the truth, I can prove, here and now, in public, that you are telling a huge lie. You claim that your princes have given you power to slay or to free anyone, but you have only the power to take life — you lack any other power. Of course you can say that your rulers have made you the minister of death, but if you claim anything more than that, you lie, for the limits of your power are clear.'

Now Maximus was very angry. 'Stop your arrogance at once and sacrifice to our gods! Now! I don't care what error you are suffering from — I can accept it as your philosophy — but I cannot allow you to say these things about our gods.'

But Cecilia answered him calmly: 'Oh, you fool! You have not said a single word to me that did not demonstrate your ignorance or that showed in any way that you have any wisdom and are more than a stupid man and a false judge. There is nothing wrong with your eyes to account for your blindness, but this god, as you call it, we can all see is nothing but a stone — as everyone can attest. Since your eyes seem to have failed you, I suggest you touch it or even taste it, and you shall soon know that it is nothing but a stone. What a shame that everyone will scorn you and laugh at your foolishness, since we know that almighty

God resides in the high heaven, and that these statues, as you can easily see, can do neither themselves nor you any good, because they are worthless.'

She said this and much more, making the judge angrier and angrier, until he finally pronounced his sentence: 'Take her home to her house and burn it down with her inside, to die surround by red flames.' And they did as he commanded, tying her down in her bath and building a fire underneath it — enough to last for weeks.

For one long day and night Cecelia sat comfortably in that bath without feeling the heat. But her life's end was inevitable, for that wicked Almache sent one of his servants to kill her. This evil man struck her across the neck three times with his sword but, for all his might, he could not sever her head from her neck. And since there was a law that no-one could be punished with more than three strokes, he dared not strike her a fourth time. Instead he left her to lie there half dead, with her neck sliced open. But her fellow Christians caught her blood in sheets they wrapped around her, and she lived in this torment for three days, ceaselessly preaching her faith to them the whole time She taught them, she distributed her goods and entrusted everything she owned to Pope Urban, telling him: 'I asked the heavenly King to live for three days and no more, so that I could commend these souls to you and to ask you to turn my house into a permanent church.'

Pope Urban and his deacons then secretly took up her body and buried it, under cover of dark, with the other saints she knew. After her death, her house became known as the Church of Saint Cecelia, consecrated properly by Pope Urban, and to this day people carry out services there in honor of Christ and His ministry."

The Nun finished her devout tale with these words, and there was general silence among the pilgrims. Perhaps one or the other of them were about to say something — we had neared the community of Boughton under Blee — but any comments that might have been made were cut short by the abrupt arrival of two men on horseback, one all in black, with a white surplice peeking out underneath. His dappled grey horse was so drenched in sweat that he must have been putting the spurs to it for at least three miles. The horse of the Yeoman riding with this seeming cleric was also sweating and breathing as if it could go no further. Foam was standing an inch high around the horses' collars, and they both looked as if they were dappled, so flecked were they with foam.

There was a bag draped over the front of the first man's saddle but it seemed that he had little baggage, as he was dressed for summer. I was wondering just exactly what he was, but then I noticed that his cloak was sown to his hood and, after some consideration, I decided he was probably a Canon.[63] Fortunately his hat was attached by a cord, so it hung on his back, nearly separated now, what with the insane speed at which they had been riding. Under his hood, there was a large tree leaf to keep his head cool and to absorb the sweat that poured from his pate. It was a treat to see him sweat like that! The drops fell from his forehead as if his head had been a still producing healing potions.

Already before he had reached us, he shouted out: "May God save all of you in this jolly group! I have ridden as fast as possible to catch up with you because I simply had to overtake you to join up with this merry troupe." And his Yeoman most courteously joined in: "I can tell you all, gracious Sirs, that early this morning when I saw you riding out of your inn, I right away alerted my lord and master, as he was eager to ride along with you for the entertainment you would no doubt provide, for he enjoys nothing more than good conversation."

Our Host was the first to answer him: "God bless you for this information, my friend. It surely looks like your master is a learned man, if I am any judge. I dare lay a small wager that he is

---

[63] Canons were priests living under a common set of "canons," or ecclesiastical laws. They were usually assigned to specific cathedrals or important churches.

a merry sort, too! Does he know a good story or two we would all find entertaining?"

"Who, Sire? My Lord? Absolutely, and you can take my word for that! He knows more about joking and having a good time than anyone. Also, Sire, you can trust me that if you knew him as I do, you would be amazed at all he knows how to do and do well — nearly anything. He has taken on tasks so difficult that hardly anyone here could accomplish them unless they might learn how to from him. As unpretentiously as he has joined you here, if you got to know him, you would certainly benefit from it. I would wager everything I own that getting to know him would be worth its weight in gold to you. He is a man of incomparable judgment — take it from me — this is one outstanding human being!"

"If all you say is true," asked our Host, "is he then a scholar? Tell us if that's it!"

"Oh no," answered the yeoman, "he is far more than a scholar. Let me tell you briefly just a little bit about his many skills. I assure you that my master is so smart — and, let's be clear that I cannot do full justice to his abilities, even though I assist his work to a certain degree. He is so smart that he could level all the countryside between here and Canterbury and pave it over with gold and silver."

Our Host exclaimed: "May God take me for an ape, but it makes no sense to me that a man endowed with such great abilities, someone who has earned such high esteem, would care so little about his appearance! God knows that for someone who is really as you say, he's wearing a pretty shabby cassock — it's all ripped and filthy! Can you explain why he dresses so slovenly if, according to you, he clearly has the means to buy better clothes — unless you're not being straight with us. Is there any way you can make explain that?"

The Yeoman was taken aback. He looked around to see how close his master was and lowered his voice so that he could scarcely be heard: "Don't ask me to explain! But as God is my witness, my master never succeeds!" His voice fell to little more than a whisper. "I cannot swear to what I'm about to tell you, and I beg of you to keep it to yourself! He is too smart for his own good — that's what I think. He overplays his hand and never reaches his conclusion — to put it in terms scholars use."

He looked around to see how close his master was to him, and then continued in that same low voice.

"It's a terrible, terrible vice. In this one thing, I find him to be ignorant and foolish. He's a bit like men who are too smart for their own good — often they misuse their abilities. This is definitely my master's problem. And it is maddening to me! Only God can amend it — that's all I can say now."

"Don't worry about it, my good man," our Host softly answered him. "Since you seem to know all about your master's prowess, tell me more about how he does what he does, please." And now, more audibly: "Why don't you start by telling me where you live?"

"On the fringes of a town — we lurk in hidden places and blind alleys that robbers and thieves make their ghastly hideaways and where they ply their trade — folks that may not show themselves in public. If truth be known, that is exactly how we live, too."

"Good," said our Host to him, "now can you tell me why your face is so discolored?"

"By Saint Peter, may God damn it to hell! I spend all my time blowing in the fire and, it seems, that has altered my complexion. I don't have much chance to look at myself in a mirror, because I must spend all my time working away at this and learning how to transmute base substances into silver and gold. We stumble around, staring in the fire, and still never succeed — we always fail in the end. We trick many people into letting us borrow their gold, just a pound or two — or ten or twelve — and sometimes much more than that, by making them think that at the very least we can turn one pound into two. Of course it's all a lie, but we live in the hope that it will eventually work. So we keep at it. But the deep secret of that practice is just out of our reach and keeps sliding farther away from us, though we are sworn to pursue it. In the end it will make beggars of us all."

Now, while the Yeoman was speaking faintly like this to the Host, the Canon had worked his way closer and closer to him until he could overhear what the Yeoman was saying. It was beginning to look as if this Canon had reason to be leery of what people had to say about hm. As Cato tells us: a guilty man always fears that people are talking about him. And that is why the Canon was edging ever closer, so he could hear his Yeoman. When he finally succeeded, he shouted at him harshly: "Shut up right now, and don't you dare say another word, or you will pay dearly! You are slandering me to these people, and you divulge what you should conceal!"

"No, not at all," our Host answered him and then reassured the Yeoman. "Don't let him intimidate you! Just keep talking!"

"If I'm going to be honest," the Yeoman said, "I've just scratched the surface!"

Hearing that, the Canon realized that there was nothing he could do to stop the Yeoman from unmasking him completely and, with that, he hastily spurred his horse and rode off, never to be seen by us again.

"Finally," the Yeoman sighed, "at last we can get down to it! I will tell you everything now!

Now that he's gone, may he end in the company of the foul fiend! Believe me, never again will I consort with him, for penny or pound! He was the one who first introduced me to that game, and for that I curse him to unending sorrow and shame until the day he dies. His game was serious enough for me, I swear! I don't care what anyone says; I mean it!"

He paused for a moment and slowly shook his head. "And yet, for all the pain and all the grief, despite the heartache, the drudgery and the frequent mishaps, I was never able to walk away from it — there was no way I could do that! I can only hope that God lets me explain well enough everything that is part of it!"

He shook his head again, more vigorously this time. "Despite all that, I will tell you what I can. Since my master is gone, I will skip over nothing — I will tell you everything I know."

And so he began his tale.

The Canon's Yeoman's Tale

"I have spent seven years with this Canon and know no more about his science than I did when I started. If anything, in the process, I have lost everything I ever had . . . God knows, others have lost much more than I. When I was young, I wore fine clothing, always stylish — now I wear an old stocking on my head; and where I used to have a fresh, ruddy complexion, now I am pale with a leaden hue. I have become a living warning not to follow my path, a path I can barely see, as my vision is blurred from my activities.

Blame the wonders of alchemy, the art of turning base metals into gold!

This false science has so impoverished me that no matter where I might go, I have nothing. On top of that, I am so in debt because of all the gold I have borrowed that I can never repay it all, no matter how long I live — and that is no exaggeration. Let everyone learn by my example! Anyone who pursues and continues on that path may as well say goodbye to everything he possesses. For, as God is my witness, in that endeavor he will gain nothing except an empty purse and a barren mind. And when, through his own madness and folly, he has lost everything by his needless risks, he has no choice but to enroll others in his scheme so that they too will lose everything, just as he has done already. For scoundrels like nothing better than to see others in pain and distress. I learned that a long time ago from a certain learned man — but that does not matter now — I want to tell you about our venture.

When we show off our unnatural craft, we look like we are wondrously smart, as we make use of rare, scholarly and quaint terms. All the while, I am blowing on the fire until I feel like my heart is about to give out. It would be meaningless for me to tell you the exact proportion of the materials we work with — five or six ounces of this or that — it might be silver or something else — or to recall all the names of arsenic, bone ash, iron flakes, all ground up small enough to look like dust — how we put it all in an earthen pot that already has salt and pepper in it and then cover it all with a glass lantern.

I could tell you much more about lots of the other things we rely on: the pots and vials stopped with clay so that the air cannot escape, or the lively fire we make or, how meticulous we try to purify our components in blending and in calcination of quicksilver, also known popularly as unrefined mercury.

But for all our cleverness, we are always unsuccessful.

Our arsenic and our refined mercury, our ground lead and our purified marble, each in an exact specified amount — none of them result in what we want. All our efforts are in vain. Neither our vaporized spirits nor the materials extracted in the bottom of our containers help us to achieve what we seek in our work. Our sweat and blood are spent for nothing, as is the expense that we have racked up — cursed be the devils in hell!

There are, of course, many more things connected with our craft. Even though I cannot remember them all in the right order, since I am not a learned man, I will nevertheless tell you of them as they come to me, even if I don't put them in the right places. For example, we use Armenian bole, verdigris, borax and various containers made of clay and glass, flasks, retorts, vials, crucibles, sublimation vessels, not to forget gourds and alembics, and other stuff not worth a leek — there is no reason to mention all of these things — the coloring agents and bull's gall, the arsenic compounds, ammonium and sulphur, and all the herbs that I could list, like agrimony, valerian, and moonwort, and the rest, if I wanted to go on.

We work by lamplight both night and day to achieve our goal; the same for our furnaces used in calcination and the coloring of liquids, what with the unslaked lyme and egg whites, various powders, ashes, dung, piss and clay, waxed bags, saltpeter, sulphates, burnt and solidified materials, clay mixed with horse or human hair, cream of tartar, potash, yeast, unfermented beer, potassium, ratsbane, and a wealth of soaking liquids. And then there are the compounds of our own making — too many to list — and the materials to create a silvery tint, to fuse materials in heat and in fermentation, our molds and containers for the metal, and many other things — too many to keep track of.

I will gladly, however, tell you about the four spiritual elements and the seven metals, just as they were taught to me, in order, as I frequently heard my master talk about them and as I have them by heart.

The spiritual elements are quicksilver, arsenic, sal ammonia, and brimstone. And here's how I remember the seven metals: the sun is gold, and we call the moon silver, Mars iron, Mercury quicksilver, Saturn lead, Jupiter tin, and Venus is copper, by my own kin!

No one who practices this cursed craft shall ever benefit from it; rather he will lose everything he puts into it — of that I have no doubt! Let anyone who wants to be a fool in front of the whole world step up and study transmutation, and let anyone who has anything in his treasure chest, let him come forth and become an alchemist. Does anyone believe that this craft is so easy to master? No, no, it is not!

God knows that monk, friar, priest, canon, or anyone else, though he sit at his desk with his books night and day studying this unnatural craft, wastes his time and, as God is my witness, much worse than that. For an unlettered man to learn these skills — fie! Don't even think of it, for that will never happen. But educated or uneducated, no matter — the outcome will be the same. I would wager my salvation that both will succeed to the same degree in transmutation when all is said and done — and I say it with absolute certainty. They will fail!

Oh, but I have to tell you about acidic liquids and metal fillings and of softening, as well as of hardening, bodies — it would be impossible to mark it all down even in a book bigger than the largest bible ever created — that is why it is best if I stop listing things now. I believe I have told you enough by now to where you could conjure up an evil spirit, scabrous though he may be.

Ah, no! Never! Alas! Forget about the philosopher's stone — called 'elixir' by some — that so many people are searching for. If we possessed that we would be set. But I swear to you now, by the heavenly God, no matter how good we are at the craft, when we have worked it all, applied each of our schemes, and done everything we know, what we seek will not materialize. It has made us waste much of our earthly goods, nearly driving us crazy. We were ever hopeful in our hearts, always sure that no matter how much we suffered, in the end we would be rewarded handsomely. That assumption and that hope — they are both insidious and enduring, I must warn you — means an unending search.

Their reliance on hope has made many people lose everything they owned, yet they will never be satisfied by that craft, for it is bitter sweet — that I know. If all they had to their name was a single blanket with which to keep from the cold at night and no more than a woolen cloak to wrap themselves in during the day, they would definitely sell both and spend the proceeds on this cursed craft. They won't stop until they have nothing left and, wherever they go, men will know them by the whiff of brimstone which surrounds them. They stink like goats, a smell so strong and hot that people notice it from a mile or more away — trust me! And that is how, by their stink and their threadbare clothes, everyone can tell what they are about. And if you ask them about their poor clothing, right away they will whisper in your ear that if they are discovered they will be killed for their practices. Alas, they corrupt everything they touch.

But enough of that — back to my story.

Before the pot, filled with a certain quantity of metal, is placed on the fire, it is mixed by my master and only by him. And now that he is not here anymore, I will say that by everyone's account he is most skilled at it. Nevertheless, despite his reputation, he often encountered problems. And do you know how? Quite regularly the pot would break and then, farewell, all was lost.

These metals are so powerful that the walls of our containers cannot resist them, even if they are made of lime and stone. They explode and pierce the very walls. Some pieces bury themselves deep in the ground — and that means a loss of many pounds — and some are scattered all around on the floor — some fly up to the roof. I have no doubt but that the very devil, even though he does not show himself, is surely there with us, that goddamned scoundrel. For in those moments when our pot blows up, more woe, more anger or disagreement is impossible to feel, not in hell itself, where Satan rules. Everyone involved is enraged and feels like the victim of the entire world.

Of course, everyone there has an explanation: some say that it sat too long on the fire, others blame the blowing on the fire — which always caused me terror, because that was my responsibility. 'The hell you say,' chimes in another. 'You're silly and stupid! It's clear that the pot was not tempered properly!' 'No, that's not it,' says the fourth accomplice. 'Shut up and listen to me! It's because our fire was not made of beech; by my life, that's the only reason this happened.' This second-guessing goes on for some time — who knows how long — but I can attest to the fury of the exchange.

'Alright,' then says my master, 'it's over. I will figure out what happened soon enough. I am certain that there was a crack in the pot. Whatever happened, let's not be dismayed. As we have before, let's get to it and sweep up. Buck up, look alive and cheer each other up!'

We would sweep the rubbish into a pile, put down a canvas to cover the floor, sift through the remains, and throw a lot away.

'By God,' one of us might observe, 'we've salvaged some of our metal, though we've lost some. But even if things didn't go right this time, the next time they will. We have to trust in the future. Rich merchants did not have only profitable deals along the way. Some days goods are lost at sea and some days they arrive safely in the harbor.'

'Enough,' my master would say. 'I will figure out how to make everything work out the next time. And if I don't, I will accept the blame. It's clear that something wasn't right.'

There was always someone who blamed the fire for being too hot, and I don't know who was right, but I know this: we never succeeded. Every time we failed we just continued to rave on in our madness, even though, when we were all together pursuing our ends, we all thought we had the wisdom of Solomon.

But all that glitters is not gold, as I have been told, nor does every beautiful apple taste good, however much people may yell or complain. That's the same way it was with us. He who seems the wisest, by Christ, is the most foolish when push comes to shove. And he that seems most honest is the thief. Although this is all I want to say about it, for now, that is the lesson I want you to learn from me before I leave you.

I happen to know a Canon who can fool an entire city, one as large as Nineveh, Rome, Alexander, Troy and three more. Were he to live a thousand years, I am certain that no man could sum up properly this Canon's ability to deceive and his infinite capacity for lying. He has no equal in deception in this entire world, as he can wrap himself so effectively in his terminology and speak to everyone so cleverly that he will certainly make another person act the fool, unless — like himself — he is also a fiend. He has a lifetime of deceiving people and will continue to do so as long as he lives; nevertheless people go out of their way to seek him out and to meet him, not knowing how false he really is. But if you give me a chance to do so, I will tell you all about him.

But I beg all you worthy Canons out there, do not think for a moment that I am slandering your profession, just because of what my story says about one of you. Every order, God knows, has some scoundrels, and God forbid that all the members of a group should pay for the folly of one of its members. It is certainly not my intent to disparage you — only to correct what seems to me to be amiss. This tale is told for the sake of all, not just for one.

You remember how among the twelve apostles of Jesus there was only the one traitor, Judas. We certainly don't blame the other eleven who were guiltless, do we? I think of you the same way, except for this — don't ignore this — if you have a Judas among you, get rid of him as soon as possible. If you fear being shamed or losing goods, I advise you to do it now. And please do not take any of this the wrong way, I beg you, as you hear what I have to say.

One day, this evil Canon of whom I speak came to visit a Priest in his private chamber and begged him to loan him a certain amount of gold that he would pay back quickly. 'Lend me one mark, and I will return it to you in a mere three days. But if you find that I have deceived you, you can hang me by the neck afterward.'

Without hesitation the Priest gave him a mark and the Canon thanked him profusely and left. Three days later he returned the money, and the Priest was very happy and grateful. 'You can be sure,' he said, 'that it is no trouble to lend a man a note or two or three or whatever I happen to have, if he turns out to be so honest that nothing can make him break his word — I can never say no to someone like that.'

'What?' responded the Canon. 'Surely you don't believe that I would cheat you? Never! That would be a first! I will always be true to my word, always, til the day that I crawl into my grave — God forbid that I ever act differently! You can believe this as you do God's holy creed! I thank the Almighty above and I am proud to say, that never was any man who lent me gold or silver not paid back fairly. Nor have I ever intended to be false to any man. In fact, my friend, since you have been so kind to me and treated me so nobly, I want to show you something to reward you and, if you hear me out, I will gladly teach you a whole lot of what I know about alchemy. Pay attention, and you will see with your own eyes the amazing things I will do before I leave here today.'

'Really?' asked the Priest. 'Tell me more, my good friend. Will you, indeed? By the Virgin, I can only hope you do so!'

'I am at your command; you have no reason to doubt me,' the Canon assured him. 'God forbid that I would ever be anything but true to you!'

By Christ's anointed hands, I will never stop being amazed at how cleverly this thief presented his argument!

Of course, experience tells us — and this you can count on — that unrequested offers like his smell to high heaven, and I will show you soon enough how this is borne out in the action of this Canon, who is the root of treachery and, evermore, delights in and gets joy from leading Christ's people to constant mischief — inspired to such evil by the devil himself! May God keep us all from such wicked deception!"

Here, he and many of the pilgrims near him crossed themselves. Then he continued.

"This poor Priest did not know with what kind of man he was dealing and he could not imagine what he was getting into. Oh, you foolish Priest! Oh, you poor innocent! You are blinded by your own greed. You poor unfortunate fool, ignorant of what is happening, you are not aware of the deception this sly fox is preparing for you. But you will not escape his subtle tricks.

So, I will move quickly to the results your sorry actions always lead to, you unhappy man, and describe quickly your stupidity and foolishness, as well as the wickedness of that other wretch — as much as I am able to."

The Canon's Yeoman looked around our group carefully before he continued.

"Now some of you may be tempted to think that this Canon was my own master. But, my worthy Host, as God is my witness and by the Queen of Heaven, I am talking about a different Canon, not at all my master, who was a hundred times more cunning. He has deceived many people many times over, and I am embarrassed even to talk about it.

Whenever I find myself speaking of all his deceptions, I blush for shame. I am not naturally ruddy, that I know but, as I told you before, my present ruddiness is the result of metal fumes that have eaten away at and destroyed my natural hue.

But let me tell you about this Canon's wickedness, the one whom this story is about!

He told the Priest: 'Sir, send your servant to acquire two or three ounces of quicksilver, and when he returns with it you will see a marvelous thing, unlike anything you have ever witnessed.'

The Priest was delighted and said: 'Sir, it shall be done at once!' He ordered his servant to get the quicksilver, and that man went out immediately and soon returned with it. Then the Priest gave these three ounces to the Canon, who placed them very carefully and told the servant to bring him some coals so that he could do his work. When they had been fetched, the Canon took a crucible that had been hidden in his clothes and showed it to the Priest: 'Take this container and put an ounce of the quicksilver in it. With that you will take the first step to becoming an alchemist, knowledge I am willing to share with very few people. You will see with your own eyes that I will transmute this quicksilver — there will be no trickery. I will turn it into silver as pure, as refined, as malleable as you will ever find in your purse or mine, or anywhere else. And if I do not succeed, you can declare me a charlatan to the whole world. So, let me show you my secret potion — one that I paid dearly for. This is what will make all this happen, the secret ingredient that lets me work the kind of miracle you are about to witness. Send your servant away so that he does not bother us, shut the door, and we will then, in all secrecy, with no one to observe us, do our alchemy.'

Following the cursed Canon's instructions, the Priest then placed the crucible in the fire and blew on it and did everything he was told. The Canon put a powder into the crucible — don't ask me what it was — something made of glass or chalk or something — whatever it was, it was worthless, and its purpose was only to fool the Priest. Then he instructed the Priest to arrange the coals so that they covered the crucible. 'Now,' he said, 'as proof of my affection for you, I will let you do, with your own hands, what I am teaching you to do.' This made the

Priest very happy, and he said: 'God bless and reward you always for this,' arranging the coals just as he had been told to do.

And while he was busy with this, the false Canon — may the devil himself take him — secretly took out of his shirt a piece of beech wood shaped like a coal, but with a hole in it that could be filled with an ounce of silver metal fillings. This hole was stopped with wax that kept the fillings from falling out. You need to understand that this hollow device had been prepared beforehand, along with other things the Canon had brought with him. Those I will tell you about when the time comes.

He had planned all along to deceive the Priest, even before he went to him, and that is just what he did before they parted. He was not about to stop before he had skinned this rabbit. I can barely stand to speak of him, and I would dearly love to get even with him for his deception if only I knew how, but he is never in one place for long. He can be here or there, moving about so much that he does not have any one place he calls home.

Now, for the love of our bleeding Savior, listen very carefully! The Canon took the coal that I described to you just now and secretly placed it in one hand while the Priest was arranging the coals exactly as he had been instructed. Then the Canon said: 'Look here, my friend, you haven't got that just right. Let me help you put the coals in the proper position. The whole process will take a little while, and I'm sorry that you have gotten so hot. I can see you sweating hard — here, take this cloth and wipe your face.' And while the Priest wiped his face, the Canon — villain that he is — took his wooden coal and placed it right above the crucible and then blew on it as hard as he could until the coals were all burning brightly.

'Now,' he said, 'let's have a drink. It's all coming together now — count on it. Let's sit and enjoy our time together while we wait.'

Now when the Canon's hollow wooden coal burned up, all the silver fillings slid down into the crucible below, just as they were arranged to do by their placement directly above it. But the foolish Priest knew nothing of this! He thought all the coals were the same, and he did not understand how he had been duped.

In due time the alchemist said: 'Alright, here we go, Sir Priest. Stand here next to me — I don't suppose you have a metal mold on you? Good enough, why don't you go and find a block of chalk, and I will do my best to shape it into a mold. We will also need a pot full of water, and you will soon see the great result of our work here. But to make sure that you can have absolutely no doubt about me or anything I may have done while you are gone, I will stay with you the entire time, going and coming with you.'

They left the chamber, carefully shutting and locking the door behind them, making sure they had the key. When they came back — I will not delay the story any further — the Canon carved and shaped the chalk into the form of a mold, just as he said he would.

But now listen to what he did: he secretly took from his sleeve a small chunk of silver — may he rot in hell — no more than an ounce in weight. Now, pay attention to his wicked deception!

When he had shaped the mold to be exactly as long and as wide as the silver piece, so slyly that the Priest had no idea what he was doing, he hid the silver in his sleeve again, took the material that the fire had produced and, smiling sweetly, slipped it into the mold and threw that into the hot water. Then, after a while, he said to the Priest: 'Let's see what is there. Reach into the water and feel around. I think you will find silver there — I am sure you will.'

What else, you devil straight from hell, what else could he find? After all, shavings of silver are silver, are they not?

The Priest put his hand in the pot and detected a chunk of silver, making him entirely happy and thoroughly delighted. 'May you be blessed by God and his mother and all the saints, Sir Canon,' said the Priest, 'and may I be damned to hell if you don't agree to teach me this noble craft and all its tricks. So help me God, you can count on me forever!'

'Be patient and let's try it again so that you become expert at it. Then, any time I am not with you but you have need of it, you can use this knowledge and work this subtle science alone. Take another ounce of quicksilver right now and do just as you did with the first which, as you know, is now silver.'

The Priest did everything the Canon — cursed villain — instructed him to do and blew hard on the fire to hasten the achievement of his desire. Of course the Canon was deceiving him every step of the way — this time with a stick that had a hollow end — oh, you must be ever careful and prepared for deception — filled with exactly one ounce of silver shavings (just as the coal had been the first time) and stopped with wax to keep the shavings from falling out prematurely. While the Priest was busy carrying out the Canon's directions, the Canon tossed the powder in the fire, as before — I pray to God Almighty that the devil flay his skin as payment for his trickery, hopeless and false villain that he was. Then he began to stir the coals with his hollow stick, right over the crucible that had been placed there. He stirred until the fire melted the wax again — just as every man, fool or not, knows well that it must — and the silver contained in the stick slid right into the crucible.

Now, good Sirs, what else could possibly be the outcome? When this Priest was tricked once again, even though he truly thought everything was as it seemed to him, he was so happy that there is no way for me to describe adequately his joy and delight. No wonder that he pledged himself to the Canon, body and soul. 'Indeed,' said the Canon, 'I may be poor, but I am quite clever. And I tell you now that there is more to learn.' He asked the Priest whether he knew of any copper thereabout.

'Of course, Sir, I know very well where we might find some.'

"If you don't have any on hand, go and buy some, and do so without delay. Go, good Sir, on your way, and hurry!'

The Priest immediately left and returned soon with an ounce of copper, which he delivered into the hands of the Canon.

Lord, how I wish my tongue, as the agent of my wit, were nimble enough to describe adequately the duplicity of this Canon, source of all wickedness! He always appeared to be friendly to strangers, while underneath it he was all evil in everything he thought and did. It tires me out to recount all his subterfuges, but I will nevertheless tell you, so that no one can say he wasn't warned — that is the only reason I am telling you all this!

He placed the chunk of copper in the crucible and put it back in the fire, added his secret powder and had the Priest blow on the fire again so that he was bent over it as before — and the whole thing was nothing but a trick! Once again he made a fool of the Priest, just as the time before! Meanwhile he shaped more chalk into a mold and placed it in the pot of water. Now remember that this cursed wretch had in his sleeve a chunk of silver, which he took out when the Priest was not looking, and dropped into the bottom of the pot also. Then he groped about in the water, to and fro, and found the copper chunk and, without the Priest's notice, hid it away. Now he turned to the Priest and said — all a part of his plan: 'Now reach into the water, as before — and note that you are doing this all by yourself now. Put your hand in there and see what you find.'

And, of course, the Priest found the silver that the Canon had dropped into the pot, and the Canon said: 'Let's take these three silver pieces that we have produced here to some goldsmith to determine their quality, for I swear by my hood that they are of the finest silver there is, and this shall be shown without delay.'

They took the silver to a nearby goldsmith and had it assayed by fire and hammer, and there was no doubt but that it was exactly what the Canon had said it would be.

Then who was more delighted than this greedy, stupid Priest? Never was a bird happier to see the dawn, no nightingale ever inspired to sing in the season of May, no lady more energetic in caroling or — if we speak of love and the service of ladies — no armed knight more eager to do great deeds in order to win fair lady's grace, than was this Priest now committed to learning everything about this dismal science. So he said to the Canon: 'For the love of God who saved us all, and to repay you as is proper, tell me now what this will cost me. Please!'

'By our Lady,' answered the Canon, 'I have to warn you that it is very expensive, indeed. Except for me and one friar, there is no one else in England who knows how to do this.'

'No matter! Sir, for God's sake, what shall I pay you? Please tell me, I beg of you!'

'As I said, it is quite costly, but I will tell you if you are serious about obtaining this knowledge. As God is my witness, it will cost you forty pounds. And if it were not for the friendship we share, it would be much, much more!'

Without a moment's delay this Priest fetched the sum of forty pounds in nobles and gave all of it to the Canon for this information that we know to be nothing but fraud and deception.

'Sir Priest,' the Canon said, 'you can understand that I dare not be known for practicing my craft and would rather keep this between us. As you are my friend, please don't tell anyone about this. For if the world knew about my skills, I swear to God, I would be the subject of such envy because of my alchemy that I would be killed for it. And that is God's truth!'

"God forbid! What are you saying to me? I would rather spend every penny I have and go mad on top of it, if ever I was responsible for any ill that might befall you!'

And with that the Canon went on his way, never to be seen again by this Priest. But when the time came for this Priest to try out his newfound knowledge of alchemy, fare thee well! Nothing happened. Behold how he was fooled and tricked! This is how the Canon played his game of destroying everyone he met.

Consider, Sirs, that no matter what social class people inhabit, there is always conflict over money, sometimes to the point where none is left. Alchemy blinds so many people that, in good faith, I believe it to be the greatest cause of poverty. Alchemists talk about their craft in such obscure ways that people cannot comprehend it, no matter how smart they may be. Then again, they might as well jabber away like magpies and devote all their desire and pain to the proper terms, but they will never achieve their goal. If he so wishes, any man can easily learn to multiply everything he has into nothing!

The only profit in this trickery is that it will turn a man's joy into sorrow, emptying purses no matter how large or heavy they may be. Those who have spent their wealth on it have simply paid for the right to curse those who have deceived them.

Oh, fie! For shame! Are people simply unable to stay away from the fire? I can only counsel you who practice it to stop before you lose everything you have. Better late than never! This is too much time invested in the enterprise of failure! No matter where you prowl, you will never find it.

Like Bayard, the blind horse, you blunder about without paying heed to the havoc you create, as likely to run into a wall as you are to miss the path entirely.

I say that this is exactly what alchemists do!

And if your eyes are indeed blurred, look to it that your mind does not suffer the same fate. For no no matter how closely you look and observe, you will not profit in this business; instead you will lose everything you gather and seize.

Do not light that fire, for it will burn out of control. I am telling you never to meddle in that art because, if you do, you are bidding goodbye to your own well-being. If you don't believe me, at least heed the wisdom of ancient philosophers in this matter.

Here is what Arnold of New Town says in his alchemical treatise, the Rosarie: 'No man can transmute mercury without the assistance of his brother, sulphur.' And this was first stated by Hermes, the father of all alchemists — he said that the dragon does not die unless he be killed alongside his brother, and he was, of course, calling Mercury the dragon and brimstone his brother, as both emerge from the sun and the moon. 'And therefore,' he said — listen carefully — 'let no man commit himself to seeking this knowledge unless he understands both the intent and the language of alchemists. And if he does, he is but a fool, for this science and this knowledge is the secret of secrets, by God!'

There was also a disciple of Plato, as is written in the book of Zadith, who once said to his master and, truly, these were his words: 'Tell me the name of the secret stone.' And Plato answered: 'It is the stone that is called Titanos.' The disciple asked: 'Is that the same as magnesium?' Plato answered: 'It is, indeed! But this is *ignotum per ignocius*, trying to explain the unknown by the more unknown. What, pray tell, is magnesium if it is not a liquid made up of all four elements?"

'Well, then, be so kind as to explain the essence of that element to me.'

'Never!' answered Plato, 'I will never do that. Alchemists are sworn never to tell anyone else about it. And it has never been written down in any book because it is so important to Christ that he does not wish it to be discovered. For God likes to use it to enlighten and to confuse men, just as He chooses. And that is all there is to it!'

And so I conclude that since the God of all creation does not want alchemists to tell us the name of the philosopher's stone, I advise everyone that it is best not to pursue it. For he who chooses to antagonize God by doing something contrary to His will is surely not going to thrive — no matter if he devotes his entire life to the effort to transmute. That is my point and this is the end of my tale. May God remedy the wrongs of every honest man!"

The Host responded at once to the Canon's Yeoman: "May God bless us all for this timely story. You are absolutely right, Sir Yeoman, to warn us against seeking secret knowledge. Surely there are things God does not want us to know — things He has, in His divine wisdom, kept from us to protect and safeguard us all.'

"Indeed, Sir Host,' the Student interjected. "Do you really think that the God who gave us reason and the desire to know is keeping secrets from us? Surely neither you nor our worthy Yeoman believes that!'

The Canon's Yeoman frowned and rejoined: 'The proof, my dear Sir, is all around us.'

"What is all around us, dear Sir,' the Student answered, somewhat caustically, 'is evidence that we are to use our senses and our reason in every way we can to know more about this wondrous world that God has given us."

Now the Parson audibly cleared this throat and said, loudly and firmly, "If we but read the holy book, we can see that God has only one commandment he gives Adam. He forbids him to eat of the Tree of Knowledge, and his failure to do as God instructed him has condemned us all to a life of labor, of suffering, and of sin — outside of the Paradise that God first intended for us to inhabit for all eternity. Surely there can be no argument about that!"

"Well said, worthy Parson," the Knight imperiously contributed. "There can be no argument with holy writ, no matter what our students are taught these days at Cambridge or Oxford. God's word is clear on this matter."

The Student tried once more: "Of course God's holy word must be observed. But, at the same time, God gave us an ever-changing world and we are constantly learning new and wondrous things. Can we question that God created us to be creatures who seek always to stretch the narrow boundaries of what we now know?"

"I agree that it is time to stretch, Sir Clerk," the Host said, chuckling at his own little joke, "as we are getting ever closer to the blessed martyr's shrine, but we have not yet heard from everyone, and it is my duty to make sure all here tell their tale."

The Student sat back in his saddle and shrugged his shoulders, accepting the fact that he cold not win this argument, for now.

The Host looked around, and his eyes lit on the Manciple.[64] "If memory serves me, Sir Manciple, you have not yet graced us with a story. This is a good time for you to share with us some tale you have heard in your frequent forays for your betters. Please tarry no longer."

The Manciple bowed and began his story, without further ado.

---

[64] A representative of an institution charged with the acquisition of food and other supplies.

The Manciple's Tale

"Ancient stories tell us that in the time when Phoebus Apollo still lived here on the earth, he was the most eligible bachelor in the world, not to mention being the best archer. In those days he put a fatal arrow into the serpent Python where he lay sleeping in the sun and, if you read those old stories, you will learn about all the many other noble things he did with his bow. You will also learn how he could play every known musical instrument and sing so beautifully that his unaccompanied voice could create a powerful melody. No one, not even Amphion, the king of Thebes, whose music built the walls of the city, could match him. On top of that, since the beginning of time, there has never been anyone as handsome as he. Words cannot do justice to his appearance, for in the entire world there was no one who was as good looking. Moreover he was filled with nobility, honor and perfect worthiness.

This Phoebus, then — so the story tells us — the very flower of knighthood, both in bearing and in chivalric acts, enjoyed carrying his bow in his hand at all times, in remembrance of his victory over Python.

He also kept in his house and took care of a crow that lived in a cage. Over time he taught it to speak, as people do with magpies.

Now this crow was as white as a snow-white swan, able to mimic the speech of everyone he had ever heard say anything. And, amazingly, he sang a hundred thousand times better and more joyfully than any nightingale, anywhere in the world.

In addition, Phoebus had in his house a woman whom he loved more than life itself; he tried constantly to please and honor her, doing everything he could to make her happy. But — If I am to speak truthfully — he was very jealous. Like every man in his position, he did not want to be deceived — for all the good that does us.

Now I say that a good woman, proper in her thoughts and deeds, should not be restricted; that I know. And, by the same measure, any effort to control a shrew is a waste, for it will not happen. In the end, any effort to govern women is foolish — and wise men from ancient days on agree on that.

But back to my tale: Phoebus did everything he could to please her, and he was certain that no man could come between her and him, based on his treatment of her, as well as his manliness and general behavior.

But God knows that no man can restrain something that nature has implanted in one of her creatures. Take any bird and put it in a cage, and then do everything you can to treat it well with food and drink and all the treats you can think of, and keep it ever so well. Even if the cage were made of gold, this bird would twenty-thousand times rather live in a wild and cold forest, eat worms and miserable things like that. A bird will do whatever it can to escape from its cage. If there is any way, a bird will always seek its freedom. Or take a cat and feed it lovingly with milk and soft foods, and give it a bed of silk. If that cat sees a mouse flitting past the wall, its appetite to eat that mouse will be so strong that it will ignore the milk and food and everything else. Behold, here desire dominates and appetite conquers discretion. A she-wolf is naturally churlish; when she is in heat and seeks a mate she will accept the worst wolf, with the worst reputation, that comes her way.

I mean t apply these examples to unfaithful men — not women. So driven are men by lechery that they would rather have their way with low-born women than with their wives, be they never so fair, never so true, and never so attractive. Our flesh is so bedazzled with novelty, worse the luck, that we are incapable of finding pleasure in anything virtuous.

In this case, Phoebus, who was ever guileless, was still deceived, despite his attractiveness, as his woman had another alongside him — a man of terrible reputation, not equal to Phoebus by any comparison. More's the pity; this happens often, always ending in much harm and sadness. And so it happened as soon as Phoebus was away, his woman sent for her lover.

Her lover? Forgive me! I must apologize for this churlish language. I am sorry. But the wise man Plato tells us that the word must match the deed; if we are to describe a thing accurately, the words must fit the actions. I am a plain man and use plain speech. If they do wrong, there is no difference between a woman of high degree who is not chaste and a poor wench. Of course, the noble woman who strays shall still be called 'lady,' while that other, the poor woman, will be known as a wench or a lover. And God knows, my own dear brother, that men place the same low value on each of them.

I say that the untitled tyrant, the outlaw and the common thief are all equal — there is no difference. As was told to Alexander, the Great: because the tyrant has more power and can slay more people with his army, burning house and home, and razing everything, we call him a captain. But, the outlaw, who has little power and cannot cause harm as great nor bring entire countries down, is referred to as a common outlaw or thief.

I am untutored in scholarly texts, so I cannot cite any of them, but I will simply return to my tale, as I left it: at the moment when Phoebus' woman had sent for her lover and they indulged in their foolish lust.

The white crow in its cage saw everything but did not say a word. However, as soon as Lord Phoebus had returned, it sang out: 'Cuckoo, cuckoo, cuckoo!'

'What is it, bird,' asked Phoebus. 'What song are you singing? I am used to hearing you sing with such joy that my heart rejoices at the very sound of your voice. Alas, what kind of song is this?'

'By God, Phoebus, I am not singing falsely. Despite your great nobility, despite your handsomeness and your gentleness, despite your beautiful singing and all of your ability as a minstrel, despite all your watchfulness, you have been deceived by one of little reputation, not to be compared to you. I watched someone worth no more than a gnat, so help me God, screw your woman in your own bed!'

What else is to be said? The crow then described, with great detail and clear words, how his woman had been lecherous with another, how she had shamed Phoebus and treated him badly, and how the crow had observed this with his own eyes on many occasions.

Phoebus sank down, feeling like his heart would burst with sadness. At once he took his bow, placed an arrow on it and, in his anger, killed his wife right then and there.

What else is there to say?

In his sorrow he destroyed all of his musical instruments, as well: his harp, his lute, his zither and his psaltery, and then he broke his bow and his arrows, saying to the crow: 'You traitor! You have brought me to this state with your scorpion's tongue. Alas that I was ever made.

Why am I not dead?

Oh, sweet woman! Oh, jewel of delight! You were always so trustworthy and true to me. Now you are lying here lifeless, your face pale and ashen. You are without guilt, I swear it! Oh, rash hands, to do such a foul deed! Oh, troubled mind! Oh, reckless anger that struck the guiltless without thinking. Oh, distrust filled with vile suspicion, what has happened to your intelligence and judgment?

Oh, men, listen to me and beware of recklessness. Trust nothing without strong evidence. Don't smite too hastily before you know why. And don't ever kill someone without first gaining every bit of counsel and wisdom, rather than letting your anger fuel your suspicion. Alas, a thousand people have let their reckless anger undo them and bring them down. Alas, I may kill myself for very sorrow.'

And turning to the crow, he continued: 'Oh, you false thief! I will pay you for your vicious lie. You once sang like a nightingale, but now, malicious scoundrel, you will lose your song and all of your white feathers, and never again in your life shall you speak.

This is how people will be avenged on a false traitor. In return for making me slay my woman, you and all your descendants shall forever be pitch black in color, and you shall never again make a beautiful sound but be capable only of summoning rain and storm with your voice.' And with that he ran to the crow and pulled out every white feather there, turning him black, bereft of song and speech. Finally, he threw him out of his door, condemning him to the devil.

And that is the reason all crows are black now.

Gentlemen, this is an example meant to convince you to be careful and watch what you say. Don't ever tell a man that another man has screwed his woman, for he will only profoundly hate you. As wise clerks tell us, Solomon says to keep a quiet tongue.

But, as I have said, I am not learned. All I know and remember is what my mother told me—

'My son, God help you never to forget the crow.

My son, hold your tongue and keep your friend. An evil tongue is worse than the devil.

My son, learn what you can from the devil.

My son, in His eternal wisdom, God encircled our tongue with a wall of teeth and lips so that we humans think before we speak.

My son, too often have men lost their lives, as learned clerks teach us, over what they said, but rarely, if ever, has anyone been punished for saying too little.

My son, restrain your tongue at all times, except when you are doing your duty to speak with God, honorably, in prayer.

Hear me well, my son: the primary virtue is to restrain and keep your tongue in control. This is what children learn in youth.

My son, too much speech is ill-advised when less talk suffices and causes no harm.

I teach you only what I was taught. Too much talk is usually sinful.

Do you know what good comes of a reckless tongue? Just as a sword cuts and slices an arm in two, my dear son, just so does a tongue slice a friendship in two.

A chatterer is an abomination before the Lord. Read Solomon, a wise and honorable man; read David's psalms; read Seneca.

My son, say nothing and nod your head. Though you can hear, pretend to be deaf; chatterers say dangerous things. The Flemish tell us something you should take to heart: a little chattering results in much wrong.

My son, if you have spoken no evil you need not fear betraying someone's confidence. But he who has misspoken, I dare say, he cannot call back his words. What is said, is said, and it goes out into the world, though he may be as sorry as can be. He is beholden to whomever he has said what will now be repaid with evil.

My son, be careful that you are never the first to spread news, whether true or false. Wherever you go, among the low or the mighty, hold your tongue and remember the crow.'"

"Great God!" exploded the Host. "Enough. We will all remember the crow and your mother's advice. Be it ever so sound, you have yourself failed to follow it today. By saying it over and over again, you have done the very thing your mother advised you not to do. I can only hope you are a better manciple than you are a listener or a story-teller."

The Manciple was clearly not pleased by this comment but the Host just as clearly did not care, as he turned to the Knight's Yeoman and said: "Now then, my dear Yeoman, you have not said much on this journey. I believe it's time for you to tell your story."

The Yeoman bowed graciously and said: "Sir Host, most of the stories I have heard in my life's work are not stories I can tell in this company. But, knowing the time would come for me to speak, I have been going over one in my mind that I can tell. This is a story I heard a long time ago when my Lord and I were in Jerusalem, besieged as we often were and whiling away our time.

A knight who died in that siege told it one evening, and I will do my best to tell it to you all now."

The Knight's Yeoman's Tale

"This story begins in France, and it is a true story about real people known personally to the knight who told the tale to me.

Not too long ago, the King of France and his son, both to defend their kingdom and also to spite their adversaries, raised a great and powerful army, consisting of all the knights of their kingdom, as well as their kindred and allies, to make war against their enemy in the east.

Of course they could not leave their kingdom without someone trustworthy to serve as governor for the duration of the war and after, appropriate discussion, they settled on Gaultier, Count d'Angiers, whom they knew as a wise and worthy person, entirely devoted to their interests, and a proven expert in military affairs.

Gaultier, a veteran of many battles, wars and much martial toil, had been looking forward to a life of ease and inactivity with his wife and two children but, being the man he was, fully devoted to his king, willingly accepted this new position.

Having named Gaultier to be Viceroy in his absence, the King set out on his expedition, assured that his kingdom was in good hands and that he could devote all of his attention to the demands of war.

As expected, the Count executed his new office with all due care and discretion, conferring, before he made any decisions, with the queen and her daughter-in-law, and always treating them with the respect and honor they were entitled to as his mistresses and superiors, even though they were now subject to his guidance and authority.

Gaultier was a very attractive man, about forty years of age, and as good-natured and agreeable as any man could be.

Nowhere in the world could be found a more complete gentleman in all respects.

However, soon after the King had departed for the war, deep sadness touched Gaultier's life, as his beloved wife died, leaving him to take care of their two children, a boy and a girl. Now, as he spent a great deal of time in the presence of the Queen and her daughter-in-law, consulting with them on the affairs of the kingdom, the king's son's wife cast her eyes upon him, and being struck both by his worthy person and his noble manners, privately conceived a violent passion for him.

Of course she was younger than Gaultier and had all the passion of youth. She easily convinced herself that she had no impediment to her love for Gaultier except the difficulty of uncovering her feelings to him, but she soon overcame those concerns and decided to let him know just how she felt.

One day, as she was by herself, she thought it a fit opportunity to pursue her plan, and she sent for the Count to discuss matters of great importance. Gaultier came at once, expecting to discuss pressing matters of state. He had expected the Queen to be there with her daughter-in-law but found the princess to be alone.

He sat down beside her on the couch, requesting with all due respect that she tell him what she wished to talk about. At first, she said nothing, and he had to ask her twice without receiving any answer. At last, propelled by passion, trembling and blushing, her eyes moist with tears, with broken and confused words, she began: 'My dear lord and friend, it cannot have escaped your most acute judgment, how great is the frailty of both the sexes, and, for diverse reasons, how much more it displays itself in one individual than another.'

Though surprised by this topic, he answered her politely: 'Indeed, most gracious Lady, I cannot disagree.'

She continued: 'I am also certain that you know from experience how the very same offense will be judged and punished differently by an equitable judge, according to the varied quality and status of the offenders.'

Gaultier could only nod, still mystified by her words.

'Besides,' she persevered, 'who will deny that a poor man or woman, who has no other subsistence but what is earned by his or her daily labor, is more blamable when seduced and carried away by love, than a lady of wealth and leisure, who has nothing to do but to think of but how to divert and please herself?'

Puzzled more and more by her observations, all Gaultier could offer was agreement.

She pressed ahead: 'Everyone must acknowledge that distinction.' A slight pause, while she collected herself, and then: 'Surely then, this will be a sufficient excuse for a lady who gives way to such a passion, supposing that she, at the same time, makes choice of a wise and worthy person on whom to fix her affection.'

The baffled Count, somewhat uneasy now, wondered where this conversation was going, but he did not have to wait long for her conclusion.

'Having such circumstances concurring for me, and considering my youth and the absence of my husband, may I expect that they have their due weight with you and that you will afford me the advice and assistance I now require from you?'

'My Lady, of course you can count on me to assist you in any way—'

But she would not let him finish, now compelled to complete her revelation without further delay.

'I must confess then,' she blurted out, 'that, not being able, on account of my husband's distance from me, to resist my most earnest desires, living also a life of ease and indolence, as you know, I have suffered myself to be quite led astray by them. I am, however, convinced that, though it would redound but little to my credit should it be known, yet, so long as it is a secret between us, there can be no room for reproach.

I share with you here and now that love has been so gracious to me, that far from taking away my understanding, it has rather enlightened it, by presenting you to me as an object worthy of my affection, a person whom I esteem as the most accomplished nobleman this day in France — and one at present without a wife, as I am without a husband.'

Gaultier had become more and more apprehensive as she spoke, and this conclusion left no doubt as to her intent, even as she concluded: 'Wherefore I entreat you, by the tender regard I have for you, that you would vouchsafe to show the same towards me . . . pity my youth, which is consumed for your sake by my deep passion for you, even as ice melts before the fire.'

Tears pouring down her cheeks so fast that she could say no more, she was overcome with emotion, and let her head sink upon his bosom. The Count being a person of the strictest honor, naturally shrank back, trying to formulate an appropriate response, now fully aware of what she was proposing, as well as certain that his answer would spell the difference between life and death for him.

'Madam, I assure you that . . . my most worthy Princess, I can only say . . . as God is my witness I must—'

Impatiently she threw her arms around his neck, only to have him disengage as gently as possible, saying: 'No, no, my dear Princess, this is not . . . I cannot, dare not . . . under no circumstances can we . . . . Madam, I would rather die a thousand deaths, be pierced by hundreds of arrows, be shamefully drawn and quartered than that I would ever so wrong anyone else in this fashion — least of all my master, the King, or his son, the Prince, your lawful husband.'

She had heard enough.

This response made it immediately clear that her freely-offered love, her heartfelt but shameful confession of her feeling for him, had been rejected and rebuffed with such clarity and finality that there was only one thing for her to do. Far more quickly than her passion had over time led her to this moment, it now washed away in a flood of anger and the need for retribution.

She pushed him away and shouted: 'What, villain, do you treat me thus? Shall my offer to you of all I am and everything I have be abjectly despised by you in this manner? Do you dare?

What foolishness persuades you to reject this gift of my honor to your wicked, dastardly self? You maggot, you wretched miscreant. Do you know what I can . . . nay . . . what I will do to you? By God I will see you dead and your children banished to lives of abject misery!'

Having now heard, for his part, all he needed to hear, Gaultier rose, bowed deeply and swiftly made his way from the chamber, certain that his word would not prevail against the customary envy of the court, and that more credit would surely be given to the princess's wicked story than to anything he could say or do. His hasty departure was accompanied by the ever-louder shrieks of the Princess: 'Help ! Help! the Count d'Angiers would force me. He has violated me! Help me now! Chase down this villain and make him pay for his wickedness!'

Her cries were quickly rewarded with an onrush of her maidens and servants, who were now treated to a sobbing, convulsed rendition of the heinous violation perpetrated against her by the monstrous Count d'Angiers. They reacted just as Gaultier had feared they would, believing everything the Princess told them and determining without doubt that he had always been a scoundrel whose debonair appearance and demeanor at court had been nothing more than a pretense assumed expressly to effect his guilty purpose. At once, some ten of her servants set out to capture Gaultier at his palace.

But he had arrived there well before them and, without a moment's delay, had gathered his two children, placed them on horseback, and galloped off — unbeknownst to them or anyone else — in the direction of Calais. Discovering that he and his children had escaped them, in their bloodthirsty but helpless fury, the servants of his accuser stripped his palace of everything valuable, razed it to the ground, and set afire the remains. It did not, of course, take long for the news of Gaultier's reprehensible seduction of the Princess to reach the camp of the King and Prince and, being understandably outraged at the claims of the Princess, the King immediately sentenced Gaultier, Count d'Angiers, and all his descendants, to perpetual banishment from

France, offering — as well — a sizable reward to anyone who should deliver him up alive or dead.

Meanwhile, the Count realized that his flight had eliminated any chance he might have had to offer his side of the story, as it would be construed as an admission of his guilt. This grieved him immensely, but he was certain that he could no nothing else but flee, in order to save the lives of his children. Arriving at Calais he was careful not to make himself known to anyone but went on directly to England, arriving in London in mean apparel, but having on the way taught his children two essential things: never to reveal whence they came, or whom they belonged to, if they had the least regard for his life and their own, and, to bear in all patience the poverty to which fortune had reduced them through no fault of theirs. Fortunately, the Count's nine year old son, Louis, and his seven year old daughter, Violante, both attended more to their father's admonition than could have been expected from their youth, and Gaultier was most grateful for this. Nevertheless, thinking it best for their greater security, he changed their names. Thus, as they were reduced to going about the city asking for charity like common French beggars, he referred to his son only as Pierrot and to the daughter as Jeannette.

One morning, as they were waiting for alms at a church door, a certain great lady, who was wife to one of the king's principal officers of state, saw them and asked the father where they had come from, and were those his children? He told her that he was from Picardy, and that the shameful behavior of his oldest son, who had turned out very badly, had obliged him to quit his country with these two other children. The lady, who was of a compassionate temper, was pleased by their appearance, and said to him: 'My good man, I like the looks of your daughter so much that, if you are content, I will take her to live with me and, if she behaves appropriately, I will in due time provide her a husband, so that she shall live comfortably all her life.' Gaultier rejoiced at this offer and, with tears in his eyes, resigned his child to the lady, bidding farewell to her in the most affectionate manner imaginable.

Well-satisfied with how and by whom his daughter would be provided for, he decided to stay in London no longer and, his son at his side, he begged his way across the island until, at length, deadly fatigued, as he was not accustomed to traveling on foot, he reached Wales, where he had heard there was a great lord, an officer and true servant of the English king.

This noble lord was known to assist all who were in need and, as they approached, it happened that the lord's son and some other young noblemen were diverting themselves with running, leaping, and other youthful exercises. Pierrot joined in and soon was outdoing the others in every activity. The nobleman, seeing this, was mightily pleased with the boy and inquired whom he belonged to. Told that he was a poor man's son who was there to beg alms, the lord asked the father to let the boy stay with him. The Count, very pleased by this offer, freely consented, though he was deeply sad at leaving his remaining child in this manner. But having now provided for both his children, he determined to stay no longer and, as soon as he had an opportunity, passed into Ireland, arriving at Stanford, where he hired himself out to a certain knight belonging to the retinue of an earl, and there he carried out, for some years, the duties of a common servant.

Violante, known now only as Jeannette, lived with her Lady in London, increasing in beauty, stature, and every possible accomplishment. Small wonder that she became the delight both of her Lord and Lady, as well as of everyone else. Her Lady had no other notion of her quality than what she had assumed about Jeannette's father. But God, who rewards all merit, knowing that this young woman was nobly born and the innocent victim of other people's wickedness, was pleased to ordain otherwise.

Jeannette's Lord and Lady had an only son of whom they were both exceedingly fond, deservedly so, on account of his excellent disposition and character. He was about six years older than Jeannette and, having seen her extraordinary beauty and merit, fell so deeply in love with her that he cared for no other woman. However, believing her to be of low extraction, he was afraid that his parents would not approve and, fearing reprimand for placing his affections so low, he kept his love for her smothered in his breast. This of course meant that he suffered even more than if he had divulged his feelings, till he fell into a grievous fit of sickness. The several physicians who were sent for explored one symptom after another until, not being able to make out what his disorder was, they concluded they could not help him. His parents suffered nearly as much as did he, frequently asking him why he was so sad, but he made no answer except to sigh and continue to waste away.

One day a certain young but profoundly skillful physician was sitting by the young man's bedside, feeling his pulse, when Jeannette, who attended carefully upon him at the request of his mother, came into the room. Upon seeing her, the young gentleman — without a word or outward sign — conceived more strongly in his heart the passion of love and, at once, his pulse began to beat higher. The physician, who happened to be monitoring his pulse, noted this with some surprise and continued to check his pulse, to see how long that difference would last. As soon as Jeannette left the room again the pulse abated, causing the physician to suspect that he had discovered a possible cause of the disorder. Pretending that he wanted to speak to Jeannette he had her called back while he continued to hold his patient's wrist. When she returned the young man's pulse beat more highly, as before, but subsided at her departure.

The physician, now certain, took the father and mother aside and said to them: 'I believe that no physician can heal your son, for the power to do that seems to lie solely in the hands of Jeannette, whom I am certain your son loves desperately — although it seems equally clear that she is totally unaware of this. I have no doubt about what must happen if you want your son to live.'

The Lord and Lady were equally pleased to hear there was a way to save their son's life as they were fearful of having to do something they most dreaded — namely, having him marry someone well below his station. After the physician was departed, they went together to their son, and the Lady said to him: 'Although we are surprised that you have concealed your wants and needs from us, especially since your not being gratified in that respect has been attended with such evil consequences, we are more saddened to think that you did not know we would move heaven and earth to ensure your ease and welfare. But since this is what you have done, God has been more merciful to you than you would be to yourself, for we now know that it is all occasioned by unrequited love. Why, dearest son, have you kept this from us. Were you ashamed? Is it someone unworthy of you? Please tell us, for all this is natural to one of your age — indeed, were you not moved to love at your age, we should be deeply concerned.'

Although it was clear to his mother that the young man found her words uncomfortable to hear, she nevertheless continued. 'We beg you to open yourself up to us and to rid yourself of all that drooping and melancholy which has brought this disorder upon you. Be assured that there is nothing you can desire of us in which we would not gratify you to the utmost of our ability, for we love you as dearly as life itself.'

And his father joined in: 'Put away this bashfulness and tell us plainly how we can be of service regarding this love of yours, for if you find that we do not mean what we are saying, then you have every right to think of us as the most cruel of parents.'

During this time, the young man's hue changed multiple times, but in the end he trusted his parents' assurances and realized that only they could resolve his dilemma. So he took them at their word and told them: 'Beloved parents, I have kept my love a secret because of what I have observed in many people as they grow older, namely that they forget that they ever were young. Here, however, I find you so understanding that I shall admit your suspicion to be true. I will name the person to you, provided you will, in keeping with your promise, do your utmost on my behalf — and by doing that you will most certainly save my life.'

'Mother, father, I have been brought to this sad condition by the beauty and graciousness of the lovely Jeannette — who has done nothing amiss, except to be oblivious to my love for her, which I have up to now revealed to no one. But now, unless you make good your word to me, you may soon expect my life to come to an end.'

His parents were quite surprised and somewhat taken aback by this news but, with a kind smile, his mother simply said: 'So this is why you have languished for so long? Be of good cheer and leave this matter to me.'

This exchange with this parents raised the young man's hope immeasurably, and his health began to show immediate symptoms of improvement, to the great comfort of his parents, who now privately — but only to one another — expressed their concerns about their son marrying a woman of Jeannette's status. But in the end they realized that they would have to do what they could to ensure their son's happiness and his very survival.

So the mother set out to explore the topic of love with Jeannette.

She called Jeannette to her and casually asked her if she had ever had a sweetheart. Jeannette blushed deeply and replied: 'Madam, it ill becomes a poor young woman like myself, driven from her own house and subject to other people's will and pleasure, to think of love.'

But her mistress retorted: 'My dear, if you have no lover, I will procure one for you, for so pretty a girl as you are should never be without one.'

Now Jeannette blushed even more deeply and said: 'Madam, as you have taken me from my father, and brought me up like your own child, I am forevermore indebted to you and bound to do all in my power to please you. But I beg you not to put me in such a position.'

'What do you mean? What are you saying?'

'Most gracious Lady, if you mean to give me a husband, him I shall respect, but only if we are married. For, of all that my ancestors possessed, there is nothing now remaining to me but my virtue, and this I intend to keep as long as I live.'

'But if a young nobleman should have a fancy for you, would you deny him?'

Blushing ever more deeply, Jeannette nevertheless responded firmly: 'His lordship might use force, but he should never have my consent, unless it be on honorable terms.'

Pleasantly surprised but not yet convinced, the Lady was determined to put her to the test. She said to her son that, when he got well, she would put him and Jeannette into a room together and he might do with her as he pleased. The young man responded to this offer by relapsing into ill health. When his mother perceived this, she once more approached Jeannette but found her more resolute than ever.

The Lady's husband being made acquainted with the whole matter, the parents agreed (though much against their inclinations), that their son should marry this woman. There was no doubt but that they preferred their son's life with a wife much beneath him in status to his death without one. Matters were soon settled, to the great joy of Jeannette, who thanked God for His blessing on her. She did not, however, reveal any more about her history, continuing to say only that she was daughter to a person in Picardy.

I will leave her and her husband for now, happy in their new life together.

When last we left Pierrot in Wales he had been taken in by an important officer of the English King, whom he much impressed. Being graceful and manly in person and more expert in military exercises than any one in the country, he became known as Pierrot the Picard.

Having been gracious to his sister, God was equally kind and merciful to him.

Then the plague broke out in that country, sweeping away half the people, while a great number of those who were left fled for refuge into other lands. Among the dead were the lord and lady, their son, and their near relations — all except for an only daughter, just of age to marry. When the plague was over, the daughter chose Pierrot for her husband and made him lord of all her inheritance. And it was not long before the King of England, hearing of the late lord's death and knowing Pierrot's worth and valor, appointed Pierrot in his place as ruler of that lordship.

Who would have thought that the pitiable children of Count d'Angiers, whom he had left destitute, would find such success in the world as adults?

As for their father, having suffered great hardship in Ireland for some twenty years, he became increasingly desirous to know what had become of his children. His physical appearance had changed a great deal over time, but he was as robust as ever because he had made his living with his hands. So he left the service where he had been and set out for England. Of course he was delighted to learn that Pierrot was a great, powerful, and healthy lord, but he could not rest until he knew what had become of Jeannette. When he arrived in London he cautiously inquired about the lady with whom he had left his daughter and discovered that Jeannette was married to her son. Of course, to find both children alive and prospering pleased him immensely and made all his past sufferings worthwhile.

As he wished to see his daughter with his own eyes, he went to her estate dressed as the poor man he was, and there he was noticed by James Lamiens, Jeannette's husband, who had pity on him and ordered one of his servants to give him relief.

By now Jeannette and James had several beautiful children, the oldest of whom was about eight years old. Noticing this poor man, the children gathered around him and were as much pleased with him as if by instinct they knew him to be their grandfather. He, aware that they were his grandchildren, showed a thousand little fondnesses towards them, which made them unwilling to leave when their tutor called them. Hearing this, Jeannette was upset with them, but the children began to cry, saying that they wanted to stay with this man, who loved them better than their tutor did — which caused some concern to their parents.

The Count humbly greeted his daughter, as a poor man does a great lady, but she did not recognize him with his long beard, grey hair, and swarthy, meager countenance. Seeing how unwilling the children were to leave him, she let them stay a little longer.

In the meantime, her husband's father came home. Sadly, he continued to hold his daughter-in-law in low esteem because of her supposed low birth, and he said, 'Let them stay with this miscreant; may mischief be theirs! This is how they show whence they are descended; beggars on their mother's side — of course, they are drawn to beggars.' Gaultier heard these words and was much grieved, but he was forced to bear this insult just as he had done many others.

When James saw the beggar with his children, he too was uneasy at their fondness for this stranger, but the poor man was so tender with them that, rather than make them uneasy, he gave orders that if this man was willing to stay in his service, he should be allowed to do so. Gaultier was most pleased by this and was assigned to look after the horses, a task in which he was well-experienced. It would soon become customary for him to play with the children when his work was finished and he had free time.

It then came to pass, that the King of France died and was succeeded by that son whose wife had occasioned the Count's banishment. But soon another bloody war broke out, and the King of England, kinsman with the French crown, sent large supplies and many soldiers to fight with the French. They were under the command of Pierrot, one of the king's most respected generals, and James Lamiens, the son of another accomplished general. Gaultier accompanied the soldiers, took care of the horses and, by outstanding service, valor and good counsel, played an important role in the ultimate victory.

Shortly before the war's end, the Queen of France chanced to be taken ill, and finding herself past all hopes of recovery, made a confession of all her sins to the Archbishop of Rouen, esteemed by all as a most holy person. Among other things, she mentioned the great wrong she had done so long ago to the Count d'Angiers. She also made this declaration in public, before many other worthy persons, desiring their intercession with the king and asking for the restoration of the Count and his children to their former estate if they were still alive — all this shortly before she died.

The King was much distressed by this news and immediately issued a proclamation, stating that any person who could give tidings of the Count, or his children, should be well rewarded, since His Majesty meant to exalt him to the same, or even greater honors than he enjoyed before. Of course, the Count went immediately to James Lamiens and Pierrot and said: 'Most esteemed Lords, I am none other than Gaultier, the former Count d'Angiers and you, Pierrot, called the Picard, are my son, while you, James Lamiens, have married my daughter, dowry-less at your wedding. I intend, therefore, that you, James, shall have the benefit of the king's proclamation by introducing to him — first — Pierrot, as son to the Count d'Angiers; secondly, Jeannette, your wife and his sister; and lastly, myself, who am the Count d'Angiers and Pierrot's father.'

Now Pierrot recognized his father and, with tears in his eyes, fell on his knees before him. Penitent and blushing for the little respect he had showed this man, his father, he humbly asked pardon, which the Count readily granted. James, for his part, was so overcome with wonder and joy, that he scarcely knew what to say. When they had shared their stories — now in tears, then again in laughter — they planned their next steps. These included the Count refusing to put on suitable apparel, for he wished James Lamiens first to secure the reward, presenting the Count as he was, in order to increase the shame of the court for his past ill treatment.

James then told the King that he could produce the Count, as well as his children, and the King immediately ordered a most magnificent present to be given to him. James then presented the

Count as his servant, and Pierrot as himself: 'Behold, Sire, the father and son; the daughter has become my own wife, whom you will see before long.' The King studied the Count carefully and, notwithstanding the changes the passage of time had wrought, recognized him. Sobbing and apologizing for past treatment, he raised Gaultier from the ground, kissed him and shook him by the hand. He welcomed Pierrot just as warmly and provided clothes, servants, horses, and everything suitable for Gaultier. Of course, he treated James Lamiens with great respect and would not rest until he had heard everything that had befallen the families.

After James had received the promised reward, the Count said to him. 'I wish for you to enjoy this royal bounty at the hands of His Majesty in lieu of the dowery you did not receive when you graciously married my daughter. I ask only that you make sure your father knows that your children and my grandchildren are not meanly descended on their mother's side.'

James and Jeannette, Pierrot and his wife were all soon reunited with the Count, to whom the King restored all he had lost, with large additions of fortune. Eventually his children and grandchildren returned to their homes, while Gaultier stayed at the court in Paris until his dying day, living in more repute and glory than ever."

When the Yeoman had ended his tale, he humbly accepted the appreciative responses accorded to him by the Knight and several other pilgrims. The Knight approvingly patted his Yeoman on the shoulder and said, for all to hear: "A tale well-told, Robert. This was a story after my own heart."

He paused.

"In all the years we have spent together, I have never heard you tell — I have never heard you speak so long or say so much. I have learned something about you today, Robert."

"Indeed, my Lord. I am most happy to please you and hope to do so for many years to come."

"How wonderful," the Miller chimed in sarcastically,, following his observation with an enormous belch. "Let's have more stories about good things happening to lords and ladies who suffer with the patience of Job while their masters enjoy life at their expense."

The Clerk could not suppress a smirk — nor did he try to.

By this time, the sun had descended in the south so far that, by my judgment, it was at no more than twenty-nine degrees. I would guess that it was about four o'clock, as my shadow was more or less eleven feet long, if a foot is one of six parts of a man's height. Also, the moon in Libra was beginning its ascent,.

Now the Host continued. 'Gentle pilgrims, we have heard a moral tale and I'm sure we are all glad of it. But we are drawing ever nearer to Canterbury and we still have a few stories to hear.'

He turned to the Plowman, who was riding quietly on his humble farm horse next to his brother, the Parson. 'I don't remember your name, Plowman, and I am certain you have one.'

The Plowman looked up, smiled gently at the Host, and then looked down again.

"Well, Plowman? You must have a name, sir! And, by our agreement, a story for the rest of us."

The Plowman smiled at the Host again, but said nothing. Now the Host was frowning and staring at him, waiting for a response, but then the Parson spoke up.

"My worthy Host. My brother's name is Will, and it is an apt name, for he is always willing to help anyone in need. He is a good man, a better man than I or most people I know, for he has taken a perpetual vow of silence.'

A murmur ran through the pilgrims.

The Host, slightly aggravated by this, said: "But Sir Parson, we all agreed to tell a tale. Why did your brother not tell us then?"

"As I have said, he has taken a view of silence."

He crossed himself and continued.

"I apologize. The fault is mine, I should have told you earlier. But he has not spoken in ten years now, ever since his wife and their three children fell victim to a plague that killed many in our village. He vowed at that time not to speak again, to expiate for whatever evil he had done that might have caused all that suffering and those deaths. Of course I tried to dissuade him, to make certain that he knew none of it was his fault. He is one of the best people I know — wouldn't hurt a fly. He is always doing something to help someone else, but he has never wavered — not said a single word since then."

Now I remembered that on the evening before we set out, when I spoke to all of the pilgrim to learn who they were, the Parson answered my questions briefly and without elaboration, while the Plowman was quite agreeable but, this is true, smiled but said nothing, while the Parson spoke for him but without telling me much of anything particular. I now recalled that when I first began talking to the two, the Plowman left to fetch us some more ale and then returned without ever saying a single word. I had forgotten, but now it all fit together.

I was astonished. I have heard of people — outside of monasteries — who take vows of silence, but I had never met one, until now. I had liked the Plowman that night, but now I thought I had reason both to admire and to pity him.

His brother continued.

"It is true that all of you, our fellow pilgrims, are right to think we have entered into our agreement with you at some degree of deception, as my brother and I knew from the beginning that he would not tell a tale."

There were nods and some utterances of agreement.

"For this I most heartily apologize — it was a sin of omission. We took advantage of you and the safety you offered to complete this pilgrimage with you, and for that I — on behalf of Will and me — apologize most profoundly and ask for your forgiveness. We are most grateful to you for your welcome and companionship. After all, did not Our Lord Himself teach us that wherever two or more of us are gathered, there He will be, also?"

Murmurs of agreement.

"And so, if you will allow my brother to maintain and honor his sacred vow and accept a story from me that I offer to you from both of us, we would feel blessed by your actions and by your willingness to allow us to continue as members of this community as we approach the Holy Martyr's shrine."

Now he turned directly to the Host. "My dear Host, unlike my beloved brother, I have not taken a vow of silence and could not, considering my holy orders and my life's work in the world. And, Sir Host, if I am not mistaken, I am the only one remaining who has not yet told a tale. I am ready to do so, if you wish. And I can only hope that you will take it as an acceptable action to make up for my brother's silence."

"I can only hope," offered the Miller loudly, for the first time on our journey slurring his words a bit, 'that you don't make up for it with an endlesh shermon about how mosht of ush will surely go to hell for our shins! I don't need that kind of making up for your bloody brother and hish bleeding vow."

The Parson just smiled, but the Host was not pleased by the Miller's words. "Enough, you drunkard! There's no need to speak to the Parson like that, especially when you're . . . ." He was more or less sputtering, but then he stopped short: "Enough! I think we have heard quite enough from you, Sir Miller!"

"Oh, no," the Miller mocked. "God blesh my shorry pickled ash. Does that mean I won't be winning the prize . . . because you don't like me, Sir Hosht?" He made a sweeping bow and laughed loudly, barely maintaining his balance on his horse after the bow.

But the Host ignored him and continued: "You are correct, Sir Parson, to say that yours is the only story lacking."

Turning to the rest of us, he announced: "My duty and my responsibilities are nearly at an end now, as we have heard from everyone else. May God bless all of you who have joined in so eagerly as we have gone along our journey.

Now, as regards this honorable Parson and his request to tell one tale for the two stories we should have heard from him and his brother" — here the Host sat up straight in his saddle, clearly pleased with the request from the Parson and the opportunity to wield his power over us one more time — "I grant, most happily, that you now tell your tale, that it be the last, and that your brother be excused from our agreement — for good and admirable reasons."

He paused, to let all this sink in.

"So, Sir Priest, I cannot tell whether you are a vicar or maybe a parson with only one village to serve — by my faith, we would be glad to know more about you. But whatever you may be, I am pleased that you wish to honor our story-telling agreement here. Now that we have heard all of the other stories, I ask you to open your treasure chest and share with us what it contains as we approach the holy shrine. By the looks of you, and by your speech, you might have just the right tale to end our adventure with what we need. So, for cock's bones, tell us something fabulous."

The Parson frowned at this oath, shook his head, and answered: "You will hear nothing fabulous from me, Sir. The great Apostle, Saint Paul, writing to Timothy, admonishes those who would sacrifice truth in order to tell fables and such wretched lies. You can rest assured that I will never misuse my hands, filled with wheat, to sow chaff, praise God!

That is why I say clearly to you all: if you want to hear a tale of high morals and virtue and you want to pay full attention to that, I will gladly, with the help of Jesus, provide you with righteous pleasure, giving it my all. But you must be able to tell from my words that I come from the South of England and know not how to alliterate words, and I don't think much of rhyme, either. So, if you find it acceptable — I will not beat a dead horse — I will tell you something engaging that will conclude all the tales we have heard and prove a fitting end. And I pray meekly that Jesus will give me the grace and the wit to show all of you on this journey the way to complete the perfect glorious pilgrimage to the heavenly Jerusalem. So, with your permission, I will begin my story shortly, asking your consent — that is the best I can do.

But I can tell you, Sir Host, that I am merely a village parson, happy to place all this under the jurisdiction of those more intelligent than I, untrained in scholarly texts as I am. I provide what is substantive only, and I am more than willing to be corrected. However," and here he paused and looked around at our assemblage, taking his time, "I will not be interrupted by those who do not wish to learn about things that are essential to our salvation, be they drunk or sober, malicious or of good intent. For I will explain to you the seven deadly sins, how to avoid them and how to repent for our sins, so that we may all achieve salvation in our next, our one, true life."

He ignored the massive belch the Miller now offered, as many of the rest of us assented to the Parson's request because it seemed right to end with some virtuous considerations, and to give the Parson this opportunity and our attention along the way. And we encouraged our Host to tell the Parson that all of us requested him to tell his tale.

So, our Host spoke for nearly everyone when he said: "We all wish you well, Sir Priest! Please go ahead and share your holy thoughts with us, but do not delay, for the sun will set soon. We hope you get it all in, because there is not much time left to us, and so we all pray that God shed his grace upon you. Say what you have to say, and we will happily listen to you."

And with that the Parson began.

The Parson's Tale

"It is the most profound wish of our sweet Lord, our Father in Heaven, and the Holy Spirit that emanates between them, that no man should perish, but that all should come to know the most sacred Trinity and to achieve eternal life. Of course, there are many paths to salvation, but the noblest and most suitable, that fails neither man nor woman who have lost the way to the heavenly Jerusalem, is penitence. And that is why it is essential to know what penitence is, why it is called penitence, the workings of penitence, its various kinds, what is part of it and what prevents it.

Saint Ambrose says that penitence is the admission of guilt for our sin and the resolve to avoid it in future. Weeping while continuing to sin is insufficient. No matter how many times a man falls, penitence allows him to rise again. And Holy Mother Church considers anyone who ceases to sin, certain of salvation. In the end, the great mercy of Our Lord assures that salvation.

Penitence plays a role, first, when a sinful man is baptized; second, after baptism, when men commit mortal sin; and, third, when they commit daily venial sins. That is why Saint Augustine says that the penitence of good and humble folks takes place daily.

Formal penitence occurs in exclusion from church attendance for killing children and that sort of thing, as well as sin that is known to everyone and is punished by penance visible to all. Public penitence occurs when a priest requires someone to atone in public, for example, going on pilgrimage barefoot or naked. Private is that which is performed by an individual following confidential confession of sin.

True and complete penitence requires genuine contrition, oral confession, and reconciliation. Penitence redresses three activities which anger our Lord Jesus Christ: dissolute thoughts, reckless speech, and sinful acts.

And penitence, which counteracts these evils, may be likened to a tree.

The root of this tree is contrition, concealed in the heart of the true repentant as the roots of a tree are buried in the earth. From this root emerges a trunk that bears the branches and leaves of confession and the fruit of reconciliation. And by this fruit people know this tree.

A seed of grace also springs from this root — it is the mother of certainty. at once harsh and keen, for it is God's reminder to us of the day of doom and the pain of hell, as well as the love of God and the desire for eternal bliss. It draws man to God, as it makes him hate sin. Nothing is sweeter to the sinful man than his sin, but from the moment he turns to God he finds nothing more abominable. For God's law is God's love.

You must understand what contrition is, what things move one to contrition, what it means to be contrite, and the benefits of contrition for the soul. Contrition is the sorrow for his sin that a man feels in his heart, his intention to confess, to do penance and never to sin again. Saint Bernard tells us that this sorrow is sharp and searing because our sin angers Him who delivered us with His precious blood.

Now a man may be moved to contrition for six reasons.

First, he becomes conscious of his sins.

Second, people tire of being enthralled by sin, for there is nothing as hideous as persistence in sin.

Third, there is the fear of hell and eternal damnation.

Fourth, men will be moved to contrition by remembrance of the good they have yet to do and the good lost forever.

The fifth thing that ought to move men to contrition is the memory of our Lord Jesus Christ's suffering for our sins, as we can never atone for His suffering, endured for our salvation.

And sixth, the hope for three things: the forgiveness of sin, the gift of grace, and the glory of heaven.

Contrition must, of course, be complete and total — for all sins. Sinners choose and delight in their sins, in full knowledge that they act against God's law but overriding reason to do so. Dwelling too long on the delight of sinning leads to sin, and no mortal sin was ever committed without loving the sin. Sin occurs in wicked words as well as wicked deeds, and true contrition for sin must be perpetual.

You must also understand that contrition delivers a man from sin. It destroys the prison of hell, defeats the devil, restores the gifts of the Holy Ghost, purifies the soul and delivers it from the clutches of Satan to the communion of believers.

The second indispensable part of penitence is confession, which is really a sign of contrition. Confession consists of telling your sins to a priest, and that means all of your sins, hiding nothing.

Now, as Saint Paul tells us, sin entered the world through Adam's breaking of God's commandment. As all mortal sin, this original sin began with temptation, pleasure in the sin, and consent, overriding reason. It was passed down to each new human soul, born into concupiscence that leads us to greed, sins of the flesh, and all others. Baptism corrects but never fully quenches our desires, and you should not believe those who claim that they have conquered their fleshly desires.

You must also understand how sin grows or decreases. It begins with concupiscence, a fire fanned by the devil into temptation which, if resisted, is no sin. But giving in kills the soul, always in the same way: temptation, pleasure and consent. And sins are either venial — loving Jesus less than we should— or mortal — loving anyone or anything more than Jesus. Of course, the more a man indulges in venial sins, the more likely he is to move on to mortal.

Eating or drinking too much, speaking idly or too much, ignoring the plight of the poor, failure to fast, sleeping too long, tardiness for Mass, using one's spouse for other reasons than procreation or to pay the marriage debt, failing to perform works of mercy, loving spouse or child excessively, flattering more than is appropriate, blandishing food too much, slandering, breaking promises, disparaging one's neighbor, being suspicious — or innumerable other ills — all, these are sins. While no one can avoid all venial sins, this can be bridled by receiving Holy Communion, using holy water, giving alms, general confession at Mass, blessings by ministers of the Church, and doing good deeds.

It behooves us to consider in depth the seven deadly sins — deadly because they are the chief evils, and from them spring all lesser evils.

The root of all the deadly sins is pride, and from it grow the branches of sin. Among other evils, pride causes lack of obedience, boasting, hypocrisy, contempt, arrogance, impudence, joy in evil-doing, insolence, vainglory, impatience, presumption, irreverence, babbling pointlessly, and entitlement.

Pride can exist interiorly, or externally, as in extravagant dress. Clothes that use excessive amounts of cloth, trains that are too long, dress that mocks poverty, or clothes that do not cover the body modestly or that show off the swollen member or the buttocks — these all demonstrate pride, as do superfluous servants and entourages that exploit their own masters, and excessive feasting, using needlessly precious utensils and containers.

The sources of pride can be found in nature, fortune and grace. The body and its goods: health, strength, beauty, etc.; the soul and its goods: wit, understanding, virtue, memory, etc.; fortune and its goods: wealth, nobility and reputation; and the goods of grace: knowledge, resilience, generosity, virtuous contemplation, and resistance to temptation — all these are gifts. They should never be the source of pride but often are.

The remedy for all of this of course is humility, which resides in our heart, our mouth and our actions. Humility is shown in knowing ourselves to be worthless before God, refusing to despise others, being impervious to the low opinions of others, and taking humiliation in stride. It is seen in tempered and humble speech, consistency between what we say and what we do, and the willingness to praise others. It is demonstrated in those who put others before themselves, those who find the lowest seats at the table, those who seek and accept good counsel, and those who treat their lords with appropriate respect.

Now I will speak of the foul sin of envy, that emanates from malice and, more than any other, is a sin against the Holy Ghost. It opposes all virtue and goodness and, uniquely among sins, lacks pleasure. The envy of another man's goods and joy in his harm leads to backbiting: praising another, but ending with 'but'; turning another's good intentions into evil ones; undercutting the goodness of another; undercutting praise by praising another even more; and supporting evil speech about another.

Envy takes the form of grumbling against God or other men, as well, although this can also be caused by pride. Servants often grumble unjustly, and this may be caused by anger. The result is usually bitterness, scorn, accusations, and ill will. The remedy for envy is love of God and of one's neighbor, including one's kin, and this love consists of good will, kind words and deeds, lack of covetousness and love of one's enemy — not to be diminished because your enemy offers you hate, ill words and wicked deeds. Love is the medicine that treats the illness of envy.

As for wrath, it is caused by both pride and envy. Wrath is the relinquishing of reason to harm those we hate. We should be angry with wickedness and the misdeeds of man, but never angry without thought or reason. It is merely a venial sin when a man's reason does not consent to anger, but it is a mortal sin to commit a crime or to carry out vengeance with evil intent.

Wrath produces hate, strife and murder, but murder actually has ghostly as well as corporeal forms, shown in hate, backbiting, false rumors, malicious counsel, withholding wages and alms; and there is physical murder, such as legal execution, killing in self-defense, intentional death, death by negligence, willful prevention of conception, and killing of children. Wrath also causes men to hate God and His ministers, as well as to commit sacrilege on the consecrated host. It is wrath that makes men condemn what they consider harsh penance or to deny their sin outright. Believers in divinations, incantations and charms are, of course, acting contrary to God and His Holy Church.

Wrath may come in many forms: fruitless lying and lying to gain an advantage, to save one's possessions or self, lying for the joy of lying, to support one's word, reckless lying, to name some. Flattery in the service of wrath and wrongful praise are worse than detraction, for detraction can correct a proud man but flattery makes a man think more of himself than is true. Cursing others and reproaching them falsely are rooted in malice and light the fire of anger in others. Scorning people is contrary to God's law of love, and false counsel only turns on him who provides it. Christ also hates the sowing of discord, duplicity, treachery, threats, idle words, and mockery.

The remedies for wrath are kindness and patience. Kindness is long-suffering, and patience tolerates all grievances. There are four kinds of grievances, which must be remedied by patience: wicked words, damage to possessions, bodily harm, and extreme labor. Patience begets obedience to God's teachings.

The deadly sin of sloth makes men sluggish, passive, and lazy. Envy and wrath instill bitterness in us, and that bitterness is the mother of sloth, making us incapable of loving the good. Sloth troubles our hearts and causes us to be annoyed, fretful, inactive, and to rely on excuses. Sloth endangers our very life, since it makes us ignore temporal necessities.

Sloth leads to despair, known as the sin against the Holy Ghost. Idleness, spiritual paralysis, and laziness cause spiritual and temporal poverty and destruction, spiraling into lack of devotion and dread, suicide and death. The only remedy is fortitude, which resuscitates the soul to withstand the horror of sloth. Courage, reliance on reason, discretion, faith and hope will lead us back to certainty, good works, and spiritual stability.

Greed, "the root of all harm," according to Saint Paul, is the deadly sin that seeks comfort in worldly things rather than in God. Covetousness is merely the desire for things we don't have, but greed is the desire to keep everything we don't need, replacing love for Jesus with ardor for earthly possessions. Greed makes noble men abuse their attendants and cheat their overlords. It was greed that first made slaves of men, but sovereignty is a gift from God, not to be abused.

Merchants perform a proper role in buying and selling goods, but the buying and selling of spiritual benefits is simony. As for gambling, it cannot be practiced without sin. Greed also spawns deception, theft, bearing false witness and false oaths. Especially wicked is spiritual theft, a serious sacrilege.

The remedies for greed are, of course, mercy and pity. Mercy allows us to empathize with others, imitating Our Lord Jesus, and it lets us pity those in need. We should not forget that wasting earthly goods is also a sin.

The deadly sin of gluttony consists of excessive eating or drinking, the sin committed by Adam and Eve. Gluttony makes us vulnerable to all other sins. It shows itself in drinking or eating to excess, thereby negating reason. The five fingers of the devil's hand can be seen in eating too soon, seeking unusual delicacies, eating to excess, extraordinary adornment of food, and devouring food greedily.

The remedy for gluttony is abstinence, carried out not for the sake of body welfare, but for virtue's sake. Abstinence is shown in moderation, shame, satisfaction, sobriety, and frugalness.

The deadly sin of lust is gluttony's kinsman. One horrible manifestation of this sin is adultery and the desire to commit this sin, for it crushes body and spirit. Here is the devil's other hand with the five fingers of lustful sight, carnal touch, lecherous speech, lascivious kissing, and copulation. And copulation may occur as adultery or fornication between those who are not married to each other, depriving a woman of her maidenhead. A maidenhead can never be restored, and adultery is the foulest theft there is, worse than stealing sacred vessels from a church, because it is theft of body and spirit.

Adultery committed by those who have taken religious vows is the worst form of this sin, but just as evil is the adultery that occurs in marriage when husband and wife copulate solely to satisfy their lust. Equally evil is lechery between those who are related to each other, or that abominable sin of which the scriptures tell but with which I will not defile my mouth, and finally the pollution that occurs in sleep, as the result of gluttony, or foul thoughts or general physical frailty.

Of course chastity and celibacy are the remedies for lust, and the greater the restraint, the greater the heavenly reward.

Now God himself established the sacrament of marriage in the Garden and Himself chose to be born in marriage. Marriage was constituted to sanctify fornication and to ensure the perpetuation of the Church; it unites married couples and makes the mortal sin between them merely venial. Marriage is prefigured by the relationship between Christ and His Church. The husband is the wife's head and she cannot have more than one head, because that would be confusing. She could not be expected to please so many people, there would never be peace among them, and she would be uncertain as to who fathered her children.

Husbands should be patient with and respectful of their wives. God made Eve not from Adam's head (so she would not claim equality), nor from his foot (that would be too far beneath him), but from his rib (to make her his companion). And they should love them as Christ loves the Church. Women should obey their husbands, serve them well, and be modest in dress. They should always be moderate and discrete in appearance, in bearing, and in laughing, and always faithful — as should husbands also. Husband and wife may have intercourse to have children, to carry out their marital duty to one another, to overcome lust, and to avoid mortal sin. The first two can be meritorious, the third is only a venial sin, and the fourth is accomplished by maintaining the proper ends of intercourse. Widows and fallen women cleansed by confession and penance who maintain chastity earn great merit. So do virgins, the spouses of Christ — who was born of a virgin and was ever virgin Himself.

Lust can also be remedied by avoiding luxury, excessive eating and drinking, sleeping late, and the company of those who present temptation.

Now that I have characterized for you, as best I could, the seven deadly sins, their various aspects, and their remedies, I would like nothing more than to scrutinize with you the lord God's ten commandments. But I leave such matters to learned theologians—"

"Thank God," the Miller broke in, belching loudly to emphasize this words. "By Christsh's bony knees, all I can say ish, thank God that you leave such things to others. You've told ush more than anyone will ever need about the sheven deadlies, and I wish by the bleeding wounds of Jesus that you had left the plowing to your brother, for you have carved up, sheeded and harvested all the land between Southwark and Canterbury with your . . . what? Parables? What are they? What is this sermon that you are preaching at ush?"

He looked around as if seeking an answer from the other pilgrims. But all he got was a strong reprimand from the Man of Laws. "Sir, you go too far. In your unfortunate and churlish drunkenness, you do not know what you are saying . . . and you have said more than enough in attacking this most worthy Parson, as he shares the words of salvation with us all. Nay, nay, Sir, we are fortunate to hear from this Priest, and you could do well with a little less bravado and a little more humility!"

In response, the Miller relieved himself of a mighty fart, loud enough to be heard by the entire group.

The Cook nearly fell off his horse, shaking with utter delight and joy, while a few of our companions attempted to hide any signs of mirth the Miller's boorish act might have elicited.

Now a variety of response were heard, most of them in accord with the words spoken by the Man of Laws, although a few of the pilgrims seemed to agree with the Miller.

The Knight held up his arm until all were silent again, and then spoke: "Worthy Parson, I too must apologize for this interruption in your noble and godly efforts to teach us all about repentance and reconciliation with our Lord and God, and I beg you to continue your teachings, so that we may all share in your complete wisdom before our pilgrimage is at an end. This is a fitting ending of our pilgrimage, as it prepares us for our time with the Holy Marty's shrine."

The Parson, who seemed to be entirely untroubled by all that had occurred, nodded gracefully to the Knight and continued as if he had never been interrupted.

"I will end my tale with a few final words about the subtle ways in which various elements aggravate sin. We may be more prone to sin because of who we are, with whom we commit our sins, the circumstances in which we sin, how long we have persisted in particular sins, the physical spaces in which we commit our sins, how often we repeat certain sins, the causes that make us sin, and the nature of our sins.

The first requirement for a true and proper confession is sorrow, which is demonstrated by shame, humility, weeping, fearlessness in confessing sin, and willingness to accept the assigned penance. Confession should occur soon after sin is committed and must be carried out in proper preparation, confession of all sins to one man, and admission of all sins committed since the last confession. You must confess of your own free will, you must be a true Christian, your confessor must be ordained in the Church, and you must accuse only yourself and no-one else, unless you cannot validly confess without naming another person. You may not lie, you must confess orally and speak plainly to a priest who can advise you properly, and you may not be hypocritical in your confession. You must confess at least once a year and never lightly.

The last aspect of penitence is atonement, which usually takes the form of good works and bodily pain. Good works consist of contrition, charitable deeds, and providing good counsel. All men need food, clothing, shelter, good advice, visitation in prison and illness, and proper burial. As for bodily pain, this takes the form of praying, waking, and fasting. The *Our Father* was given to us directly by Jesus and we should never tire of saying it. Prayers must always be said with all humility and in conjunction with good works. Waking is done in memory of the words of Jesus: 'Wake and pray, lest you enter into temptation.' And fasting consists of forbearance from food and drink, worldly joys and deadly sin, and involves donations to the poor, spiritual lightness of heart, not fasting grudgingly, and eating reasonably and at the proper time. Bodily pain also includes self-discipline and wearing hair shirts or uncomfortable clothes, but only if these actions do not embitter you. Self-discipline may also involve scourging yourself, patiently suffering wrongs done to you, accepting illness or the loss of worldly goods, of your wife, of your children and of friends.

But there are four things that disrupt penance: fear, shame, hope and false hope. Fear can be overcome by thinking about how little this penance is compared to an eternity of suffering. To overcome shame remember that no one is perfect and that your temporal shame is nothing compared to the shame all will feel at the last judgment. Hope can interfere with penance if it is based on the expectation of a long life and the opportunity to repent at the end, or if it is actually arrogance rooted in the reliance on God's mercy. False hope comes from the conviction that you are too sinful to be pardoned or that you cannot maintain a life without sin.

The ultimate fruit of penance is eternal heavenly bliss without harm, without the pain of hell, in the company of the saints, in a perfected body, in a place where there is no hunger, thirst or cold, but every soul rejoices in the sight of God. All that is attainable through spiritual poverty, glorious humility, endless joy through suffering, and eternal life at the death of sin.

Amen."

When the Parson stopped speaking, there was, at first, a deep silence among the pilgrims. Some, deeply moved by his words, continued to contemplate all he had said and how it related to their own lives, while the rest — and I suspect, most — of our company had long ago simply stopped listening, so often had they heard the same things from various preachers that they had surrendered to their habit of simply following their own daydreams while one or another spiritual leader droned on endlessly in an attempt to change the innermost beings of those they perceived as sinners.

Finally, the Host, who, I deem fell somewhere in the second of the groups I believe we constituted, emerged from his revery and spoke.

"Worthy Parson," he addressed our final story teller, "you have given us much to think about. Unlettered as I am, I have learned many things about the seven deadly sins and about confession and penance. I will have to ponder many of the things you have told us."

The Knight chimed in: "Our Host says what I am certain many of us are thinking, most reverend Parson, for I too am grateful for what you have taught us here today."

"Look where we are," announced the Miller, rather too loudly. "We are at the gatesh of Canterbury — behold the cathedral towers and the shity wall."

"Praise be to God," the Prioress tinkled in her lady-like voice. "I have been looking forward to this moment when we achieve our goal and will soon have the chance to worship at the tomb of the blessed Saint Thomas."

The dutiful crossing of themselves by many of the pilgrims, that now ensued, almost sounded like a flock of birds welcoming us to the city.

A little later, when we reached the north gate and began to enter Canterbury, there was some jostling for position and a few exchanges, as the guard in chain mail looked at us languidly and clearly bored by the arrival of yet another troupe of pilgrims, come to pay their respects at Thomas a Becket's shrine. I considered asking him how many other groups had passed this way just in this one day, but he had begun to search and rummage about in a bag he was holding, no doubt looking for a piece of cheese or whatever he kept there to munch, perhaps as much in boredom as in hunger.

When the last of us had passed through the gate and were now inside the walls of Canterbury, our Host, who had been waiting for everyone to reassemble, addressed us once more. He somewhat shouted, to be heard by all: "As you know, we are all staying at the same inn, and we are expected there for the night. If you will follow me, I will take you there so you can find your beds and settle in. We will meet again shortly, at dusk, in order to share our last meal together. It is then," he paused for dramatic effect, "that I will announce who has won the prize and who will therefore be enjoying that meal at the expense of all the rest."

We dutifully followed him and prepared to meet again in the common room of the inn at dusk.

The Epilogue

When we were assembled once more, it took the Host quite some time to gain the silence he insisted on before speaking. By now a number of the pilgrims had taken advantage of the plentiful ale available to them in the inn. This meant, of course, that some of our companions were even more drunk than they had been on much of the last few days. This did not augur well for the peaceful passing of the evening. Before the Host began though, I counted heads and realized that we were back to our original number — the Canon's Yeoman, who had accompanied us into the town, must have slunk off somewhere to pursue whatever people such as he do in Canterbury. This seemed to have gone without the notice of my companions, for no one asked about him or commented on his absence.

"My worthy pilgrims, one and all," our Host began. "I know that we all recall our agreement, as it has come up on our journey several times. But, just to remind you, you all agreed to tell a tale on our ride to Canterbury and that I would then decide which of you told the best tale and therefore would be rewarded with supper at the expense of the rest of us. But I must also remind you of your assent to this: that whoever disagreed with my judgment would pay for supper for everyone else. Sooth to say, there is a large price to be paid for disagreeing with me. Let us remember that when I tell you who has told the best tale.

I think we can all agree that some wonderful tales were told along the way. There were noble tales of lovers, as told by the worthy Knight, of love rewarded in the end, and other tales of love's rewards in other ends, as told by the Miller." The Miller was happy to stand up and take several bows, accompanied by the guffaws of many in the room. "And," the Host continued, "there were moral tales about faithfulness to our heavenly Father, told by the noble Prioress and the Man of Laws, or faithfulness to moral principles, as in the Knight's Yeoman's Tale."

"If I may say so, Sir Host," the Clerk broke in, "I would argue that there were other moral tales, one in particular was that told by the Summoner—" loud boos and hisses filled the room, but the Clerk was not to be deterred. He waited for quiet to be restored, and then said: "Surely, you must admit that, as the Summoner demonstrated so plainly, even intentional evil can lead to good, God willing."

"Y-y-yes, you c-c-c-c-an wipe m-m-m-y ass w-w-with your m-m-moral tales, f-f-for all I c-c-c-care," interjected the very drunk Haberdasher, only to be drowned out by a chorus of shouts that prevented him from finishing whatever he wanted to say, despite his repeated attempts to be heard. What could be heard, however, was the Miller's loud, mocking imitation: "W-w-w-ell s-s-s-aid, m-m-m-m-y f-f-f-f-riend!" The Haberdasher responded to the Miller with an obscene gesture.

Finally, the Knight's voice rose above all others and he succeeded in quieting everyone down: "Listen to me, my fellow pilgrims. If we continue on in this manner, our gentle Host will never have the chance to tell us who won the contest." There was general agreement with this point. "So, I would ask that we all stop interfering with his task and let him get on with it. I think none of us are getting less hungry as time passes — and there are some who are getting deeper and deeper in their cups, and that can neither be denied . . . nor is it a good sign for the rest of us."

"Our noble Knight is correct," the Lawyer now joined in. "But, at the same time, it is clear that some of our group wish to say their piece about who told the best tale, as well — some of that may be self-serving, but nevertheless, perhaps it would be a good idea if those who wish to say a word or two about their favorites were allowed to do so before the host make this final judgment."

"That is well-said," said the Physician. "But might we add the caveat that no one can praise his own story?"

The Host, somewhat grudgingly, said: "I would not object to that, although — I must warn you — my judgment has been made, and I am quite certain as to who has told the best tale."

The Franklin jumped in: "My worthy fellow pilgrims. Surely there can be no doubt but that the noble Knight told the best story about good, moral, gentle people who were faithful in difficult circumstances and were all finally rewarded with exactly what they had prayed for. And," he hastened to add, while many in the room murmured unhappily, "the other story deserving much credit must certainly be that told by our gentle Squire, even though it was not finished. It showed such promise and would no doubt have been wonderful too, had it been completed."

The Franklin bowed to the smiling Squire and sat down, greatly satisfied with his words to us all.

"It seems to me," the Clerk now spoke, "that incomplete tales, no matter how much promise they showed, should not be considered." General assent could be heard. "I would propose, however, that, despite the rather long-winded preparation for the tale itself, the story told by our worthy Wife from Bath should be considered the best tale for—" he held up his hand to quiet the crowd "—not only did she tell a good story well, but her story answered the age-old question that surely all men wish to know the answer to: 'what do women really want?'" He sat down, clearly enjoying the broad, gap-toothed smile with which the Wife rewarded him. I think that the slight smirk on the face of the Nun's Priest was noticed by myself, only.

"While it is difficult to say," the Physician interjected, "which tale was the best, I want to state that — as all things that God put on this earth — stories should always help heal our ills, no matter what their content. So, I hope our worthy Host keeps that in mind in making his judgment."

"Heal your own bleedin' ass," the Sailor rudely responded. "Give me a goddamn jolly tale any day, by the broken bones of Christ, like the ones told by my good friend," and here he knocked cups so hard with the Haberdasher that ale splattered on everyone near them, "about putting the bloody devil back in bloody hell again — and that's a moral story, your honor, my Host!" He mock-bowed to our Host and then took another big drink of ale before continuing his private conversation with the

Haberdasher. The Prioress and her Nun crossed themselves many times over, shaking their heads in horror at the Sailor's unabashed blasphemy.

"Many worthy tales have been told by our group," the Man of Laws now added, "and our noble Host has, on more than one occasion, requested a moral tale, something to make us all more noble. And I heard a number of tales that were indeed moral. Both of the tales told by our pious nuns, for example, were uplifting and told about moral characters who acted nobly in the face of adversity. And my friend, the Physician, told a wonderfully moral tale of a father and a young maiden who sacrificed her life rather than be debauched by an evil judge. The tale I myself told — although I am not at all asking that it be judged the best tale — I merely mention as another example of a noble woman who was ever constant in the face of many evils. I mention these tales to call them once again to the Host's attention as he ponders which of the tales told here was indeed the worthiest."

"Since you have not at all praised your own tale, Sir," the Wife of Bath answered the Lawyer, giving him a broad, gap-toothed smile, "I feel the need to remind us all that a tale told by a woman may indeed be the best. It is true, there are only a few women here, and I did not recognize any women that I have ever known in the tales our two worthy nuns told, but perhaps the learned Clerk deserves to be listened to more closely in his recommendation." Again she smiled irreverently at the Man of Laws before settling back into her chair and having another sip of ale.

The Nun's Priest, whom I had observed closely the entire pilgrimage because I found him to be such a likable fellow, sat silently throughout, composed as ever, occasionally having a sip from his cup and smiling a bit now and then. I thought he was about to speak to us all, but he seemed to think better of it, and merely said something to his mistress, the Prioress. Not unlike him, the Monk also sat without speaking, but he was more withdrawn than was the Nun's Priest, as he hardly ever spoke to anyone and had not, the entire journey from London. But now the Pardoner spoke.

'I suppose it is no more likely that the Host will choose my tale than that he will buy one of my powerful pardons . . . something he so much has need of. But I am content with sharing the many blessings I have here in my buckler with any of you that still wish to partake." He said something else, but that was drowned out by a chorus of voices condemning and even cursing him and his kind, before the Parson entered the fray.

"May the blessings of the Almighty Lord be upon us all," he made a large sign of the cross in the air over us, "and may we learn how to cease fighting amongst ourselves." He paused, and by now there was general silence, which he held for a moment longer and then said: "It saddens me to see that none of the things about which I preached to you as we neared Canterbury has taken root, as I see many of the very sins I spoke of being practiced right here, in front of me. Surely, as we prepare to offer our prayers and our donations to the Blessed Saint Thomas tomorrow at the place he died for all of us, we should attempt to put ourselves in a more pious and holy mode than we are practicing here."

The group seemed properly chastised, but not for long, as the Friar now spoke up: "Of course, you are right, worthy Priest, and we did indeed learn much from you, but we still live in a sinful world and are surrounded at all times by sinful people."

"And so we are," the Summoner jumped on, "and you Sir, are the most sinful of all, attempting to besmirch me once again with the devilish words that proceed from your wicked tongue, even now, like honey from the devil's beehive." Had he not been separated from the Friar by a few chairs, tables and pilgrims — as well as perhaps his own, unproven courage — he would surely have physically attacked the Friar, but he was pulled back onto his seat by the Carpenter, who then rose to speak.

"As you all know, we are five guildsmen pilgrims, and I am spokesman for us."

"S-s-s-ince w-w-wh-en?" the Haberdasher blurted out. But the Carpenter ignored him and went on.

"As spokesman, then, I wish to say that we have talked one to another and we are decided that the tale I told should be considered the best." General hubbub, with the Haberdasher trying to object but not getting out the words. "I know, I know," the Carpenter continued, "that we are not to speak for our own tale to win the prize, but this is the opinion of us five and I am merely delivering the message." He sat down quickly, trying hard to ignore the general unrest his words had stirred up. Then the Merchant rose to speak.

"I am no judge of stories or how well told they are, but I wish to say that not everything is always what it seems to be." He sat down, leaving us to feel again the general confusion most of us felt whenever the worthy Merchant spoke to us.

Now it was clear that the Host had heard enough and was getting rather impatient to announce his decision and to move on. He stood, arms outstretched, until the room was quiet.

"Thank you one and all for your . . . thoughts about the best tale. While I have found your comments very interesting, I need not remind you that I am the sole arbiter of which was the best tale." There was a low murmuring of begrudging consent. "I have given much thought to this and have considered carefully the moral tale told by the Knight and — by his Yeoman — the various stories about the importance of diverse trades, the bawdy — and I must admit, often entertaining — tales told to gratify our basest instincts, the stories that I wish my wife had heard to her benefit . . . and mine — the stories of love — requited or not — the stories told quite cleverly at the expense of other pilgrims, tales of warning and tales of instruction, parables and saints' stories — indeed, a treasure chest of many fine stories but," he paused to let his next words sink in, "I have decided," another pause, "there can only be one winner. And so," he looked around slowly, while we all waited impatiently, "I have decided that the best tale was told by . . . our learned friend, the young Scholar from Oxford."

After a brief silence, all hell broke loose. I cannot do justice to all that was said, or shouted, or the efforts of various pilgrims among us — the Knight, the Parson, the Man of Laws, even the Carpenter — to calm everyone, though futile for some time. Finally the various shouts and curses abated and the Host again gained the upper hand.

"Come, come, my friends, you all agreed to let me be the judge, and that is what I have done — I have judged and that is my decision."

The Cook was not satisfied.

"Decision? Were you not listening this whole time? How could that be the best story? Did you think about the tale told by the Reeve? Now that was a great story that I will always remember, long after this pilgrimage has ended."

That was too much for the Miller.

"The Reeve's shtory? By the shweet blessed bones of Jesus, did you not hear my shtory where I requited the Knight and then showed what a miserable shcoundrel the Reeve ish? Did you not hear that?"

"Did you not hear my story?" The Sailor now joined in the chorus. "That was a story your wife should have heard? Or should I ask first if you yourself heard it? Or did you sleep through it?"

"S-s-sl-eep th-th-through it? Th-th-that's it! He s-s-sl-slept th-th-through it!" The Haberdasher joined in, laughing so hard he could hardly be understood.

But now the Host would hear no more objections.

"Enough!" He shouted. "Enough!"

And when everyone had fallen silent, he continued with his ultimatum.

"That will do! The next one of you who objects to my decision will indeed pay for the supper of all in this room. And that's all there is. We are finished talking about this. I will collect money from each of you to help pay for the Clerk's meal, as we have all agreed."

Whatever final disagreements remained now subsided into a low murmur, and the Host went about his business of collecting from each of us to pay for the Clerk's meal.

And so our journey to Canterbury ended, and we all did have a fine supper, while the Clerk perhaps enjoyed his more than the rest of us did.

This ends the tales told by these pilgrims on their way to the Holy Martyr's shrine. I leave you now in the hope that you found something in all these tales that pleased you, and if you did not, I am sorry indeed, but you should not blame me, for all I did was to tell what happened.

And with that I leave you to your own pilgrimages and your lives. May you be blessed, one and all, in each and all of your endeavors.

Translator's Final Note

And so ends the only complete version of **The Canterbury Tales**, — nothing less than preserved for us in Chaucer's own hand, without the usual intermediary scribe to filter whatever Chaucer's own words might have been.

I hope the reader will appreciate the genius of this medieval poet, who produced the first frame story in our tradition with characters plucked from reality and experience, who interact and are thoroughly human, even if they never existed and, predating us by six centuries, would be long forgotten, had they lived anywhere but in Chaucer's art.

Acknowledgements

This book is the result of years devoted to studying and to teaching Chaucer to undergraduate and graduate students of English literature. It follows **This Passing World**, a novel based on the fictional journal Chaucer supposedly kept in the last thirty months of his eventful life. Both books constitute an effort to reintroduce Chaucer to our contemporary world because he produced entertaining, thought-provoking, and challenging literature that show us how we have changed — and how we have not — as humans in the last six centuries.

This book would not have come about without Michael Koep and Andreas John of Will Dreamly Arts Publishers. The former listened to me think and talk about this project for years, and the latter showed great faith in my writing by agreeing to publish both **This Passing World** and this version of **Pilgrimage: The Only Complete Version of Geoffrey Chaucer's** *Canterbury Tales*. I also owe much to the indirect pushes Ken Pickering has given me over the years, inspiring me to think about Chaucer more broadly through his continuing work as one of the shining lights of contemporary dramatic activity in England.

I must express my gratitude for the unintentional encouragement I have received from colleagues and scholars who have questioned and challenged, for many different reasons, my — for some — sacrilegious efforts to complete what Chaucer did not. For the sake of completeness, I must here also thank the primary mentor of my career as a student and teacher of literature: Franz Schneider. The extraordinary standards he himself practiced throughout his distinguished history as an educator, and challenged me to reach, have impacted everything I have done in my professional and personal life.

More than anyone else, however, I have relied on the patience, the constant support, and the assistance of my wife, Jean, who has read and reread numerous versions of this book at various stages and proven to be not only a first-rate editor but a thoughtful and invaluable critic. I am deeply grateful to her and to the generations of students who forced me to think ever more deeply and creatively about Chaucer and his art.

My main hope for the books about Chaucer that I have produced is that many people who have heard of him, who may have read some of his work or studied it in high school or college, and the millions of people who know neither of him nor of his work, will come to appreciate the marvelous legacy he left for his contemporaries and for us, more than 600 years after his death.

Michael B. Herzog, Ph.D.

Professor Emeritus of English

Gonzaga University

Works Consulted

Benson, Larry D. **The Riverside Chaucer**. 3rd Edition. Houghton Mifflin Company.
>Boston, 1987.

Cole, Joanna. **Best-loved Folktales of the World**. Anchor Press/Doubleday. New
>York, 1983.

Crane, Thomas Frederick. **Italian Popular Tales**. ABC-CLIO, Inc., 2001.

Dorson, Richard M. **Folktales of the World**. University of Chicago Press, 1965.

Mayhew, A. L. **A Concise Dictionary Of Middle English**. CreateSpace Independent
>Publishing Platform, 2012.

Ovid. **The Metamorphoses**. In *Oxford World's Classics: Ovid: Metamorphoses,* Oxford
>University Press.

Also from Michael B. Herzog

It is 1398, and all of Europe is abuzz about the duel to be fought in September between Henry Bolingbroke, Duke of Hereford, and Thomas Mowbray, Duke of Norfolk, to settle the question of which one has committed treason against King Richard II. Geoffrey Chaucer, courtier and well-known poet, is unexpectedly drawn into the intrigue surrounding the impending duel and compelled to perform an act so heinous that he is shaken to the core.

The journal Chaucer begins and keeps for the remaining two and a half years of his life chronicles his unlikely rise as the son of a middle-class wine broker to become not only the pre-eminent poet of his age but the brother-in-law of John of Gaunt, uncle to the king, at times the most powerful man in England and, with his three wives, the ancestor of every ruler of England since the year 1400. This novel provides a fascinating look into life in late 14th century England, the women and men Chaucer loves, the intrigues of the Richardian court, and what compels someone who holds some of the most important jobs in the English bureaucracy to spend his nights writing poetry that is still being read and studied 600 years after his death.

This Passing World
by Michael B. Herzog
ISBN 978-0-9976234-6-8
Will Dreamly Arts Publishing

Where books are sold.